FULL BLOODY CIRCLE

Miles to Vietnam
Book 4

**A Novel By
William Peter Grasso**

Copyright © 2023 Grasso Joint Revocable Trust
All rights reserved
ISBN: 9798378987580
Cover design by Alyson Aversa

FULL BLOODY CIRCLE is a work of historical fiction, not a history textbook. Events that are common historical knowledge may not occur at their actual point in time or may not occur at all. Apart from the well-known actual people, events, and locales that figure in the narrative, all names, characters, places, and incidents are products of the author's imagination and are used fictitiously. Any resemblance to current events or locales or to living persons is purely coincidental. The designation of military units may be actual or fictitious.

Sign Up For New Release Announcements at:
williampgrasso@gmail.com, with Mailing List as the Subject

Visit the Author's Website:
https://williampetergrasso.com

Connect with the Author on Facebook
https://www.facebook.com/AuthorWilliamPeterGrasso

Follow the Author on Amazon
https://amazon.com/author/williampetergrasso

Novels By William Peter Grasso

Miles To Vietnam
Butter Bar, *Book 1*
Reports Of Their Demise, *Book 2*
Forever And A Wake-Up, *Book 3*
Full Bloody Circle, *Book 4*

Jock Miles-Moon Brothers Korean War Story
Combat Ineffective, *Book 1*
Combat Reckoning, *Book 2*
COMBAT: Parallel Lines, *Book 3*
COMBAT: Magic Bullet, *Book 4*

Moon Brothers WWII Adventure Series
Moon Above, Moon Below, *Book 1*
Fortress Falling, *Book 2*
Our Ally, Our Enemy, *Book 3*
This Fog of Peace, *Book 4*

Jock Miles WW2 Adventure Series
Long Walk to the Sun, *Book 1*
Operation Long Jump, *Book 2*
Operation Easy Street, *Book 3*
Operation Blind Spot, *Book 4*
Operation Fishwrapper, *Book 5*

World War II Standalone Novels
Unpunished
East Wind Returns

Dedication

To the artillerymen: the cannon-cockers
Knights of the King of Battle
Their value, in the words of Kipling:
The guns, thank God, the guns

Author's Note

To those of my generation, the Vietnam War was a transformational waypoint in our lives, whether one served in that conflict or not. To most who answered their country's call and made that trip to the other side of the world, it was a period of confusion, contradiction, and frustration. In no way does the fictional story presented here mean to denigrate the hardships and sacrifices of the individual American soldiers, marines, airmen, and sailors forced to fight a war they—and often their commanders—did not understand.

Dialogue often uses terms deemed derogatory for people of various Asian ethnicities, African Americans, and other nationalities. The use of those terms by the author serves no other intent than to accurately represent the vocabulary of military personnel in the 1960s.

It would take a host of maps to fully depict the locations and battles visited in this novel. Since it focuses on the exploits of fictional characters and doesn't intend to be a history textbook, I've chosen to include no maps. Those readers who wish to put the fictional action into a geographic context can visit a number of online sources. Here is a helpful link:

https://libguides.nps.edu/vietnamwar/maps

Chapter One

A Shau Valley, Republic of Vietnam
Fire Support Base Signal Hill

22 April 1968

First Lieutenant Jif Miles, US Army, hoped he wasn't watching another helicopter resupply mission on the cusp of failure. He told Captain Knapp, his battery commander, "I'm not sure those pilots can even see us, sir. I hope to bloody hell there's still enough light to do the drop."

There was a good reason for his uneasiness; it was already pitch dark on the valley floor below. But there was something he and the captain couldn't know: on this lofty peak called Signal Hill, there was still enough twilight for the pilots of the CH-54 Skycrane heavy-lift helicopter to see the layout of Charlie Battery, their artillery unit. The mountain's designation hadn't been a random pick; there was a radio station collocated there that relayed communications from combat units along the A Shau Valley to 1st Cavalry Division's base at Camp Evans some twenty miles to the northeast.

Even with the small margin of visibility, the Skycrane's task was a challenging one. Like all the helicopters that had serviced the firebase since its inception three days ago, the massive ship struggled to hover in the thinner air at 5,000 feet above sea level.

Buffeted by swirling mountain gusts, the big chopper rocked and rolled as she crept toward the peak. The pallet of ammunition that hung on slings beneath her swayed and twirled menacingly, its seven-ton mass threatening to smash into men and equipment on the firebase below.

Captain Knapp was anxious enough to pull the plug on the delivery. "We've got to wave her off," he screeched over the roar of the *Crane*. "If that stuff smacks the ground and blows up, we're all going to buy it."

"We really need that ammo, sir," Jif replied, just as concerned but not quite as fatalistic. "Maybe we hold off a second on that wave-off?"

Knapp didn't reply. He was already running toward the LZ, his arms flailing over his head in the abort signal. It was wasted effort; the pilots didn't see his shadowy figure. They were fixated on the guidance from the lighted wands of the signalman, who couldn't hear the captain shouting to him over the noise of the helicopter.

The men on Signal Hill didn't realize they'd been cut a break; the cooler temperature of evening had provided the flying machine a small boost in performance, something unattainable in the daytime heat at this high altitude. The ship's gyrations settled down as the signalman inched her to the designated drop point. The hefty pallet, containing almost three hundred rounds of 105-millimeter howitzer ammo, was placed exactly where it was wanted. Her load released, the Skycrane wasted no time making an escape. The pilots were eager to get back to the club, just a twenty-minute flight away, where they could regale their fellow aviators with a triumphant tale of pushing the envelope once again.

When Jif caught up to Knapp at the pallet, the captain was no longer the overwrought commander he'd been a few moments before. He'd become the stern evaluator, critiquing his XO's judgment. "You like to take risks a little too much, Miles," he said. "That's probably the Australian in you coming out. Every Aussie I ever met was a wild man. You got lucky on this one, though…but I'm here to tell you that one of these days, you're going to get bit in the ass real bad when that luck of yours runs out." He turned and started toward the radio relay bunker, saying, "I've got to check in with Divarty. Carry on, Lieutenant."

Sergeant First Class McKay, Charlie's chief of firing battery—the position commonly known as *Chief of Smoke*, or simply *The Smoke*—was standing nearby and heard every word. He'd been the signalman who guided the Skycrane to the mark. He asked Jif, "What's the BC bent out of shape over?"

"The captain wanted to call off the drop, Smoke. But I thought maybe we shouldn't be so hasty."

"Oh, so that's why he was crawling up my ass. He's mad we didn't abort?"

"Something like that," Jif replied. "And by the way, he thinks I'm reckless."

"Nah, you're not reckless, Lieutenant. He's just pissed off because you called it right and he jumped the gun. Without that drop, we'd be hurtin' for certain tonight if we got a bunch of missions to shoot. We would've run out of rounds for sure."

*****

Twenty minutes later, Captain Knapp returned to the drop point. He was surprised to find most of that massive load of ammunition had already been distributed to the guns. "The rest will be parceled out in just a few more minutes, sir," SFC McKay told him. As he spoke, a pair of cannoneers appeared out of the darkness, hoisted another of the hundred-pound boxes between them, and hustled back to their section.

"This is amazing work, Sergeant," the BC said. "How in the world did you motivate these men to do the job so quickly?"

"It was simple, sir," McKay replied. "The XO asked them to, that's all." The Smoke let that sink in for a minute before adding, "It was a lucky break when we got Lieutenant Miles to fill the slot at the last minute like we did. I was worried about him at first...thought he might've been just a tad brash. But it turns out he's real good people, and the men are really warming up to him." He smiled as he added, "And he doesn't need any adult supervision."

Knapp asked, "So where is the prodigal son, anyway? You do know that his daddy is a retired general, right?"

"I'm well aware, sir...and Lieutenant Miles is over at FDC."

FDC: the battery's fire direction center, where target information called in from observers in the field was processed into firing data for the howitzers, enabling those guns to hit distant targets their crews couldn't see with indirect fire.

"Very well, Sergeant. Join me there. Something's come up we all need to talk about."

*****

"As *Operation Delaware* moves to its next phase, Division has entrusted us with a fire mission of highest priority," Captain Knapp told Jif, SFC McKay, and his battery's FDC, a five-man section headed by the assistant XO, Second Lieutenant Hammond. Spreading an acetate-covered map across one of the plotting tables, the BC continued, "Tonight, we're going to destroy some anti-aircraft weapons that have suddenly appeared near the old damaged airfield at *A Luoi*. Those Mohawk recon planes we see blasting down the valley below us sniffed them out just a few hours ago. The target locations are only four to five kilometers from here…and about three thousand feet down, of course. It'll be like shooting fish in a barrel. It's a shame we couldn't've hit them in daylight, but it took a while to process the intel from the recon ships. No real loss, though…Divarty figures a night bombardment will have maximum shock effect."

He marked the target locations on the acetate: several points along a kilometer-long ridge line containing alternating areas of dense and sparse tree cover. The ridge was southwest of Signal Hill and straddled Route 548, a hard-packed dirt road that was the only thoroughfare through the A Shau Valley capable of heavy vehicular traffic. *Five-Four-Eight* was the path over which the North Vietnamese funneled supplies and equipment in vast quantities into the northernmost combat zone of South Vietnam. This zone, the first of four covering all of South Vietnam and numbered with Roman numerals, was officially called I Corps Tactical Zone. Americans immediately took to calling it *Eye Corps*. The name stuck.

Knapp continued, "Now that First Cav has established LZs with firebases at the northern end of Delaware's zone of operation, the Cav's next move will be an air assault into the middle of the zone just south of the old airfield at A Luoi, right below us here on Signal Hill. Holding that airfield will allow large fixed-wing aircraft to land and offload heavy cargo, but it's going to take a lot of work by the engineers to make the runway usable again. In addition, Division has intel of an NVA base camp in the vicinity. Exactly where it is, we're not sure. But it's got to be eliminated."

When the captain paused for a sip of coffee, Lieutenant Hammond, the AXO, rolled his eyes and said to the group, "Gee, Division's got more objectives than Carter's got pills, doesn't it?"

The BC didn't appreciate the comment. His reply: "So you don't approve of their plans, Lieutenant Hammond? I'm sure the brass couldn't give a shit less…and neither do I."

He let the edgy silence reinforce Hammond's embarrassment for a moment. Then he continued, "Our mission is to make sure those anti-aircraft guns are neutralized. Our chopper force has taken something of a beating in these opening days of Delaware. They've already lost half a dozen Hueys and a couple of Chinooks to triple-A. We don't want tomorrow's assault adding to that tally. Completing this mission successfully will be a big bright feather in Charlie Battery's cap."

Sergeant McKay muttered what he and everyone else was thinking: "What the captain really means is that it'll be a big bright feather in *his* cap."

Jif had been studying the target locations on the map. He asked Knapp, "That ridge we're targeting isn't very steep or very high above the valley floor, sir. The jungle density looks light enough in spots that light trucks can probably find a way to the top without much problem. Are we thinking the NVA might've hauled some bigger weapons up there than the usual ZPU heavy machine guns?"

"The intel doesn't specify what type weapons, Lieutenant. But you're probably right on the money that they're ZPUs. The only question is whether they're single, double, or quad mounted."

"Begging your pardon, sir," Jif replied, "but there is another question, too."

"Oh? Like what, Miles?"

"We're not that far from the target, sir. Even their lightest caliber triple-A could theoretically reach us up here. The odds of an accurate hit on this peak are very small, I realize, but—"

"Then don't worry about it, Lieutenant," Knapp replied, cutting him off.

"Roger that, sir. I reckon we'll be doing our own observation and adjustments for this mission?"

"Exactly right, Miles. This is a rare opportunity for our gunners to see the results of their indirect fire. There aren't too many places on God's green earth that afford us an opportunity like this."

SFC McKay chimed in, asking the BC, "To stay on target, sir, we're going to need to use plenty of illum rounds. That ridge is invisible in the dark. Division doesn't have a problem with that, do they? They wouldn't want us lighting up friendlies accidentally."

"There'll be no problem, Sergeant," Knapp replied. "We'll use as many illum rounds as necessary."

"Damn good thing we got some, then, sir. We were down to just a couple until that ammo drop came in tonight."

Jif winced when those words came out. *Maybe Sergeant McKay isn't trying to needle the BC,* he told himself, *but it sure sounds that way.*

If the remark had annoyed Knapp, it didn't show. He asked Jif, "Which piece will fire the illum?"

"Let's use Guns One and Six to start with, sir. Once the adjustments are dialed in, I'll switch Six to HE rounds in the fire-for-effect phase."

"You really think it's necessary to use two guns for illum instead of just one, Miles?"

"I reckon so, sir. We never saw those triple-A weapons in broad daylight, and we sure as hell aren't going to see them in artificial light. I just want to make sure we illuminate that bloody ridge so well that we don't miss it…or anything that tries to move off it once the fun starts. Vehicles in motion should be easy to spot beneath illum, even partially concealed ones."

"All right, we'll do it your way," the captain replied. "The show begins at twenty-thirty hours. That gives you an hour and a half to get ready."

Jif asked, "And if other missions pop up in the meantime, sir?"

"The triple-A position gets priority, Lieutenant. It's our time to shine."

"Who terminates the mission, sir?"

"I do, Miles."

*****

The meeting at FDC over, Jif was walking back to the guns when a voice called out, "Hey, Miles…got a minute?" He turned to see the leader of the *LRRP* platoon, 1LT Mike Carpenter, jogging over to him. The LRRP outfit—pronounced *Lurp* and short for long-range recon patrol—were the men who'd rappelled from Hueys onto this mountaintop three days ago, claiming it despite sporadic but determined uphill assaults by NVA forces who'd probably outnumbered them. The efforts of Carpenter's platoon allowed the establishment of a small LZ that quickly grew into this firebase and relay station. They were still providing Signal Hill's much-needed perimeter security.

Jif replied, "What's on your mind, Mike?"

"What you said about that triple-A being able to reach this peak…was that on the level?"

"Theoretically, it's possible, I reckon," Jif replied. "Practically speaking, though, I kind of doubt it. Since you and your guys are rotating out of here in the morning, what are you worried about?"

"I'm worried about *tonight*, man. My positions down the west side of the slope could be real vulnerable to ZPU fire, even at long range. I don't need my guys getting splashed by random shit. They don't deserve that after what they've been through…not during their last night on this damn rock."

"At least your guys will be down in their fighting holes, Mike," Jif said. "Mine will be upright, manning their pieces. Those low parapets they work behind only stop incoming from the knees down. It's the nature of the beast with the one-oh-deuce howitzer, low as it sits to the ground."

Even in the darkness, Jif could see the outline of a weary smile on Carpenter's face. "Yeah, I guess it sucks sometimes to be a cannon-cocker," he replied. "Are they really not flying in any bunker-building material for you guys?"

"Aside from crates full of empty sandbags and that tiny bulldozer the engineers are using, nope. According to the powers that be, we don't need it. Our little haven in the sky is supposedly safe from enemy artillery and rockets."

"Do you believe that, Jif?"

"Not for a bloody minute. But I worry more about those NVA infantry probes. I just hope the outfit that relieves you is half as alert as you guys have been."

"Never fear, man...they're Lurps, too. They'll be great."

Carpenter looked around to make sure they were still alone. "Can I ask you something else, Jif?"

"Sure."

"That bracelet you're wearing...is that some hippie peacenik thing? Or is it from the Montagnards?"

"It's not a hippie thing, Mike," Jif replied. "The *Yards* gave it to me after a pretty hairy patrol I did with them. It's a token of friendship and respect."

"Geez, Miles...I heard they don't give those things away too easily. It's one of those deals where you've got to see the elephant, right?"

See the elephant: an expression describing wisdom gained by overcoming a great challenge.

"Roger that," Jif replied. "I reckon I've seen a few elephants. Maybe more than a few."

*****

At 2015 hours—fifteen minutes until showtime—Captain Knapp plopped down onto a camp stool between Guns Four and Five. Binoculars draped around his neck and a map board on his lap, he was readying himself to call the fire mission on the suspected triple-A location. To those watching, though, the captain looked more like he was getting ready for some bird-watching instead of a tricky night fire mission.

Sergeant McKay stifled a laugh as he thought, *All the BC needs is a little table, a checkered tablecloth, and a pot of tea.* He and Jif had already set up an observation post between Guns Five and Six, complete with field telephone wired into the battery network. Unlike the captain's position, theirs would provide an unrestricted view of the targeted ridge since they didn't have Gun Five blocking the southern end.

McKay told Jif, "I'm kind of surprised the BC didn't drag out the periscope binoculars. They'd be about as useless for this mission as tits on a boar. And speaking of useless, somebody better go tell him he's in the wrong place."

"And you reckon that *somebody* is me, right, Sergeant?"

"Affirmative, sir." Raising his open hands wide like a priest giving a blessing, McKay intoned, "Go now and enlighten the man on how it should be done."

Captain Knapp didn't take kindly to the correction. He fumed, "Are you absolutely certain where that ridge is down there, Miles?"

"We've been looking at it for three days, sir, so yes...I'm certain where it is," Jif replied. "The darkness is going to make this mission hard enough, and trying to look through a gun pit will make it even harder. And we've hooked up a phone over there so somebody doesn't have to relay our commands."

The captain picked up his stool and followed Jif to the other side of Gun Five. His tone combative, he asked, "Have you ever been a forward observer on top of a mountain like this, Lieutenant?"

"Yes, sir. During the Hue fight we called fire from a mountaintop OP for a couple days. It wasn't quite this high, but the principles are the same."

"At night, too?"

"Affirmative, sir."

"And how'd that work out, Miles?"

"Not bad. The biggest problem we had was getting a battery to support us, short on artillery as we were at the time. I don't reckon that'll be an issue here, not with our own guns shooting the mission."

Jif didn't bother to ask the captain about his experience as an FO in combat. From what he'd gathered, the man had none. But Knapp was still the boss. On his command, Guns One and Six fired their first illumination rounds simultaneously at precisely 2030 hours. Fourteen seconds later, one of the flares popped exactly where expected, high above the targeted ridge but at eye level to the men on the lofty observation post that was Signal Hill.

The other illumination round should've ejected its flare at the same time but didn't. Five seconds later, a vast stretch of jungle beyond the ridge lit up in quivering pulses of brilliant light. Distracted and paying no attention to the target area below the correctly positioned flare, Knapp groaned, "What the fuck just happened, Miles?"

"The round malfunctioned, sir," Jif replied, his eyes fixed on the ridge. "The flare didn't eject until the shell hit the ground. Now it's lit but bouncing through the jungle at a pretty good clip, lighting fires along the way. It'll stop moving in a minute and then burn out."

SFC McKay added, "We've got a pretty old lot of illum rounds, sir. The gel inside some of them must've gotten a little thick. We can fix that." He immediately relayed the solution to the guns: "Rap all around the circumference of the illum rounds with the fuze wrench before you set them into the cartridge. That oughta break up the jelly."

Jif stayed focused on the fire mission. He told Knapp, "We've got good visibility on the target area, sir. No sign of any triple-A weapons, but that's not surprising. If they're really there, they'll be hidden among the trees as long as they don't try to move. We can shoot an HE adjustment round as soon as the next pair of illum is in the air."

"Are you sure, Miles? I didn't see much of anything that time around."

Jif replied, "I'm sure, sir." What he didn't add: *If you hadn't let yourself get distracted by that bizarre light show, you'd be sure enough to shoot the high explosives, too.*

The second pair of illum rounds was in the air thirty seconds later, their firing timed to provide continuous illumination of the target area. The first HE adjustment round was fifteen seconds behind them. This time, both flares popped at the correct point in their trajectory, bathing the ridge below them in silvery artificial daylight as they floated down to earth on parachutes.

The phone to his ear, McKay called out, "Splash." He was relaying FDC's alert that the HE adjustment round would impact in just a few seconds. But that time came and went and they saw no flash of impact. The sound of its explosion—if there was going to be a sound—would take fifteen seconds to travel the five-kilometer distance.

An agitated Captain Knapp asked, "Where the hell is that bastard? Don't tell me we've got a lost round."

"It's not lost, sir," Jif replied. "It just fell real close behind the ridge and got masked."

"But we should be able to see it, anyway, dammit. The ridge isn't that high." As the captain said it, the muted *boom* of the round's unseen impact floated up to Signal Hill, covering the five-klick distance on schedule.

"The ridge is high enough, sir," Jif replied. "Just drop one hundred and try again."

They took Knapp's silence as tacit agreement, and McKay called in the correction. No sooner had he done that than FDC reported a new mission, a request for illumination at coordinates seven kilometers—over four miles—to the northwest of Signal Hill. The area to be lit up was on the valley floor along Route 548.

"Tell them to give it to some other battery," the captain said. "We're busy with a priority mission."

Brigade's rapid reply could be summarized like this: *Everybody else is pretty busy, too, sport, so how about a little help?*

The request—an order, actually—shouldn't have come as a surprise. There could be no doubt just how busy the other batteries in the area were. The rumble of distant guns had been a constant since nightfall. Yet Knapp seemed confused, as if the brass had changed the rules on him in mid-game, diluting the importance of his critical and potentially career-enhancing assignment.

Jif appealed to the BC, saying, "Sir, we'll have enough light on the ridge now with just one gun firing illum. We can easily shift Gun One to help them out up north."

The captain took issue, replying, "But then we'd be shooting three damn missions at once, Miles. We'll overload our FDC, and nobody will get fire when they need it."

"Not if Sergeant McKay helps them out as an extra computer, sir."

The Smoke had already handed the telephone to Jif and started running toward the FDC bunker.

The first thing Jif heard from the handset: "Splash, over."

This time, they saw the adjustment round land. It hit the front face of the ridge no more than thirty meters from the crest. Knapp was ecstatic as he said, "Add five-zero, fire for effect."

No sooner had Jif called in that correction than the first burst of green tracers began to arc through the night sky toward Signal Hill. They looked like fireworks from hell.

Chapter Two

"They aren't even coming close," Jif said as the green tracers struck the western slope of Signal Hill. "Doesn't look like the Lurp LPs down there are getting hit, either. Just gotta watch the bouncers. Lucky there aren't too many of them, though."

"Those ricochets won't make it up here to the peak," Captain Knapp said. "They've already lost most of their energy." His words sounded more like wishful thinking than a confident pronouncement on ballistics.

"It's going to depend on what they bounce off of, I reckon," Jif added. "And there's got to be some bouncing of ball rounds going on we can't bloody see."

The arcs of the tracers seemed deceptively listless, but the artillerymen were fully aware of their deadliness. Watching those projectiles try to reach the peak against near-impossible odds, they couldn't forget that between each of those streaks of green light were four or five ball rounds that didn't glow. If one of those invisible rounds ricocheted, you'd have no idea what its new trajectory was until it struck something.

But the near-constant bursts aimed at the firebase on Signal Hill yielded one benefit: the tracers betrayed the NVA weapons' firing point. "The stupid bloody bastards," Jif said as he estimated the necessary shift to the now-revealed target. "They just gave their position away for nothing. I reckon they forgot tracers work both ways. I call it left five-zero, fire for effect. Check or hold?"

He'd expected an immediate answer from the BC, whether it be a confirmation—a check—or rejection—a hold—of his estimate. It was, after all, the captain's fire mission, but he was mulling it over, saying nothing. As precious seconds dragged on, Jif said, "We've got to go with bloody something, sir," and called in his correction.

No sooner had FDC acknowledged the adjustment data than Knapp said, "Negative. As you were, Lieutenant. That's not enough of a shift. Make it left one hundred."

"Too late, sir. We'd better let them shoot. It'll just cause confusion and more delay if they don't."

The firing data was set; rounds were in the tubes. Jif told the battery to fire.

"You'd better pray you're right, Lieutenant," the captain said. "Otherwise, you just wasted four rounds."

It would take fourteen seconds for the volley to reach the ridge. As those seconds ticked away, a tracer struck the slope and bounced higher than any before it, dropped onto the peak, and set fire to Gun Five's canvas-roofed ammo hutch. Then the glowing round lodged in a parapet sandbag and quickly burned out.

The fire atop the ammo hutch threatened disaster. Jif and the captain were only yards away from the blaze as it spread quickly across the canvas.

Distracted by the flames, Knapp hadn't seen the rounds land. Jif was the only man watching the impacts on the ridge. They were right where he'd wanted them, but they'd struck slightly to the left of the still-firing triple-A. He didn't bother pointing out that if they'd used the captain's desired correction, they would've missed by a hell of a lot more.

The fire at Gun Five was still raging.

Jif didn't bother asking the BC's adjustment this time. He told FDC, "Right two-zero, repeat fire for effect."

Two more green tracers bounced up to the firebase, headed for the radio relay bunker.

Intent on commanding the firefighting effort at Gun Five, Knapp left the observation post. He called back to Jif, "Take over the mission, Miles. We're going down the tubes here!"

Take over? That's funny...it feels like I've been calling the bloody thing all along.

The situation wasn't quite as far down the tubes as the captain feared, but he failed to recognize that fact. At the able direction of their section chief, Gun Five's cannoneers had wrenched the flaming tarp from the hutch and tossed it over the parapet, where it could burn without threatening any explosives. But in the process, smoldering fragments from the canvas had fallen among projectiles and cartridges waiting to be joined together once their powder bags were cut to the proper charge. Just one spark could set off a cartridge's bags, creating a conflagration that couldn't be extinguished quickly by any means at hand. If that blaze persisted long enough to cook off even one projectile, the devastation would be no different than a direct hit by enemy artillery...

And *long enough to cook off* could be measured in seconds.

As men worked feverishly to move the ammunition away from the flames, a burning canvas fragment floated into the open end of an upright cartridge they hadn't gotten to yet. Only one cannoneer saw it happen. Trying to reach the propellant-laden cartridge and snatch it away to safety, he crashed headlong into Captain Knapp, who was darting around the parapet, screeching orders that seemed unnecessary and at cross purposes to those issued by the section chief.

"MAKE A HOLE, SIR," the frustrated man pleaded with the captain, trying to reach around the obstacle Knapp had become.

He didn't get there in time. A blowtorch-like flame shot upward from the cartridge as the top bag—Number 7, the largest one in the propellant charge—ignited. Both men were driven back by the searing heat.

There were six more bags stacked beneath Number 7, each smaller than the one above it. They'd light off in a heartbeat.

"I'LL GRAB IT," the BC said. "STAND CLEAR."

Knapp had never dealt with an uncontrolled propellant fire before; most artillerymen hadn't. They all burned huge piles of unused powder bags from rounds fired at less than full charge on a regular basis, but that was always in a controlled setting, where the impossible task of extinguishing the blaze never entered into the equation. SOP was to allow the bags to burn themselves out fiercely, safely, and quickly.

The captain's instinctive reaction was to adapt the procedure for a hangfire, which was designed for a round already loaded into a howitzer. If that round failed to fire, the canister would be ejected from the breech, its base thrown backward into the grasp of a cannoneer's outstretched hand. He'd then fling the bags out into the safe zone behind the howitzer in one sweeping motion. If they ignited, they'd individually burn out very quickly and cause no harm.

But this cartridge wasn't in a breech. It was sitting upright on an empty ammo box. Even using both hands, grabbing the base of the brass cylinder as it spewed a tongue of brilliant orange flame was a tricky proposition. Somehow, Knapp picked it up without burning himself outright. All he had to do now was fling out the bags while still hanging on to the base firmly.

And that's where it all went wrong.

In an instant, the brass became too hot to hold in bare hands as more of the bags inside ignited. Knapp tried to launch the burning contents with an underhand motion, much like a softball pitcher's delivery. But he lost his grip along with a layer of skin from each of his palms. The cartridge sailed a few yards across the gun parapet and struck Spec-4 Danby, the crew's gunner, in the shoulder as he tried to duck out of its way. His utility shirt was ablaze instantly.

As Danby fought a losing battle to peel off the shirt, a quick-thinking PFC tackled him and smothered the flaming garment with a flak jacket. It saved the gunner's life but couldn't prevent the severe burns that would cover his arm and back. His war was over.

Still on fire, powder bags from the hurled canister spilled into the ammo hutch just inches from some unopened boxes of rounds. The cannoneers quickly dragged those boxes clear of the flames, which died out on their own a few moments later.

The fiasco had taken all of twenty seconds.

Firing data for the next volley had already been sent to the guns shooting HE. All of them had rounds in the tube except Number Five, still deep in its own chaos. Realizing there was no one at the gunner's station, Jif jumped into the gun pit and assumed Danby's duties.

While setting the deflection, he shouted the elevation to the assistant gunner on the other side of the piece, who'd just performed double duty by grabbing a round and ramming it into the breech. Jif gave the command for the battery to fire.

The volley on the way, he stood on the gun chassis, preparing to observe its impact on the ridge.

It hit just where he'd wanted. The green tracers being lofted toward Signal Hill stopped suddenly. There was an unexpected bonus: he could see movement on the ridge. Vehicles of some sort were heading east, no doubt trying to flee.

Jif was startled as SFC McKay's voice rose above the din of men shouting, trying to sort out the shambles inside their parapet. "Looks like a good hit, sir," the sergeant said, "and I think you've got some gooks on the run, too. I'd chase them, if I were you."

"Where the bloody hell did you come from, Smoke? Why aren't you at FDC?"

"They don't need me there, sir. Lieutenant Hammond figured out how to shoot three missions at once all on his own. You sure as hell need some help out here, though. Keep playing FO and gunner at the same time until I sort out the clusterfuck going on in this gun pit, okay?"

"Sounds like a plan, Sergeant."

Jif was thinking the same thing as his chief of smoke: *Chase them. Now that the incoming's shut off, all I've got to do is figure out where those vehicles doing a runner are trying to go. Maybe they're towing guns...*

And with a little luck, we can ruin their whole day, too.

Telling FDC to *wait one*, he pulled out the map and studied it in his flashlight's beam, looking for a likely route the vehicles could use to escape the ridge. *They're headed east,* he reasoned, *and our illum rounds are helping them out by lighting the way. Still, their exit route can't be too steep or clogged with trees...*

So how about this draw where the ridge gets L-shaped? It's a shallow downhill slope, the vegetation is light according to the map, and it ends at a trail leading straight to Route Five-Four-Eight.

A moment's study of the illuminated terrain through binoculars confirmed his suspicion. There was definitely movement down that draw, disappearing and reappearing as it passed beneath crowns of trees. It had to be vehicles...

Or we've scared a small herd of elephants into a stampede.

All I've got to do is guess where they'll be in about forty seconds.

His mental calculation complete, he told FDC, "Left two hundred, drop two hundred, fuze VT, repeat fire for effect."

Let's give them those perfect airbursts with VT fuzes. Shift the focus to the personnel on board instead of the vehicles themselves.

As FDC did its computations, there was the flash of an explosion on the ridge at the impact point of the last volley. It quickly developed into a continuous fireworks display, with glowing projectiles being shot in a variety of directions.

Ammo's cooking off, Jif told himself. *Looks like we bloody well hit something.*

Seeing the airbursts might be difficult; they'd be nothing but momentary pinpoints of intense light in the silvery wash of an illumination flare. But he saw them clearly enough, as well as the dust devils they stirred on the ground below.

Right where I want them. But did I hit anything?

The motion of vehicles that had been so obvious a moment ago could no longer be seen.

Do I shoot another volley of airbursts as insurance? Or do I go back to point-detonating fuzes?

What about shooting white phosphorous? That works real good against vehicles.

He decided on the white phosphorous—usually referred to as *willy pete* or *WP*—and told FDC to repeat fire for effect. The voice on the phone had changed; it wasn't one of the RTOs, but Lieutenant Hammond.

"Roger on the willy pete, XO, but we've got a big problem," Hammond said. "Brigade is calling for maximum effort against that target up north by *La Dut*, the one we're lighting up with illum from Gun One. Must be some big shit going on...they want every battery hitting it ASAP with HE. And as far as our mission against the triple-A goes, they want it wrapped up like yesterday."

"Stand by," Jif replied. "Gotta check with the BC. The triple-A mission is his baby."

And I've stepped on his toes enough already. Let him decide this one.

Captain Knapp was still immersed in the havoc he'd caused by setting Danby on fire. The medic, who'd just arrived, was shaking his head in disbelief as he carefully cut away what was left of the gunner's charred shirt, unable to fathom how such a screwup could happen. Jif couldn't make out much of what was being said, but everything out of Knapp's mouth sounded both overbearing and defensive in the same breath. The sentiment *it was just an accident* seemed present in every sentence he spoke. The enraged gun crew wasn't buying it; *you fucked up* was the expression they preferred, and the murmurs were growing louder. Chief of Smoke McKay defused the confrontation by telling the captain, "Sir, we need you back at the OP running that mission on the triple-A. Lieutenant Miles is wearing too many hats right now."

As soon as the WP volley was fired, Gun Five's section chief took over at the gunner's position. As Jif climbed over the parapet, Knapp demanded, "Where do we stand, Miles? I see lots of stuff burning down there."

"With any luck, you're about to see even more, sir. Take a look."

A few seconds later, the WP rounds impacted in the draw, erupting in brilliant balls of orange flame.

Knapp erupted with, "What the fuck, Lieutenant? Why in the name of God are we not hitting the ridge?"

Jif explained how he'd sighted the movement off the peak. Then he told him of Brigade's demand for maximum effort against the northern target at La Dut.

"That's just fine and dandy, Miles, but is this mission finished? Yes or no?"

Jif scanned the target area, hoping to see vehicle fires from the WP and more ammo cooking off. None of that was happening...

But nothing's moving.

All I know is we got at least some of the triple-A, and if there's any left, it's not posing a threat to us at the moment.

But there are some guys north of here who must need supporting fire pretty badly.

I reckon they should come first.

Knapp repeated his question: "Are we finished here or what, Miles?"

"Affirmative, sir. I think we've done all we can do."

"You'd better hope so, Lieutenant. Now make Brigade happy and shoot their damn mission." As he started to walk away, the captain snarled, "I'll be at the CP. Let's try not to have any more clusterfucks tonight…and keep watching for any signs of that triple-A."

The BC kept waggling his hands, as if they were causing him great discomfort. Having no idea they'd been burned by the hot canister, Jif asked, "Something wrong with your hands, sir?"

"No, Miles. There's not a goddamn thing wrong with these mitts."

"What about Specialist Danby? Are we getting a night medevac for him?"

"All we can do is ask, Lieutenant. The rest is up to the rotorheads."

*****

The guns of Fire Base Signal Hill didn't fall silent for another hour. A medevac chopper was on the way for the badly burned Spec-4 Danby, ETA roughly 2200 hours. The *rotorheads*—the helicopter pilots—gave no guarantees they'd come within a klick of the peak unless it was lit up like Times Square. José "Joe" Contreras, Charlie Battery's first sergeant, was busy cobbling together a beacon and floodlight array for the LZ with the help of the engineer detachment. They were desperate to get it right; this was the first time aviators had expressed any willingness at all to come to Signal Hill in total darkness, and they wanted to make sure it wasn't the last. Danby needed to be in a hospital, not spending an agonizing night at a mountaintop aid station. If he could be moved to Quang Tri or Da Nang tonight, he'd probably be in Japan or on an evacuation flight back to the States by noon tomorrow. Contreras told himself, *It's a cryin' shame it happened at all, but we're damn lucky he's the only man who got hurt tonight. But are we going to count him as wounded in action or an accident victim? I've got a hunch the captain's going to lean real hard toward WIA.*

*****

SFC McKay told Jif, "We'd better plan on firing illum over that ridge until sunrise, Lieutenant. Unless they start shooting at us again, that's the only way we've got a shot at spotting those triple-A bastards...if we didn't already waste them, that is."

"Copy that, Smoke. How much illum do we have left?"

McKay yelled that same question to the battery recorder, who checked his clipboard and replied, "Forty-six rounds, Sarge."

"Here's what I want to do," Jif said. "We'll keep lighting up the ridge but no more than three illum rounds an hour...and not on any regular schedule."

"Copy that, sir," McKay replied. "I'll make it happen."

There were two other casualties from the triple-A attack on Signal Hill; both were pieces of equipment. The water trailer—known as a *water buffalo*—had held three hundred gallons when it was struck by a ball round bouncer that passed completely through the tank, leaving a jagged hole an inch in diameter at the top and bottom. As water poured from the lower puncture, the men of the mess section caught as much as possible in jerry cans and stock pots, managing to save a third of the tank's contents. "That's only going to last us a day, Top," the mess steward, Spec-6 Nick Panakis, told First Sergeant Contreras.

"Tell me something I don't know," Contreras replied. He was well aware they weren't scheduled to receive a new, topped-off water trailer for another two days. "I'll see if we can get the buffalo delivery bumped up to tomorrow."

They'd need that water badly. The regular delivery of water buffaloes by Chinook was the only way to adequately and efficiently feed and water the artillerymen, signalmen, engineers, and Lurps on the mountain. Together, they numbered just over one hundred fifty men.

"If they don't bring us one ASAP," the steward said, "we're going to be catching rainwater and eating C rations. That ain't gonna work for too long with this bunch."

"Again, Nick, tell me something I don't know," Contreras replied.

The second inanimate casualty: the radio bunker. The tracers seen bouncing that way had done some damage, too. An antenna mast and cable had been severed, the resulting short circuit causing internal damage to one of the station's two transmitters, knocking it off the air. It could be fixed, but the technicians needed parts that had been placed on board the medevac chopper coming for Danby. Until repairs could be made, the station's ability to handle traffic would be slowed significantly. But it was still on the air, at least.

Lieutenant Carpenter's Lurps manning the listening posts on the west slope endured some terrifying moments as triple-A rounds splashed dangerously close to their fighting holes. Even though the NVA fire had stopped, they were still jumpy.

"Every five minutes, they think they've spotted another bunch of gooks trying to climb the mountain, coming right for them," Carpenter told Jif. "But all they've really seen so far are shadows from your illum rounds."

"And that's probably all they're going to see," Jif replied. "The west slope is too steep for man or beast. The gooks haven't come that way yet, and I doubt they ever will."

"I hope you're right, dude...because your howitzers can't cover that direction with direct fire."

"Mike, we can't cover *most* of the slopes up this hill with the howitzers. They're too bloody steep. The tubes just don't go down that low. The only direction we can cover is the southeast...and that would only work with killer juniors."

"What about beehive, dude?"

"Beehive is worthless up here. We've got some, but it won't touch anybody on the slopes. If we use it on the peak, we'll be killing each other."

That sounded like a sad state of affairs to Carpenter. "You really think a couple of M60 machine guns are going to cover those slopes if the gooks decide to come up en masse?"

Jif replied, "Those machine guns, plus Claymores, gunships, and the fire from other batteries up north, will have to do the job."

"All I can say is that I'll be glad to get off this rock, Jif."

*****

The medevac chopper was on the radio, calling in range. First Sergeant Contreras looked to Captain Knapp and asked, "Time to light the place up, sir?"

"If we must, Top," the BC replied. "Crank it up."

With the signal from Contreras, the LZ was suddenly outlined in the darkness by strings of generator-powered marker lights staked to the ground. The mutter of the approaching Huey grew louder, although no one could see her muted navigation lights through the glare of the markers. The first sergeant stood ready with illuminated wands in each hand—one red, one green—to guide the medevac in.

The ship finally crept into sight, two hundred feet above him. He raised the wands high above his head...

And that's when the first mortar rounds exploded on the peak, dangerously close to the LZ.

Chapter Three

The medevac pilot's voice on the radio was emphatic: "You've got five seconds, then we're out of here."

Everyone on Signal Hill was surprised he'd set the chopper down at all with enemy mortar rounds splashing around her. But there'd only been three impacts so far, one roughly forty yards off her nose and two more in a twenty-yard radius of her tail. Jif said, "I reckon the pilots only saw the one at her one o'clock. Good thing those other two landed behind her. If they'd seen them, they would've sworn the ship was being bracketed and aborted for sure."

Chief of Smoke McKay replied, "You've got that right, sir."

First Sergeant Contreras' detail had no trouble making that five-second window. Danby's stretcher was hustled on board while several boxes of supplies were kicked out the chopper's door. The Huey was gone before the next three-round volley of mortar fire struck the firebase. They caused no damage, either, but kept everyone on edge.

The medevac accomplished, Contreras gave the order to kill the LZ's marker lights. While his team scurried away with the boxes the Huey had delivered—one of which contained the parts needed to fix the radio station's second transmitter—the first sergeant straddled one of the impact craters, inspecting the jagged hole with his flashlight. Jif ran to join him.

"It's coming from the southeast, Lieutenant," Contreras said, sighting down the longest dimension of the crater's oval. "Just like we figured it might. Looks to be eighty-two millimeter."

Jif pulled the map from his shirt pocket. They were well familiar with its depiction of the topography to the southeast. The rising terrain formed a narrow, kilometer-long table jutting from the mountainside six hundred feet below the peak on which they stood. They'd already sighted in and recorded the gunnery data that would enable the howitzers to pour fire down on its key points. It would be a torturous climb for the North Vietnamese carrying the one-hundred-twenty-five-pound mortars plus ammo up to the table, but the enemy rarely shied away from physical challenges.

"So they're somewhere in this one-klick-long box," Jif said, "at a range of between one and two klicks."

"Roger that," the first sergeant replied. "Again, it's just like we figured."

Another mortar volley landed, but it was only two rounds this time. Both hit the south side of the now-deserted LZ, tearing up some marker lights but nothing else.

"They're just shifting the stuff around in the blind," Contreras said. "They can't have eyes on the top of this peak no matter where they are…and either they're running out of ammo already or their third tube shit the bed on them."

Even though he had a counterfire plan ready to go, Jif asked, "Where's the BC? I'm sure he'll want to add his two cents about what to do next."

"He'll be along," the first sergeant replied. "He's still with the doc, getting those burned hands of his fixed up. In the meantime, we'd better start shooting back before the gooks get lucky."

"Sure, Top, but we need to get the Lurps out of their LP in that sector. One mistake launching time fuzes set to almost nothing over their heads can cause—"

Captain Knapp's voice boomed out of the darkness, cutting Jif off. "There won't be any damn mistakes, Miles," he said. "I expect you to see to that. Get that counter-battery fire up and running right now."

"We're on it, sir," Jif replied. Then he told SFC McKay, "Guns Five and Six, use data for target Mike, one round, fire at will."

The gun crews spun their guns to the predetermined deflection, cranked in negative elevation for the downslope shots, and set the mechanical time fuzes on the projectiles to just under two seconds. Captain Knapp misconstrued how the gunners were aiming their pieces. He called out, "Miles, what the hell are you doing? Are you shooting direct fire against a target you can't even see?"

The two guns roared in near-perfect synchronization. There was barely time to blink before the low airbursts flashed in the darkness below, followed seconds later by the delayed *crack* of their detonations. Jif commanded, "Shift to target data Foxtrot, one round, fire at will." Then he explained to the captain, "We don't need to see the aiming points at all, sir. We already dialed in the data with the direct fire scopes during daylight. Those points won't move."

"But temperature changes and wind can make you miss," Knapp sputtered, "and you can't adjust fire on targets you can't see."

"We shouldn't need to adjust, sir," Jif replied. "At these short ranges, temperature and wind don't matter a whole lot."

Guns Five and Six roared again. The recoil from low elevation and high charge caused them to jump viciously, loosening the hold-down stakes driven through their firing plates. At each piece, a cannoneer with a mallet was pounding those stakes back into the ground moments after the round was on its way.

As Knapp watched the gun crews work with stunning efficiency, 1SG Contreras said, "The firing data we're using is written on the battery defense plan you approved, sir. The XO sighted it all in on day one—three points along that table labeled *November* for near, *Mike* for mid, and *Foxtrot* for far. Consider it short-range harassment and interdiction fire, combining killer junior techniques with indirect fire procedures."

Killer junior: high-explosive rounds with mechanical time fuzes set to extremely low settings, fired from light and medium howitzers at low elevation to create short-range airbursts very near the ground. They were equally effective against personnel whether in the open or down in the cover of fighting holes.

"And we don't even need to waste illum rounds, either," Contreras added. "We won't see much of a mortar and its crew, anyway. Not unless they get much closer."

Knapp demanded, "Did anybody even try to look for them with the starlight scope?"

Doing his best to stay calm and reassuring, Contreras replied, "Affirmative, sir, but nothing showed up within the scope's range."

Another two mortar rounds crashed down, missing the peak completely but landing a hundred yards down the eastern slope near a Lurp listening post. Even more perturbed now, the BC told his first sergeant, "Check with Lieutenant Carpenter, Top. See if his men are okay."

Jif commanded a shift to target data *November*, the nearest point on the table but still a kilometer away. He added, "Maybe third time's the charm."

As Guns Five and Six fired their next set of rounds, Contreras assured the agitated captain that the Lurps were not endangered by the mortar rounds; they weren't even at the LP anymore. "You don't need to worry about them, sir," he added. "They know the score. They beat feet up here to the peak as soon as our first rounds left the tubes."

Jif was sure the first sergeant was needling the BC over his earlier lack of concern for the Lurps, when he demanded the counter-battery fire commence without regard to their potentially endangered position...

But he slipped the knife in so gracefully that the captain didn't even feel the pain... and with all due respect, of course.

That's an art I'm still working on.

The captain went back to grilling Jif. "What's your plan if this third volley doesn't stop the mortars, Miles?"

"Then we walk our rounds back down the table fifty meters at a time, sir."

"Have you got the firing data for that? You still can't see anything."

"Simple interpolation, sir," Jif replied. "Close enough for government work, you know?"

As he spoke, one of the other howitzers lofted an illumination round toward the triple-A site. Knapp asked, "What the hell are we shooting now?"

A few seconds later, the flare popped high in the sky over the ridge, answering the question.

When the plan for random illumination of that previous target was explained to him, the captain replied, "Only two or three flares an hour? That's not enough, Miles. We'll talk about it after you shut down those mortars."

Jif couldn't stop glancing at the captain's burned hands. The white gauze wrapped around them glimmered in the darkness. His first thought: *I hope he doesn't have to handle a personal weapon anytime soon. He'll have a big problem getting his finger into the trigger guard of that forty-five on his hip...if he can even hold the bloody thing.*

He was going to suggest that maybe the captain should carry an M16 instead. At least then he could use the cold-weather mitten option and open the lower bar of the trigger guard for better access. As cranky as Knapp had become lately, though, he decided to say nothing.

An entire minute passed in relative silence. No mortar rounds landed on Signal Hill, no howitzers needed to hurl their rebuttals into the darkness below. Jif was computing what the next correction for the guns would be—the walking down the table he'd described to Captain Knapp—if the mortars continued their barrage…

Which they didn't.

Two minutes later, the quiet was shattered by small arms fire on the north side of the perimeter. But it wasn't the usual riotous exchange of Soviet-bloc and American weapons. Contreras said, "Sounds like nothing but a handful of *Sixteens*...no AKs, no SKS, no nothing. That's pretty damn strange...and on the north sector?"

The relay station and engineer camp were the only installations on the north side of Signal Hill. They'd been positioned there—the sector deemed most impervious to assault—since it bordered on the steepest and least accessible path to the peak.

"Mountain goats couldn't climb that slope," the first sergeant added.

Knapp's RTO was listening to nothing but silence in his handset. He told the captain, "I'm not believing this, sir, but I can't raise the relay station...and they're only like two hundred meters away. Something's really fucked up here."

"Let's take nothing for granted, Top," Knapp told Contreras. "Get the reaction force moving that way like right fucking now. You and I are going, too."

The BC turned to Jif and said, "XO, load beehive on Gun Three." Then he added, "Just in case."

Just in case: Jif took that to imply that if the north side of the perimeter was, in fact, being overrun, any Americans not already dead at the relay station or engineer camp would be deemed expendable. In Charlie Battery's crescent-shaped formation, Gun Three—the base piece in the open jaw of that crescent—was the only one of the six howitzers that could possibly employ beehive rounds in that desperate scenario. They'd turn the weapon into a giant shotgun that would not discriminate between friend and foe as it hurled thousands of flechettes across the flat, open space of the peak, cutting anyone above ground in their path to ribbons.

The other five howitzers had no use for beehive, positioned as they were along the edge of the western slope. The ground-skimming flechettes would be worthless against attackers on the mountainside; the tubes couldn't depress far enough to hit them. Turning inward and firing across the peak would only shred other battery personnel. That's why the twenty rounds of beehive in the battery's inventory were stacked only at Gun Three...

And nobody expected to ever use them.

As he ran off to join the reaction force, Captain Knapp didn't get more than a few steps before becoming a slapstick parody of a Wild West gunslinger. He'd managed to draw his .45 caliber from its holster, but he couldn't hold on to it with his bandaged hands. The pistol fell to the ground once and then again as he tried and failed to retrieve it.

Watching the spectacle, a cannoneer mumbled, "Maybe he should forget the forty-five and just set the gooks on fire. He's real good at that."

SFC McKay dressed the man down immediately. "Knock that bullshit off, smartass," he said. But the rebuke was difficult to deliver with conviction. The battery wasn't likely to let the BC off the hook for Danby's injuries for quite a while, if ever.

Jif jogged over to the struggling captain, popping open the trigger guard of his M16 with the tip of a ballpoint pen along the way. Even bandaged fingers would be able to fire the weapon now. Handing the rifle to Knapp, he said, "Here, sir...tuck this under your arm. It's an easier carry...there's more to grab. I'll take the forty-five."

There was no hint of gratitude in the captain's reply. "Very well, Lieutenant," he said. "Now get that beehive ready." Then he was just another silhouette vanishing into the darkness.

Jif and McKay moved to Gun Three. The chief of smoke said, "It sure sounds like we're getting way ahead of ourselves with this beehive order, Lieutenant."

"I agree, Smoke. I don't think we're that desperate yet."

"But are we going to put one into the tube like the man wants?"

"Not exactly," Jif replied. "Traverse the gun north and line up three beehive, ready to load. Minimum fuze setting. Chamber a round only on my command."

"He's going to think you're countermanding his order, sir."

"*Load* can be taken with a grain of salt, Smoke. I'm sure you can think of a whole lot of reasons you wouldn't put a round in the tube until you absolutely had to."

"Sure I can. But still..."

"Look, Smoke...if we actually need to use beehive, God forbid, we'll still be ready."

McKay didn't sound completely convinced as he replied, "As you wish, sir."

"In the meantime," Jif said, "have Gun Two put another illum over the triple-A site and up the rate to four per hour. I reckon that's what the boss wants, and it's a little harder to weasel out of that order."

The reaction force, an ad hoc battery defense team of eight artillerymen armed with M16s and with two machine guns, crept up to the relay station. Inside, they found nothing but three nervous radio operators crouched behind their equipment, clutching their rifles. The sound of gunfire had faded away, replaced by frenzied voices coming from some distance down the slope, shouting in English. They were bellowing things like, "YOU DIE TONIGHT, GOOK," along with assorted insults regarding the virtue of North Vietnamese mothers and sisters.

First Sergeant Contreras asked the lead radio operator, "Just what in blue blazes is going on here, Specialist? Is that your men doing the yelling?"

"I don't know those voices, First Sergeant."

"Then what do you know?"

The man replied, "All I can tell you is that our techs were outside, working on the antenna that got damaged. They lost one of the parts...an element. It rolled down the slope a ways. They had to have it for the fix, so they went looking for it."

"Okay," Contreras said, "so how many of your men are wandering around down there in the dark?"

"Four."

"Give me their names, quick."

As the man wrote them down on a message form, Contreras asked, "Who the hell do they think they're shooting at?"

Pointing to a stack of M16s in the corner of the bunker, he replied, "I don't think they're doing the shooting, First Sergeant. All their weapons are over there."

"Dammit, it's got to be those engineers, then," Contreras said. "They've got LP duty in this sector tonight. Dial up the switchboard, have them get *LP Easy* on the horn…"

As the radioman cranked the field telephone, the first sergeant added, "Before we kill our own guys…if we haven't already."

That was the moment Captain Knapp stormed into the radio bunker, demanding an immediate situation report. Eyeing the BC's empty holster and the M16 slung on his shoulder, Contreras asked, "You didn't misplace your forty-five, did you, sir?"

"No, Top, I did not," he replied. "Now give me the sitrep."

"The switchboard can't get through to LP Easy," the radioman reported.

"Then have them connect us to the engineer compound," Contreras said.

Knapp demanded, "Are we engaged in an enemy assault?"

"Don't believe so, sir," the first sergeant replied. He was halfway through his report to the captain when the radioman said, "We've got the engineer compound on the horn." Knapp grabbed the phone from him.

The engineer section chief was equally clueless about what was happening down the slope. He, too, had been trying to contact LP Easy without success and was seeking help from the Lurps over the radio. Before the captain could formulate a plan, the first sergeant was already on his way out of the bunker, taking his RTO and two others from the reaction force with him. When Knapp called out to stop him, he replied, "I've got this covered, sir…but put the Lurps on standby, please. They'll confuse things even more."

Seeing that the captain still lacked a grasp of the situation, a sergeant from the reaction force explained, "He didn't want the whole team wandering around down there in the dark, sir. That's just more guys to get lost…and maybe shot by friendly fire. He's got the radio if he needs help."

"Understood," the BC replied, although he still didn't understand much of anything. But desperate to feel necessary, he continued, "I'll take care of the Lurps."

He was about to add, *Get your people out on the perimeter, Sergeant*, but they were already headed that way.

*****

First Sergeant Contreras and his three men didn't waste time wandering the steep slope in the dark. Instead, they ran straight to the engineer camp, picked up the telephone line running to LP Easy, and followed that wire down to the listening post. It took only a minute of half-walking and half-sliding on their backsides to reach it. Just feet from the LP, they realized why its phone was dead; the first sergeant had the bare wire ends in his hand. They'd been yanked from the phone, no doubt another accident in the chain of screwups plaguing the north side.

The two engineers manning the LP were so in the grip of an imagined enemy incursion that they didn't hear Contreras coming. When he growled, "Which one of you dipshits is in charge here?" they spun around in panic, nearly dropping their M16s.

"I guess I am, Sarge," an overwrought spec-4 replied.

Contreras said, "You *guess*? You're *not sure*? That figures. You're shooting at your own guys, numbnuts. If you've hit any of them, it's your ass. What direction are they and how far?"

When the specialist answered with great certainty, the first sergeant replied, "At least you're showing me excellent terrain appreciation. Now go get them."

Both engineers responded to that order with looks of abject horror.

"I'll make it easy for you," Contreras continued. He called out, "MALINSKI...YOU STILL DRAWING BREATH DOWN THERE?"

It took a few seconds for a terrified voice to reply, "YEAH. I'M OKAY. GOT A BAD CASE OF THE BROWN DRAWERS, THOUGH."

"HOW ABOUT THE OTHER THREE?"

"SAME-SAME."

Turning back to the senior engineer, the first sergeant said, "Well, son...good thing you can appreciate the hell out of terrain because you can't shoot worth a shit. I say again, go get them."

*****

Shook up but otherwise unscathed, Malinski and the other commo techs were returned to the relay station. Their near-fatal misadventure was actually a success story; they'd found the lost antenna part. But they'd ventured outside the perimeter without ever bothering to learn the day's challenge and password. Trying to ascend the slope back to the relay station, the techs became disoriented and stumbled to within fifty meters of LP Easy. Then, pinned down in terrified, bladder-emptying silence behind a fallen tree, they became pop-up targets in a shooting gallery.

After explaining it all to Captain Knapp, Contreras added, "It's amazing that even when there's no way to go but up, you can still make a wrong turn."

The BC asked, "So there is no evidence of NVA intruders on the north slope?"

"Negative, sir. Just our own dimbulbs stumbling around in the dark."

"And the radio station is back on the air?"

"Affirmative, Captain. At full capacity."

"Excellent, First Sergeant. We have our happy ending. But I want you to personally re-educate the radiomen and engineers on perimeter security procedures. We don't need any more clusterfucks like that one."

"As you wish, sir."

Knapp had one more potential calamity to avert. He raced back to the firing battery and found Jif at Gun Two, which was shooting another illum round to light up the triple-A site. The BC asked, "Anything new turning up down there, Miles?"

"Not a bloody thing, sir."

"Excellent. Let's hope it stays that way. Now listen up…you can stand down with the beehive. We won't be needing it now."

Jif feigned a sigh of relief. "That's real good to hear, sir."

"I take it you've fired beehive in battery defense before, Lieutenant?"

"Affirmative, sir…several times. And it's not something I ever want to do again."

He didn't bother asking the captain if he'd ever faced an imminent overrun, with beehive the last-ditch chance for salvation. He knew the man hadn't.

Knapp's face grew stern as he said, "You know, I walked past Gun Three on the way over here. You didn't put a beehive in the tube, did you?"

"No, sir, just aimed the piece and set the fuzes." His tone wasn't defiant or defensive, just matter-of-fact.

"And why did you stop there, Lieutenant?" It seemed like he was offering Jif the rope to hang himself.

But his reply was still straightforward: "Because after we didn't use it, we'd just have to ram it out to shoot a different type mission. Punching a round out of the tube takes a ton of brute force. Fragile as those beehive canisters are, I didn't want to end up with a damaged round we could never shoot. If it was really needed to stop a horde of gooks inside the perimeter, we could've rammed and fired one in less than two seconds."

Knapp did a slow burn for a few moments while Jif picked up an M16 from the parapet. Offering it to the BC along with the forty-five from his trouser pocket, he asked, "Could I have my weapon back now, sir? It's zeroed in for me."

The captain handed over Jif's rifle. Then he asked, "Where'd this other sixteen come from?"

"It was Danby's, sir. He doesn't need it anymore. You'll make better use of it now."

Knapp wouldn't take the rifle. He snatched up the forty-five with both bandaged hands and stalked off into the darkness.

Chapter Four

It was just before 0200 hours when Captain Knapp called Jif on the battery phone network. "You can knock off the illum of the triple-A site now," the BC told him.

When asked what caused the change of heart, the captain replied, "Brigade orders, Miles. Is that good enough for you?" Then he rang off without another word.

He sounds testy, as usual, Jif told himself. *But just as well...we were probably wasting those illum rounds, and there's no guarantee when we'll get more, not with another big air assault in a few hours tying up the choppers for who knows how long. I reckon Brigade's worried that if we light up the same place all night, we'll be giving away the LZ location for the next assault...*

And the odds are pretty good we took care of the triple-A on that ridge, anyway...or whatever it was.

A solitary form ambled out of the darkness: Lieutenant Arthur Hammond, the assistant XO. Hammond was coming to relieve him as duty officer. It was Jif's turn to catch some sleep.

The AXO asked, "I guess everything's quiet now where that triple-A was?"

"Like a graveyard, Art," Jif replied.

"Well, that's good, isn't it? Do you think we got those mortars, too?"

"Looks that way," Jif replied, "but they could've just run out of ammo. If they can hump more rounds up the mountain, they'll hit us again."

"Hope not...but what are you still doing here? I'm your relief, man. Aren't you going to catch some sleep?"

"In a minute," Jif replied, thumbing through his pocket notebook by flashlight. "Looks like I've got only one thing to tell you about...the recoil cylinder on Gun Four is leaking pretty badly. We've filled her up again, and she can probably fire a dozen or so rounds before she'll need more oil. The seals we need for the fix should be on the next resupply chopper, hopefully. Until then, top her up whenever she gets low. Don't shoot her dry."

"Copy that, Jif. Otherwise, somebody gets docked for the damages out of his paycheck on the installment plan, right?"

"Maybe. But that could be the least of our worries right now."

As Jif stood to leave, Hammond said, "I've got something to pass on to you, too. I overheard the first sergeant talking to the BC. He was telling the old man that he thinks your shit doesn't stink. The sun may even rise out of your asshole."

Even though the AXO didn't sound in the least bit sarcastic, Jif had to ask, "Really? You're not pulling my leg, are you?"

"No shit, dude. This is the straight skinny."

"All right," Jif replied. "So what'd the captain have to say to that?"

"He agreed with the top. Said you're an even better XO than Harding, the dude you replaced."

"I'm a little surprised to hear that, Art. You sure you heard him correctly? I mean, the terms *pinko*, *commie*, or *subversive son of a bitch* never came up?"

"No, never. Why would anybody call you that?"

Jif gave the thumbnail version of his mother's anti-war essay in Foreign Affairs magazine and the blowback he'd taken for it back at base camp.

Hammond asked, "So your mother's a lefty college teacher, eh? She's your Australian half, right?"

"Correct." He didn't bother mentioning that his mother was also one of the wealthiest women in Australia.

"And isn't your father some retired general who's a big wheel at the State Department now? That's what I heard, anyway."

"I don't know how big a wheel he is," Jif replied, "but yeah…he works at State."

"Damn…that sounds like your parents have one hell of a political problem."

"Not really. I think they just agree to disagree on a lot of stuff."

"Well, more power to them," Hammond said. "What does your dad do at the State Department?"

"I wish I knew, Art." It wasn't meant as a deception. He'd never been told much about his father's job on the Southeast Asia desk, and he'd always assumed such vagueness was part and parcel of a diplomat's portfolio.

As Jif started walking to his hooch, Hammond called after him, saying, "And for what it's worth, I agree with the first sergeant. I'm damn glad you're here, man. You really know your stuff. Everybody thinks so."

Jif took some small comfort in that sentiment, telling himself, *And this was the guy who hated my guts a week ago. He thought I took the job that should've been his, although he didn't know his ass from his bloody elbow at the time. In a lot of ways, he still doesn't. But he's learning fast.*

The path to his hooch—a small earthen bunker with a roof of cut logs covered in canvas and sandbags—took Jif past the battery command post. Inside that much larger bunker, he could see an RTO manning the bank of radios, his face lit by the green glow of their dials. Aside from two dozing medics with mercifully nothing to do, there was no one else inside.

But he could hear the hushed yet heated voices of Captain Knapp and 1SG Contreras coming from behind the CP, barely rising above the purr of the bunker's generator. *I shouldn't be listening to this*, Jif told himself, *but screw it…I'm going to.* He squatted against a sandbagged wall so as not to be seen.

"I hear what you're saying, sir," Contreras told the captain, "but I need to make sure we're real clear on this before I start putting entries on the morning report. Specialist Danby's injuries…were they a direct result of enemy fire, or were they an accident?"

"They were obviously a direct result of enemy fire, First Sergeant."

"I'd like to believe that, sir. I really would. But I've heard more than a couple of stories…and I've got no way to sugarcoat this…they say *you* were the cause of his injuries. The gun crew had the fire well under control until you—"

"That's a crock of bullshit," Knapp interrupted. "You weren't there, Top. I was. I want Danby declared WIA, not an accident victim. End of discussion. Copy?"

There was a pause that hung in the air like silent disagreement. It lingered a few moments until Contreras said, "As you wish, sir."

*****

Jif didn't think he'd caught more than twenty minutes of actual sleep during his three-hour period off-duty. He couldn't shut out the events of the past day and night still churning in his head. The one he found most puzzling: the contentious discussion he'd overhead between Knapp and Contreras.

What's going on with the BC? When I first came to this battery, he seemed an easy-going bloke who gave people plenty of room to do their jobs, including me. That was kind of surprising, since I was an unknown, a last-minute replacement for a man who, by all accounts, really had his act together.

But now he's turned into a bloody asshole, breaking everyone's balls over just about everything, sticking his nose into places it's not needed. I'm definitely getting the feeling he's just an admin type—a REMF—who's better off in some office back at base camp. He's not very comfortable out here in the field...

And he's certainly no expert on gunnery.

I'm not sure why the first sergeant is questioning Danby's status. As far as I can tell, he deserves to be counted as WIA and get that Purple Heart...even if the captain did accidentally contribute to his injuries. Stuff like that happens all the time—one guy's mistake gets another guy wounded. But Knapp sounds like he's trying to cover something up.

I'd be the first to admit I wasn't an eyewitness to Danby getting injured...I was too busy playing FO and gunner at the same time. But I do remember the captain swearing up and down at the time that it was an accident.

Now he's changed his tune...
And I don't understand why.

*****

At 0430 hours, Jif made his way to the mess section for some breakfast. He'd be back on duty in another thirty minutes, and it promised to be a day of intense activity. If he didn't eat a decent meal now, he might not get another chance for quite a while. At the chow line, he crossed paths with 1SG Contreras.

"Glad I caught you, Lieutenant," the first sergeant said. "FYI, we've got an inbound chopper at first light. She's bringing us some aviation talent."

"What's that mean, Top?"

"Brigade wants air liaison officers above and below the usual early morning cloud deck down in the valley. Lately, it's been hanging about five hundred feet above the valley floor and two thousand feet below us. The brass are thinking that with trained eyes on both sides of the clouds coordinating the choppers, they won't have to wait until it burns off to get the assault forces on the ground."

"I'll bet the pilots hate that idea," Jif replied. "Flying blind is not high on their list of favorite things. But it would be a great thing if it worked."

"Let's hope so," Contreras said. "And I hear there'll be an Air Force-type ASO on board that chopper, too."

Jif thought that made a lot of sense. "Yeah...this mountain's perfect for an air support officer. He could function like a command and control ship that never runs out of fuel."

As he downed his last swallow of coffee, the first sergeant added, "One more thing, Lieutenant...FDC has the data on the restricted fire areas for this morning's assault, which become effective at zero-six-thirty hours. We won't be shooting anything south of grid line double-zero until those restrictions are lifted."

Jif asked, "Grid double-zero...that runs through the north end of the old airfield at A Luoi, right?"

"Bingo, sir."

"Well, that makes it easy, Top. Hey, you got a minute? I really need to ask you something."

"Can we do it walking, Lieutenant? I've got to make sure the marker lights at the LZ are ready to go for this incoming bird. It may still be a little dim when she gets here."

"Sure," Jif replied, scooping up his paper plate of scrambled eggs, bacon, and biscuits while stuffing a banana in his pocket. "I'll just take all this to go."

He began to explain—more of an apology, actually—how he'd overheard the first sergeant's conversation with Captain Knapp. By the second sentence, Contreras laughed and said, "I know you heard it all, Lieutenant. My RTO told me you were right outside the CP the whole time. No need to apologize. And don't worry...the captain doesn't know you were eavesdropping. What is it you want to ask?"

For openers, Jif said he didn't understand why Danby's wounded-in-action status might be controversial.

"It has to do with the captain trying to cover his ass, Lieutenant," Contreras replied. "He's up for major...goes before the promotion board very shortly, probably as soon as this operation is over. Maybe even before."

"What does that have to do with whether Danby gets a Purple Heart or not, Top?"

"To make a long story short, sir, an accident in his command just might hurt the captain's chances of a promotion more than his combat casualty numbers, believe it or not. Accidents—or allowing situations that can lead to accidents—can be made to imply that he's a weak leader who's sloppy about procedures being followed. I've been told he's already got one pretty juicy incident on his record. That letter of reprimand will be in his file until someone on high decides to expunge it...if that ever happens."

"You're not talking about Lieutenant Harding's jeep accident, are you, Top?"

"Hell no, sir. The captain couldn't have done a damn thing to prevent that one. That unfortunate mishap is on the lieutenant, I'm afraid."

Contreras went on to describe the *pretty juicy incident* Knapp should've prevented.

"The captain commanded another battery a few years ago, a nuclear-capable eight-inch-howitzer unit in Germany. I've been in one of those nuke outfits over there myself. I was chief of smoke, and let me tell you, sir, that assignment was nothing but a pain in my ass. Don't get me wrong...I'm one hundred and ten percent on the side of safety. But when you've got nuke ammunition on your books, you spend just about every hour of every day complying with a long list of procedures for its care and handling. You don't even have to worry much about the Russians invading, because despite all their tough-talking bullshit, they aren't coming, period. Instead, you've got nuke inspection teams up your ass constantly, making sure every regulation is being followed to the letter. That's where Captain Knapp got himself in trouble. Some staff sergeant working for him was in a storage bunker full of nuclear rounds, and the dumbshit had a cigarette lighter in his pocket. I mean, there are only signs about every ten feet telling you that *no incendiary devices of any kind* are permitted in or around the nuke storage areas. An inspector caught that sergeant red-handed, and our good captain has carried that piece of paper with him ever since. You know the drill…when you're in command, you're responsible for everything your unit does or fails to do."

Jif understood where this was going. "So an accident that resulted from something like poor ammo handling practices within his unit—Danby getting set on fire, for instance—might be a career-ender for the captain?"

"Exactly, Lieutenant. No promotion, no career. And can you imagine if an investigation found he was personally involved in the incident? The board would have a field day with that. So he wants to sweep Danby into the WIA column…and in the meantime, he's going crazy trying to make sure there are no other fuckups that'll drag him down."

Jif added, "And as the promotion board draws closer, he's going to get more and more uptight."

"Correct, sir. So don't take it hard if he bites your head off. It's not just you he's riding. He's doing it to everyone." Then Contreras said, "If he does get that promotion, we'll be getting a new BC. Majors don't command batteries. That's a job for a company grade officer...maybe even you."

"I kind of doubt that, Top. I've heard there are captains all over Nam just begging for combat command time. One of them would get the slot, I'm sure."

As they drew near the XO's post being manned by Lieutenant Hammond, the first sergeant spoke softly as he added, "Just to be clear, sir, I ordinarily wouldn't talk out of school about my commander, so I'm telling you all this in confidence. I don't want to see a good officer like you get down on himself because his BC is playing ass-covering games. And I know an old Army brat like you is wise enough to keep what I just told you under your hat."

They parted ways as Contreras headed to the LZ.

Hammond brought Jif up to speed on the little that had transpired in the past several hours. The only thing the battery had done in that time was fire a few illum rounds to help a lost infantry patrol reorient itself. Surprisingly, Jif hadn't heard those shots. *Maybe I did get some sound sleep after all*, he told himself.

"You heard about the inbound chopper traffic, Jif?"

"Yeah, the first sergeant filled me in. I'll take it from here, Art. Get you and the boys in FDC fed, if they haven't eaten already. We're going to be very busy today." Handing the paper plate and banana peel to Hammond, Jif added, "Trash this for me, will you?"

"Why are we using paper plates? What's wrong with mess kits?"

"Nothing, except they need to be washed in hot water or we'll all get the shits. Water's a commodity we're a little short on right now...and will be until we get another water buffalo."

*****

The rising sun was a vibrant orange disk perched on the edge of the South China Sea when the chopper called in range. Jif had expected a Huey, but it turned out to be a *Jolly Green Giant*, an Air Force HH-53. The big helicopter flew majestically to the mountaintop with all the assurance of a ship equipped with an inertial navigation system, technology the Army choppers lacked. Even the swirling mountain winds seemed to relent in honor of the Jolly Green's approach. She touched down, offloaded her four passengers and their gear, and was airborne again in less than fifteen seconds. Captain Knapp escorted the new arrivals to the XO's post.

"Check out the magnificent view from up here, gentlemen," Knapp told his guests. "Not only can you look well out to sea, you can observe the entire A Shau Valley. LZ Cecile, the objective of this morning's assault, is directly below us. Lieutenant Miles here is not only an excellent executive officer, but he has considerable experience as a forward observer. He'll help you get organized. Now, if you gentlemen will excuse me, I've got a conference with Divarty."

The Army air liaison, an aviator named Ellis with the rank of major, seemed unimpressed as he took in the panoramic view from the firebase. "So this is the famous Signal Hill, eh?"

"It bloody well is, sir," Jif replied.

"What the hell are you, Miles? Australian?"

"Only half, sir."

"The half that talks, I see," Ellis replied. "This mountain strikes me as one big target. Are you getting hit much?"

Jif explained that he originally viewed the mountain the same way: one big target. But so far, the firebase had only received sporadic probes by infantry, mortar fire, and triple-A guns.

"Division is telling its aviator-types that your outfit wiped out an anti-aircraft battery last night," Ellis said, his tone doubtful. "Is that really true, Lieutenant?"

"As near as we can tell, sir," Jif replied.

Still skeptical, Ellis asked, "But you've never been hit with NVA artillery? How hard could it be for big guns just across the border in Laos to nail this place?"

"Pretty hard, I reckon, sir. The terrain's really tough for vehicles along the border, so the closest they could set up their guns is about twenty klicks from here. That's pushing the range of even their biggest weapons. And unless they've captured some of our maps from the ARVN, all they'll have is old ones—probably Japanese—which aren't very precise about vertical terrain. So for them to hit this peak, it would be sheer luck. In fact, it would be sheer luck if NVA artillery in Laos hit *anything* in this entire valley with precision. It's not like it was when we were near Khe Sanh, where the terrain wasn't quite so vertical and we got hit from guns across the border at Co Roc."

"I'll take your word for it, Lieutenant...for now. My RTO will set up our radios right over there, if that's okay with you. Don't want to be crowding this cozy little bunker of yours."

"That'll be fine, sir," Jif said. "If you're going to be here for a while, I can get the engineers to dig you a bunker."

"No need, Lieutenant. We're just here for the morning."

The Air Force ASO, a captain and pilot named Fisher, chimed in with, "I'll take you up on that bunker, Miles. I expect my RTO and I will be here a couple of days."

*****

Just before 0700 hours, Major Ellis announced, "The first wave of assault helicopters is inbound, five minutes out. We'll know for sure if you really knocked out that triple-A pretty soon, Miles."

From their vantage point on the mountaintop, it was hard to believe a helicopter assault was about to happen down in the valley. As it was most mornings, a solid deck of cloud was suspended above the entire length of the A Shau Valley, its cottony blanket fifteen hundred feet below the peak of Signal Hill. A scout helicopter flying below the cloud deck reported a ceiling of seven hundred feet.

They could hear the rumble of dozens of invisible choppers below the overcast. Major Ellis explained, "They're coming out of the south flying at five hundred feet, a little below all that white junk. The lead ship already has eyes on the old airfield. LZ Cecile is right next door, so finding it should be a piece of cake."

A minute later, he said, "Lead flight is on the ground. LZ is cold. Repeat, LZ is cold. Now comes the hard part."

The hard part: keeping the empty Hueys that just delivered their assault troopers clear of the next wave of inbound choppers. With limited visibility in the valley and little room to maneuver laterally within it, the outbound ships had to climb expeditiously through the cloud deck. Once above it, they could turn south, safely overfly the incoming waves, and return to base camp for another load. Ellis and the air liaison on the LZ would work together to stagger the ascents of the departing ships so they wouldn't collide with each other while blind in the soup.

Viewed from above, it was an amazing spectacle as the rotors of rising helicopters whipped the frothy clouds like cotton candy machines. A dozen ships broke through the overcast into the morning sunlight before turning south in what seemed a game of follow the leader.

But this game could turn deadly. A Huey emerged from the clouds that seemed to have two main rotors, one above the other. The lower rotor, though, belonged to another ship climbing faster than her sister directly above. With a sickening *crunch*, like wooden beams being snapped apart, the two aircraft met, shearing the main rotor from the lower ship. She fell back into the clouds, plummeting to the inevitable completion of her destruction.

The upper helicopter, still climbing but out of control with her tail rotor broken away, began a death spiral toward the western face of Signal Hill.

Chapter Five

The twirling Huey vanished from sight behind trees on the mountainside, but the sound of her crash—like a big tin can being crumpled—left no doubt of her demise. She'd come to her final rest just a few hundred feet below the firebase. For several anxious moments, those who'd watched her crazed, climbing pirouette from the peak of Signal Hill thought she might impact among them. There were more than a few sighs of relief when she didn't rise quite that far.

But within seconds, that relief turned to a sense of urgency. Chief of Smoke McKay said, "Those guys could still be alive. Somebody's got to help them."

Jif was already planning what they'd need for the rescue. He told McKay, "I'll take the guys from Gun Four, the one with the leaking cylinder. We shouldn't be shooting that piece much until it's fixed, anyway, unless it's a flat-out emergency."

McKay replied, "Roger that, sir…but maybe this rescue is a job for the Lurps?"

"Negative. They're still scattered all along the other three quadrants of the peak. It'll take Lieutenant Carpenter too long to round them up, and we need to do this quickly. And if we did pull them from the perimeter, who'd be watching our back door? But I'm going to call them because we'll need their climbing ropes and Jacob's ladder. There are some pretty steep spots down that slope. We may need to supply our own steps."

"Yeah, I see your point, Lieutenant. Getting down is easy, but you may need some help getting back up, especially with survivors. You're taking a medic, too, right?"

"Yeah," Jif replied as he dialed up Carpenter. "Do me a favor, Smoke...get one of the docs ready to go—make sure he's got his sixteen with him—and tell the BC what I'm doing."

"Maybe you should tell the captain yourself, sir. He's right over there with that visiting aviator," McKay said.

Major Ellis looked like a man desperately trying to continue the mission while deflecting blame for the tragic mistake that had just been made. The first thing Jif heard him say to Captain Knapp was, "I'm telling you, that wasn't my damn fault. If some nineteen-year-old hot stick warrant officer decides he's going to ignore the rate-of-climb instructions, it's on him, not me. The damn fool got himself and his crew killed for not keeping with the program." He ended his self-absolution with the standard Army phrase, "Sorry about that," delivered in the usual, uncaring tone that conveyed no sympathy at all.

Of all the expressions that had become standard jargon in Vietnam, Jif hated that one the most. It always meant the same thing: *Tough shit, pal. Nothing I can do for you.*

Jif almost had to admire Ellis' rapid transition to blame-avoidance mode. He remembered one of his father's axioms on Army culture: *The first item on the agenda after any calamity is immediate blame assessment, usually inflicted on the lowest-ranking officer in the vicinity. It doesn't matter whether or not the designated fall guy has anything to do with the fuckup, just so he's there to take the rap.*

Jif thought that the major must be familiar with that axiom, as well: *The sound of the crash is still echoing and he's already getting his exculpatory ducks in a row.*

Captain Knapp was thinking blame avoidance, too, wondering to himself if Brigade would decide a failure to neutralize the triple-A site—*his* failure— would be labeled as the cause of the mishap, although nobody had reported any anti-aircraft fire yet. But even if fabricating his guilt hadn't crossed their minds at Brigade, Knapp expressed the concern out loud that they might still suspend the airmobile assault until the valley's cloud cover cleared, which probably wouldn't happen for another two hours.

No such order was being issued, though. Ellis theorized why: "We took the gooks totally by surprise coming in through the overcast. That's something we usually don't have the balls to do. But the element of surprise is gone now. We've got less than a full battalion on the ground. If we don't bring in the rest of our guys immediately, the first element will get their asses riddled within the hour." With the choppers of the second wave already approaching the LZ, he went right back to preparing for another round of blind departures, with a special command radioed to each crew to read back the climb-out instructions down to the last detail.

Jif told Knapp of his plan to lead a rescue party to the crash site. He'd expected at least a cross-examination about the possible pitfalls. Considering the BC's current state of mind, a refusal to allow the venture wasn't out of the question, either. But the captain seemed uninterested in the details. All he said was, "Sounds simple enough. Don't fuck it up."

Major Ellis added, "There were no passengers on board, Miles, just the crew."

Mike Carpenter was waiting at Gun Four with the Lurps' climbing gear in a neat pile on the ground. "I'm sure glad you're volunteering to do this thing," he told Jif. "My guys aren't much interested, that's for damn sure. All they can think about is rotating the hell out of here this morning. You sure you know how to use this stuff?"

"We'll manage, Mike. Thanks for the quick response."

"No problem, man...but since I might be gone by the time you get back from this rodeo, I'd better give you the bad news while I still can. Remember when I said another Lurp team would be replacing us? Well, somebody upstairs pulled the plug on that. You're getting a standard rifle platoon instead."

"From where, Mike?"

"I think they were part of the security detachment at Camp Evans."

"Great," Jif replied. "Bloody base camp heroes. Anybody tell Captain Knapp yet?"

"Yeah, I told him and the first sergeant both. The top is ready to spit nails over it. He said he wanted to keep working with Lurps because they don't need a whole lot of command guidance. Your BC, on the other hand, didn't seem to give a shit one way or another."

"That sounds about right, Lieutenant," Staff Sergeant Theophilus Dunn, Gun Four's section chief, interjected. "The BC's either going upside your head when it ain't about nothing, or he don't give a good goddamn about the stuff that matters." Looking to Jif, he added, "Something tells me you're down with that opinion, LT."

He spoke the rank as *el tee*, the common manner in which enlisted men addressed lieutenants. Most students of military lexicon agreed that black troopers had coined the expression, and its usage spread like wildfire to white soldiers. As with the term *dude*, it could imply great respect or none at all, depending on the delivery.

"Well, Sergeant," Jif replied, "let's just say that our BC is like God. He works in mysterious ways."

Dunn already had one of the thick coils of rope in his hands. "How about we tie this off to the base plate of my piece and play it out as we go down? If we've got to haul anyone up, it'll be ready to go. The gun-bunnies up top just gotta start pulling."

"Great idea, Sergeant," Jif replied.

"My mama didn't raise no dummies, LT. But I got one more question...which one of you two gentlemen is in charge of this little exercise?"

"He is," Carpenter replied, pointing to Jif. "I'm not going. I'm just the guy loaning you the goods."

"Suits me fine, sir," the sergeant replied. "No man can serve two masters, you dig?"

The rescue team—Jif, the medic, Dunn, and five of his gun crew—were organized and ready to descend the slope in just a few minutes. Jif gave only one order that caused a murmur of dissent: "It's too steep a climb to carry a radio, so we'll bring a field phone instead and reel out the wire as we go down. Everyone with a sixteen carry three extra magazines besides the one in your weapon, and bring two extra belts of ammo for the sixty."

Sergeant Dunn protested, "What the hell we wanna be carrying all that shit for, LT? I thought this was just a rescue mission, not some commando raid. Ain't we already humpin' plenty of stuff with the ropes and ladder? Gonna be tough enough without—"

"Let me put it this way, Sergeant," Jif interrupted. "My mama didn't raise no dummies, either. Bring the bloody phone and the extra ammo."

*****

"I'd feel a lot better if we could see the *sumbitch*," Dunn told Jif as they walked downhill, clinging for extra support to the rope they'd tied off at the peak. "We sure that chopper didn't roll downhill?"

"With all these trees to catch it? Not likely. It's down there...shouldn't be too far now."

When they found her a minute later, they realized why the crashed ship had been invisible to them until that moment. She was tucked into a depression on the mountainside, compacted by the force of her violent return to earth, and covered with the detritus of fractured rotors and shorn tree limbs. The twisted, olive-drab fuselage was barely recognizable as the remains of a Delta-model Huey. Though the smell of leaked jet fuel was strong, nothing was burning.

"I ain't believing this," Dunn said. "The crew's still alive."

"We'll need the Jacob's ladder," Jif told the team. "Set it up right here."

The ladder, rolled into a cylindrical bundle, would be more than long enough once unfurled to handle the forty-foot drop from the ledge where they stood to the wreck. After another moment evaluating the challenge they faced, Jif added, "How much rope do we have left?"

"About a hundred feet, LT," one of Dunn's men replied.

"More than enough. You stay here, Sergeant. Keep the sixty and the phone with you. I'll go down with the doc. If I need more guys, I'll holler." As he scanned the area around the wreckage once more, he was about to add, *Set up all-around security*, but there was no need. Dunn was already doing it.

Jif was first down the ladder, with the medic right behind. The Huey's crewmen were conscious but dazed. The aircraft commander was unable to move from his seat. His broken ankle was pinned beneath the crushed instrument panel. The battered co-pilot was seated on the cockpit rear floor, his back against the center pedestal, groaning in agony. The medic, Spec-5 John Clayton, quickly diagnosed the man's main problem: "His shoulder's separated. I've got to reset it, or we'll never get him out of this damn hole. No medevac ship with a hoist is going to be snuggling up to this slope."

There was one more crewman, half-in and half-out of the mangled cabin. After a quick evaluation, Clayton said, "He's pretty beat up, but I don't think anything's broken, LT. His name's Trudeau. He's the crew chief and one of the door gunners. But where the hell is the other gunner?"

Jif was about to ask the same question. The usual crew on a Huey was four men—two pilots and two gunners. He asked Trudeau, "Where's your partner?"

Pointing down the slope, the gunner replied, "He ran off that way."

"So he's not hurt?"

"If he is, it's not stopping him, sir."

"What's his name?"

"Hanson. Spec-Four Kevin Hanson."

"Do you think you can climb that ladder on your own, Trudeau?"

"I'll give it a damn good shot, Lieutenant." He began a slow but determined ascent up the rungs, seeking the salvation awaiting him at the top in Sergeant Dunn's outstretched hands.

The co-pilot wailed mightily as Clayton gently maneuvered him to his back on the cabin floor. He told Jif, "I'm going to need a little help here, LT. Keep him still and distracted while I do the deed. Tell him about the best sex you ever had. That usually works."

Jif began to relate the first story that popped into his head: doing it in a banyan tree with Suzy McCauley when they were Brisbane teenagers. He'd only spoken a few sentences—all setup and no sex—when the co-pilot's body went rigid, as if hit by an electric shock. As the waves of surprise and pain subsided, Doc Clayton said, "See? That wasn't so bad, was it, Chief? And quick, too. Maybe too quick…I was kind of hoping we'd get to the punch line of the lieutenant's story. It was starting to sound real interesting. All this time, I thought only monkeys fucked in trees."

As he fashioned a sling from his own belt, the doc grumbled, "Damn pilots with their flying jumpsuits…they never have a belt of their own when you need it. Between all the slings and tourniquets I've had to apply, I've given so many away I'm lucky I haven't lost my britches yet."

Climbing the rope ladder with only one good hand and a shoulder still in searing pain wouldn't work, so they fashioned a donut at the tail end of the lifting rope in which the co-pilot could sit. He then clung to the tackle with his good arm while Dunn and his men hauled him up.

Once they freed the aircraft commander from the cockpit, they used the same donut to lift him to Dunn's position. From there, men at the firebase began the task of pulling the wounded crewmen up to the peak.

Jif told Clayton, "You go up, too, doc."

"Aren't you coming, sir?"

"I want to see if I can find the other door gunner first. Tell Sergeant Dunn to send down one of his guys to—"

"Why do that, Lieutenant? I'm already here. I'll go with you."

"That's not your job, doc."

"Maybe not, sir…but every second we wait could put this guy Hanson deeper into the shit. He could be hurt…maybe even concussed and not thinking clearly. That could be why he ran off."

As Jif considered Clayton's suggestion, the medic added, "And if he is hurt, I'm just the guy you want to have along." Holding up his M16 while he patted the holster carrying his forty-five, he added, "And I've got these babies, too."

*****

After they'd descended another hundred meters, the slope became almost level. A thickly forested table—small in area—lay before them, its boundaries obscured from their sight. Jif told Clayton, "I'll bet the drop-off at the end of this table is bloody steep."

They'd seen no sign of Specialist Kevin Hanson. Clayton asked, "Maybe I should call out the dude's name a couple of times? If he hears your accent, he might think it's a gook trick."

Jif found that funny. He'd met some Vietnamese who could sound almost like Americans when speaking English...

But I've never heard one who could sound Aussie.

He told Clayton, "Go ahead...call him. But make sure your ass is behind a big tree when you do it."

"How come, LT?"

"Because the NVA could be close enough to hear you."

The medic did as he was told before he bellowed the man's name.

There was no answer...

But Jif saw movement among the trees just fifty meters away. It was more than one person. Clayton was about to call out again when Jif told him, "Be quiet. We've got contact."

"Is it Hanson?"

"If it is, he's not alone." He pointed to where the movement had been just a moment ago.

"What do we do now, LT?"

"Stay where you are and cover our backs. I'm going to slide over a few yards. I think I've got a better shot from there."

No sooner had he moved than two NVA emerged from behind a stand of trees, spraying bullets from their AK-47s. But the shots were wild, as if they weren't sure where Jif and Clayton were. None of the rounds came within twenty feet of them. After several bursts, the enemy soldiers jumped back into the cover of the trees.

They're reloading, Jif told himself.

There was more movement among the trees. A much taller man in a flying helmet—Hanson, no doubt—his hands bound behind his back, was being led by a rope leash around his neck.

I'd have no problem taking out the gook with the leash, Jif thought. *But there are at least two other NVA soldiers...*

Any one of them could kill Hanson.

And any one of them could kill us if we expose ourselves.

I have no idea if Clayton can shoot worth a damn. This is a bloody tough call.

Jif was about to signal the medic to hold his fire when he got the break he needed. As the three NVA and their prisoner entered an area where the vegetation was less dense, the handler jerked hard on the leash, a command for his captive to move faster.

The pull of the rope caught Hanson by surprise. He fell flat on his face...

And the NVA were suddenly stationary in plain sight...and still only fifty meters away.

Jif took down the handler with his first shot.

The other two enemy soldiers began firing, this time with a far better idea of where their adversary was. As bullets smacked into the tree he was crouched behind, Jif dropped the second NVA with another single shot.

The third, still firing, began to run. But he'd only taken a few steps when he, too, went down in a cloud of pink mist. Jif had been lining up on the man but never got to squeeze the trigger.

"DID I GET THE FUCKER?" Clayton shrieked, his voice an octave higher than it had been a few moments ago.

"Yeah, you bloody well got him," Jif replied. "Right in the head. You do much shooting, doc?"

"Not me, sir. I haven't even fired this thing since in-country orientation."

Okay, so maybe he's a natural, Jif told himself. *Or maybe he was just lucky. The target was pretty close, but he was moving fast. That made it a tough shot.*

Hanson had struggled to his knees by the time his rescuers reached him. As Clayton checked the NVA soldiers for signs of life, Jif cut the rope binding the door gunner's hands. The empty shoulder holster prompted him to ask, "What happened to your weapon, Hanson?"

Pointing to the man Clayton had shot, he replied, "Hang on a second, Lieutenant." He rolled the body over with his foot and retrieved a .45-caliber pistol, US issue, from the man's belt. Then he fired two bullets from that .45 into the already-shattered skull. Returning the pistol to its rightful place in his shoulder holster, he said, "My weapon's right here, sir."

After examining the two men Jif had shot, Clayton shook his head and said, "One's dead, LT, and the other's not going to make it."

"Then let's get the bloody hell out of here," Jif replied.

*****

As they hurried back to the crash site, Clayton asked Hanson, "Where the hell were you running to, man?"

"Trying to get back to the LZ."

"But what about the rest of your crew? Didn't you even try to help them?"

"Dammit, doc, I thought they were all dead. I got pitched out of the ship when we hit the trees. I called out, but nobody answered, nobody moved. What was I supposed to do?"

Clayton was examining Hanson with a practiced eye. The cuts, bruises, torn flight suit, and scratched-up flying helmet seemed to jive with tumbling from a chopper into the undergrowth. He decided the gunner was on the level.

Jif was satisfied with the explanation, too. He said, "You'll be happy to know that the rest of your crew isn't dead. They're a little broken and battered, but they'll be okay."

Hanson was relieved to hear that. But he still seemed embarrassed... or perhaps ashamed. It sounded like an apology as he said, "I didn't mean to drag anyone else into my shit, Lieutenant. But how'd you know where to search?"

"Trudeau told me."

"I can't imagine how the hell he saw me. He sure didn't look alive."

"Don't worry about it, Hanson," Jif said. "We all do strange things sometimes. When you're scared shitless, it's allowed."

They were within sight of the wreck—and the Jacob's ladder—when a firefight erupted on the ledge where Dunn and his men waited.

*****

Sergeant Dunn's machine gunner saw the NVA soldiers first, a dozen or more of them just twenty meters to the north, struggling upslope toward the peak. He let loose with a wild burst from his M60 that did more damage to the trees than the enemy. The NVA dropped into concealed positions and returned fire. The machine gunner's assistant was promptly hit in the arm.

What followed was a mad minute in which both sides expended prodigious amounts of ammunition to little, if any, effect. To add to the chaos, Captain Knapp's shrill voice spilled from Sergeant Dunn's field telephone, demanding to know if the Claymore mines emplaced on that side of the perimeter should be fired.

"NEGATIVE, NEGATIVE," Dunn screamed into the phone. "NO GODDAMN CLAYMORES. FRIENDLIES DOWNRANGE. REPEAT, FRIENDLIES DOWNRANGE."

Knapp replied, "Roger, copy. No Claymores."

But then there was another voice on the phone network, considerably calmer than the captain's. It belonged to Lieutenant Carpenter, the LRRP platoon leader. "I can see where you're at," he told Dunn. "Give me a vector from you to the gooks."

"To our right—due north—about thirty meters," the sergeant replied.

"Roger, stand by for bloopers."

In a rare split-second of silence when no one happened to be firing, Dunn thought he heard the unmistakable *ploomps* of M79 grenade launchers, called bloopers, bloop guns, thumpers, or a variety of other nicknames. They were firing from somewhere behind him.

A moment later, two grenades exploded in rapid succession near the NVA position. The impacts were short of the target. But not by much.

"Add another five meters," Dunn said. He was playing the unlikely role of forward observer for the first time in his Army career.

The next two grenades were on target. The NVA gunfire stopped abruptly. Whether the enemy had been killed or forced to flee was of no importance to the Americans. They were just glad the fight was over.

Dunn, cradling the telephone handset, had to laugh at himself: *I didn't even want to tote this damn phone that just saved my ass. I am one dumb sumbitch.*

*****

Jif, Clayton, and Hanson could only hear the firefight as it raged above them. Hunkered down against the shattered Huey, they could see nothing of what was happening on the ledge and had no idea how to help Dunn and his men. They didn't dare attempt to scale the Jacob's ladder while the shooting was going on: *It would be bloody suicide.*

The fight had lasted less than two minutes but, as with all firefights, seemed so much longer. In the unsettled silence that followed, Jif yelled up to Dunn, "Are you still up there?"

"Still here, LT."

"Is everybody okay?"

"Got one wounded. Need the doc ASAP."

Once up on the ledge, Jif said, "I heard a hell of a lot of shooting going on. Have you guys got any rounds left?"

Each man with an M16 was well into his last magazine. The machine gun was on its last belt.

Dunn said, "That was a damn good call about taking the extra ammo, LT. Did you have a notion we'd get into trouble?"

Jif replied, "Like I said before, my mama didn't raise no dummies."

"Amen to that, LT."

Chapter Six

By 0900 hours, the airmobile insertion of infantry forces near A Luoi was complete. The overcast shrouding the A Shau Valley had cleared, and there had been no other helicopter collisions to mar the operation. Not waiting for their own artillery to arrive, the Brigade's three battalions began pushing out from LZ Cecile in an expanding circle to secure the abandoned airfield at A Luoi.

As Major Ellis had presumed, the NVA were taken by surprise, never expecting the American helicopters to assault through a low overcast. But the element of surprise had expired quickly; enemy resistance was strengthening rapidly. As the Brigade's assault began to bog down, they made repeated calls for artillery fire, but the guns on Signal Hill were forced to remain silent. The *no-fire below grid double-zero* restriction had still not been lifted.

Jif asked Captain Knapp, "What the bloody hell is the holdup, sir? The assault choppers are gone. We should've already returned to normal flight safety procedures."

"I hear you, Miles," the BC replied, "but the relay station is all backed up. There's so much radio traffic that commo with Camp Evans has really slowed down. Be patient…we'll get clearance to fire soon."

"Be patient, sir? Are we going to tell that to the grunts down in the valley getting their brains beat in?"

"At ease, Miles. Orders are orders."

"But it doesn't make sense, Captain. We can see the bloody coordinates where they want fire. We know there are no airspace conflicts with the choppers because we can see that, too. Hell, we can see almost everything from up here. If we're going to get the clearance eventually, anyway, why don't we just go ahead and shoot the mission now? There are a bunch of guys down there who'll thank us for it. I reckon everybody will thank us."

"Negative, Lieutenant. You're thinking above your pay grade. Don't worry about those grunts so much. At the moment, they have gunship support if they need it."

Jif looked across the wide expanse of the A Shau below him. There was not an aircraft of any type, let alone a gunship, within five klicks of the airspace between Signal Hill and the target being called.

Back at the XO's post, SFC McKay told Jif, "Sir, I can tell by the look on your face that he's not going to let us shoot."

"You're bloody well right, Smoke."

With little they could do but wait, they looked down on the abandoned airfield, the first objective of the day's assault. McKay said, "How long do you figure it'll take Brigade to secure that place?"

"If they don't get some fire support from us real quick, it's going to take quite a while," Jif replied. "*Abandoned airfield*, my ass. I reckon it's crawling with NVA by now."

"Yep," the chief of smoke replied. "And once we take it, the cranes and shithooks still have to fly in the engineers and their equipment to rebuild the place. That won't happen overnight, either."

"You're saying we're going to be here for a while, Smoke?"

"Damn right, sir. But maybe it'll be worth it once those big Air Force cargo planes start landing there, instead of dumping those para-drops all over the place. That blue-suit ASO's been busier than a one-armed paperhanger trying to keep them on target. Once they can land, though, they'll be bringing in ammo and supplies by the pallet-load. Vehicles, too…and we'll get them all instead of losing some of those chutes to the NVA."

"Won't do us a bloody bit of good way up here, though," Jif said. "Nothing but choppers are ever going to reach us."

First Sergeant Contreras joined them with news to share. "Speaking of helicopters, we've got a Chinook inbound with the replacement platoon for the Lurps. About three minutes out…should be visible real soon. There's more good news, too. It's supposed to be bringing our water resupply, as well."

Jif asked, "Are you sure, Top? A platoon on board with all its equipment plus a water buffalo slung underneath? That's just about max gross weight for a shithook at sea level. I can see a pilot refusing to haul that load way up here."

"We'll just have to wait and see, Lieutenant," Contreras replied.

The boxy shape of the Chinook, still miles away, was coming into hazy view. Looking at her through binoculars, Jif said, "There isn't a bloody thing slung under that chopper."

"Maybe they manhandled the water buffalo up the ramp and into the cabin, sir," McKay offered. "She'd fit...and they sure have enough guys to do it."

"That'd be a first," Jif said. "If that thing broke loose in the cabin, it'd be six thousand pounds on wheels rolling around out of control, smashing things up like crazy. I don't think any flight crew would set themselves up like that."

The battery recorder yelled, "FDC's on the horn, XO. Looks like we've got the no-fire hold lifted."

"Better late than never," McKay said.

"Let's hope we're not too late," Jif replied. Then he told the first sergeant, "Advise the chopper we'll be firing, Top. She can approach in any direction she wants except out of the west."

"Copy that, Lieutenant," Contreras replied.

McKay asked Jif, "Are we still standing down on Gun Four, sir?"

"Negative, Smoke. Let her shoot. Just watch that oil level like a hawk."

*****

The gun crews enjoyed being able to watch the impact of the rounds they'd just fired, a benefit only a lofty firebase like Signal Hill could offer. Jif enjoyed it, too. "It's just like being up on a ridge at Fort Sill," he said, "where you can see the guns firing from your OP, follow the rounds through the sky, and then watch them hit down below in the impact area. It's the best training in the world for a cannon-cocker."

The battery was firing its third fire-for-effect volley as the Chinook settled onto the LZ at Signal Hill.

Thirty men in full field gear spilled from the ship's ramp, some carrying boxes full of C rations, the rest carrying five-gallon water cans. The moment they were clear of the ship, Lieutenant Carpenter's LRRP platoon scrambled on board, along with Major Ellis, his RTO, Sergeant Dunn's wounded man, and the four-man crew of the crashed Huey. In less than a minute, the big ship was airborne again.

First Sergeant Contreras did a slow burn as he tallied the water cans: there were twenty, yielding a total of one hundred gallons. "That's not enough to last this firebase a goddamn day at normal usage rates," he said. "And these C rations…they know we can't prepare food without water, so they were nice enough to send us more box lunches, the bastards."

McKay offered, "Maybe another chopper's going to bring in the buffalo, Top."

"The only other incoming flight we've got scheduled is an ammo drop. Do you want the water instead?"

That question answered itself. They could get by on minimal water, but they were useless without ammunition.

Contreras asked, "Did you at least get the parts you need to fix Gun Four?"

"Looks like it," McKay replied. "Sergeant Dunn's tearing into it right now."

"Good luck, Smoke," the first sergeant said. "I've got to get this new security platoon squared away. Where the hell is their lieutenant, anyway?"

"Not my turn to watch him, Top," McKay replied, trying to be funny. "But I think he's over with the XO."

The leader of the security platoon, a second lieutenant named Pat Gruner, appeared to believe he'd been handed a cushy assignment. To Jif, he was *too clean* and *too green*, the type of inexperienced officer who could only react rather than initiate. Case in point: his platoon milled around on the LZ, apparently waiting for somebody to tell them what to do...

Something he should have made sure his sergeants had under control before they even got off the bird. I don't think there's anyone in charge of this route-step outfit.

Gruner asked, "So, when do we get started?"

"You started the minute you touched down," Jif replied. "The first sergeant has the firebase defensive scheme ready to lay on you. He's right over there."

Gruner was confused by all the urgency. He asked, "You really haven't had much trouble with the NVA on this big ol' mountain, have you?"

"That depends on how you define *much*. We've been in two firefights already this morning."

"Really? Where?"

"At the site of a chopper crash just down the west slope."

Sergeant Dunn at Gun Four called out to Jif, "Need you and the Smoke over here, LT."

"Look, the shit's really hopping right now, Gruner. Get with the first sergeant. Maybe we'll talk later." He left the newcomer and met up with McKay, who said, "That new platoon leader looks like he has his thumb about a mile up his ass."

"It's that bloody obvious, eh?"

At Gun Four, Dunn said, "Need a second opinion...and maybe a third. One of the seals they sent us showed up damaged. We changed out all the others, but I can't use this one, so I put the original back in. I know we're not supposed to, but it looked pretty good, so…"

Jif deferred to McKay, asking, "What do you think, Smoke?"

"I'm okay with it, sir…tentatively. Let's shoot her. If she starts blowing oil, we'll shut her down and do this all over again."

"Roger that," Jif replied. He told Dunn, "Jump right into this fire mission, Sergeant."

A few moments later, Gun Four added her round to a volley. As the tube returned from recoil, both sergeants took a look at the repair. They found no oil leak.

"Good job, Theo," McKay told Dunn. As a joke, he added, "Why don't you take the rest of the day off?"

"Don't play with me, Smoke. It's been that kind of day, you dig? And it ain't even half over yet."

Walking back to the XO's post, Jif said, "Things are going to be really busy today. Do we have an ETA for the next ammo drop?"

"Negative, sir," McKay replied, "but as backed up as the relay station is, we may not get the word for a while. If you ask me, somebody back at Camp Evans is doing a piss-poor job of prioritizing messages."

*****

By 1000 hours, Charlie Battery was shooting its eighth fire mission of the morning, targeting a trail junction one klick west of the A Luoi airfield. The FO with the assault troops was calling for repeated airbursts against enemy personnel in the open, burning through the battery's limited supply of VT fuzes, the radio-controlled devices that ensured a perfect airburst height without the need for adjustments. "Tell that dude that we have to switch to mechanical time fuzes," Jif said to Lieutenant Hammond in FDC. "He's running us out of VT."

The FO replied that it wouldn't work. Hunkered down in a wooded area with limited visibility, he couldn't observe the airbursts. Without the ability to see their detonation, he couldn't adjust the mechanical time fuzes for optimum burst height and the resulting maximum effect on the ground below.

"Maybe he can't see them," Jif replied, "but we can. His target coordinates are less than four klicks from here. We'll adjust the bloody airbursts for him."

After a brief but pointed radio exchange, the FO reluctantly agreed.

Hammond was still confused. As his computer worked up the required time fuze setting, he asked, "But how can you tell how much to adjust, Jif? We've got this big vertical angle that'll mess up the scale in the binoculars."

"Don't sweat it, Art. We'll be close enough for government work. A few meters one way or the other won't make a bloody bit of difference. Come on out and watch. Your boys can live without you for a couple minutes."

The computer—a spec-5 who was sharp as a tack—laughed under his breath as he thought, *We can live without Lieutenant Hammond forever, if necessary.*

By 1200 hours, they'd fired ten more missions. Fortunately, there'd been enough time between the missions so they didn't have to pour water on the tubes to cool them, water they didn't have.

On his way to the XO's post, Captain Knapp did a tally in his head of the ammunition remaining. It wasn't encouraging; at the current rate of expenditure, they would use up all the HE rounds by late afternoon.

"I've got Divarty's assurances that we'll have an ammo resupply by fifteen hundred hours," the BC told Jif and McKay. "If I'm reading between the lines correctly, Division is having trouble keeping all its helicopters in the air."

"That's surprising," Jif said, "considering the chopper losses look pretty light this morning, not counting the two that collided. Actually, since the main lift ended, there haven't been a whole lot of helicopters at all operating down in the valley, just the occasional gunship and medevac."

"I don't think their problem is out here in the A Shau, Lieutenant. I think it's back at base camp. When I find out more, I'll let you know. But speaking of information, I've got good news and bad news. Which do you want first?"

"I'll take the bad news first," Jif replied. He turned to McKay and asked, "What's your choice, Smoke?"

"Definitely the bad news first, sir."

"So be it," Knapp said. "The bad news is that the cavalry battalion commander in the lead at A Luoi has a case of the ass over how long it took to get artillery support. Like that's our fault, right? I've logged the time to the second when we got the message to lift the no-fire restriction as well as the time our first rounds left the tubes less than a minute later. He knew what the Brigade orders were, so he can pound sand."

Jif and McKay exchanged jaundiced looks. They were both thinking the same thing: *Technically, the captain was correct sticking to the letter of his orders, but correctness seems irrelevant in this case. We all knew what needed to be done. Our guys needed fire support, and some of them probably died because they didn't get it right away.*

Sometimes, a commander has to have the stones to do what's tactically required, even if he's administratively prohibited from doing it. We all knew what was going on and what had to be done. It shouldn't have been a tough call.

Jif asked, "So what's the good news, sir?"

"The battalion assaulting the ridge south of the airfield—the one we were tasked to engage last night—has found the burned-up remains of four heavy anti-aircraft weapons," Knapp replied. "Brigade is quite pleased with our work. Those guns would've made mincemeat out of the assault choppers. Division is very pleased, too. They're giving us a big *attaboy* for our efforts."

That ought to help the BC with his promotion board, Jif thought. *Now he has something else to show for that fire mission besides a pair of burned hands.*

*****

Fifteen hundred hours came and went without the arrival of an ammo supply chopper. While Captain Knapp was at the relay station repeating his plea for a delivery before sundown, a brawl erupted outside the mess bunker.

It started when a white PFC from Lieutenant Gruner's security platoon wasn't happy with the C ration selection he'd drawn for supper, the universally hated ham and lima beans. Flying into a rage, he dumped out the box and started flinging the cans as if throwing rocks. The biggest can—containing the ham and lima bean entrée—struck a black spec-4, also from the security platoon, in the chest. A slugfest ensued involving at least a dozen of Gruner's men, the opposing sides broken down almost evenly along racial lines.

First Sergeant Contreras had happened to be passing by when the chaos began. He'd almost gotten the combatants separated when the ration-thrower who'd started it all taunted, "Hey, why don't you porch monkeys complain to Martin Luther King? Oh, wait…you can't. The son of a bitch got his ass shot dead."

It was like throwing gasoline on a smoldering fire. The pushing, shoving, and punching began all over again.

On the other side of the firebase, Charlie Battery was shooting its twentieth mission of the day. The mixed-race gun crews knew a race riot when they saw one. More than a few across the various ethnic groups looked ready to bolt and join the melee, even though they had no idea what it was about. But the gun section chiefs quashed their departure immediately, making sure they stayed where they were and kept doing their jobs. As SFC McKay reminded his NCOs, "Make no mistake: they leave their posts, they go straight to the LBJ."

The LBJ: the Army's principal prison in Vietnam at Long Binh, its lengthy name reduced to simply Long Binh Jail or, more commonly, the initials it shared with the current President of the United States, Lyndon Baines Johnson.

Even from a distance, Jif could see that none of the other three officers on the firebase were dealing with the skirmish. He told McKay, "I've got to get over there. Wish me luck."

"Looks like you're going to need it, Lieutenant. Don't worry…I'll keep order on this side." Watching as Jif laid down his M16, he asked, "You sure you don't want to take a weapon of some sort, sir?"

"No weapon, Smoke. The volume on this thing looks like it's been pumped up enough already. Got to cool things down."

He trotted off, helmet tucked under one arm, the other hand in his pocket. The casual pose belied the seriousness of what he knew had to be done. Watching him go, McKay thought, *I hope he knows what he's doing, because he looks like a lamb going to the slaughter.*

As he drew closer, Jif could tell that those in the fight were taking great care to ensure that they didn't lay a finger on First Sergeant Contreras. They were well aware that striking an NCO—or an officer, for that matter—was a sure ticket to a court-martial. But the top was just one man trying, and failing, to get control of a rabid mob on his own. Still in his relaxed pose, Jif waded into the middle of the brawlers.

Seeing only his white skin, a black trooper lunged for him, not noticing the bar on his collar until he was just an arm's length away. Too late to check his momentum, the trooper slammed into him, bounced off his unyielding form, and ended up on his knees at Jif's feet.

There was no doubt what the look on the man's upturned face meant: *I just fucked up, big time.*

The brawl ground to a halt as the realization of what had just happened rippled through the mob: *The fool laid his hands on an officer. He's gonna do a dime at Leavenworth.*

All eyes were glued to Jif and his would-be assailant. Nobody wanted to miss one bit of what they were sure was going to happen next: the unbending bludgeon of military justice.

But they were all in for a surprise.

Jif looked down on the apprehensive trooper and said, "You don't need to kneel before me, my son. I'm not a king, just a lieutenant."

The men of the security platoon had never heard Jif speak before. His accent stunned them. A voice from the mob called out, "What Army you in, LT?"

As he helped the man to his feet, Jif replied, "The United States Army, same as the rest of you. Who's the ranking man from the security platoon?"

He already knew the answer; one of the white brawlers was a staff sergeant, his rank made obvious by the old-style chevrons and rocker on his sleeve. After Jif glared at him for a few moments, the man finally said, "I am, Lieutenant."

The name strip on his utility shirt was obvious, too. "All right, then, Sergeant Harrison. Explain to me why you didn't do your job and stop this little dustup before it even started."

He began a semi-coherent tirade about *those people still being uppity* over the murder of Doctor King, but Jif cut him short, saying, "You still aren't telling me why you didn't do your job and stop it."

After stammering a few more deflections and evasions, Jif interrupted him again, asking, "Have all your men drawn their rations?"

When Harrison nodded yes, he added, "Then march them back to their posts. While you're up here playing grabass, the NVA are quietly turning your Claymores around. And yes, the NVA are that close. Trust me on that one. Now move out."

The sergeant did as he was told and led his subdued but seething men away.

Now that all was quiet, Lieutenant Gruner suddenly appeared. He'd been inside the mess bunker—just a few yards away—the whole time.

"Nice of you to show up," Jif told him. He didn't bother explaining what had been going on outside the bunker. Gruner already knew. He'd been hiding too close to it not to know.

"I'll tell you the same thing I just told your useless Sergeant Harrison: do your bloody job and handle your platoon." After letting Gruner squirm for a few moments, he added, "It'd be a shame if you got reassigned to some outfit down in the A Shau instead of staying up here on God's front porch."

Gruner started to ramble on about his platoon of misfits and troublemakers, especially PFC Garrity, the man who'd started the brawl.

Jif replied, "Bloody hell, you even know who started it! You saw the whole thing and did fuck all about it." He paused before adding, "Aren't you ashamed?"

"I'm telling you, man, it's all that fucking Garrity's fault. He just got busted down from specialist for stealing guys' stuff in some other platoon. What are you going to do with a scumbag like that?"

"I'll tell you what I'd do, Gruner. I'd make him bunk with one of your black troopers, a big dude with a sense of humor and a high tolerance for bullshit. That should make sure nobody in your outfit gets fragged in his sleep. And while you're at it, take a stripe or two from your Sergeant Harrison. He's not up to the job. Find somebody else."

As Gruner wandered off, a disgruntled 1SG Contreras told Jif, "Well, you sure put out that fire, Lieutenant, but dammit, that's not the way things are done. Striking an officer is a criminal offense. Are you serious about not pressing charges?"

"Affirmative, Top. There's no need for that. That wasn't the problem, anyway, just a sideshow."

"But that jackass threw a full-on body block at you, sir. I'm still surprised you didn't go down."

"I reckon I'm a little tougher than that, Top. We play football in Australia without helmets, you know?"

"That's not the point, sir. We can't let breaches in discipline like that go unpunished. The world will come tumbling down around us."

Jif replied, "Have you ever heard the expression *there are no bad troops, only bad leaders*? That's what we're dealing with here, bad leadership. And because of that, I'm worried the security of this firebase is in jeopardy with that bunch covering our asses."

Their discussion was brought to an abrupt end as Captain Knapp came running from the relay station. Full of enthusiasm, he said, "We've got choppers inbound."

First Sergeant Contreras asked, "Is it ammo, water, or both, sir?"

"We're about to find out, Top."

The inbound choppers turned out to be just a lone Huey. All she carried were three passengers: one of 1st Cav's two assistant division commanders, a brigadier general; an artillery bird colonel from MACV; and an imposing sergeant major, also from MACV, named Sean Moon.

Chapter Seven

Brigadier General Barker, assistant division commander-A of 1st Cav, practically brushed past Captain Knapp, who'd raced to the LZ to greet his helicopter. "I want to talk to the radio people right now, Captain," the general said. "We've got to get to the bottom of these commo problems before this whole damn operation falls on its face."

"Roger that, sir," Knapp replied. "I'll take you over there right—"

"I know where the goddamn relay station is, Captain. You can see all those antennas for miles. The colonel riding with me needs to talk with you, anyway."

The colonel—the artilleryman from MACV who'd accompanied Barker—told Knapp, "We may be making some changes on this hill, Captain. Give me the two-dollar tour so I can see if those changes are going to work out." Nodding to Sean Moon, he added, "In the meantime, the sergeant major here wants to talk with your XO. Where is he?"

"I believe you'll find Lieutenant Miles in FDC," the BC replied. "But may I ask what you need from my XO, Sergeant Major?"

"I'm an old family friend, Captain," Sean replied. "I worked for the lieutenant's dad in Korea. Just want to say a quick hello."

"You came all this way just to visit with Miles?"

"There are a few other issues, too, sir," the sergeant major replied, "all of considerably greater importance to the MACV commander." Pointing to the bunker whose antenna array was surpassed only by that of the relay station, he added, "I take it that's FDC?"

*****

The NCO-in-charge of the relay station didn't sugarcoat the communications problem for General Barker. "It boils down to this, sir—we're only supposed to be handling traffic that needs a relay to or from Camp Evans, but the units down in the valley keep bogging my operators down with local requests for artillery and Air Force support. I know why they're doing it…they're afraid their signal might be too weak to get through otherwise. But that hasn't been the case. They're perfectly readable when talking directly to the batteries and the air support officer without a relay. Hell, the ASO is right on this mountain, too. You can even see him…he's sitting about two hundred meters away, looking down into the A Shau. If the guys in the valley are in range to talk to me, they sure as hell can talk to him…and my people wouldn't have half the traffic to deal with. I've been trying to tell Division that all day, but I'm not getting anywhere."

General Barker replied, "I see your point, Sergeant. Give me a clear frequency to Camp Evans. We'll fix this problem immediately, if not sooner."

*****

The artillery colonel from MACV got right to the point, telling Captain Knapp, "We want to blanket more of the Laotian border with artillery fire. It's looking like the most efficient way to do that is to upgrade the howitzers on this hill to one-five-fives. The Cav doesn't have any to spare, but we can attach some from First Field Force Artillery." The colonel took one more panoramic look at the firebase before adding, "Trouble is, I don't believe we can cram another battery along with your one-oh-fives onto this mountaintop. And since the Cav could use more easily movable direct-support batteries down on the valley floor, I'm going to recommend that we send your battery downstairs and bring one-five-fives to Signal Hill."

Knapp hated the idea but had to bite his tongue. There was something very special about being the King of Signal Hill, and he wanted to stay there as long as he was BC. He asked, "Wouldn't it be better to put the one-five-fives down on the valley floor and leave us up here, sir? That would entail a whole lot less air-lifting, and they could still easily reach the border."

"No, Captain, it would not be better. We'd only achieve one of our two objectives that way. Sure, we could still reach Laos, but one-five-five batteries just aren't as movable as yours."

Knapp decided it was time to shut up. Being argumentative wouldn't help his promotion prospects at all.

*****

Jif was hunched over a chart with several FDC personnel as they collectively figured out if it was possible for Charlie Battery to place fire on a target that was masked behind a tall and distant ridge. He didn't see the formidable presence of Sean Moon enter the bunker until Lieutenant Hammond tapped him on the shoulder, whispering, "Look sharp, man. We've got serious company of the E-Nine variety."

When he saw who the company was, Jif broke into a grin matching the one on Sean's face. With mock seriousness, he asked, "Are you lost, Sergeant Major? Can't you see we're busy here?"

The other men in the bunker thought their XO had lost his mind smartassing a very senior NCO like that. But then he and the visitor engaged in a hearty handshake. "I ain't lost, Lieutenant," Sean replied. "But I thought you might be. What's a boonie rat like you doing on this rock, anyway?"

His Brooklyn accent seemed almost as out of place as Jif's in an Army where nearly everyone spoke with either the passionless intonation of Middle America or the drawl of the southern states.

"Still plying my trade as an artilleryman, Sergeant Major, just on the other end of the trajectory. But I reckon you already knew I was here. You MACV types know everything that's going on in country."

"Not exactly everything, but enough," Sean replied. "Got a minute to talk?"

"Sure. Give us a second to put the finishing touches on this firing data."

Once they were alone outside the bunker, Sean explained, "There's a bit of a clusterfuck going on with the Cav, and I'm part of the team scoping it out for General Abrams."

"You mean the commo problems?"

"More than that, Lieutenant. There's talk that this mountain needs bigger artillery with longer range. But that ain't the worst of it—the Cav's suffering through a self-induced aviation fuel shortage, and it's looking like it's Divarty's fault. They severely underestimated the fuel they'd need for their part of Operation Delaware, and the idiots at Division Supply accepted their figures without double-checking. We're already scrambling to ferry as much fuel to Camp Evans as we can on short notice. But in the meantime, after flying the crap out of everything this morning, about half your chopper force is now sitting on the ramp with no gas."

Jif asked, "So that's why we haven't gotten our ammo or water resupply yet?"

"Affirmative, Lieutenant, and we're going to fix that right quick. But anyway, how the hell are you doing?"

"Staying alert, staying alive, Sergeant Major. Seen my dad lately?"

"As a matter of fact, that's what I wanted to tell you. I expect to see him in a couple of days down in Saigon. Anything you want me to pass on?"

"I think he's got it all, but thanks for asking."

Sean asked, "Did your R&R in Brisbane go okay?"

"Wait a minute...how the bloody hell did you know I was in Brizzie? My travel orders said Sydney."

Sean replied with just a knowing smile. Jif took it to mean that MACV knew he'd gone out of bounds but had cut him some slack. *Like Dad said, it's good to have friends in this Army*, he told himself.

"R&R had its moments, Sergeant Major, mostly good ones but with a few that could've been better. It all worked out, though. Are you going to be here long?"

"It's General Barker's chopper, so it's his call. But I don't figure we'll be here too long. We've still got a lot to look at down in the A Shau and back at Camp Evans."

*****

Fifteen minutes later, the VIP guests flew away, their Huey descending to the valley floor for visits with the assault commanders at A Luoi. Assembling the firebase cadre at the XO's post, Captain Knapp briefed them on what had transpired during the visit. "General Barker has promised us ammo before sundown," he began. "We're going to have to wait until tomorrow for another water buffalo, though. I know it'll be hard getting through the night with so little water available…and I agree we're all getting pretty ripe and in need of a good helmet bath. On the bright side, the forecast is for a storm later tonight, so the first sergeant and mess steward will be ensuring that all sections collect as much rainwater as possible. Even though it'll be on the cool side, I expect some of the men will be skinny-dipping in Mother Nature's shower, as well. Anything for good hygiene, right?"

Lieutenant Gruner, the security platoon leader, asked, "We hear a rumor that the battery is going to be leaving. Is that true, sir?"

"I was just getting to that, Lieutenant. It's possible we'll be moving, but nothing's set in stone yet. It all depends on how soon they can get a battery of one-five-fives ready to replace us on this mountain. That's no small feat, and it'll need to employ a lot of helicopters Divarty doesn't have available at the moment. Whatever happens, it won't be for a few days, at least."

Seeing his battery leaders react with obvious displeasure to the news, Knapp continued, "Now, I know you don't think it's fair to be pulled out of a position after you've put in so much work to build it up. But the big picture is more important than our little inconveniences. I know you like it up here…so do I…but you didn't really think we'd be here forever, did you? In a dynamic situation, no unit stays put for very long."

Jif tried not to laugh at that slice of flawed tactical wisdom: *No unit stays put for very long? I've been on firebases in country that have been in place so long, they're set in concrete. I'm sure the NCOs are thinking the same thing. They know the score better than me, probably.*

I reckon he's not going to mention the aviation fuel fuckup. Just as well…there's nothing anyone up here can do about it, anyway. But until it's straightened out, nobody is going anywhere.

*****

General Barker was true to his word. Two Skycranes raced the sunset to deliver a plentiful supply of howitzer ammunition to Signal Hill. The gun crews were still breaking the pallets down when the thunderstorm began. Sopping wet but undaunted, the cannon-cockers completed the distribution by 2000 hours.

Oddly enough, it wasn't raining down in the A Shau Valley. Dug into their perimeters for the night, the assault troops continued to call for artillery fire against enemies real and imagined. It was inevitable that some of the fire missions would include requests for airbursts with VT fuzes, the radio devices that provided maximum effectiveness against enemy personnel in the open or with limited cover.

Jif answered in advance the question he knew Hammond was going to ask: "We will not—repeat, *will not*—use VT fuzes in this heavy rain."

"But why, Jif? It's not raining down in the valley."

"Listen to me, Art...rain can create a false target for the fuze's receiver. At best, we waste rounds when they detonate too early in their trajectory. At worst, those detonations are so close to us that we kill some of our own people."

Hammond asked, "C'mon, man...I know what the manuals say, but have you ever really heard of that happen?"

"Yeah, I have. No bloody VT fuzes until I say so. End of story, Lieutenant."

Chief of Smoke McKay, who'd overheard the conversation, told Jif, "Couldn't have said it better myself, sir."

Captain Knapp, who was in FDC, overheard the conversation, too. Convinced Jif was being too cautious, he was about to overrule his decision when 1SG Contreras pulled him aside and said, "The XO's absolutely right, sir. The last thing you need right now is to be hauling off some of your own men in body bags."

He paused, not sure he wanted to say the next thing on his mind. But he said it, anyway. "And we'd be hard pressed to score those casualties as WIA. They'd be accidents caused by negligence, plain and simple."

In the stark shadows of FDC's bare-bulb lighting, the expression on Knapp's face changed rapidly from denial, to anger, and finally to acceptance. When the first call for *fuze VT* was radioed in, he stood by silently as the forward observer was told, "Negative on the VT. Shooting *fuze time* due to weather."

*****

The only good thing about the stormy night was the firebase was collecting a decent amount of rainwater. First Sergeant Contreras told Captain Knapp, "We've got about fifty gallons so far, collected from a variety of non-sterile places. We can keep about a hundred gallons in the damaged water buffalo, but we don't have the chemicals to make that much water potable all at once. Can't boil much, either, since too much of that'll burn up gasoline we need for the generators, and there's not enough wood left on this peak for a decent fire. Each man is going to have to keep treating his own canteen. For that, we've got enough purification tablets to last about three days."

Knapp asked, "We can use the untreated water for washing, though, can't we?"

"Negative, sir. About the only thing we can do safely with the untreated water is scrub the gun tubes. Any other use—even for helmet baths—is going to give us the shits. Guys are going to eat something with their supposedly clean fingers, and that'll be all she wrote. We'll have half the battery hovering over the latrine, going like the hammers of hell."

"Speaking of the hammers of hell," the BC said, "we've lucked out that nothing's been struck by lightning."

Contreras replied, "We'd better not count our chickens quite yet, sir."

*****

At a listening post on the north side of the firebase, two of Lieutenant Gruner's men had no intention of getting soaked by the chilling rain. Dug into the steep slope some fifty meters down from the peak, the fighting hole they occupied had been turned into a covered shelter. Snapping their waterproof ponchos together, they'd fashioned a broad lean-to that kept out the water. But this attempt at creature comfort restricted their ability to hear much of anything outside the hole; the racket of tropical raindrops pelting the taut fabric of the ponchos masked all but the loudest sounds.

One of the men at the LP was PFC Garrity, the ration-thrower who'd triggered the race riot a few hours before. His partner in the hole was another white man, a PFC named Boyer; Lieutenant Gruner hadn't taken Jif's suggestion to pair Garrity with one of his more astute black troopers. He'd rationalized his lack of action this way: *Miles can say whatever the hell he wants because it's not his platoon. He doesn't have to deal with the backlash when changes are forced on people.*

Boyer watched as Garrity curled up on the ammo crates that formed a floor, keeping them out of the mud at the bottom of the hole. When he protested that they couldn't sleep on LP duty, Garrity replied, "Oh, yeah?

Just watch me. If you weren't such a fucking Boy Scout, you'd be taking a nap, too."

"But we've got to check in every fifteen minutes. The sarge will have our asses if we don't."

Garrity's reply began with an outstretched middle finger. "Fuck the sarge…and fuck you, too, Boyer. If anybody tried to check on us…and they're not gonna, not in this storm…we'd just tell 'em the rain knocked out that piece-of-shit phone. Happens all the time." Then he pulled his field jacket over his head, adding, "Don't fucking wake me until our relief shows up."

"I don't understand you, Garrity. You just got Article Fifteened down to E-3. Aren't you afraid of getting screwed over again?"

"So I got busted…big fucking deal. The only difference is that since I'm a PFC again, I've gotta pull KP with all you assholes. Everything else stays the same ol' shit."

In a few moments, Garrity was snoring.

*****

Thirty minutes later, he was still snoring. Boyer thought he heard something besides his partner's sleep noises and the patter of raindrops on the lean-to. But he could see only a watery blackness beyond the LP…

Until the roof of ponchos was ripped away and he saw the glint of a thrusting bayonet about to pierce his chest.

*****

Just outside the mess bunker, Spec-6 Panakis, the mess steward, was marking a few cans of water that had been boiled on his stoves as *potable*. He was distracted by the darkened shapes of two men a few yards away, wandering among another group of containers. He yelled out, "Hey, assholes…don't mix those cans up. Those ones over there ain't fit to drink."

There was no reply.

Then one of those men raised a rifle to his shoulder. As Panakis jumped back into the mess bunker, he thought he saw a bayonet on the muzzle of that rifle.

Ain't none of our guys walking around with mounted bayonets…not even that bunch of fuckups in the security platoon.

He grabbed the shotgun the first sergeant had assigned to his section and crouched at the bunker's entryway, drawing a bead on where he'd seen the intruders…

But they were gone.

We've got gooks on the firebase, Panakis told himself. Then he grabbed the flare pistol and fired a red star cluster into the air—the signal that the enemy was in their midst.

Chapter Eight

There was always that moment of disbelief that followed the sudden arrival of something you didn't want to happen. Every man on Fire Base Signal Hill was living through that moment as he caught sight of the red star cluster drifting down through the rain. For some, that moment would linger too long, causing dangerous inaction. For Jif, it didn't last a heartbeat. He grasped the deadly nature of the warning immediately.

This is a really dangerous time, he told himself. *Having gooks inside the perimeter is bad enough, but even if this is only some panicky false alarm, just the thought that they're inside drives the risk of friendly fire incidents sky high. Throw in the confusion of darkness and pouring rain, and this becomes a bloody nightmare.*

He wasn't surprised when McKay, a phone pressed to his ear, said, "The BC wants some clarification as to what the hell's going on."

Jif replied, "Wouldn't we all? But we don't have bloody time for that. We need to light this place up right now. Tell every gun section to throw out a ground flare as far as they can toward the middle of the firebase. Do we know who shot the red star cluster?"

"Working on it, sir," McKay replied.

There was a short burst of gunfire from the vicinity of the relay station on the opposite side of the peak. An explosion came right on its heels. It seemed too strong a blast to be a grenade, more like a mortar round or satchel charge. Jif couldn't tell what, if anything, had blown up.

Slowly—too slowly—the ground flares were being hurled into the open space behind the gun sections. Their pinpoints of light, though brilliant, did a barely adequate job of illuminating the crescent-shaped battery.

At least the rain isn't dousing them, Jif told himself.

"Got an answer on who shot the flare," McKay said. "The mess section. Claim they saw two intruders."

"You know the drill, Smoke...if they think they saw two, there are probably ten running around the place. Any word on what the security platoon's up to?"

"Negative, sir. But hang on..."

McKay listened intently to the phone for a moment more before adding, "The captain wants the reaction force to assemble at the CP."

Jif replied, "Is he kidding? Doesn't he realize they stand a bloody good chance of being shot by our own guys as they try to cross the firebase? Everybody needs to stay in position. Anyone moving outside those positions is a target."

Offering the phone, the Smoke asked, "You want to tell him that, Lieutenant?"

Before Jif could answer, there was another explosion, again from the other side of the firebase but closer to the engineer section. This time, there was no doubt something had blown up; there was a secondary flash and *boom* as tendrils of flame shot into the air.

"That's not ammo cooking off," McKay said. "Looks more like fuel. I think the gooks got the engineers' mini-dozer. No doubt about it, sir...we've got sappers in the house." Pressing the phone tight to his ear again, he relayed, "Dead gook near the radio bunker...apparently threw a satchel charge...didn't hurt anything." Another pause, and then he added, "BC wants to know the status of the reaction force."

A crackle of gunfire—M16s by the sound of it—erupted near Gun Two, lasting just a few seconds. As it died out, Jif told McKay, "Tell the captain that the reaction force is already engaging intruders right at the gun sections." He considered adding, *And he's welcome to join them*, but held his tongue.

"We've got a fire mission coming down, Lieutenant," the Smoke said. "Put it on hold?"

Jif was about to say, *Hell, no...we'll shoot it*. But he changed his mind, telling McKay, "Ask the BC for his blessing."

They'd expected a quick yes or no answer. Instead, Captain Knapp told them to stand by because he was calling for illum over Signal Hill from Bravo Battery down in the A Shau.

Jif said, "Did you tell the man that illum won't do us a whole lot of good? We can practically reach up and touch the bloody cloud deck over us. All the flares will do is light up the top side of that deck."

"I'm trying, sir," McKay replied. "I'm trying."

"In the meantime, tell the gun sections to put one man on backdoor security while the rest of the crew stands by for a fire mission."

The battery recorder, the other man with Jif and McKay at the XO's post, yelled out, "I SEE MOVEMENT NEAR THE BURN PIT, LT."

The burn pit: that was actually a misnomer. It was the place well behind the guns where the battery safely burned off their unused bags of propellant. Rather than a physical pit, Jif had had the engineers craft a rectangular earthen platform roughly twenty feet on each side and just a few inches above the actual ground level of the peak. Higher in the middle, it had a slight slope toward its sides so water wouldn't collect in the burn area when it rained.

Not that the stuff doesn't burn when wet, Jif had said at the time, *but it's bloody hard to light off in standing water.*

The numerous fire missions they'd shot today had been of mostly short and medium range, each round fired contributing three or four unused powder bags to be burned off. There were currently several hundred bags of the highly flammable propellant in the pit, creating a mound several feet high. It would yield a tremendous bonfire that would burn fiercely for three to four minutes, but with helicopters bringing ammo deliveries, the onset of the storm, and now intruders in their midst, there hadn't been a chance to light it off.

The recorder was right; there appeared to be a few men taking cover behind the mound. "They've got to be NVA," Jif said. "Our guys wouldn't go anywhere near the burn pit unless it was their turn to light it off."

"Are you sure about that, Lieutenant?"

"I bloody well am. Those aren't our men."

McKay offered, "In that case, sir, those gook bastards could do us a favor and throw a satchel charge into that pile. Might even burn themselves up in the process."

"You just gave me an idea, Smoke." Jif took a ground flare from its shipping can and started a hunched-over run toward the burn pit, hoping to make himself as small a target as possible. When he figured he was close enough, he lit the flare and hurled it like a grenade onto the pile. Then he sprinted back to the XO's post.

In the seconds it took him to return, the powder bags still hadn't lit off, although the flare was obviously burning. McKay asked, "You sure that's going to work, Lieutenant? Those bags are pretty wet..."

"And that magnesium flare is bloody hot, Smoke. Give it a couple more—"

He stopped in mid-sentence when a small flare-up ignited on the top of the pile. In seconds, the entire mound of wet bags became a roaring blaze, spewing steam and lighting the firebase like the biggest campfire in history. There was no darkness for intruders to hide in any longer.

Two NVA sappers popped up behind the inferno. One proved a difficult target as he began a full-tilt run toward the north side of the firebase. The other was on fire. He managed only a few stumbling steps before he dropped to his knees, wrapped in flames. As the human torch toppled over, the satchel charge he carried cooked off. The explosion vaporized him, leaving behind nothing but a few smoldering embers, which the rain quickly put out.

As Jif predicted, this *most dangerous time* for friendly fire incidents was upon them in full force. There were at least half a dozen NVA still running across the firebase, exposed in the orange glow of the blaze. One tried to hurl his satchel charge at the relay station but was cut down by a long burst from a radioman's rifle. He'd been hit only twice; the other four rounds in the burst flew across the firebase to strike Gun Two's position. A bullet destroyed one of the section's two collimators, the devices that provided deflection references for the piece. The other rounds ripped into the low parapet, flinging dirt from torn-open sandbags into the eyes of two cannoneers. They'd be temporarily blinded until treated by a medic.

Another sapper set his sights on blowing up the generators behind the CP bunker as he made his escape from the firebase. But the hail of gunfire that cut him down didn't prevent him from throwing the satchel charge. Landing on top of the parapet surrounding the two generators, its detonation knocked out one of them. Two radios in the CP's bank of four were now without power.

One of Panakis' cooks, who was outside the mess bunker protecting the water storage area, came face to face with two sappers escaping to the north slope. In a wild exchange of point-blank gunfire, he shot one of them dead. The other NVA took revenge, shooting the cook before vanishing over the edge of the peak.

The mass of burning powder bags would continue to light the firebase for a few minutes more. There was nobody moving through its open spaces now. A flurry of gunfire from down the north slope lasted only seconds.

Then there was no sound but the steady hiss of rain.

Captain Knapp had lost interest in calling for illumination rounds from another battery; on this overcast and rainy night, the blaze had done the job of lighting the firebase more effectively, anyway. As his CP struggled to compensate for the loss of half its electrical power, he was on the battery phone network, telling Jif, "You can commence that fire mission now.

Also, I want the reaction force to sweep the entire firebase. There may still be intruders in our midst. Make it quick, before that fire dies completely and we're in the dark again."

After telling McKay to get the guns firing, Jif tried to process what the BC had just told him:

Is he telling me to lead the battery's reaction force? Per SOP, that's the first sergeant's job. Things could get real confusing—and real dangerous—if two people try to do the same job while the shit's hitting the fan.

Unless something's happened to Contreras...

But he never had the chance to ask. Perhaps someone had read his mind—maybe Knapp or, more likely, 1SG Contreras himself—because the captain added, "The first sergeant is on his way to your position, Miles. He'll take charge of the reaction force."

The first rounds of the fire mission were on their way less than thirty seconds after McKay put the howitzers back in business. As he watched his crews flawlessly do their jobs despite the darkness and chilling rain, he told Jif, "One thing's for damn sure, sir…there would've never been gooks in the perimeter if Lieutenant Carpenter's security platoon was still watching our asses. This new bunch has some shit to answer for, I'm afraid."

*****

It didn't take long for 1SG Contreras to figure out how the perimeter breach had happened. From the firebase switchboard, he called every LP. All replied except one on the north slope. A team from the reaction force quickly found two dead men from the security platoon in that fighting hole: Garrity and Boyer, lying in a puddle of rain and their own blood. Their rifles were stacked in a corner, plastic bags still over the muzzles to keep out the rain.

"I wouldn't be surprised if the poor, dumb bastards were asleep," Contreras said after taking just one look. "There wasn't any fight here at all, I guaran-damn-tee it." Assigning two of his own men to the LP, he added, "This north slope is going to be a pain in our asses as long as we're on this mountain."

It took another few minutes to finally raise Lieutenant Gruner on the radio. His voice full of excitement, he gushed, "We've got one! Captured the gook bastard alive! We're bringing him to the CP."

When Contreras reached the CP, Gruner and several of his men were standing outside, waiting to present their prisoner to Captain Knapp, who was, at the moment, consumed with re-establishing communications on the command net; it had been lost when the radios died along with the sabotaged generator. Pumped up by their illusions of triumph, the captors milled around, taunting their kneeling captive while slapping each other on the back in congratulations for the *bitchin' job* they'd just done.

But Contreras was fairly sure that he was viewing the second biggest fuckup of the night, the debacle at the LP being the biggest. He had no problem determining that the *prisoner*—on his knees, hands bound behind his back with engineer tape, too aggravated to speak—was not, in fact, Vietnamese. "Get away from him, for cryin' out loud," the first sergeant growled. Then, crouching behind the captive to cut his hands free, he asked, "Are you okay? Did these people hurt you?"

"No, Top, I'm not hurt. But the minute I get untied, they're gonna be."

"Negative, Joey. I'll take it from here."

Contreras returned slowly to his feet, as if the weight of the stupidity he was being forced to deal with was almost too great to bear. He told Gruner, "This is one sorry state of affairs, Lieutenant. What on God's green earth made you think this man was Vietnamese? He's a little on the tall and beefy side to be a gook, wouldn't you say?"

"Don't be pointing fingers at us, Top. Look at him…he's Asian!"

"Negative, sir. *Negative*. Let me introduce you to Sergeant Joseph Ka'anā'anā from the engineer section. Most of us can't come close to pronouncing his name properly—I only know it because I've had to write it on reports a few times—so we just call him Joey Aloha. He's Polynesian, from the great state of Hawaii."

"But he's all dressed in black, Top! And he's got Ho Chi Minh sandals!"

Joey Aloha asked, "Can I say something, Top?"

"If it's helpful, go right ahead."

Addressing Gruner, he said, "I'm not dressed in black, Lieutenant. I'm wearing an OD tee shirt and utility pants. They're soaking wet so they look black in low light, just like everyone's clothes do right now. As to my sandals, they're Zoris—you know, flip-flops—like everyone wears in the shower. I wasn't on watch, so I was relaxing when the shit hit the fan. I was trying to save the bulldozer from being a total loss when these douchebags—I don't mean you, Lieutenant—decided to *capture* me. But if you thought I was the enemy, what stopped you from just shooting me?"

One of Gruner's men answered, "Well, you didn't have a weapon..."

"Sounds like another clue I wasn't an intruder, doesn't it?"

"All right, let's wrap this clusterfuck up," Contreras said. "Are you aware, Lieutenant, that two of your men manning an LP on the north slope are dead?"

The dumbfounded look on Gruner's face was all the answer the first sergeant needed.

"They both got run through, no gunshots...might've even been asleep on duty," the first sergeant continued, "so it's not surprising that nobody heard a damn thing. That's how the gooks got in here, I'll bet...right over that hole. Now, I suggest you all get back to your designated positions immediately...my guys will cover that north slope LP for you. Tonight's fun and games may not be over, so for God's sake, stay alert. When the dust settles, Lieutenant, the captain will want to see you and your platoon sergeant at the CP."

"It'll have to be me and my acting platoon sergeant, Top. Our actual platoon sergeant didn't come out on this mission."

"Why the hell not?"

"Said he had stuff to take care of."

And you bought that, you dumb shit?

"Well then, sir, that's something else we'll be correcting."

*****

It was near midnight when the rain stopped. The battery activity had slowed to the usual illumination requests, with an occasional H&I—harassment and interdiction mission—thrown in, firing at a likely location of enemy movement or assembly. While the intelligence people tried to put great weight on the term *likely*, as if based on serious amounts of irrefutable intel, most H&I targets were, at best, the result of a SWAG: a scientific wild-ass guess. At worst, they were the product of wishful thinking.

Gathering his combat leaders at the CP, Captain Knapp conducted a debrief of the night's events. First Sergeant Contreras gave the casualty numbers: "On our side, we've got two KIA from the security platoon. There are three WIA, all from Charlie Battery. Two men from Gun Two got crap in their eyes, but the doc says they'll be okay—nothing a good eye flush and a tube of Tetracaine won't fix. PFC Woodard from the mess section got shot, but he's lucky—it's a through-and-through to his left flank that apparently didn't hit anything major. Doc's got him stable, and we've called for the medevac. Don't have an ETA yet, but it'll be an Air Force chopper. At least those blue-suit flyboys know how to requisition enough fuel to keep flying. Captain Fisher, our ASO, is working to make it happen ASAP. As far as NVA casualties, we have five confirmed dead. If there are enemy wounded, we're unaware of the number at this time."

Captain Knapp said, "In other words, looking beyond that tragic lapse in the security platoon, we did an excellent job repelling the attack."

"You might say that, sir," Contreras replied, "but let's not forget that in addition to the mini-dozer, we lost a generator, too, and that's hurting the CP's commo capabilities."

"Both items can be easily replaced," Knapp said. "You've already requisitioned them, correct?"

"Affirmative, sir...but we're going to have to make a choice here. Considering how few heavy-lift choppers they can put into the air with their restricted fuel supply, Division is asking which we want first—the water or the dozer. Once we get one of them delivered, though, there's no telling when we'll get the other. And I've got to advise you, sir, that they're pushing real hard for the dozer to be first."

Nobody was surprised to hear that. It was a foregone conclusion that Division would replace them with a 155-millimeter battery within a few days. Reinforcing that conclusion was the fact that just hours after General Barker's visit, the engineers had been radioed instructions outlining the earthwork modifications the larger howitzers would require. The dozer was key to accomplishing that work in a timely fashion. Every day without that vital piece of equipment would delay the project immeasurably, and no general was going to tolerate an indefinite wait for his plans to be executed.

As Knapp pondered the choice, Contreras opened his canteen and swallowed the little that was left inside. Then he held it upside down, letting one last drop spill to the bunker's wooden floor.

"I get your point, First Sergeant," the captain said, "but you know as well as I do there are bigger considerations at stake here." He didn't surprise anyone when he added, "We'll take the dozer first."

"Very well, sir," Contreras replied, his tone respectful yet dissatisfied. "There's one more thing to discuss...this raid tonight was not some day trip by NVA from down in the valley. Climbing this mountain on foot is a major mountaineering effort, especially with weapons and equipment. They're living up here...and probably very close. We've had too much contact with the NVA for them not to have one or more camps on these slopes. We just haven't found them yet. That said, should we put in another request for a mortar section to be based up here with us? I realize Division's shot down that request twice already, but the short-range fire and illumination capabilities are something this place really needs—tonight's festivities prove that, I think—especially if they replace us with one-five-fives. Their battery defensive capabilities will be much less flexible than ours."

"I'll ask, Top," Knapp replied, "but don't get your hopes up. Division still seems to think this mountain is Shangri-La."

Captain Fisher, the Air Force ASO, had left the CP a few moments before when summoned to the radio by his RTO. He was back now with important information: "The *Jolly Green* is on the way, one-five minutes out."

"I'll get the LZ lit up, sir," Contreras replied.

"And another thing," Fisher said. "Night air recon with infrared has reported a huge hot spot just west of the airfield at A Luoi, about three klicks from here. Brigade thinks it might be the main NVA base camp they're looking for."

"That's great," Captain Knapp replied. "No doubt we'll be getting the order any second for every gun in Divarty to hit that spot."

"Negative, Captain," Fisher replied. "Brigade's requested that *Spooky* level the place, and Special Ops Squadron just approved the request. ETA on the gunship is three-five minutes from now. Stand by for the greatest fireworks show on Earth, y'all."

Chapter Nine

The drone of Spooky's engines announced her approach nearly a minute before they sighted the aircraft from Signal Hill. As she drew closer, the blue-orange glow from the exhausts was all that could be seen of her in the night sky. The AC-47 gunship—one of a dozen or more relics from WW2 given new life as aerial gun platforms—passed a few thousand feet above the firebase, flying northeast to southwest toward the suspected NVA base camp near A Luoi airfield. Not known for speed, the old aircraft leisurely skimmed the scattered moonlit clouds the storm had left behind.

"We'll be retiring the likes of her real soon," Captain Fisher, the Air Force ASO, told Jif and Captain Knapp. "Within a few months, we'll be seeing bigger, faster aircraft with even more devastating firepower than that old girl carries."

That didn't come as any surprise to the Army men. They'd already heard the stories of the two aircraft types that would replace Spooky: C-119 *Flying Boxcars*, aging cargo planes in the USAF inventory since the Korean War, now flying only in the Air Force Reserve and Air National Guard, were being modified to AC-119 *Shadow* gunships for Vietnam service; early-model C-130 cargo aircraft, founding members of the Air Force's current workhorse fleet, were becoming the AC-130 *Spectre*.

But for this place and time, Spooky was still the only game in town.

Jif, who'd seen the type in action a few times before, asked Fisher, "She's a little high for flare drops over the valley floor, isn't she? When's she going to start losing altitude?"

"Any second," the ASO replied. "Once she's clear of all these mountains on the east side of the valley, she'll spiral down, drop her flares, and commence the cone of death."

Jif had never heard the expression *cone of death* until now, but it seemed fitting. Orbiting a few thousand feet over a target, the tracers from her mini-guns would sketch a dazzling cone in the sky as thousands of rounds devastated a targeted area in seconds. From a safe distance, it was exhilarating to watch...and terrifying.

We'll be looking down on the ship while she's doing her worst, Jif thought. *I've never seen that mayhem from above. That's a view you normally only get from another aircraft.*

Just seconds after passing overhead—and to the surprise of the men on Signal Hill—Spooky's crew kicked out their first parachute flare, a million-candle-power beacon that illuminated the firebase and the entire western slope of Signal Hill in its brilliant light. Fifteen seconds later—to their even greater surprise—her crew kicked out another flare.

"What the bloody hell are they doing?" Jif asked. "Aren't they dropping the line in the wrong place? They're about a klick and a half off to the east."

"Relax, Lieutenant," Fisher replied. "Those good ol' boys know their job." He sounded like he was trying to convince himself as much as the men around him.

"I'm not so sure about that, sir," Jif replied. "The wind being what it is, I reckon that first flare is going to hit the ground somewhere on our west slope and keep burning for a good while. I hope everything is still soaking wet down there or we may have a forest fire to deal with."

Captain Knapp added, "The damn thing better not land on the firebase. That's all we fucking need...if it falls into a pile of ammo, we'll have our second blaze of the night... and maybe even cook-offs that'll rip this place apart."

"Oh, ye of little faith," Fisher said, still trying to sound confident and calming. But even the biblical reference wasn't helping his case.

Spooky kicked out a third flare, this one closer to the mark. Her crew radioed Fisher, asking, "How are we looking, *Golden Eye*?"

Unsure how to reply, the ASO asked Knapp, "How far from the target area do you make her?"

The BC punted the question to Jif, saying, "You're the crackerjack FO around here, Miles. Let's hear your guess."

"I put her over the airfield now," Jif replied, "so she's about two klicks out and way too high for a gun run."

"Yeah, I've got to agree with you there," Fisher replied. He relayed that information to Spooky's crew.

Their answer—a dithering combination of excuses and what-ifs—confirmed what everyone was thinking: *Even with all those flares lighting up the valley, they're afraid to drop down into it. They may know exactly where the target area is, but they don't have a real good handle on where the mountains around it are. Granted, if they misjudge where that high ground is, it'll ruin their whole day...*

But isn't that ship equipped to navigate in the dark better than this?

As Fisher struggled to help the flight crew get oriented, the first flare kicked from the aircraft dropped onto the western slope as if the Sun had come to Earth, landing about six hundred meters down from the peak. It showed no inclination to burn out anytime soon. But as Jif had hoped, the woods were still wet; the flare hadn't started a forest fire. At least not yet. Everyone on the firebase was aware that if it did start a blaze, the prevailing wind would push the flames their way. Though the peak was cleared and had no vegetation left to burn, there was no telling if small bits of smoldering debris lofted into the air would settle onto some ammo or fuel storage area. If those stealthy incendiaries weren't detected and extinguished immediately, they'd have a new blaze on their hands, one that was completely out of their control.

Despite Fisher's best efforts, Spooky's crew was still hesitant to descend into the valley. Their big issue: "We can't see the damn peaks. Sure, we can see the side of your mountain all lit up like that, but we've got no visual on the top...or any other top, for that matter."

First Sergeant Contreras, who'd joined the group, offered, "Look, Captain Fisher...if they need a reference for the peak, we can light up the LZ again. Sure, we shut those lights off once the Jolly Green medevac flew away, but we can crank them right back up. It'll only take a minute, and then they shouldn't have any question where the peak is. I can even make those lights blink in Morse Code, if your crew wants."

Jif added, "And if Spooky can lock in on this peak, they should be able to figure out exactly where every other peak is...they've got the same maps we do, and a lot more sophisticated navigation gear. That valley's over a mile wide. Surely they can keep her in a box that big."

Knapp told Contreras, "Go ahead and do that, Top. Light up the LZ." As an afterthought, he asked Fisher, "If that's okay with you?"

"That'll be mighty fine," the ASO replied. The flight crew agreed, too, asking only that the lights cycle on and off every few seconds for positive identification.

Chief of Smoke McKay, who'd been with the gun sections, came running over. "You've got to see this, gentlemen. The flare that just hit the slope lit it up real good, and we've got gooks running all over the damn place down there."

"How far away?" Knapp asked.

"About six hundred meters, sir. Right where that flare landed."

"How many?"

"Hard to tell for sure, sir...could be ten, could be a hundred."

Jif and the BC started to follow McKay back to the guns, but Fisher called out, "Hey, wait a minute...how about one of you staying and helping me out? We haven't put this thing to bed yet."

Knapp said, "I'll work with the Air Force, Miles. You sort out what's going on down the slope. Keep me informed."

Sure, I'll keep you informed...for whatever bloody good that'll do.

*****

McKay hadn't exaggerated; there were dozens of NVA in the vicinity of the flare, silhouetted in its blazing light, darting about as if their only objective was to get far away from it.

"Can't say I blame the bastards," McKay said. "They're a lot more night-blinded than we are right now...and will be for a long time. You don't think they'd be stupid enough to come up here, do you?"

"I wish," Jif replied. "They'd be such easy targets. But I reckon they're trying to go laterally or toward the valley. It's a bloody shame we can't point the howitzers downhill."

"Damn right, sir," the Smoke replied. "But this sure answers the question about whether there are gooks living on this mountain. The first sergeant hit the nail right on the head."

An anxious section chief called out, "What are we supposed to do, LT?" His section was already crouched behind their gun parapet, rifles at the ready, artillerymen fearing they were about to fight as infantry.

Jif replied, "Don't waste ammo on them. They're too far away. Just be ready if they get closer."

Turning back to McKay, he added, "But we've got to do *something*. I'm going to get with the BC and ASO. Maybe we can work up a plan." That said, he headed for the two captains.

Lieutenant Gruner intercepted him, asking, "Do you think I should pull back my LPs on the west slope?"

"No, not until the gooks start coming up the hill...*if* they start coming. That flare's not going to last much longer, and then we'll need those LPs more than ever."

"Copy that, Jif. When you're night-blind and can't see worth a shit, all you can do is listen."

"Remember, the gooks are having the same problem, Gruner. Just sit tight."

In the minute it took Jif to rejoin Captains Knapp and Fisher, the flare on the west slope had burned out. The BC asked, "What's the story, Miles?"

"Looks like there's about a company of NVA down there. They aren't moving toward us at the moment...not quite sure where they're going. We'll try to keep tracking them with a starlight scope now that the flare's out."

"Good idea," Knapp replied. "Make it happen."

Jif could hear the conversation Fisher was having with Spooky. The ship was lining up for another flare run farther to the southwest, away from Signal Hill and closer to her intended target, the suspected NVA base camp. He asked the ASO, "Is she ever going to get lower?"

"Have a little patience, Lieutenant. After this flare drop, their pucker factor should be toned down and they'll go in for the gun run. By the way, lighting up the LZ helped a lot."

"It'd be great if after she hit that target down in the valley, she'd work over the west slope for us."

Fisher shook his head. "Negative, Miles. Shooting up a mountainside as steep as this one is against all the attack profiles. She can't orbit, so she can't be effective. They're still too scared of this mountain to get near it, anyway, even in the light of flares...which they'll be running out of real soon at the rate they're kicking them out the door, because we weren't her first customers tonight. Besides, by the time Squadron gave us approval for a new target—*if* they gave approval—Spooky would be low on gas and ammo, too."

"So we've got to get Bravo Battery down in the valley to hit the slope for us," Jif said.

Fisher's bristling reply: "That's your call, gentlemen, but bear in mind that if you think you need to put artillery rounds in the air immediately, that forces Spooky to leave the area immediately, too, and the mission against the base camp gets scrubbed."

Captain Knapp added, "We're just going to have to wait until the Air Force is done, Miles. It won't be long."

"Yeah...but long enough for the gooks to scatter," Jif replied.

"You can't have everything, Lieutenant," Fisher said. "Spooky is for high-density, high-priority targets. We'd never have her chasing a handful of gooks on a mountainside in the dark. That's a shamefully inefficient waste of a precious asset."

Returning to McKay and the gun sections, Jif fumed, "Bloody Air Force...being around them is like sitting in some corporate board meeting, listening to some suit and tie blow hot air about assets, priorities, and efficiencies. I thought LBJ shitcanned that corporate whizbang McNamara and all his bullshit theories about applying industrial management principles to the military. The way those flyboys talk, though, it doesn't sound like anything's changed. As far as I'm concerned, we—and by we, I mean every swinging dick down here on the ground—are the highest priority asset in this fight.

We should be calling the targets without needing the approval of some brass in an air-conditioned office on the other side of the country...or the other side of the world."

"Not disagreeing with you or anything, Lieutenant," McKay replied, "but how many corporate board meetings have you ever sat in at your tender age?"

"A bunch, Smoke. Back when my mother was running a major corporation in Australia, before she decided it was better to pay others to deal with the day-to-day aggravation, I ended up sitting through more than a few. She considered it a learning experience. I went to a few board meetings of an American corporation, too, when I interned for it in college."

"So I guess you know what you're talking about, sir. I stand corrected."

"No worries, Smoke. Hey...it looks like Spooky's finally in the right place and at the right altitude. Let the show begin."

*****

The gunship's reign of fire was every bit as formidable as the other times Jif had watched one in action. The howitzer crews, most of whom had never seen the spectacle before, were transfixed by the sight of thousands of 7.62-millimeter rounds streaming down as if from a fire hose. From the distance of three kilometers, that deluge of steel shimmered in ribbons of red and white.

But the cannon-cockers' fascination had McKay worried. "I'm glad they're liking the show, Lieutenant," he said, "but they can't be forgetting we've got gooks dancing around not too far below us. This isn't the time to be getting distracted." He stalked off to redirect their attention downslope.

Spooky's work was done within two minutes. Then she droned south through the valley, still well below the peaks, her engines straining for every bit of altitude the old bird could muster.

"Looks like she's hardly moving," a gunner said. "Probably be easy pickings for some triple-A site."

"I'm pretty sure the flyboys know that," Jif replied. "I reckon it's a question of what they're more scared of right now…hitting a mountain or getting shot up by ground fire. My guess is it's the mountain."

"How come she can't help out with these gooks down below us, LT? It seems like it would only take one pass to do the job."

"I wish I could answer that," Jif replied, "but the Air Force thinks it's too risky for them."

"Too risky, eh?" Grabbing his crotch, the gunner continued, "I've got their *too riskies* right here, LT. The poor babies better hurry back to their air-conditioned quarters and ice-cold brews. God forbid we douchebags living outside in mud holes and drinking rainwater put their precious asses at risk."

The gunship now gone, Captain Knapp sought and received permission from Fisher to resume artillery operations. With Jif acting as FO, Bravo Battery—located down in the A Shau, five klicks to the south—began pounding the west slope of Signal Hill. He had little choice but to blindly sweep the fire across a broad area in hopes of finding the NVA; the starlight scope that had looked for them out to a range of nearly eight hundred meters had detected no motion; they couldn't see any trace of the enemy when Jif requested several illum rounds from Bravo, either. With Knapp's blessing, the fire mission was terminated after five inconclusive fire-for-effect volleys.

The night returned to the all-too-familiar pattern of occasional fire missions, interrupted sleeping shifts, fear of another intrusion by the enemy, and the hope that the morning would reveal their actions had actually accomplished something.

*****

Thirty minutes past sunrise, the rumble of a Skycrane stirred the sky around Signal Hill. Even though the big helicopter was still a few miles away, her sling load was easy to identify with binoculars: "Here comes your replacement bulldozer," 1SG Contreras told the engineer section chief. "Try not to lose this one."

"Not funny, Top," the sergeant replied. "That's a hell of a note after the favor I just did for you."

"Favor? What the hell are you talking about, amigo?"

"You'll see."

As the mini-dozer touched down at the engineers' camp, the *favor* became apparent: fifteen five-gallon jerry cans of water were strapped to the vehicle.

Contreras was thrilled. "Whoa! What a sport," he said. "Another seventy-five gallons. That should keep this place in business another day. How'd you pull that off, Ray?"

"I just asked my C.O. back at Camp Evans to send them along. Sometimes it helps to have friends, you know?"

Contreras knew it all too well: *Friends are great, especially ones who know how to bypass the supply chain.*

That wasn't the only favor the Skycrane would provide. After releasing the dozer, she hopped over to the firing battery, where gun crewmen snapped multiple A-22 cargo bags full of expended shell canisters onto her load hook. The weight of the roughly one thousand pieces of brass—about twenty-five hundred pounds—was child's play for the heavy-lift chopper. She lifted the bags effortlessly and headed back to Camp Evans.

"It's about time we got a trash run," the first sergeant said to Captain Knapp. "I've been begging for one, but I didn't expect they'd accommodate us so soon. We had enough expended brass stacked up around here to build a shrine to Saint Barbara."

Seeing the quizzical look on the captain's face, Contreras explained, "You remember, sir...Saint Barbara, the patron saint of artillerymen?"

"Oh...of course," Knapp replied, trying to pretend he'd known the answer all along. "How many canisters were in those bags?"

"Hang on a minute, sir, and I'll get you an exact number."

He yelled over to the recorder at the XO's post, posing the same question.

The answer: "One thousand forty-eight, First Sergeant."

"That's a lot of shooting," Knapp said. "It didn't seem like that much."

"The numbers don't lie, sir. But it was a lot of shooting…and they'd better come through with another ammo drop today or we'll be shooting doodly-squat by supper."

The BC smiled and said, "I wouldn't worry about it, Top. I've got a feeling the troubleshooting team from MACV has crawled so far up Division's ass that everything is going to go like clockwork from now on. That little fuel fiasco of theirs is the kind of stuff that ends careers."

*****

Captain Knapp was right; the MACV team had, at the very least, alleviated the aviation fuel shortage overnight. Helicopters bringing supplies and ferrying troops were in abundance in the A Shau that morning. Per Captain Knapp's request, there was also a LOACH scout ship detailed to recon the slopes of Signal Hill for signs of enemy activity.

"I want that LOACH to focus on the western slope, Miles," the BC said. "You had eyes on the gooks, so guide her in as necessary."

As they watched the scout ship go to work, Jif told McKay, "Look at her…she's buzzing around real low, trying to draw fire. That takes some pair of balls, but I reckon the gooks won't give themselves away, if they're even there. They only come out at night, you know?"

"Roger that, sir."

Not surprisingly, the LOACH saw nothing to indicate an enemy presence either now or last night. Over the radio, her pilot reported, "No joy on the bad guys, but somebody sure blew the hell out of this forest. Is this your work?"

"Negative," Jif replied. "That's a little out of our field of fire. Another outfit did the job."

"Well, if they're in the lumber business, they just scored themselves a windfall. In terms of body count, though, looks like we've got zip. Nada. Bupkis."

"Shit," Jif said off the air as he kicked the parapet in frustration. "If we hadn't had to wait for Spooky to get the bloody hell out of the way, we could've..." He didn't bother finishing the sentence. Instead, he slumped down in the XO's post, letting the discontent and weariness flow over him. "Give me a minute," he told McKay.

Down in the A Shau, at an LZ near the A Luoi airfield, a dozen Hueys—enough to airlift a company—picked up a recon-in-force group for the brief flight to the area Spooky had decimated last night. As gunships loitered overhead, the troopers streamed from the choppers and scoured the suspected NVA base camp.

They found nothing; not so much as a scrap of trash inadvertently left behind. The battalion commander whose men did the recon-in-force summarized the results as follows:

Maybe the infrared readings that air recon got were a bunch of bullshit.

Or if there actually were NVA here, they were just passing through.

Either way, we got skunked.

Chapter Ten

Colonel Chastain, 1st Cavalry's Division Artillery commander, would say and do anything at this point to keep his hopes of that first star alive. But he'd run out of things to say, and every effort he'd taken to straighten out the logistical fiasco his headquarters had caused had been treated by his superiors like this: *That's outstanding, but if you'd been on the ball, you would've done it last week, and none of this mess would've happened. As it is, you nearly turned Operation Delaware into a debacle.*

The two men sitting in his Camp Evans office, Brigadier General Barker, 1st Cav's assistant commander, and Sergeant Major Sean Moon from MACV—*General Abrams' spy and asshole buddy from way back*, Chastain told himself—looked quite comfortable being his judge, jury, and executioner.

"To put it simply, Colonel," General Barker said, "Divarty is top-notch when it comes to operational planning and execution. The fire support your unit is providing in the A Shau right now is nothing short of excellent, especially when you consider the logistics handicap you inflicted on them. But administratively, your organization isn't cutting it. I'm not convinced—and neither is the division commander—that relieving your S-4 is going to magically solve all your problems. The issue here, quite simply, is little to no command oversight. Nobody—not you, not your XO, not your sergeant major—is providing adequate supervision and coordination of your staff sections. Not requisitioning sufficient aviation fuel for your needs was a shitshow, obviously, but problems have been created in several other areas of your headquarters as well."

With that verdict, Chastain knew his chances of promotion to general officer were nil. It would cause several categories on his efficiency report to be rated below par. A bad rating in one category alone was a death sentence.

But in a way, that knowledge is liberating, the colonel thought. *I won't have to kiss ass quite so fervently. I can say pretty much what I want now, and if the boys upstairs don't want to listen, fuck 'em.*

What are they going to do? Retire me? I'm already as good as out the door.

"Regarding those several areas of concern," General Barker continued, "Sergeant Major Moon has come across some festering problems in your personnel shop." He nodded to the sergeant major to take it from there.

"As you know, Colonel," Sean began, "putting a one-five-five battery on Signal Hill to replace the one-oh-five outfit currently there is a MACV priority, to be accomplished two days from now. But looking at the orders coming down from your S-1, you're creating a problem that'll put Charlie Battery of Second Battalion, the unit coming off the hill, in a real bind."

His tone surly, Chastain asked, "How so, Sergeant Major?"

"A little problem of command continuity, sir. The current battery commander, Captain Knapp, received promotion orders this morning along with instructions to report to Nha Trang for reassignment to

First Field Force Artillery within twenty-four hours. But his replacement, a captain named Ellison, isn't due to arrive at the Cav for a week. You're asking Charlie to accomplish a critical tactical movement in a sudden command vacuum."

"That's not my fault, Sergeant Major. More like a fuckup at Corps. Or maybe even MACV."

"I can assure you, Colonel, the fuckup is not at MACV," Sean replied. "Those aren't the sort of orders we process. Regarding Corps' actions, though, you could've asked for a brief hold on Captain Knapp's reassignment and backdate his promotion once the tactical movement was complete. But nobody thought to do that, and now it's too late. Once they've been set in motion, revising orders will only confuse things. It won't take long before ol' Snuffy the Private will have no idea who's in charge of his outfit."

Chastain made little effort to restrain his irritation. Ignoring Sean, he said, "With all due respect, General, I resent my organization being dissected without warning, as if this were some impromptu IG inspection. That's not the way it's done."

"Let me correct you there, Colonel," Barker replied. "It's not the way it's done when the store is being minded properly. Unfortunately, your store is not."

Chastain started to sense a real possibility that he'd be fired on the spot, or at least within the hour or two it took to get Division Headquarters to draft the order relieving him. With nothing left to lose, he offered, "It would be nice if all our ducks always lined up in nice, neat rows, General...but this is combat. The chain of command adapts. If a commander gets taken out of action, his second-in-command steps up and does the job. Why are we assuming that won't happen here?"

"We're not losing command continuity due to combat attrition, Chastain. We're losing it to administrative incompetence, and our men deserve better than that."

Sean asked the general, "If I may, sir?"

"Be my guest, Sergeant Major."

"It just so happens that I know the second-in-command of Charlie Battery personally. Fortunately, he's more than capable of jumping into the battery commander's job on a moment's notice. But asking him to accomplish a critical mission as acting C.O. and then jerking him back to XO when it's done is a raw deal, a real fucking-over. And if he was less of a leader, you'd be setting him up to fail, too."

Barker asked, "Who is this second-in-command, Sergeant Major?"

"A first lieutenant named Miles, sir, who's—"

Chastain cut him off. "That subversive son of a bitch? *He's* the one who's going to be acting battery commander?"

Surprised the colonel didn't already know that, Sean replied, "Affirmative, sir. He's the XO, so he moves up." He looked to Barker, asking, "May I add something else, sir?"

"Sure. Have at it."

"Colonel, you are aware of who Lieutenant Miles' father is?"

"Of course I'm aware...a retired two-star who's some State Department muckety-muck now. And I'm very well aware of his pinko-commie mother and her anti-war journalism, too. As far as the lieutenant goes, I don't think the apple fell very far from her traitorous twat."

Doing a masterful job of keeping his temper in check—a skill that had taken him years to acquire when dealing with unimpressive officers like Chastain—Sean concisely explained his connection to the Miles family, the privilege it had been to serve under Jif's father, Jock Miles, in Korea, and the WW2 combat exploits of Jif's Australian mother, Jillian Forbes-Miles, whose resume would make the experiences of most American soldiers seem pale by comparison. He concluded with, "Since Mrs. Miles is not a member of this man's Army, she's free to write whatever she pleases in the political journals. It's not a given that the rest of her family shares her views."

Chastain asked, "Is that your opinion, Sergeant Major, or the opinion of MACV?"

"Both, sir." There was no doubt that MACV meant General Abrams.

"So I take it you've been appointed guardian angel for this Miles kid?"

"Negative, Colonel...and believe me, he's no kid. But I do owe it to his father to mentor him when I have the chance...and every now and then I've been able to do so. I've been in a few tight spots with the lieutenant over the past few months, and I'm here to tell you that he's every bit the fighter his parents are. I have no doubt he'll rise to the occasion that you're dumping on him, but you're still fucking him over. In a couple of ways, actually."

"Oh, really? There's more than one?"

Sean explained that while going over Divarty's personnel procedures—the same review that revealed the gap in assigning a captain to command Charlie Battery—he'd uncovered a "hold" file of pending administrative actions that looked more like a dead letter office. Most were recommendations for medals; among them was a Silver Star for Jif Miles, citing his actions during Operation Pegasus, the relief of Khe Sanh.

Sean added, "According to the originator's narrative on Lieutenant Miles' recommendation, he did one hell of a job at the Lang Vei fight, and the endorsers agreed. Then, the paperwork reached your command, where it died."

"I remember that submission," Chastain said. "The youngster already has a Bronze Star. How many decorations are we supposed to hang on some green lieutenant?"

"As many as he deserves, Colonel," General Barker interjected.

Sean continued, "Sure, he's got a Bronze Star, but it's not the typical award officers have been getting for just showing up in a combat zone. It came with the "V" device for valor, so he earned it in combat, not bending his elbow in the O Club. General Abrams pinned it on the man himself."

"So are you suggesting I should approve all these requests for decoration, sir?"

Barker replied, "That might be a good start, Colonel. I mean, what does a man have to do to get a medal in your command?"

*****

The meeting with Chastain completed, they headed for Division headquarters with Sean behind the wheel of the jeep. Along the way, Barker asked, "This Miles kid…is he really as good as you say, Sergeant Major?"

"If I'm lyin', I'm dyin', sir."

"Then I'll take your word for it," Barker replied. "I was about to put the brakes on this whole change of command fiasco, but since you say Miles is up to the challenge, I'll let it slide. Like you said, it'll be less confusing all around. By the way, I had a thought on how to save a little more aviation fuel. Since you're flying straight back to MACV at Phu Bai, how about having your chopper stop at Signal Hill and pick up this Captain Knapp? He's got to be in Nha Trang by tomorrow, and he can easily catch a shuttle flight to there from Phu Bai. While you're at the hill, you can give young Miles a heads-up about the move he's going to handle."

"I'd be glad to, sir. But you know, it's still bugging me he's getting the shaft like that. It seems that once a man has to step up into a job, he should be given that job permanently. None of this *acting commander* bullshit. He's *the commander*, period."

"I hear you, Sergeant Major, but you know what career tracks are like. A captain only gets so many chances to prove his worth. Your young lieutenant will have plenty more opportunities to shine."

"Sir, if Lieutenant Miles shined any brighter, you'd need welder's goggles to look at him. I just pray he doesn't get in so far over his head that he ends up getting hurt…or worse. I figure he's used up about seven of his nine lives already."

*****

Within an hour of the meeting in Colonel Chastain's office, the warning order detailing Charlie Battery's move to a new location down in the A Shau Valley, seven kilometers south of their present position, was broadcast to Signal Hill. An attached supplemental order spelled out the travel arrangements for Captain Knapp's departure later that day.

Scanning the message forms, 1SG Contreras uttered a few choice swear words under his breath before saying out loud, "This really sucks the big wazoo. We lose a BC while we're gearing up for a major move. And once we get that move done, a new captain shows up to take the credit." Looking at Jif, he said, "Acting BC, eh? All I can say to that is BOHICA, Lieutenant."

BOHICA: military slang for *bend over, here it comes again.*

Contreras added, "I hope they kiss you when this is all over, sir, because they're sure fucking you right now. They should just give you the damn job and be done with it."

Ever since receiving his promotion orders a few hours before, Captain Knapp had been like a kid who'd just been told there really was a Santa Claus. Now, with his travel orders in hand, he rushed off to pack his gear.

As the hour of the BC's departure drew near, the first sergeant asked him, "Anything you need to fill us in on before you go, Captain?"

"Negative, Top. I have faith all of you will keep up the outstanding performance. But I would like to ask you a personal question." He pointed to a group of four Hispanic troopers from the battery. They were in a circle near the mess bunker, singing along to a boom box blaring The Kingsmen's *Louie Louie*. Instead of the nebulous English lyrics, they were belting out a Spanish version with gusto. The words *Louie Louie* were replaced by *A Luoi A Luoi*, the name—sung twice—of the abandoned airfield and village below Signal Hill. The only other lyrics Knapp could make out were *capitán* and *cojones*.

"Tell me what they're saying with that tico-tico music, First Sergeant. You know the lingo."

"Nothing important, sir," Contreras replied, stretching the truth a mile or two. "Just a little love letter to that place down below we've been shooting up…and a fond farewell to you, of course."

What they were actually singing could be paraphrased like this: *This place sucks balls and so does our captain.*

Knapp smiled tentatively, not sure whether his leg was being pulled or not. "Tell the men I'll miss them, too," he said, his words trying to sound sincere but failing. "Now get some bodies to haul my gear to the LZ like right now."

*****

The Huey touched down on Signal Hill's LZ as scheduled. Two passengers were on board: Sergeant Major Sean Moon and SFC Marcus Collins, the replacement for the deadbeat security platoon sergeant who had finagled his way out of coming to the field. There was some cargo, too: a collimator to replace the one destroyed in the sapper attack on the firebase two nights ago; a box of parts to fix the generator damaged in that same attack; another twenty-five gallons of water in jerry cans.

Sean Moon told 1SG Contreras, "We tried to get the aviators to lift a few more water cans, but they were nervous about the extra weight. Sergeant Collins alone takes up about half their allowable load."

With a big smile, Collins, a strapping black man, replied, "With all due respect, Sergeant Major, you've got some damn nerve suggesting someone is too heavy for choppers, big as you are."

"Relax, Marc...I'm just breaking your chops." Then he asked Contreras, "Where's Captain Knapp, Joe? Don't tell me he doesn't want to leave."

"The captain is still packing up his kit. Shouldn't be much longer."

"Tell him to move his ass, with all due respect, of course. How about Lieutenant Miles? Where's he?"

"He's right over yonder, headed this way, I believe. Must've noticed you standing here."

Jif arrived within seconds. As they exchanged a robust handshake, he asked, "Are you checking up on me again, Sergeant Major?"

"Actually, sir, I might be able to do you a favor. I was looking at the goose egg for your battery's move. It doesn't look like much on the map. Want to take a gander at it from the air?"

"You mean right now?"

"No time like the present, Lieutenant."

"Bloody right I want a look at it. Give me a second to get my shit together. Is there room to take an RTO, too?"

"Better not," Sean replied. "Weight might get critical. The pilots want to keep her light and nimble for this jaunt. I get the impression they don't do a lot of recon flying."

As Jif ran off to gather his map board, web gear, binoculars, rifle, and a *Prick-25* receiver/transmitter, Knapp led an entourage of porters carrying his gear to the LZ. Sean told him, "Hold off throwing your stuff on board, Captain. We're going to go for a little recon ride first. Shouldn't be more than fifteen minutes. Wanna come?"

Sounding very put out, Knapp replied, "Negative, Sergeant Major. The only place I'm going is Nha Trang. Who authorized this recon flight?"

"The Division commander, sir."

"Very well, then. I'll await your return…but I'm holding you to that fifteen minutes."

There were a number of snappy retorts Sean could've delivered in reply to that toothless ultimatum. Each of those quasi-respectful replies would leave the officer with the mistaken impression he'd been taken seriously. All he bothered to say, however, was, "Roger that, sir."

When Jif returned to the chopper, he yelled to the outgoing BC, "Wish us luck, sir."

Knapp replied with just a scowl.

*****

Before they'd lifted off, Jif and Sean had briefed the aircraft commander, a warrant officer who looked barely old enough to drive a car legally, on what they wanted to see at this new firebase location. The goose egg—the broad oval drawn on the map by higher headquarters within which a battery commander would select the exact location for his unit—encompassed nearly a kilometer-wide area on the valley floor. It included Route 548, its intersection with Route 547 out of the east, and a destroyed airfield adjacent to the equally destroyed village of Ta Bat. According to the map, roughly half of that goose egg lacked serious tree cover.

"Give me a wide orbit over this open area," Jif told the pilot, pointing out the expanse that lacked trees. "How about doing it a hundred feet off the deck? I want to get low to test this Prick Twenty-Five and make sure we're still in radio range of Signal Hill."

"I can dig it," the pilot replied. "But we don't have any units down that way, do we?"

"Not yet," Jif replied. "But by the time my battery gets lifted in, there'd better be."

Since he hadn't been given an in-depth overview of the operation, Sean began filling in the blanks. "The Cav will secure this area around Ta Bat," the sergeant major explained, "while a brigade from the One-Oh-First Airborne gets both trucked and airlifted down Route Five-Four-Seven to meet up with them. From there, a combined force will push about fourteen klicks south down Route Five-Four-Eight to cut off any river traffic from Laos along the *Rao Lao*. Once that's done, we'll have this branch of the Ho Chi Minh Trail blocked off. The NVA will be denied their main highway for infiltrating men and supplies into Eye Corps."

Even the tinny distortion of the Huey's interphone system couldn't mask the sarcasm in Jif's voice as he asked, "Deny them, you say? For how bloody long?"

Sean replied, "Long enough, hopefully, to help knock their entire logistical network out of commission. If we keep bottling up the exits from the Ho Chi Minh Trail, their whole operation in South Vietnam withers and dies."

To Jif, this exercise was beginning to smell just like the Central Highlands campaign of half a year before, where he saw his first combat. At great cost, the Americans had evicted the NVA from the mountains south of Dak To and driven the survivors into Laos.

Then the Americans abandoned the ground they'd bought with so much of their own blood.

And in a month, the NVA returned, stronger than before, to reclaim the mountains.

Seeing the jaundiced look on Jif's face, Sean asked, "What's the matter? You're not with the program?"

"I reckon it doesn't matter much whether I'm with it or not, Sergeant Major. For the moment, the only thing on my mind is laying out this move so it doesn't turn into a bloody clusterfuck."

"That's the spirit. A wise man once told me, *Success in combat is ninety percent planning and ten percent execution.*"

"Who was that wise man?"

"Your father, Lieutenant. Are you ready for some good news now?"

"Yeah, sure."

"Looks like you're about to be awarded the Silver Star."

"Really? For what?"

"Something about you holding off an NVA battalion single-handedly back at Lang Vei during Pegasus. I seem to recall the tale."

"I seem to recall you breaking my balls about it, too, Sergeant Major. Something about being dumb enough to jump out of a perfectly good helicopter."

"Hey, all's well that ends well, right, Lieutenant?"

They were getting close to the objective; the Huey's rapid descent made it obvious. As the ship began to skim the valley floor, the pilot said, "I'm a little leery about being all alone out here in Indian country, so it's going to be pedal to the metal the whole way. If we're going too fast to see anything, we'll have to do another orbit a little higher up. It's pretty flat down this way…no hills for us to hide behind."

The pilot was right; at the speed the Huey was moving, the ground zipped below them too quickly for a detailed view. Jif resorted to leaning from the open cabin door for a wider field of vision; a gunner, afraid the lieutenant might topple out, had a death grip on his web belt. Sean, working the Prick-25, got a good comm check with Signal Hill, despite the distance of four miles. *Having that relay station way up in the air helps a lot*, he told himself.

Halfway through the orbit of the area, Jif had made up his mind. He told Sean, "I'm going to put my guns in the southwest corner of the goose egg. We'll have the highway and that stream to our backs. Since I won't have the services of a bulldozer, though, I'm going to have to borrow a chainsaw from the engineers. Even with only a few trees, some will still have to be cut down for better fields of fire."

"What about drainage, Lieutenant? It might turn into a fucking swamp when it rains."

"It shouldn't be too bad. Looks like it runs off to that stream pretty well."

"How the hell can you tell that?"

"I spent a lot of time camping in the bush as a kid, Sergeant Major. This terrain's much the same. If you pick a bad spot, you wash away, so you learn to read the signs real quick."

Sean said, "If you say so. But I was pretty sure you'd choose the opposite end of the goose egg, where you could set up on one of those rises."

"I don't like it there. We might not be able to use beehive effectively if we get hit…and it's too close to that Montagnard village. I don't want to be shooting through them. They don't deserve that."

"How do you know they're not commie sympathizers, maybe even VMC?"

VMC: Viet Montagnard Cong, ethnic Montagnards forced into service as communist guerrillas; the more common VC—Viet Cong—were ethnic Vietnamese.

Jif replied, "I don't know what their sympathies are, Sergeant Major. But I reckon I'm going to find out."

The pilot's voice crackled in their headsets: "That's the whole circuit. Are we done here?"

Jif replied, "How about one more lap around the southwest end?"

"I wish you told me that about ten seconds ago, Lieutenant. I ain't gonna slow down, so now I've got to make a big, wide turn to circle back and—"

He didn't get to finish the sentence. Streams of green tracers were bracketing the sprinting Huey.

Chapter Eleven

"HOLD ON TO YOUR ASSES," the pilot screeched into the interphone, the terror of the moment making his voice an octave higher than it had been just a few seconds ago. The ship seemed dangerously close to the ground already, but he pushed her down even lower. The crowns of the few trees the Huey had to dodge were higher than she was.

But the chopper's speed had saved her. Coupled with the difficult angle, the enemy gunners found it impossible to lead the ship. She was heading north now, racing toward Signal Hill, the tracers from the enemy triple-A little more than a fireworks show in her wake.

"I hope you saw enough, Lieutenant," the pilot said, "because I sure as hell ain't going back there."

"It'll have to do, I reckon," Jif replied. "I spotted where they were coming from—the northwest corner of that old airfield. Anybody see it differently?"

Only one other man on board had seen the tracers' origins: the gunner who'd been hanging on to Jif's belt, keeping him from falling out of the ship as he scanned the terrain below. The gunner had tried to return fire, but stopped after letting loose with a few bursts that couldn't find their target. The speed and erratic maneuvering of the Huey made accuracy as difficult for him as it had for the enemy gunners.

As Jif plotted the coordinates of the triple-A site on the map, Sean, making his comment off the interphone, yelled, "Gotta love these teenaged flyboys,

Lieutenant. They've got reflexes like cats. Why go over a tree when you can go around it, am I right?"

"Just so we don't go through it," Jif replied as he handed the coordinates he'd written down to the young pilot. "See if the gunships will work the place over."

Seconds after making the call, the pilot reported, "Negative on the gunships. They're too busy up north right now. Maybe you oughta get your battery to handle it."

"We'd have to stick around to adjust fire," Jif replied. "Want to do that?"

"Fuck no, Lieutenant. I think I've crapped myself already."

Sean offered, "How about we give your Air Force buddy up on the hill a try? He shouldn't be too busy. It doesn't look like he's got anything going on in the valley except that Herc dropping supplies way up the road."

Through the windshield, they could see the tiny cruciform silhouette of the C-130 far ahead as she dispensed a string of cargo pallets, each one dropping to the ground beneath the canopies of multiple parachutes.

"By the time we get through to the ASO, we'll be back on Signal Hill ourselves," Jif replied. "We're only a few minutes out, right?"

"Roger that, Lieutenant," the pilot confirmed. "If we didn't have to climb to five thousand, we'd be there already."

*****

Back on Signal Hill, Jif was startled to find that Captain Fisher had already been advised of the triple-A site seven klicks to the south. The coordinates the ASO was busy passing on to a FAC ship were the same ones called in to Brigade less than ten minutes ago from the Huey.

"How the hell did you get those numbers, sir?" he asked Fisher. "Those are the ones I sent to the gunships."

"No shit, Lieutenant? This is your work?"

"Bloody right, sir. I was going to hand them to you personally. But air liaison at Brigade must've gotten to you first."

Fisher replied, "Can't beat that with a stick, right? That must've been some exciting recon flight. I'm told you saw two guns at the site?"

"Let me put it this way…that's all we saw firing at us."

"Did your ship get hit?"

"Negative, sir. If you've ever seen a chopper low-crawl, that would've been us."

Fisher's RTO announced, "FAC in five mikes, jets in ten to twelve, sir."

Jif said, "I hope that triple-A will still be there. They could easily be a couple of klicks down the road in ten to twelve minutes."

*****

With Knapp gone and Jif now acting BC, Lieutenant Hammond had become the acting XO. *He'll be okay under Sergeant McKay's tutelage for the moment*, Jif told himself. *His first real test comes in two days, when we move.*

But Jif's test as battery commander would begin immediately. First Sergeant Contreras was waiting for him at the CP with a question: "They're still jerking us around with the water, sir. The way it's coming in dribs and drabs, we're getting by on the potable stuff. But everybody's getting pretty ripe. We don't have enough to rig showers, and with the upcoming move, nobody gets to rotate back to Camp Evans for the three S's. I begged Captain Knapp to get a water buffalo up here today, but he let it slide. What do you want to do, Lieutenant?"

"We'll get a buffalo when we hit the new position, Top. Sergeant Major Moon is going to help us out and make sure that happens. We can scrape by without it until then."

"Copy that, sir," Contreras replied, surprised that Jif had thought ahead and pulled some strings to make it happen. Yet, he was skeptical: *It's great to have friends in high places and all, but I won't be a true believer until I see a full buffalo dropped at the new firebase.*

He continued, "We've got just enough water to cook a hot meal tonight, sir…Salisbury steak with mashed potatoes and salad greens. It'll be a good break from C rations, but we'll have to dip way into our supply of paper plates to serve it. We can't afford to be boiling any water to clean mess kits."

Then Contreras asked, "But what about the showers, sir? The men can't even take French baths. Our hygiene's going to shit."

"If the weather report holds up, Top, it's going to rain buckets again tonight. Mother Nature will provide the showers. Make sure everyone's got plenty of soap."

"Soap we've got, sir, but do you believe those weather reports out of Division? What'll we do if they're wrong again?"

"Have a little faith, First Sergeant. Even a stopped clock is right twice a day."

*****

It was 1300 hours, fifteen minutes after Jif's return to Signal Hill. Charlie Battery was firing its twelfth mission of the day, shooting repetitive fire-for-effect volleys of ever-increasing range as a cav unit pursued some NVA four klicks west of A Luoi airfield. Lieutenant Hammond, not comfortable in his new role as XO, asked Chief of Smoke McKay, "If we keep firing at this rate, aren't we going to overheat the tubes?"

"We'd better not, Lieutenant. We don't have the water to cool them down, not unless we want to stop drinking." He'd meant it to be flippant. But seeing Hammond's uncertainty turn to alarm, he added, "Seriously, sir, at the rate we're firing—no more than three rounds per minute—we can pretty much shoot all day and not have to worry about overheating."

That knowledge did very little to make the lieutenant feel better.

McKay suggested, "Why don't you check out Gun Two while they set up the backup collimator that just came in? It's a little tricky to do in the middle of a fire mission, but it's no step for a stepper."

What he didn't add: *It'll be good training for a greenhorn like you.*

Thirty seconds after they'd fired the latest volley, new firing data was already being sent to the battery.

Gun Two, which had cranked its tube back to base deflection to position the new collimator, had to stop what they were doing and pick up the mission's new deflection and elevation. They'd get back to setting up the sighting device at the next lull.

No sooner were the rounds rammed into the tubes than the call went out to HOLD; there were aircraft in the area. The fighter-bombers Captain Fisher had summoned to hit the triple-A site were a minute out from their target. The F-4 Phantoms would be streaking down the valley, right through the trajectory of Charlie's rounds. As they roared past, the aircraft were level with the peak of Signal Hill, descending at a brisk rate to their bomb release point. Every head on the firebase turned south to watch the violent spectacle the aircraft were about to unleash.

"Those fuckers better be on target," a gunner said. "I hear that's where we're going next."

"That's still two days away," a cannoneer replied. "Even if those jet jockeys wipe those gooks off the face of the earth, there could still be plenty more on hand to greet us."

From the distance of seven klicks—over four miles—the delivery of cluster bombs looked like clouds of dust and smoke billowing into tight swirls that hugged the ground as if confined in an invisible dome. The Phantoms were already gone, having pulled almost straight up, becoming vanishing pinpoints in the afternoon sky. The fading shriek of their turbine engines lingered for less than a minute, and then it, too, was gone. If any anti-aircraft fire had risen to challenge the jets, it hadn't seemed to bother them in the least.

"Funny how some explosions don't look near as impressive as you thought they would," McKay said to Jif, who was walking past the XO's post on his way to talk with the ASO. "Kind of disappointing, actually, sir."

"Just so it did the job, Smoke. How's Lieutenant Hammond holding up?"

Before he could answer, the clearance to resume the fire mission was passed from FDC to the guns. After an intense few seconds while gunners rechecked sight pictures, the battery was about to fire again.

Jif saw the problem first. The tube of Gun Two was at a noticeably lower elevation than the other five howitzers. He yelled, "MORGAN, DROP THE LANYARD!"

Spec-4 Morgan, the assistant gunner on Gun Two, did as he was told. A split-second later, every other piece fired.

Hammond, who'd been in the gun pit, turned to stare at his BC in bewilderment. A moment before, standing arms akimbo, he'd been the picture of a posturing but unseasoned junior officer as he followed the crew's actions, a novice supervising experts.

But even experts make mistakes sometimes.

The flow of the fire mission, interrupted by the air strike and coupled with his gun crew's attempt to orient the collimator, had distracted Specialist Morgan. He'd never fully cranked up the tube to the new elevation. Had he pulled the firing lanyard, the round would've landed short. Dangerously short, perhaps.

The section chief should've caught the error, but he didn't. His attention had been diverted for just a second to sort out a problem with a fuze setter.

The gunner should've caught it, too, but he was busy traversing the tube to the new deflection after dialing in the collimator.

Chief of Smoke McKay did catch it, but knew better than to open his mouth while Jif was shouting *drop the lanyard*. Two commanding voices at the same time would've muddied the message, probably confused Morgan, and allowed the errant round to fly.

But the man who bore the ultimate responsibility to catch mistakes like this was Lieutenant Hammond, who, as XO, was also the battery safety officer.

Now that the danger had passed, McKay called to Morgan, "What elevation is set on your quadrant? No, don't touch anything...just read it back to me."

Jif made note of the number. It was eighty-two mils—nearly five degrees—less than it should've been. Enough to present a small but noticeable difference in elevation when compared with the other tubes.

Not wanting to reprimand Hammond in front of the men, Jif called him back to the XO's post. McKay knew to give them privacy. He headed off to Gun Two, intent on upbraiding the section chief for his part in the screwup. All he said to Jif before leaving was, "What do you want to do with the round in the tube, sir?"

"Punch it out, set it aside, Smoke."

Once they were alone, he told Hammond, "Bloody hell, Art...you do remember the XO is the safety officer, too, don't you?"

"Yeah, sure. But the section chief should've—"

Jif cut him off. "The *buts* aren't going to cut it when we have an accident. The section chief's not the safety officer. You are. A tube out of elevation is pretty easy to spot. All you have to do is look real quick."

The cav unit calling the mission didn't want another volley, so the fire mission was terminated. Jif told Hammond, "While we've got a minute, let's go over to FDC and figure out where that short round would've landed."

When they computed the impact point for the incorrect elevation, it plotted on the edge of a no-fire box drawn in red pencil on the firing chart. That box represented the approximate location of a cav unit.

Jif said, "Arthur, neither of us needs a friendly fire incident. Not now, not ever. I've been through an investigation for one, and believe me, you don't want to be there. Remember, it just takes one slip, and you're killing the wrong people. Get your head out of your ass before somebody cuts it off."

As Jif set out once again to meet with the ASO, McKay intercepted him and said, "I guess I need to keep an even closer eye on Lieutenant Hammond than we thought."

"Bloody right, Smoke. Watch him like a hawk. All we've got to do is get through these next few days, and then he and I go back to our real jobs."

*****

SFC Collins, the new security platoon sergeant, was at the ASO's bunker when Jif arrived. "Glad you're back safe, Lieutenant," Collins told him. "By the way, I saw that tube out of line from way over here. Real good call that you stopped it from shooting. Real good."

Captain Fisher said, "The sergeant was telling me a very interesting story. Remember those gooks on the west slope we tried to blow up with fire from Bravo

Battery last night? Looks like they're still there. Maybe not all of them, but still plenty."

Jif asked, "How far down are they? We haven't seen any sign of them from the guns."

"I put them at eight hundred meters, sir," Collins replied. "Looks to be at company strength or better. I hear tell they were at six hundred when you saw them last night."

"Yeah, that's right. How the bloody hell did you lay eyes on them?"

"Sent a patrol down that way."

This is something new and interesting, Jif told himself. *In the two days this security platoon's been on the hill, they wouldn't venture beyond shouting distance of the firebase...and even at that, they managed to suffer two KIA. It's been just a few hours since they got a real platoon sergeant, and already they're patrolling well down the slope. Quite a change from how ineffective Gruner was on his own.*

It's almost like having the Lurps watching our backs again.

Jif asked, "Where is Lieutenant Gruner, Sergeant?"

"Back at his hooch, filling out requisitions, sir. This platoon came out to the field a little light, shall we say? We're short all sorts of grenades, for openers...frags, smoke, even forty mike-mike. Those damn bloop guns got like a dozen rounds between them. That's only three per launcher. It's all because the lieutenant depended on that no-account Ledbetter, and he fucked him over, as usual."

"Ledbetter...he's the platoon sergeant who didn't come out to the hill?"

"That's him, sir. The talk is that battalion's gonna take a stripe and put him supervising some gook laborers at base camp. He'll find a way to fuck that up, too. That's for damn sure."

Fisher asked Jif, "So what do we do about these gooks on the hill?"

"Good question, sir. How about a napalm strike? Eight hundred meters is a safe margin from us, and there's no other cav unit anywhere close."

"Last night, everyone was worried about a forest fire climbing the hill and torching the firebase," Fisher said. "Why the change of heart?"

"The wind, sir. It changed, too."

The ASO replied, "Give me some coordinates. Let's get this barbeque started."

*****

A Chinook deposited her sling load of artillery ammunition near the howitzers before swinging around to the LZ. There, she landed and disgorged small arms ammo, rations, another hundred gallons of water in jerry cans, and other assorted supplies.

Her outbound load consisted of expended shell canisters, a dozen empty jerry cans, and the body bags containing PFCs Garrity and Boyer of the security platoon, killed the night before last during the sapper intrusion.

"I didn't know the remains were still here," Jif said to SFC Collins, who was supervising their loading.

"Lieutenant Gruner said they couldn't get them on that Air Force medevac chopper in time, sir. Didn't think to ask about putting them on Sergeant Major Moon's chopper, either. This is the next chance we got."

As they cleared the LZ for the chopper's liftoff, Collins added, "It's a cryin' shame those boys had to die like they did, but in a way, they did the platoon a favor."

"How's that, Sergeant?"

"It's simple, sir...nothing tightens up an outfit like having to bag up some of their own."

Jif nodded. He already knew that. All too well, in fact.

*****

Once the Chinook lifted off and cleared the mountaintop, she made a sharp turn east, away from the flight path of the incoming napalm strike. Two minutes later, the jets arrived, homed in on the smoke rockets the FAC had laid down, and turned a swath of the west slope several hundred meters long into an inferno. The flames belched thick black smoke that drifted lazily northward in the gentle wind.

Watching the carnage, 1SG Contreras said to Jif, "What do you think, sir? Crispy critters?"

"Let's hope so, Top. We've got enough on our plate without another nighttime visit from the loyal opposition."

"You got that right, sir. Funny, but I seem to remember the brass assuring us that *Altitude is our friend. This mountaintop is impervious to attack*."

"Too bad nobody told the gooks," Jif replied.

"By the way, sir...I set aside a can of water if you want to clean yourself up."

Jif bristled at the suggestion. "Negative, Top, and I don't want to see any of our section leaders taking a bloody bath. If our men can't do it, we can't, either."

"Very well, sir."

Though outwardly stolid, Contreras was smiling inside as he thought, *Well, he passed that test. I shouldn't be surprised, though. Lieutenant Miles doesn't seem hung up on this "rank has its privileges" stuff. On the other hand, Captain Knapp—that self-serving cabrón—would've had his rubber ducky out as soon as I'd made the offer.*

*****

Just past 2100 hours, a steady rain began that would last an hour. In that time, every man on Signal Hill took the opportunity to rinse their filthy utilities. Then, stripped naked, they lathered up with the soap bars the first sergeant had passed out. Courtesy of the heavens, the men enjoyed a good cleansing while responding to three fire missions.

Nobody seemed to care how chilly the night had become. Very few of the men donned ponchos or field jackets. Jif's only worry: *I just hope we all don't get bloody pneumonia.*

Most had at least their trousers back on quickly. But one cannoneer—PFC Arroyo—decided he was just as comfortable ramming rounds into the tube wet and naked as wet and clothed. As he danced the cha-cha on his way to the breech, holding the round as if it was a female partner, he sang *La Bamba* at the top of his lungs.

He was up to the second chorus when his section chief, a slow-talking Texan, told him, "Careful there,

Pepe…you're gonna get your pecker lopped off by the breech block. Put your fucking britches on, hombre."

As Arroyo complied, he defiantly offered this: "Nothing's ever gonna cut off my *pito*, Sarge."

Another cannoneer replied, "Small as it is, Pepe, I thought that might've happened already."

Chapter Twelve

The move was scheduled for first light of the following day. Charlie Battery had done all the packing they could, but the final preparations would have to be done at the last minute. They still needed to be able to provide fire support right up to the moment of their stand-down order, which wouldn't come until choppers were en route to airlift them.

"We sure haven't been shooting much today," Chief of Smoke McKay said to Jif. "Looks like we'll have more ammo than we can drag to the new position in one lift. Plus, we won't have enough cargo bags for the excess, anyway, so how do you want to handle it?"

"Just leave it where it is," Jif replied. "If it's in the way of the one-five-five battery, they can move it. We've got enough to do."

"Roger that, sir. And there's always the chance we'll get busy and shoot off the excess once First Brigade starts moving south."

"I don't know, Smoke. The Air Force is pounding the hell out of the valley. Like you said, it's been pretty quiet for us today."

"Some would say too quiet, sir. Are you planning another chopper recon of the new spot?"

"Nope. I've seen all I need to see for now. The Top and I will handle any glitches that come up when we go in with the advance party."

By midafternoon, maneuver units of 1st Brigade were being shuttled south by a flock of Hueys and the occasional Chinook to secure Ta Bat. Watching the procession, 1SG Contreras said, "Tomorrow, it'll be us down there. Let's hope those crunchies make it nice and safe for us."

"Admit it, Top," Jif replied, "you're going to miss it way up here."

"I won't miss the nosebleeds and the cold nights, that's for damn sure, sir."

*****

The morning sun was still rising from the South China Sea when the rumble of heavy-lift helicopters began to rattle the air. "Those can't be our lift ships," the first sergeant said as he monitored the radio traffic. "We haven't even gotten the stand-down order yet."

A quick look with binoculars confirmed his suspicion. The choppers were a mix of Skycranes and Chinooks, ten in total. Each ship had something slung beneath her. "They'd better not be coming here," Contreras mumbled under his breath.

But Signal Hill was obviously their destination; there'd be no need for them to climb so high otherwise. The lead ship was on the radio, announcing herself as carrying the command element of Alpha Battery, 2nd of the 87th Artillery, the 155-millimeter unit taking over the fire support duties on Signal Hill. The chopper then requested a smoke marker and signalmen to guide the ships to their drop areas.

Jif had been at the relay station, expecting to receive the stand-down order any minute. When he heard the helicopter's in-range call, he raced to the LZ. In the minute it took him to get there, the lead ship—a

Chinook—had landed and was in the process of off-loading Alpha Battery's commander and his advance party. The commander, a captain named Gray, strode urgently away from the chopper, his irritation apparent even at a distance.

His raised voice barely audible over the helicopter's whine and thrum, Gray asked Jif, "Who's the BC here, Lieutenant?"

"I am, sir. The name's Miles."

"What the fuck are you doing here, Lieutenant Miles?"

"I was going to ask you the same thing, sir," Jif replied.

As they spoke, Bravo Battery's base piece fired the first adjustment round of a new fire mission.

Gray, his arms raised as if beseeching the heavens, asked, "And why the hell are you still shooting?"

Jif explained that his battery was still active. They'd received no stand-down order. He added, "And obviously, our choppers haven't shown up yet. It's not like we can drive down the road to our next position."

While Gray stood there fuming, watching the helicopters transporting the rest of his battery flying a lazy orbit to the east of the mountain, Jif said, "Something tells me Phu Bai and Camp Evans aren't talking to each other very well this morning. This replacement of my battery with yours is a little out of sync."

"No shit, Sherlock," Gray replied. "But I worked Phu Bai from the chopper through that relay station over there. They say I've got to get my boys on the ground immediately, if not sooner. You're the landlord here for the time being, and those choppers are burning gas like crazy. I can't have them divert on me. How the hell do we cram my guns in here, Lieutenant? I don't want to be left standing here with just my dick in my hand."

Jif led him to the CP, where they were joined by 1SG Contreras, who was already putting together a plan to get Alpha Battery on the ground quickly. All it needed was the approval of Jif and Gray. "It's best if we put your battery down between the LZ and the engineer compound, Captain," the first sergeant said. "You won't be in our way when it comes time for us to leave, which, by the way, will be one hour from now. Just got that word from Camp Evans. Some kind of emergency up near the DMZ tied up our choppers, but they're refueling now and will be on their way in thirty mikes. That's when our stand-down kicks in."

"Wait a damn minute," Gray said as he surveyed the firebase. "My guns can't shoot from way over there. They've got to be where your guns are, on the edge of the peak."

Jif replied, "Once we're gone, those positions are all yours, sir."

Gray's face reddened with annoyance. Growing louder and with spittle flying, he raged, "How in God's green earth am I supposed to get those six-ton monsters across this firebase? They're not exactly man-portable, and the choppers aren't going to hang around to drag them over."

"Of course not, sir," Jif replied, "but you've got a bulldozer at your disposal." He asked Joey Aloha of the engineers, who'd been summoned to the CP by 1SG Contreras, "Isn't that right, Sergeant?"

"Yes, sir," Aloha said. "At your service."

Gray wasn't buying it. "That dinky little bulldozer on the other side of the firebase? That's the one you're talking about?"

"It's the only one we've got, sir. But believe me, if it can push a couple tons of dirt, it can sure as hell tow six tons on wheels. The dozer will put those suckers right where you want them. It can drag your ammo pallets into position, too, no sweat."

The captain asked, "But how the hell long is that going to take, Sergeant?"

"I've seen how much time it takes a one-five-five outfit to set up, sir. It won't hold you up much at all."

*****

Thirty minutes passed in what seemed like seconds. Charlie Battery was now officially stood down for its relocation to Ta Bat. SFC McKay was keeping Lieutenant Hammond on a long leash, allowing him to make on-the-spot decisions to expedite the final closeout while keeping tabs on the acting XO's orders.

But nobody could see everything when there was a whirlwind of activity going on. As 1SG Contreras inventoried the equipment to be loaded on the BC's advance-party chopper, he came up with two critical items missing: the battery's aiming circles, the magnetic instruments used to orient the howitzers. When he told Jif of their absence, he added, "How much you want to bet the XO's packing them with his gear?"

"I reckon you're right, Top," Jif replied. "Send someone to get them."

But the PFC tasked with the retrieval returned without them. "Lieutenant Hammond won't give them to me, sir," the man said. "He says they belong with his section."

Jif spat out a *Bloody Hell* before storming to the XO's post, now just a collection of personal gear and a few field boxes full of equipment. The aiming circles were there, too; he and McKay simultaneously discovered their presence. There could be no mistaking the meaning of the Smoke's exasperated sigh: *Chalk up another fuckup for the acting XO. Sorry I didn't catch this one before the BC did.*

Putting on his best ass-chewing voice, Jif said, "Arthur, give me the bloody aiming circles."

Flustered, Hammond replied, "But aren't they supposed to go with the guns? What happens if we get a call for fire along the way? How do we lay the battery?"

"For fuck's sake, you don't do *hip shoots* when you're being airlifted. That only works when you're moving overland in vehicles. And you wouldn't use the bloody aiming circle, anyway. You'd just rough in the tubes with a compass and shoot…give the guys who need fire something they can adjust immediately. When you're in the shit, *any* fire right now is better than fire a couple of minutes from now."

"But that's not the way they told us to do it at—"

"That's the bloody way it is here," Jif interrupted. "When you get to the new location, I'll have the circles all set up and waiting for you. Guns can be laid and firing within a minute or two after they touch down."

As he walked away, the heads of the aiming circles in one hand, their folded tripods beneath his other arm, he thought, *This is only Hammond's second move, and during the first one, all he really had to worry about was FDC. But still, he's not a total stranger to the process. How slow a learner is he?*

*****

Jif was afraid that the name assigned to their new location—*Fire Base Condon*, after a staff major who was killed in a helicopter crash at the start of Operation Delaware—would immediately be twisted by the men into something sexually suggestive. On the bright side, the water buffalo Sergeant Major Moon had promised was already there, deposited almost exactly where he'd wanted it. On the not-so-bright side, his Chinook was met by the commander of the infantry company providing firebase security, an uptight captain with white-blonde hair and soulless blue eyes named Rex Wilton.

The first words out of the captain's mouth: "I take a dim view of babysitting cannon-cockers, Lieutenant. My men should be out there scouring the boonies for gooks to kill."

Jif replied, "With any luck, sir, the gooks will come to you. Firebases tend to attract them."

Wilton spit on the ground. "It ain't the same. I'm just counting the days until another company rotates in here and I can go back to my real job."

Jif thought, *We've got something in common there. I'm counting the days until I can go back to my real job, too.*

"Y'all talk funny, Miles. Where the hell are you from?"

Jif gave him the abridged version of his origins, a concise, well-practiced monologue he could give in his sleep. He asked Wilton, "How about you, Captain? Where do you call home?"

"Jonesboro, Georgia. The heart of the South, Lieutenant. God's country. We've got the biggest KKK chapter in the state. Any of your Africans start acting up, you give me a holler, ya hear?"

Sure I will...when hell freezes over.

*****

Once the star formation of the battery was laid out with markers, Jif took a good look at the new position as they waited anxiously for the Chinooks to bring the guns. He asked 1SG Contreras, "What do you think of the place, Top?"

"To be honest, sir, it doesn't look much different from any other location out in the boonies. It'll be the same scroungy collection of mud, canvas, sandbags, and plywood before too long. Tactically, you picked a pretty good spot, though. I like the fields of fire for battery defense....excellent coverage without much work to clear them. Good thing we ordered up more beehive, though. This is the place to use it."

"Yeah, that was heavy on my mind during the recon. But we've got to sit down with Captain Wilton and make sure his guys understand the drill when using beehive. I don't want to be shredding any of them in the process."

"You want to keep the green star cluster as the signal, sir?"

"Yeah...but each gun chief still needs to shout *BEEHIVE* three times at the top of his lungs before pulling that lanyard. Give any friendly out in front of it a chance to crawl into his helmet."

"Copy that, sir. I'll get with their first sergeant and make it happen."

A few minutes later, the first of the Chinooks bringing a gun section arrived over Fire Base Condon. But while she was being guided into position for the drop, the receiving crew began alerting the signalman to wave her off. One of the cannoneers held up two fingers; this gun wasn't supposed to be first to arrive but second, according to the number on her carriage.

The signalman, wise in the ways of airmobile screwups, wasted no time jogging toward the gun's correct position while gesturing *follow me* to the helicopter. In a few moments, the howitzer, its crew, and their equipment were on the ground where they were supposed to be.

Alarmed at first at the wave-off, Jif had started toward the signalman but stopped when he saw he wasn't needed. *My guys know the drill*, he told himself as he watched the Chinook reposition. *And since we're not on a mountaintop way up in the sky anymore, heavily loaded helicopters can actually drift over to a new drop point safely without worrying about losing lift.*

When the chopper landed and the gun crew egressed, Jif noticed that Lieutenant Hammond, SFC McKay, and the battery recorder were not among them as they should've been. The section chief filled Jif in on why they'd arrived out of order. "The lead bird's got a mechanical, sir. The XO sent us first instead."

"That explains it," Jif replied, "but it would've been nice if someone let us know. They could've radioed from the relay station. Do you know who's coming next, Sergeant?"

"It should be the third ship in the original order, sir…unless something else went wrong once we left."

While Contreras stood in for the absent XO at the aiming circle and laid the newly arrived gun, Jif called the relay station on Signal Hill, seeking an update on the battery's progress. He was told the last Chinook was lifting off as they spoke. Everyone from Charlie Battery was gone.

Within fifteen minutes, five of the six guns, FDC, and the mess section had arrived at Condon. Those five guns were already laid and firing a mission in support of 101st Airborne. A brigade of that division was moving west down Route 547 toward Ta Bat, the intersection with Route 548, and a hookup with 1st Cav.

The Chinook lifting that sixth and final gun section should've already been in sight. As Contreras put it, "I hate to say it, but I think she's overdue."

Jif asked, "Nothing on the radio about her?"

"Not a word, sir."

Once another five minutes passed, there was no doubt she was overdue.

*****

The last Chinook in the lift—the overdue *White Cap Four-Seven*—had made an emergency landing roughly three klicks north of Fire Base Condon along Route 548. Roughly a minute before that unceremonious coming to earth, she'd punched off her sling load from a height of six hundred feet. It had been a futile attempt to lighten the stricken chopper and remain airborne. This was the same ship that had a mechanical at the start of the lift, but her crew thought the fluctuating parameter problem on number two engine had sorted itself out on Signal Hill's LZ. They decided to give the lift another try, but it was a bad gamble. The troublesome engine died en route as the other began to lose power, too. Shaken but not injured, the artillerymen on board considered the emergency landing a semi-controlled crash.

A kilometer farther north, her sling load—the M102 howitzer and an A-22 bag full of ammo—had come to earth in a thinly wooded area of the valley floor. The rounds and canisters were scattered over several hundred meters, most all of them torn from their packing and damaged to some degree. The howitzer itself was impaled muzzle down in the soft ground, the carriage mangled.

Several choppers responded to the stricken ship's mayday. As a gunship kept watch over the crash site, a rescuing Chinook flew the artillerymen, their equipment, and the crates of fuzes they'd carried inside the cabin to Fire Base Condon. A Huey transported the downed flight crew back to Camp Evans. Brigade dispatched a cavalry platoon to guard the dumped howitzer and ammunition. "Can't have a bunch of one-oh-five rounds falling into enemy hands," the brigade XO told the battalion commander whose men were tasked with the detail. "That's a lot of explosives to be giving away. Sit on it until we can clean it up."

*****

First Sergeant Contreras said to Jif, "Well, sir, looks like we've got a gun crew without a gun, at least temporarily. What do you want to do with the extra people?"

"We've got plenty of position improvements to do in this place, Top, so use them however you think is best for now. They should probably be the first ones to rotate back to Evans for cleanup. I reckon they'll have earned it. Are we sure none of them were hurt in that crash?"

"The doc's checking them out now, sir. So far, nobody's complaining of bumps, bruises, whiplash…nothing. But it sounds like they came down pretty hard. We're going to watch them real carefully for any back sprains that might pop up. There's another problem, though…missing Gun Five like we are, there's a gap in our perimeter defense on the west side. Want to move Gun Six over so we're a diamond instead of a star missing a point? That should keep us covered as well as possible."

"Affirmative, Top. We'll do that as soon as this fire mission is terminated. We've certainly got enough people to manhandle that li'l ol' gun a measly twenty yards. I'll let the XO and the Smoke know what the plan is right now."

*****

Lieutenant Hammond had arrived on the third Chinook. Immediately, he'd thrown himself into the XO's job, seeing to it that each piece was laid and ready to fire promptly. *Sergeant McKay's still giving him a lot of rope*, Jif told himself. *Let's see if he hangs himself with it.*

Once Gun Six had been repositioned to improve the battery's defenses, Hammond asked, "When are we going to get a replacement piece?"

"I have no idea, Arthur. All I know is that the wheels are turning in that direction."

"But still, we're only five guns. Isn't that a little light to be effective?"

Finding his XO's naiveté amusing, Jif said, "Right after Tet, I was commanding a battery of only three guns down near Tuy Hoa. We called it a platoon, though."

"Only three? Was that enough to do any damage?"

"We did the bloody job then, Arthur, just like we will now."

Brimming with enthusiasm, Hammond launched into a new topic. "I think the move went really well. So, aside from the chopper crash, how would you rate it?"

Jif replied, "If we're talking aside from the crash, I think the move went all right, except for one big problem."

"Really? What's that?"

"You weren't on the first ship to arrive like you were supposed to be. You should've immediately gotten yourself and all your shit off the broken chopper and hopped on the next one to go."

His bubble burst, Hammond replied, "Yeah...that's what the Smoke said back on the hill, too."

"You should've listened to him."

*****

Two hours after *White Cap Four-Seven's* mishap, a team from EOD—explosive ordnance disposal—was flown by helicopter to the site where the howitzer and its ammo were dropped. With one glance at the damaged weapon, the warrant officer-in-charge declared it uneconomical to repair, slating it for destruction in place with thermite grenades.

The scattered rounds and propellant canisters would require a little more work. The rounds, though scraped, gouged, and of no further use as artillery ammo, were deemed safe to be loaded into another cargo bag and flown back to the depot for disposition. "Easier than blowing them all up out here," the WOIC said.

The propellant canisters were a different story. Ripped from their shipping containers, they were now a hazard to transport. The EOD team, with help from the cav unit providing security, emptied the canisters, piling the powder bags they held, along with the broken packing tubes and crates, into a mound the dimensions of a full-sized sedan and lit it off. The blaze would rage for five minutes and smolder for another twenty.

The empty canisters would be flown to the depot with the rounds. "We don't want to leave anything behind that the gooks can use," the WOIC told his team.

A kilometer to the south, a maintenance crew arrived at the grounded chopper, flown there by yet another Chinook. Anticipating they'd find fuel contamination—a problem that couldn't be rectified in the boonies—they began preparing her for a sling ride beneath a Skycrane back to base. They'd remove the rotor blades, strip heavy equipment to lighten her a few thousand pounds, and rig the ship for the lift.

The mechanics' work would take hours. Another platoon of cav troopers settled in to protect them.

*****

Later that afternoon, Jif received a transmission from Camp Evans, relayed through Signal Hill. As he read the message form, 1SG Contreras asked him, "Good news or bad, sir?"

"Mostly bad, Top. They've already cut the report of survey on the gun we lost today. They wrote it off as 'damaged beyond repair during movement by aircraft and intentionally destroyed.' Apparently, some ordnance people torched it."

"Okay...could be worse. They might've tried to blame us for the loss somehow. But are they sending a replacement?"

"Not at this time, Top."

"Figures," Contreras replied. "Oh, and by the way, sir, you were right about the men bastardizing the firebase name. Condon became Condom real quick. But it didn't stop there."

"Really? What are they calling it now?"

"Rubber, sir. Fire Base Rubber."

Chapter Thirteen

Fire Base Condon was hit that first night. The cry "GOOKS IN THE WIRE" came just after 2200 hours. A few more seconds and the intruders, who hadn't been seen yet in the darkness of a moonless, overcast sky, would've worked their way inside the firebase. Only the sound of noisemakers hung in the concertina wire had given them away.

"GIMME SOME GROUND FLARES," the section chief on Gun Six yelled to his crew. "I THINK WE'VE GOT A SHITLOAD OF THE BASTARDS RIGHT IN FRONT OF US."

He was right. The enemy—they couldn't tell in the darkness if they were NVA, VC, or VMC—were attacking in his sector, the quadrant of the battery defensive scheme facing west. Hoping to sneak closer and hurl grenades, they hadn't fired their rifles yet. They were still dealing with the temporary obstacle of the concertina, cutting through it as quietly as they could. But the rattling of one C ration can with a few small stones inside, and then another, had announced their approach.

One by one, three ground flares were flung toward the concertina, an arc of barbed wire coiled like a child's Slinky that fenced barely a quarter of the perimeter. The flares didn't provide enough light to identify the attackers or even count their numbers, but there was no denying their presence. At the very least, it gave the Americans some shadows to engage with rifles, machine guns, and grenade launchers. Whether they were hitting anybody was another story.

Captain Wilton, his voice up an octave from the tension, was talking fast. He told Jif, "Why would those dumb bastards only hit the corner of the firebase that has wire? That's gotta be just a feint. Mark my words, the main attack will come from the north, where I've got the bulk of my men. I'm leaving them right where they are."

Right where they are meant that most of his twelve squads—comprising three rifle platoons—were positioned to primarily defend the north side. Only one squad was currently covering the west. Incomplete though the concertina installation was, Wilton felt the wire provided a significant deterrent to intruders in the western sector, so there was no reason to mass manpower there.

"We've got to talk about your mortars," Jif said. "It's taking forever to reach them. They shouldn't be on the north side but here in the middle, co-located with my combined CP and FDC, so we wouldn't have to use radio or landline to communicate. We need their illum rounds like yesterday. Those ground flares aren't much help."

Wilton's testy reply: "You think you know better than me how to deploy my weaponry, Lieutenant?"

Jif saw no point in replying. He figured his opinion on the matter was already clear.

First Sergeant Contreras joined them. His first words were to Jif: "It's a good thing we repositioned that gun, sir. If we hadn't, there'd be a gap the gooks could drive a truck through."

"Let's hope they don't have a bloody truck, Top. How do you think we're doing so far? The sixties are still pumping that good interlocking fire. I don't think anybody's gotten through it."

The first sergeant wasn't so optimistic. "Sure, sir...we can hang our hats on that until the first satchel charge goes off inside the battery."

"I reckon you want to shoot beehive, Top?"

"Isn't this what we're saving it for?"

"All right. How many tubes?"

"Two tubes, sir. Six and Four. That ought to cover the whole stretch of wire."

Turning to Lieutenant Hammond, Jif asked, "You following all this, Arthur?"

"I sure am, BC."

"Good. Then make it happen."

Contreras looked stunned. He leaned to Jif's ear and said softly, "You sure this is the time for a handoff, sir?"

"Give him a chance, Top. We've got a few seconds before things get critical. Go ahead and fire the green star cluster."

To the first sergeant's surprise and Jif's delight, Hammond gave the correct orders without hesitation or confusion. The two guns responded instantly, traversing to cover the arc of the wire as they rammed rounds into the tubes, the fuzes set to minimum range. Then Hammond did something Jif had been sure he'd forget; the acting XO kicked off the chorus of *BEEHIVE, BEEHIVE, BEEHIVE.*

That done, he turned Guns Four and Six loose to fire at will, something they both did immediately.

Hammond turned to Jif and asked, "Repeat?"

"Affirmative."

The two howitzers—now giant shotguns, really—expelled their thousands of flechettes one more time.

Watching the spectacle, Captain Wilton said, "Y'all realize you just blew the wire to kingdom come, don't you?"

"Small price to pay," Jif replied. "We'll get more. Brigade still owes us about five hundred yards of the stuff as it is. I don't understand why we haven't got it already. They could've thrown it on that last Chinook with the ammo resupply, light as that ship was."

Wilton's mortar section was finally putting up the illumination. Fired at minimum range, the four flares dimly lit a circle around the firebase two hundred meters wider in diameter than the perimeter. Surprisingly, the only enemy soldiers visible were still on the west side, and those attackers promptly went to ground beyond beehive range.

"That's the thing with the gooks, no matter what uniform they wear," Contreras said. "They can't change plans in midstream. Why they're not trying to hit us from another direction is beyond me."

"We've got to kill those bastards right fucking now," Wilton said, his voice still pitched up like an excited adolescent. "I can drop HE from the mortars on them."

Jif shook his head. "How about we keep the mortars firing illum? I reckon the gooks took cover about four hundred meters out. Anybody see it differently?"

"Sounds right to me, sir," Contreras replied.

Hammond knew where this was going. He asked Jif, "You want to shoot killer junior, right? With the same two guns?"

"Affirmative, Art."

"Roger. Two rounds apiece."

Once again, Hammond conveyed the firing orders concisely to the gun crews. Within twenty seconds, the rounds were on the way in rapid succession. Less than a heartbeat after being fired, each round detonated close to the ground with a pinpoint flash and resounding *CRACK*. Their bursting only four hundred meters from the tubes was sobering, too close for comfort...but necessary.

"That's some scary shit," Captain Wilton said. "I think I like it. Can't hide from those low airbursts, no matter how deep the hole."

"That's why some clever guy invented it," Jif replied. "You can duck under flechettes, but killer junior's going to find you anyway...and at a greater distance than beehive, too."

Wilton asked, "How close can you get those *Killer* rounds to pop?"

"You just saw it. Anything closer just might kill us, too."

"I heard some story of a round's base plate coming straight back and decapitating a cannon-cocker," the captain asked. "Is that bullshit, Miles?"

"Nope. Straight skinny."

"Well, then, y'all got some righteous firepower there, bubba."

The night was darkening again as the last volley of flares from the mortars burned out. Wilton asked,

"How long y'all want to keep this illum going? I don't have an unlimited supply, you know."

"Give us one more volley," Jif replied. "Same locations."

Seconds later, they heard the soft *ploomps* of the mortars, the four tubes shooting an unsynchronized salvo spread over several seconds. "Popcorn," Contreras said, critiquing the sloppy delivery. "A couple of your loaders must have sticky fingers, Captain. We'd get a lot more light from those measly little flares if they all fired and drifted down exactly together."

"I'll tell you what, First Sergeant...why don't you fire your own damn illum next time? Oh, wait...you can't shoot straight up, can you?"

"That's right, sir, because that isn't our job. Different strokes for different folks, like they say."

As Wilton's mind flailed for a snappy comeback, the flash of a rocket launch lit the western quadrant like a flashbulb. In those dark seconds before the next round of flares bloomed, the launch seemed a prelude to disaster.

The rocket—from an RPG-2 launcher—streaked low toward the firebase from a hundred yards out, the hissing sound of its brief but rapid flight like a boiler venting steam. It flew frighteningly close over Gun Six, crossed the firebase, and landed nearly flat on its side like a poorly thrown javelin, sliding for yards before coming to rest against the trunk of a fallen tree on the eastern sector of the perimeter. It didn't explode.

Without being told, Hammond rallied the shaken crew of Gun Six, leading them through the firing of another beehive round toward the RPG's launch area.

But the gun chief balked, asking, "How the hell are we gonna hit him with beehive, LT? He's got to be three or four hundred meters out."

"RPGs can't fire that far, Sergeant," Hammond replied. "He's no more than two hundred. Set the fuze for midrange and let him have it."

The flares were providing their maximum light now. The gunner yelled, "I see gooks running! Shoot the damn thing!"

The beehive round dispensed its cloud of tiny steel darts. It took nearly a minute for the resulting veil of dust, glimmering in the artificial light, to clear. By that time, the flares had burned out, so Jif asked for one more illum round over the western quadrant. When it popped, nobody could see any sign of movement beyond the perimeter anymore.

But the unexploded RPG in the firebase was still a wild card. Sitting just a few yards from Gun One, it was a grave threat to that crew should it decide to explode. But they didn't leave their gun. If they did, the firebase would be highly vulnerable if suddenly attacked from the east. A few of Wilton's infantrymen were using the downed tree as a makeshift defensive rampart but scattered when the grenade made its appearance.

"We can't leave that damn thing there," Wilton said, "waiting on EOD to deal with it."

"That's why we're going to blow it up ourselves," Jif replied.

"How are you going to do that? You gonna throw a frag at it?"

"No bloody way," Jif replied. "That just might fling it someplace else to blow up. We're going to burn it right where it sits."

"How, Lieutenant?"

"We'll thermite it."

Contreras broke in to suggest, "Maybe we want to use white phosphorous instead, sir?"

"Save the willy pete, Top. We've got more chance of needing it than the thermite."

The first sergeant shrugged. He couldn't argue with that.

Wilton asked, "So, who's going to do the deed?"

"Me," Jif replied. He told Contreras, "Tell the section chiefs what's going on. We don't want any overreactions when it flares up. Move all unpacked ammo and sighting equipment out of blast range. Make it a ten-meter radius from the RPG, just to be on the safe side." Then he got two thermite grenades from the CP.

Two...just in case I miss with the first one.

When Jif got to Gun One, Chief of Smoke McKay was already making sure the exposed ammo and vulnerable section equipment had been moved away. After confirming all personnel were clear, he gave Jif the thumbs up.

"FIRE IN THE HOLE," Jif yelled as he pulled the pin on the thermite grenade, let the spoon fly off, and delivered it like a bowling ball, rolling the cylinder to the RPG from a distance of five meters. When the flaring cylinder clunked to a stop against its target, he turned and hurried away.

Didn't need that second one after all.

Like a welder's torch, the grenade's intense heat cooked off the RPG in a matter of seconds. Its destruction was more a series of pops and sizzles than explosions hurling fragments. They wouldn't last long.

It did, of course, set the felled tree on fire, as everyone had expected. But as the dried-out wood was quickly consumed by the flames, it offered up a surprise: a nest of snakes hidden beneath were fleeing.

"THERE'S GOTTA BE A HUNDRED OF 'EM," a cannoneer shrieked. "THEY'RE ALL OVER THE FUCKING PLACE."

The snakes—hardly a hundred, probably no more than half a dozen—were slithering in several directions, mostly away from the firebase.

"I should've bloody known that would happen," Jif said, scolding himself. "That was a perfect place for a snake den."

Wilton asked, "You know a lot about snakes, Miles?"

"A little. I spent half my childhood in the Australian bush. Lots of nasty snakes there."

"What kind were under that tree, Tarzan?"

"I'm not sure. Couldn't tell much about them from a distance."

"Well, then, maybe you can enlighten us about the best way to handle them?"

"The best way? Simple. Don't."

The RPG and the tree had burned themselves out, allowing the crew of Gun One to return to their posts. Wilton's infantrymen covering that sector returned reluctantly to the perimeter, as well. They were still unnerved by having nearly blundered into the den of snakes.

Though it wasn't being pressed at the moment, the attack on the firebase seemed like unfinished business. Jif told his FDC chief, "I don't want to use up all the mortars' illum rounds. Get flares over this position from one of the batteries up north. Put it two hundred meters west of the firebase. One gun, make it continuous. We'll adjust as necessary."

"I'm on it, sir," the chief replied. "But one question...is the mortar section really going to move over here?"

"That's the plan."

"Outstanding, LT. That'll make working together real simple."

As the request for artillery illum rounds was being processed, 1SG Contreras said, "It was some luck that the RPG missed Gun Six. Couldn't have passed more than a couple inches over the tube."

Jif replied, "One thing's for damn sure, Top...if that piece was an ol' one-oh-one, it would've gotten hit, sticking up as high off the ground as it would've been. There's something to be said for that low silhouette of the one-oh-deuce."

"You've got that right, Lieutenant."

FDC reported, "Illum's on the way, sir. Signal Hill's shooting it."

"Good," Jif replied. "Give those boys up there something to do."

Contreras added, "Yeah, they don't seem near as busy as we were up there."

"Give it time, Top. Things will pick up for them. Especially if MACV decides to start shooting across the border into Laos."

"But a ground-pounder's not allowed to be there on foot. He can't fly over it, either, so who'd be the FO for those fire missions, sir?"

"The CIA Air Force, probably," Jif replied, referring to the agency's covert Air America operations in Southeast Asia. He was about to mention that CIA operatives on the ground at Lima sites might call fire missions, too, but he stopped himself. Even though he'd once been flown to a Lima site in Laos due to circumstances beyond his control, he'd been sworn to secrecy about their existence.

More news came from FDC: Charlie Battery had just received a fire mission from a cav unit almost four klicks to the south down Route 548. "They sound like they're in deep shit and all alone," the section chief said. "They're screaming like teenage girls at a Beatles show, asking for fire for effect right off the bat. I hope they know where the hell they are."

The battery, which had been preoccupied with the assault from the west, traversed ninety degrees to a southerly azimuth of fire. As the assistant gunner on Gun One reached for his elevation handwheel, he recoiled in shock. He never saw the snake that bit him on the forearm. The viper, a fugitive of the burning tree, no doubt, had coiled itself around the elevation mechanism.

"I don't fucking believe this," the assistant gunner said, still too dazed to feel the sting of the bite. "I'm hit…I think." He stumbled to the ammo hutch and flopped to the ground, his face pale and ghastly in the light of the flare from Signal Hill. It had just popped high overhead, beaming many times brighter than a mortar flare.

But Charlie Battery's fire mission went on. As SFC McKay held his flashlight beam on the snake, still wrapped around the mechanism, he pinned the viper against the carriage with an axe head, calling out the quadrant readings as a nervous cannoneer gingerly reached around him to crank the elevation wheel, his hand just inches from the treacherous fangs. The crew didn't miss a beat firing its round in the first volley.

Jif and the medic arrived together. While the doc tended to the bitten man, Jif told McKay, "Hold that bloody bastard still, Smoke." Then, without a moment's hesitation, he reached in and decapitated the snake with a bayonet. While the headless body writhed in its dance of death, Jif pulled it from the mechanism, holding up the remains for evaluation. What was left of the whip-like creature dangled from his outstretched arm down to his ankle.

"Man, that took some balls sticking your hand in there like that, sir," the gun chief said.

"It's no big thing, Sergeant. Just check with a flashlight that you don't have any more visitors taking up residence in your pit."

The medic walked over to Jif. In hushed tones, he said, "I don't want to spook the dude, LT, but it's a nasty bite. He needs medevac, bad. That's not a krait, is it?"

"No, it's not a krait. I think it's some kind of viper, so our guy should have a fighting chance. I'll get the dustoff coming."

"The pilots shouldn't have any trouble finding the place, all lit up with illum like we are," the medic replied.

When Jif returned to the combined CP/FDC, Captain Wilton said, "I'm going to hold off moving my mortars. We don't know if the gooks have given up trying to breach our perimeter, and y'all are busy being the King of Battle. You do know why the artillery is called the King of Battle, don't you, Miles?"

"Of course I do. Infantry is the Queen of Battle, so the King is the one who puts the balls where the Queen wants them."

"Ah, you read that book, too," Wilton replied. "But getting back to my mortars, I'm not moving them until first light."

"Wait a bloody minute, sir. I didn't agree to that. It's going to be a long night and the gooks might still want to play. How about you move the section one tube at a time? That shouldn't compromise their punch for very long, and they'll be in position to do us the most good fairly quickly."

Wilton made a face like he was sucking lemons. "Will that make you *bloody* happy, Lieutenant?"

Not as happy as getting rid of your cracker ass would make me, Jif told himself. His actual reply, though: "I'll settle for that, sir."

Lieutenant Hammond was working the relay link to Signal Hill. He announced, "Medevac's coming, ETA fifteen minutes. But they want the illum shut off. The mission we're shooting down south can continue, though."

Jif asked, "Where the bloody hell is this chopper coming from?"

"A Luoi, I think."

"Tell them to stay under five thousand feet and approach us from the northeast. They won't be in anybody's arc of fire then."

A few moments later, Hammond said, "No dice, BC. Brigade's ordering a pause in the illum."

"Give me the bloody handset, Arthur."

With as much patience as he could muster, Jif outlined the situation in detail, stressing there was a perfectly flyable approach to the firebase that would not intersect the illum rounds from Signal Hill or the fire mission Charlie was shooting in support of the Cav. The flares, he emphasized, were protecting his battery so they could devote their efforts to those needing fire support instead of battery defense.

But the voice from Brigade was adamant: the flight path Jif wanted was a non-starter. To avoid the arc of the illum rounds, the route was deemed too close to the mountains on the east side of the A Shau, a wall of doom that would be invisible to the crew right up until the moment they collided with it. If they tried to fly farther west, they'd not only be crossing the trajectory of the illum rounds, they'd risk hitting the mountains on the other side of the valley as well.

It was a bitter pill for Jif to swallow. He thought of the night flying he'd been involved with, either on board or coordinating from the ground. In each case, the pilots had always managed to stay safe and still get the mission done. The best concession he was offered was delaying the interruption in the continuous illum until the chopper was four minutes out.

He took the deal...*Even if that four minutes will be an eternity if we get hit again.*

The fire mission in support of the cav troopers to the south was still raging when the medevac chopper reported in range. The last flare fired from Signal Hill flickered and died out, plunging Fire Base Condon into darkness. There'd be no more illumination until the dustoff ship was gone.

As the mutter of the inbound Huey could be heard between the *POOMs* of howitzers firing, the first round from an enemy mortar smashed into the perimeter.

Chapter Fourteen

Two more rounds from the enemy mortar struck Fire Base Condon before the medevac chopper touched down. The flight crew never saw their bursts. The only light they'd noticed came from the ground flares delineating the LZ, the glowing wands of the signalman guiding her in, and the muzzle blasts of the howitzers. As the snakebite victim was hustled on board, 1SG Contreras leaned through the cockpit window, telling the aircraft commander, "Don't stick around here, Chief, because we're getting hit. Just get yourselves and our man out of here." As if to put an exclamation point on his statement, yet another mortar round crashed down just twenty meters off the ship's nose, the flash of its explosion capturing the pilots' full attention. They needed no further encouragement; within seconds, the Huey lifted off and vanished into the night.

As he raced back to the CP, Contreras realized how lucky they'd been so far. The firebase had taken four rounds of incoming, but no one was screaming for a medic. Nothing of any consequence seemed to be damaged, either. *Good fortune like that won't stick around forever*, he told himself. *At least we've had the extra people from the written-off howitzer to help get everything dug-in and sandbagged quickly. But holes and sandbags won't save your ass when a round drops straight down on you.*

The first sergeant was horrified to find Jif and SFC McKay perched on the makeshift roof of the

CP/FDC. He called out, "What the hell are you two doing up there? Are you trying to jack up our casualty count? And if a round doesn't get you, you're gonna bust your asses when that hodgepodge of timber and canvas you're standing on collapses."

"Relax, Top," Jif replied, concentrating on the starlight scope he held to his eye. "The Smoke has a good idea here."

"Oh, yeah? Do tell, please."

McKay explained, "That's got to be just one tube firing at us. The shell craters aren't giving much of a clue as to its direction, so it's got to be pretty close…less than a klick away. A little more height just might help us spot it."

Jif picked it up from there. "We reckon they're shooting at us over open sights, so if they can see us, we can see them. If they're dropping rounds in a tube, someone out there is moving around…and they just may be in range of this starlight scope. Since we couldn't shoot illum, the scope was our next best bet."

"The medevac's gone, sir. We can crank up the illum again."

"We just tried, Top," McKay replied. "Brigade won't give its blessing yet. That medevac chopper's headed to Camp Evans, so she's still got a lot of climbing to do just to get out of the A Shau and—"

Contreras interrupted, finishing the sentence: "And the whole time she's climbing toward Signal Hill, she might cross the arc of the illum rounds, right?"

"There it is," Jif interjected, using the one common Army expression he'd actually come to like. It was a way of saying *behold the inescapable truth* and was a regularly used item in the American soldier's lexicon.

The first sergeant asked, "Is the scope showing anything, sir?"

"Maybe," Jif replied. "I'm looking at a spot right now that's bloody suspicious. We caught some back-and-forth movement a minute ago. You got the azimuth, Smoke?"

"Yep. Almost due south, direction three-one-hundred mils."

"Great," Contreras said, "but what's the fucking range, Chuck? The scope's not going to tell us that real well."

"No, but the map's giving us a damn good clue," McKay replied. "There's a ridge that pops up in that exact direction, about six hundred meters out. The crest could be a perfect spot for a mortar. FDC's working up the data for a blind shot with killer junior as we speak."

"South, eh?" Contreras said. "We're going to let Gun Four take it?"

"Roger that," the Smoke replied. "They can fit it in between volleys to the Cav. Won't be much of a shift in deflection and elevation for the crew, either, so they won't be cranking the knobs and handwheels like crazy. Lieutenant Hammond's with the gun chief now, filling him in on the plan."

There was a hint of alarm in the first sergeant's voice as he asked, "Are we sure he's up to it, Chuck? It seems like yesterday—hell, it *was* yesterday—that our acting XO couldn't find his ass with both hands. But now we're leaving him unsupervised?"

"C'mon, Joe," McKay replied. "The young man's learning real fast. Didn't he do great with the beehive and killer junior a little while ago?"

"Yeah, he did super, I guess. But you were watching him real close."

"I'm still watching him, Joe," McKay said. "I just don't think I have to be up his ass every second anymore."

He was going to add *and the BC agrees with me*, but there was no need. Even though Jif was preoccupied with the starlight scope, he'd heard every word. A nod of his head made it plain he wasn't at odds with McKay's assessment.

FDC passed the firing data for the killer junior shot to Gun Four. Contreras said, "Well, here we go. Good luck to all of us. And let's hope this PFM fire mission of yours actually works."

PFM: pure fucking magic.

*****

The medevac ship was now clear of the A Shau; the continuous illumination from Signal Hill resumed. No one could ever know whether it was due to the flares, the PFM of killer junior, or the enemy running out of ammunition, but mortar rounds were no longer falling on Fire Base Condon. With the concurrence of Captain Wilton and 1SG Contreras, Jif terminated the illumination, requesting that the 155-millimeter battery on Signal Hill mark the mission's coordinates for further use.

Shortly after that, the cav unit to the south they'd been supporting called an end to their HE fire mission, too. All they wanted now was continuous illum. Charlie Battery responded, designating Gun Two, on the north side of the diamond, to fire it. As the first round left the tube and flew south over the heart of the firebase, Wilton erupted in anger.

"That's gotta be the goddamn stupidest fucking thing I've ever seen, Miles," the captain raged. "Dangerous as all hell, too. Why are you using the gun on the north side to fire south? You're shooting right over the heads of your whole damn battery, not to mention my head and the heads of my company."

Annoyed but trying not to sound combative, Jif replied, "I don't understand your problem, sir."

"My problem? It's a question of safety, Lieutenant. What you're doing is dangerous to your own position. You need to switch that illum mission to Gun Four on the south side."

"Begging your pardon, Captain…and with all due respect…but this is a diamond formation, designed to allow massed fire in any direction. In every mission, somebody is shooting over at least one other section. It's standard procedure. There's nothing inherently unsafe about it."

"You just don't get it, do you, Miles? What you say is true when all the guns have to fire together, but you're just shooting one gun now. You've got a choice as to which one can fire the mission, and you picked wrong. I pray to God you don't get a short round."

"I hope we don't get one, either, sir. But you do realize the odds of dropping a short round on your own battery are just about nil, don't you?"

Contreras, standing conspicuously off to the side, nodded in agreement with his BC.

But Wilton wouldn't be placated. "What about a misfire, Lieutenant? What would you do then?"

"We'd do the standard misfire procedure, sir, and that's got nothing to do with which way the tube's pointing."

"So you have no intention of shifting the mission to Gun Four?"

"Correct, Captain. And considering the amount of enemy activity that gun's already had to deal with tonight and the odds of that activity picking up all over again, another section is going to handle this mission."

"I don't think you know what the hell you're doing, Lieutenant. And I caution you to watch that smart mouth of yours."

"Your caution is noted, sir," Jif replied, although he didn't sound threatened or chastened in the least. "Now—and with all due respect—please stop telling me how to employ my weaponry."

"Oh, really? You didn't mind telling me how to employ my mortars, as I recall."

"You might also recall, sir, that your mortar section is very happy with their repositioning. It works better for everyone."

As if to reinforce Jif's point, Contreras interrupted, saying, "Speaking of mortars, sir, the starlight scope has picked up movement an estimated six hundred meters to our southeast. This looks like the perfect opportunity to—"

He was interrupted by the *ploomp* of the first mortar firing an HE round at the target, quickly followed by three more. Then he continued, "As I was saying, sir, this looks like the perfect opportunity to use some of that enhanced cooperation you made possible by co-locating your mortar section with our FDC."

Enhanced cooperation was putting it mildly; that first round was on its way just forty seconds after the target had been called in. If the mortar tubes were still in their original position—over a hundred meters away on the north side, where Wilton had originally placed them—nothing would be in the air yet. The time-consuming protocols of landline or radio communications would've slowed the crucial exchange of firing data. All it took to share that data now was a shout.

After shifting the mortar fire several times to cover the probable target box, the starlight scope revealed no further movement beyond the firebase's perimeter. The mission was terminated.

"We'll keep looking, though," Jif told Captain Wilton. "The scope's been telling us just about as much as all those illum rounds have."

"Whatever you say, Tarzan," the captain replied. Then, still miffed, he stalked off.

*****

Sunrise revealed something the flares hadn't; there were three bodies entangled in the concertina wire. "Could've sworn there were more gooks than that coming through," SFC McKay said.

But there was no evidence of the blood trails that would've been present if wounded or dead men had been dragged away. The three entangled bodies were little more than blood-drained sacks of shattered bones, each one penetrated in dozens of places by flechettes. When removed from the wire, there was no rigidity to them at all. They folded like cooked noodles, their puréed insides draining through a multitude of incisions.

"Beehive does that to a body," Contreras said. "It tears it up inside and out."

What was left of their uniforms was in tatters. There was just enough remaining, though, to determine they were NVA. All still had the shredded sacks of satchel charges draped across their torsos.

Captain Wilton looked like he might be sick from all the gore. Managing to pull himself together, he asked, "Any bullet holes in them? My men fired enough to hit those bastards a bunch of times."

Contreras replied, "When they're torn up like this, sir, it's a little hard to tell."

Surprisingly, the wire itself showed little damage aside from the breaks where the NVA sappers had cut it. Some of its length had torn from its stakes by the beehive. The concertina could be easily repaired and put back into place once the dead NVA were removed.

The first sergeant asked Jif, "What do you want to do with the bodies, sir?"

"Bag them in mattress covers and drag them over near the burn pit. We'll bury them first chance we get…hopefully before they turn too ripe. At least the pit is upwind."

"It's a shame we don't have a bulldozer like up on Signal Hill. Could've dug a mass grave real easy."

A Huey was approaching the firebase. Slung beneath it was a cargo net that looked to contain several 55-gallon drums. Wilton said, "That'll be my first sergeant, taking care of business."

"Taking care of *our* business, sir," Contreras replied. "Me and Lou Avery got a few deals going."

As Wilton hurried off to the LZ, Jif asked his first sergeant, "What sort of deals are you talking about, Top? And who's Lou Avery? Are you telling me that E-Seven following Wilton around isn't his first sergeant?"

"Nah, he's just acting, sir. Lou's the real deal. Been in the Army since Christ was a corporal. He's been wheelin' and dealin' back at base camp. We're fixing to make some stuff out of those empty drums."

The Huey dropped off the drums near Charlie's mess bunker. Then she repositioned to the LZ on the north side of the firebase, unloading two passengers and an assortment of supplies, mostly small arms ammo, carpentry tools, and mermite cans of fresh-cooked food. One of the passengers was an ARVN major, a diminutive man who looked much too clean to have ever spent time in the boonies. The other was 1SG Lucius "Lou" Avery, a giant of a black man, six-foot-five, gray-haired, but spry as a twenty-year-old.

As he watched the unloading, Jif thought, *Now isn't this something...a racist like Wilton has one of the most imposing black men I've ever seen for a first sergeant, one old enough to know the ins and outs of the Army better than all of us put together. I'm dying to see how this relationship works.*

Contreras was dying to see how it worked, too. He'd only met Avery once, when Jif's advance party had first arrived at Condon. After that brief encounter, Lou had hopped on a departing helicopter to conduct his "business" at base camp. Only now had he returned.

After giving Wilton a polite yet perfunctory acknowledgment, Avery grabbed Contreras by the arm and said, "C'mon, José...you and me gonna fix up our outfits with a shower. Don't want any more of my boys skinny-dipping in that stream over yonder. They came out with more leeches than I ever saw in one sitting. Even had a dude get one of those slimy little critters in his ear. Doc had a real bitch of a time getting that motherfucker out."

"Better than getting one in your butthole, though," Contreras replied, "or your pee hole. Never actually saw that happen, but I heard a tale."

With a simple *follow me* gesture, Avery commandeered a squad of his infantrymen. As they gathered quickly around him, he told them to grab the carpentry tools and proceed to Charlie's water buffalo. His parting words to them: "Last man there makes my shit list for the week."

The other passenger, ARVN Major Pham, approached Wilton as if he expected the American to genuflect and kiss the ring on his child-sized hand. When Wilton extended his own hand, the major ignored it, leaving the captain looking like he was thumbing a ride. Pointing to Jif, Pham, in excellent English, asked, "Who is this lieutenant?"

"I'm Miles, sir. I command the artillery battery here."

The major looked as if he'd just heard blasphemy. "Your accent! You are Australian!"

"Half, sir."

"Why are you in an American uniform?"

"Long story, sir. But rest assured, I'm an American. Couldn't be wearing this bar if I wasn't."

Pham didn't look convinced. Worse, he scowled with disdain when he saw the Montagnard bracelet of respect on Jif's wrist. But before anyone could say another word, the battery sprang to life; tubes traversed, section chiefs shouted commands, cannoneers scurried. Another fire mission was about to begin. "Excuse me, sir," Jif said, "but I've got business to take care of."

"We'll meet again, Miles."

I can't bloody wait. Who the hell is that little dude, anyway?

*****

Avery and Contreras supervised the work detail as it built a field shower. Two of the 55-gallon drums were placed atop a six-foot-high tower of cut timbers. As the men worked, the two first sergeants negotiated the terms of a cooperative deal.

Using their gasoline-fired immersion heaters, Charlie Battery would supply the hot water. Avery provided the hand pump he'd appropriated to move that hot water to the elevated shower drums. The two outfits would alternate shower days, with times of use to be determined by the first sergeants according to the demands of the day.

"If it rains," Avery added, "and the drums fill up by themselves, the showers will be at room temperature until they're depleted. No sense wasting good water."

"One more thing, Lou," Contreras said. "Lieutenant Miles is hard over that his men will rotate in small groups back to Evans for a general clean-up day. The target is once a week per man. Of course, busy as we are building up this firebase right now, it won't be possible for a few more days, at least. But I'm told your company won't be rotating at all. Let's not have any friction popping up between our guys over their different situations."

"And how do you propose we do that, Joe?"

"How about this? My battery mess will keep the hot coffee flowing twenty-four hours a day for your guys. Hell, some of them have been sneaking it already. This'll just make it legit. Also, for your guys on alert at the midnight hour, there'll be scrambled egg sandwiches on demand, just like the battery's night shift gets. And I won't even ask you for a KP."

"Deal," Avery said as they shook hands.

Contreras added, "It's a shame we just can't co-locate our mess sections…"

"Nah, I prefer it this way, Joe. As long as they fly out the hot food, my company's fine. And if they can't bring a meal every now and then, that's what C-rats are for. Infantry companies ain't like artillery batteries. My mess section would be in the way out here. Better they stay back with Battalion."

"Can I ask you something, Lou?"

"Shoot."

"How do you manage to work with that cracker asshole of a company commander?"

"You mean how does a big bad spook like me work with a Klansman?"

"Ah…yeah."

"The captain ain't no Klansman, Joe. He likes to talk tough, but when it comes right down to it, he ain't no conehead, just some chickenshit peckerwood who waves the rebel flag around. Hell, he don't even know what a goddamn kleagle is. He'd be in deep shit without me, and he's well aware of that, so he don't dare give me none of that good ol' boy bullshit. And I make damn sure he don't give any man in this outfit that bullshit, either. Don't make no nevermind if that man's black, white, yellow, green…they're all my boys and they're all gonna get treated the same. We're all gonna die out here if we ain't playing for the same team…and you won't be able to tell one man's blood from another's, no matter what color their skin is. Captain Wilton's well aware of that, too."

"But he's still a racist, Lou. That's gotta have some bearing on—"

"Who ain't a racist in this goddamn Army, Joe? Hell, you know that, being Mexican and all."

"I'm not Mexican, Lou. I'm from New Jersey."

"I ain't from Africa, either. I'm from Mississippi. You dig where I'm coming from, brother?"

Contreras smiled. He was in the presence of a master pragmatist, a force unto himself who operated a cut above the usual *go along to get along* mantra that sustained lesser leaders throughout their military careers.

"Tell me, Joe…did Captain Wilton run any patrols when I was gone?"

"Not that I could tell."

"I'll be fixing that right quick," Avery said. "They didn't send my company out here just to sit on their asses and watch you shoot fireworks. You want to hear what we call the captain?"

"Sure."

"War Crime Wilton. Back when he was a lieutenant, he pitched some VC prisoner out of a flying helicopter. They had a bunch of them on board, all tied up and blindfolded, and they were threatening them with the big drop if they didn't spill some intel. Seems Wilton got carried away, or was too stupid to realize it was all just playacting. The cover-up went all the way to Westmoreland at MACV. He's a lucky son of a bitch. He should've ended up in Leavenworth for murder."

"Who squealed?"

"The pilots, Joe. You know how those warrant officers are...they're the only guys in this man's Army with a trade union. They're not afraid to speak up when there's a fuckup, because nobody's gonna cut their dick off. They got more institutional protection than West Pointers."

*****

Jif watched Captain Wilton leading Major Pham around the firebase as if giving him the five-dollar tour. The ARVN officer seemed very interested in the battery's field of fire, delightedly whirling his hand over his head in a circle that reflected the guns' 360-degree capability. While Pham took a moment to relieve himself at the latrine, Jif went over to the captain, asking, "What's the deal with that guy? Is he a friend of yours?"

"Best friend you'll ever have in the Republic of Vietnam, Miles. He's the district chief here, and his brother-in-law is the province chief."

"District chief of what? There's nothing out here to be chief of...except this road the NVA turned into a supply pipeline."

"Miles, there are none so blind as those who will not see. Trust me...you and me need to stay on his good side."

"Why? We don't work for him. At best, he's an advisor to Brigade, and they probably don't pay attention to him. Nobody trusts Vietnamese politicians."

"You're missing the point again, Lieutenant. He *knows* things...*local* things...and that knowledge is a great source of intel. Pay attention. He might be able to help you out."

"I kind of doubt that, sir. An ARVN officer who's politically connected? I reckon he's corrupt as hell, probably working both sides of the fence. I've got a hunch he just wants to pimp Da Nang bar girls direct to the firebase. Maybe even sell the Cav drugs."

"You'd better get your head on straight, Lieutenant. He's a very important man in these parts."

Jif couldn't stop himself from laughing out loud. "Oh, I reckon he's important, all right, but not to you or me. You'd better keep an eye on your billfold while he's around. Why is he even here?"

"He wants to share some intel with us," Wilton replied. "It seems all the Montagnards in the area are VMC. That village up in the hills to the north of us, especially."

"That's real strange, considering our intel assessment says nothing about that."

"Well, don't be surprised if somebody calls a fire mission on that ville real soon, Miles."

"You can call all the fire missions you want, but that place is in a no-fire zone. Until Division decides to change that, it won't be happening."

An American Huey arrived to pick up Pham. Within an hour of his departure, the fire mission Wilton had suggested was coming did, in fact, arrive at Charlie Battery, called in from a cav unit a klick to the north on Route 548. That unit was, in all likelihood, about five hundred meters from the Montagnard village.

"Those coordinates are in the red box," the FDC chief said. "What do we do, sir?"

Jif replied, "Refuse the mission."

"But what if they're taking fire, LT? Does that override the no-fire box?"

"Negative, not without authorization. Refuse the mission."

"Are you sure about that, sir?"

"Damn sure."

And he was. For the first time in his tour, he felt no qualms about bucking a request.

Chapter Fifteen

It was 1000 hours, and Charlie Battery had just completed its fourth fire mission of the morning, each one supporting the Cav as it crept south along Route 548. A Chinook hovered overhead, placing its sling load of ammo near the center of the firebase. Then she drifted north to the LZ to offload bale after bale of concertina wire while still ten feet off the ground. That done, she cleared the airspace for an approaching LOACH.

First Sergeant Contreras asked Jif, "You know *Ripper Six* is on board that ship, don't you, sir?"

"I'm well aware, Top."

Ripper Six was the artillery battalion commander, Lieutenant Colonel Latimer. After refusing to shoot into the no-fire zone, Jif was sure the colonel would want a word with him, but whether that conversation would happen over the radio or face to face hadn't been answered until this moment. The in-person visit made him certain he was about to get an ass-chewing. Captain Wilton was almost gleeful as Jif trudged off to the LZ, saying, "I told you not to piss in their faces, Miles. You're gonna wish you hadn't refused that fire mission before too long."

But Colonel Latimer was all smiles as he climbed from the LOACH. He greeted Jif with a hearty, "How's your morale, Miles?"

"Mine's just fine, sir. My battery's is, too."

"So I heard. That's a good thing, because I've got some hot news for you."

Latimer explained that the planned leapfrogging of another battery farther south over Charlie's position was on hold. "Personnel issues, logistical problems, you name it," he offered as reasons for the delay. "That leaves Charlie Battery as primary support for the advance south a lot longer than we planned. What problems will that cause you?"

"None, sir...not as long as we keep getting regularly resupplied with what we need to defend the firebase. I don't reckon the gooks are going to stop hitting this place as long as they have the capability."

"Speaking of defending your firebase, Miles, the airfield at A Luoi is expected to be open to fixed-wing aircraft within forty-eight hours. Once the Air Force is landing the big birds there, one of the first vehicular loads will be a deuce with mounted quad-fifties. That bit of hell-on-wheels will be detailed to Condon. The firepower of those fifties should be a very effective defensive tool. In the meantime, just keep doing what you've been doing, because it's working real well. Captain Ellison will owe you a debt of gratitude. He'll have a very easy time taking over as BC in a few days."

"We're looking forward to seeing him, sir, and the quad-fifties will be great, too. But we're still down a howitzer. Any update on when we'll get another one?"

"No news, I'm afraid. Believe it or not, they're in short supply at the moment."

The colonel's mood changed all at once, darkening as if day had suddenly turned to dusk. "There's something else I need to discuss with you, Jif."

There it is. He called me by my first name with a scowl on his face. That's a sure sign I'm about to get reprimanded. The next thing out of his mouth will probably be something like, "How could you let the team down like that?"

And that'll be contentious, because I don't think I did let anyone down. I was playing by the rules...

But rules have a nasty habit of changing with the circumstances. Some call it "situation ethics."

I call it "being hung out to dry."

Jif asked, "Should I have asked higher headquarters for clearance to shoot into the no-fire zone?"

"No, Jif. Relax...you did it right. We heard that call, and if we'd wanted to amend the no-fire zone, we'd have told you right then and there. But we're getting reports of firing from that Montagnard village, none of which make a whole lot of sense. Somebody is fucked up...and I'm quite sure it's not your battery. Still, I've got to get to the bottom of it ASAP."

"What do you need from me, Colonel?"

"I see from your rap sheet you speak fluent French. Is that correct?"

"Yes, sir."

"Looks like you're the only one, then. I need you to come with me. There's going to be a conference with the One-Oh-First about divisional boundaries, and we might need to include the Montagnards. Trouble is, no one can speak their language. But your French might help...and you already wear that bracelet of theirs. It'll mean a lot to them that some tribe already respects the hell out of you."

"Aren't there any Green Beret types who can translate, sir? They used to operate in the A Shau. They must know the native language."

Latimer shook his head. "The snake-eaters washed their hands of this operation a long time ago, Jif. Can your battery do without you for an hour or so?"

*****

Colonel Latimer's LOACH landed alongside two Hueys in a secured clearing near the intersection of Routes 548 and 547. One Huey carried the Cav's maneuver battalion commander whose troops were securing this section of 548. The other carried the commander of a battalion from the 101st Airborne, whose AOR was immediately to the northeast of the Cav across the divisional boundary. They were met on the ground by a cav company commander, Captain Crocker; a company commander from the 101st, Captain Moody; and an assortment of lieutenants, NCOs, and RTOs. Jif and Major Pham, who'd arrived with the cav battalion commander, completed the group.

Lieutenant Colonel Underwood, battalion commander from the 101st, pointed dismissively at the tiny LOACH while patting the nose of his Huey. He shouted to Latimer, "Can't you cannon-cockers find any real helicopters, Bob?"

"This nimble little girl can jink around the triple-A, Larry. I'd like to see that sluggish ol' slick of yours do the same."

Dispensing with the levity, Underwood replied, "Let's settle these boundary issues first, okay?"

Moving away from the racket and rotor blast of the choppers, the officers gathered around a large, flat rock, using it as a makeshift table for their conference. A map was spread, and Captains Crocker and Moody, the two company commanders, attempted to reconstruct where their units were patrolling at the time of the request for artillery in the no-fire zone.

Not surprisingly, neither captain was sure of his precise location at the time. Their reconstructions on the map looked more like goose eggs that wandered through the no-fire zone than the results of precision land navigation. Such approximations were unavoidable; moving through unfamiliar terrain with limited fields of vision due to hills and forest, it was difficult to be exact. But it was becoming clear now what had transpired. Crocker's cav company was, in all likelihood, a hundred meters north of where they thought they were; Moody's company was at least a hundred meters south of their assumed location and well across the divisional boundary into 1st Cav territory. Between them sat the Montagnard village, less than a hundred meters from either American unit.

Upon detecting a mass of armed men they couldn't identify but assumed were hostile, Crocker's cav troopers began shooting at them. Their targets, men of Moody's company from the 101st, promptly returned fire. The intense exchange lasted an estimated twenty seconds until Crocker, whose map didn't have the no-fire zone sketched in, ceased fire, withdrew to the south, and called for artillery. Jif laid out on the map where those requested rounds would have impacted if his battery had fired them. The plot fell right in the middle of the goose egg for Moody's company.

"All in all," Colonel Latimer said, "it's a miracle that none of our boys were killed or wounded."

Crocker kept shooting dirty looks at Major Pham. In his defense, he said, "We've been getting a lot of intel that all these Yards work for the NVA. I don't understand why we're so interested in protecting them."

Pham busied himself by inspecting his manicured fingernails, pretending not to be listening. But he'd heard every damning word.

Latimer's steely gaze was fixated on the ARVN major as he replied, "I can't imagine where that intel would be coming from, Captain, considering it's one-eighty out from Division's assessment."

Crocker cut accusing eyes at Pham once again but decided he'd better not say anything else.

There was one more piece of information to add. Moody said, "When the shooting stopped, these two gooks came out of nowhere, yelling at us. They weren't armed or anything. Looked like they were just carrying farm tools, so none of my men fired at them. I have no idea what they were saying, but they weren't happy, that's for damn sure."

Jif noticed Pham scowl at the term gook, so he asked Moody, "'You mean Montagnards, right?"

"Yeah, whatever."

"I think we need to go up to the village and have a talk with the Yards," Colonel Latimer said. He said to Pham, "I understand you don't speak any of the Bru dialects?"

The major seemed insulted by the question. "Why should I, or any other Vietnamese officer, learn the language of those savages?"

Latimer had planned to ask Pham to accompany them to the village but changed his mind. The ethnic hatred between the Vietnamese and Montagnards would be an obstacle to any understanding he hoped to achieve. *And the Yards tend to be receptive and gracious to*

Americans, he told himself. *Bad enough we shot up their ville. Let's not ruin whatever goodwill might still exist by dragging this clown along.*

*****

Four Americans made their way to the Montagnard village: Colonel Latimer, Jif, an RTO, and a medic. They carried no rifles, only side arms. "Start off with this, Miles," the colonel said as they drew close and the village dogs began to announce their presence. "Explain that the medic is here to help anyone who might be wounded. He'll also assess the general health of the villagers. If there are endemic problems, we can provide medical help...if they'll accept it."

The settlement was compact, just a few longhouses surrounded by plots of vegetables, pens for pigs, and chicken coops. Jif estimated that not more than three dozen people lived there. He told Latimer, "I'm a little surprised, sir, that this place is so near to the road. I always thought these villes would be well off the beaten track."

"Well, live and learn, Miles. Everything about these people is a mystery to me."

Three middle-aged men came out to meet them before they'd gotten to within fifty yards of the nearest longhouse. They had weapons slung on their shoulders, American carbines of WW2 vintage. While they seemed cautious, they gave no sign of hostile intent.

Jif called out to them in French, hoping that differing dialects wouldn't lead to misunderstandings. He introduced the four Americans and offered assurances they had come in peace. He made sure they noticed the Montagnard bracelet of respect he wore.

After the spokesman for the three introduced himself as H'Ving, he replied, "Then why do your soldiers shoot at us? We are fortunate no one is injured."

When Jif translated that for Latimer, the colonel said, "Tell them our troops incorrectly believed that Montagnards were shooting at them. This was due to bad intelligence about their allegiances. We know now that that intelligence is not correct, and we apologize for it."

When that was relayed to the Yards, H'Ving replied, "That was not intelligence. It was a lie of the Vietnamese gangster, Pham."

Latimer couldn't help but smile at the translation. "These people seem to have a pretty good handle on the district chief, don't they? Ask them what they've got against him."

The answer to that question went on for several minutes. It came as no surprise when H'Ving told of Pham selling narcotics and women to the NVA. He'd even tried to drag some Montagnard women from other villages into prostitution. But when three of his henchmen arrived to take young girls from their village, they were promptly killed. H'Ving pointed to the pigsty and said, "They're buried under there, where they belong." Neither Pham nor his men had bothered them since.

"So the bastard's trying to use us to exact his revenge," Latimer said, "peddling all kinds of bullshit about these people." He told Jif, "Assure them again that we're their friends—their allies—and no harm will come to them from our troops."

Jif relayed the message and then smiled at the reply. "We're going to have to drink on that, sir," he told the colonel. The two spent the next hour participating in a *Nam Phe* ceremony of friendship with the village leaders, sipping potent rice wine from a communal urn through bamboo straws. The medic took that time to run a clinic for the villagers.

As they headed back to the LZ and their restive LOACH pilot, Latimer—a little tipsy and unsteady on his feet—said, "That little party took a lot longer than I expected, Jif. Good thing we had my RTO with us to stay in touch, or they might've thought we were MIA."

When the colonel returned to his CP at A Luoi, Major Pham was nowhere to be found. His XO told him, "I think the little bugger jumped on a chopper to Phu Bai. Had all his bags with him, too. Looked like he was going on vacation."

Sober now from the cool, refreshing air at altitude, Latimer replied, "If he ever shows his face again, make sure he's put under arrest."

*****

Walking back to his CP after the LOACH dropped him off at the firebase, Jif was confronted by a taunting Captain Wilton, who told him, "I guess you'll be shitting real easy for a while after the reaming you just got."

"There was no reaming. But be advised...everybody from your battalion commander on up knows Major Pham is a double-dealing son of a bitch. Don't feel too bad, though, sir...you weren't the only one who got sucked in by his bullshit."

"What the fuck are you talking about, Lieutenant?" Wilton wasn't just being combative. He sounded truly worried.

"Just like I thought, he was running whores and selling drugs. That's a shining example of why the ARVN are screwed up. Too many of their officers look at war as nothing but a business opportunity. The NVA don't seem to have that problem. Sometimes I think we're fighting the wrong gooks."

"There you go again, Miles, sounding like a true California commie-pinko subversive."

"But at least I'm not a gullible one, Captain."

*****

First Sergeant Avery quickly made good on his word to get his company patrolling again, looking for budding threats in the rolling, lightly forested terrain around Fire Base Condon, or, as even he was now calling it, Fire Base Rubber. Two patrols had gone out that morning while Jif was with Colonel Latimer. While they'd not run into any NVA, they found much confirmation that the enemy had lingered in close proximity.

"All sorts of crap out there," a squad leader who'd led one of the patrols reported. "Ammo cans, some GI flashlight batteries, rice sacks that still looked half-full, even a couple of Coca-Cola bottles, one of them unopened. And one roll of bandages, too, not even used. Who said the gooks don't waste nothing?"

When Avery asked him about the suspected mortar site from last night, the sergeant replied,

"Couldn't find a trace, Top. We might've been in the wrong place, but there was zip."

"Tell him about the pumpkin, Sarge," a PFC from the patrol said.

Sure enough, they'd found a pumpkin placed in the V of a spreading tree, just high enough to reach. But the squad leader hadn't let any of his men touch it.

Listening in, Jif said, "Good move, Sergeant. I reckon it was booby trapped."

"Fucking-A, sir."

"Wait…there's more," the PFC said. "We mentioned to your battery's mess steward—Panakis, I think his name is—that it was out there, and he wants the son of a bitch so he can bake a pumpkin pie."

"I'm sure Specialist Panakis was pulling your leg," Jif replied.

"No way, LT. He was dead serious."

"Well, he probably got the dead part right. Where is this pumpkin? Can we see it from here?"

They could, but they had to stand on the elevated shower drums to get line of sight. Jif said, "Tell you what…if somebody can shoot that pumpkin, I'll see what I can do about getting some of the orange buggers shipped in from Camp Evans. Nobody knows what to bloody do with them there, anyway. It'll be pumpkin pie for everyone."

Another man spoke up. "That tree's pretty damn far, LT."

"It's only about six hundred meters," Jif replied. "Your sixteen can shoot a practically flat trajectory at that range."

First Sergeant Avery stepped forward and said, "You're on, Lieutenant. I'm your man."

"Outstanding, Top. I'll give you three shots."

Avery climbed the drums and, standing tall, weapon at the ready like a statue at some war memorial, ripped off three shots in quick succession. They all missed. The pumpkin was still intact, mocking him.

"Gimme another shot, Lieutenant," he said. "I think I've got the range now."

"Negative, Top. My turn. Come down from there."

Avery let out a laugh. "What? A cannon-cocking officer is gonna take me on?"

"Three shots," Jif said as he scaled the drums.

It only took one. The pumpkin exploded with the fury of the several grenades that had been packed inside the booby trap. After the chorus of *holy shits* died down, a dumbfounded Avery muttered, "Damn fine shooting, Lieutenant."

"Thanks," Jif replied. "Now think of something else you want to eat. Something that won't eat you instead."

The first sergeant just nodded and walked away.

Later that afternoon, among the resupply items dropped off at the firebase was a crate full of pumpkins. Beaming as he beheld the bounty, Avery told Jif, "Begging your pardon, Lieutenant, but you ain't the only one who has friends at Camp Evans. When are we gonna have that pie?"

Chapter Sixteen

If the night hadn't been so clear, the men of Fire Base Condon—a place they now universally called Fire Base Rubber—wouldn't have seen the light show from the top of Signal Hill. Seven klicks away—just over four miles—and towering thousands of feet above the valley floor, the mountain was a hazy colossus among lesser giants in daylight. Once the sun went down, it vanished from sight until the next dawn.

But this night was different. The 155-millimeter battery that had replaced them on Signal Hill was firing a mission. The near-synchronous muzzle flashes of the medium howitzers resembled bolts of lightning in the dark sky. Their barely audible thunder took some twenty seconds to reach Rubber, like the sound of a distant storm.

"Those tubes have to be pointed our way," Jif said as he watched the flashes. "We wouldn't be seeing the muzzle flashes so clearly otherwise. Has anyone heard rounds impact around here? I certainly haven't."

Lieutenant Hammond asked, "Do you think they're shooting into Laos? The border's so close to here."

Spec-5 Signorelli, the FDC chief, had been busily scanning the fire control channels, trying to listen in on the mission in progress. "I can't find it, LT," he told Jif. "They must be operating on some super-secret freq."

Jif replied, "Call the FDC at Battalion. Ask them what Signal Hill is shooting at."

The evasive reply from that higher headquarters boiled down to *none of your damn business.*

"Sounds suspicious, doesn't it?" Jif said. "Signal Hill's firing toward us and the border, but the rounds aren't landing anywhere near here, and the commo is on a freq we can't monitor. So if they're shooting into Laos—in the dark, yet—who's the FO calling the mission?"

SFC McKay asked, "You think it's some CIA dude, sir?"

"It bloody well might be, Smoke."

"Last time I checked, shooting across the border was against the rules of engagement, right?"

Jif replied, "As far as I know, it still is."

First Sergeant Contreras raised another possibility. "You don't think we put a target acquisition radar set on one of these mountains, do you? They could be using that to adjust fire."

McKay replied, "We would've known if that happened, Top. And with all these other mountains in the way between here and Laos, it wouldn't work worth a damn, anyway. The best they could get was trajectory intercept data, and that doesn't exactly lend itself to precision fire."

"I don't know a bloody thing about radar," Jif added, "but putting a set on one of these mountains sounds like a great way to lose it. Unless there was a battalion protecting that site, the NVA would overrun it in a heartbeat."

*****

Captain Gray, commander of the 155-millimeter battery on Signal Hill, was determined the "special" fire mission his unit had been assigned would go without a hitch. He'd taken over the job of running the gun sections from his XO, sending the lieutenant he'd displaced to FDC. There, the XO was to coordinate with a team of four civilians using specialized radio gear, none of which was compatible with the tactical radios Army divisions used. The civilians wouldn't reveal their names, identifying themselves only as government employees on a secret, high-priority assignment.

The XO, an experienced first lieutenant who was annoyed that Captain Gray had bumped him from his job for this exercise, told the civilian team leader, "Why don't you just come out and say it? You're spooks from the CIA, right? We've seen your type around base camp before. And we can all damn well read a map, so we know where you're shooting, and it isn't in the Republic of Vietnam."

The CIA leader replied, "I don't have to remind you and everybody else in this fire direction center of your orders to remain silent about this operation, do I, Lieutenant?"

"No, sir. We read you loud and clear. I figure the only reason I'm wasting time here instead of doing my real job is to make sure my people don't say a damn word about it."

*****

The weapons Captain Gray's battery fired, six M114 medium howitzers, were relics of wars past. They were no different in principle and operation than the first rotating-breech guns developed a century before and were just as cumbersome to operate. At ninety-seven pounds, its separate-loading ammunition was far more labor-intensive to handle than the forty-two-pound round and canister combination of the 105-millimeter howitzer. Despite its slower rate of fire, the larger shell delivered a geometrically greater amount of explosive power than the 105.

It took four cannoneers just to load the 155 projectile. Two men would hold the round on a tray at the mouth of the breech while two more rammed it into the chamber. The ramming process required a single coordinated thrust with a purpose-built staff, the motion resembling two teammates pulling together on the rope in a tug-of-war. The strength of the ramming thrust was crucial; a poorly seated round might fall short. It might not even leave the tube at all.

Due to the shuffling of personnel to cover men who were sick, on R&R, or had rotated back to The World, this was the first day the two rammers on Gun Four had worked together. Their thrust on the count of three wasn't quite as simultaneous and powerful a motion as it could've been, but it was adequate for the three rounds they'd loaded earlier. Then, one of them—PFC Slattery—was detailed to the ammo receiving team, breaking down and distributing the pallets of rounds and propellant the Chinooks had deposited on the mountaintop. It was backbreaking work. After two hours of humping the ammo, an exhausted Slattery returned to his gun crew just as Gun Three—the battery's base piece—was firing the first adjustment round of the "special" mission.

When that mission reached the fire-for-effect stage and it was time to load all the guns, Slattery faltered. Gun Four's round was rammed almost entirely by the efforts of his partner.

It wasn't enough. The section chief saw their weak effort and said, "Goddammit, you two got the punies or something? That gotta be the sorriest fucking ram I ever saw." But the rest of his crew seemed oblivious to his concern. They kept right on with their duties, placing the powder bags into the chamber, closing the breech, and inserting the primer. The gun was ready to fire.

Determined to stop a problem before it happened, the chief yelled, "DROP THE LANYARD."

The assistant gunner immediately did as he was told.

Captain Gray, who was about to give the command for the entire battery to fire, bellowed to the section chief, "WHAT THE HELL'S GOING ON, SERGEANT? WHY ARE YOU NOT READY?"

"We've got a weak ram, sir. I can smell a short round coming. Maybe even a stuck round. We've got to punch it out."

"Negative, Sergeant! Negative. Fire the damn thing before it cooks off."

"It's a cold tube, sir. She won't cook off."

"I gave you a direct order, Sergeant. Pick up that lanyard."

The chief of firing battery spoke up, telling the captain, "Maybe shooting that tube's not such a hot idea, sir."

"At ease, Sergeant. I take full responsibility."

Damn right you do, the Smoke told himself, *and there are at least ten witnesses to you saying that.* To the captain, he replied, "As you wish, sir."

Gray gave the order to fire. Five guns responded with their robust report. But there was obviously something wrong with the firing of Gun Four. For just an instant before her muzzle flash, there was a shriek of gas escaping the tube under incredibly high pressure. Then, there was a thunderous *POP,* as if a giant champagne bottle had launched its cork.

The round had been fired, but without any authority. Had it been daylight, the men on Signal Hill could've seen it wobble in a feeble trajectory that quickly decayed to an end-over-end tumble, like a place-kicked football.

Rather than the nearly nine miles it was supposed to fly, the short round only traveled two, falling into the command post of a 1st Cavalry maneuver battalion just west of the A Luoi airfield.

*****

Four members of the Cav—including the battalion commander—were killed by the short round, with another eight injured. The morning following the incident, Divarty's preliminary investigation of the friendly fire disaster was quick and brutally decisive. Despite his proclamation of taking full responsibility, Captain Gray tried to deflect that responsibility several ways, but there were too many witnesses among his own people for any of his excuses to ring true. In the formal investigation that would follow, the only technical reason for the accident that would withstand scrutiny was the firing of an inadequately rammed round, something the section chief had tried to stop only to be overridden by Gray. The captain's desire to be seen as a man who got things done by higher headquarters had clouded his judgment, leading to tragedy.

Colonel Pratt, the newly installed Divarty commander who'd replaced the lackluster Colonel Chastain, had been in the job only a day when the incident occurred. He told Lieutenant Colonel Latimer, "This is a hell of a start to my new command, Bob. I'm going to need a favor from you to help put things back on course."

"Sure, sir. What can I do for you?"

"This kid Miles who's the acting BC of your Charlie Battery...how's he performing?"

"Just fine, Colonel," Latimer replied. "Lieutenant Miles is doing an excellent job, in my estimation."

"Does your estimation include his being ready to assume command for real?"

"Absolutely, sir."

"You said that without any hesitation, Bob. Are you really that high on the young man?"

"You might say that, Colonel."

"All right, I'll say it. Put Miles in full command of Charlie."

Latimer asked, "Fine, sir, but what do I do with Captain Ellison when he arrives?"

"He won't be coming to you. I'm giving him the one-five-five Battery on Signal Hill, so he'll be reporting directly to Divarty. As to Captain Gray, he's relieved of command, effective immediately. I'm shipping him back to First Field Force. He's their problem now. Ellison has plenty of big gun experience, coming from the European command. He'll be a better fit for Alpha than anyone else who's available."

*****

At Fire Base Rubber, there were two things to celebrate. The first: their snakebit assistant gunner was going to be all right. "He should be released from the hospital at Phu Bai in a couple days," 1SG Contreras said. "Then the lucky bastard returns to good ol' Charlie Battery."

"Lucky, my ass," a section chief grumbled. "Just make damn sure he goes to the bottom of the rotation list back to base camp, Top. He's already been."

"Mind your own damn business, Pitrowski," Contreras replied. "And don't ever tell me how to do my job again...not unless you want to go to the bottom of the rotation list, too."

The second cause for celebration: no longer did Jif Miles have the word *acting* in his job title. He was now officially the BC. The mess section whipped up a lunchtime feast to mark the occasion: roast turkey with all the fixings and pumpkin pie for dessert.

Spec-6 Panakis had worked magic with the shipment of pumpkins, baking enough pie in sheet cake pans to serve every man in the battery as well as Captain Wilton's infantry company. First Sergeant Avery, whose connections at base camp had provided the pumpkins, was treated to the first bite. He gave the pie his seal of approval.

As the sections and platoons cycled through the mess bunker, each offered their congratulations to Jif along with their own profane variations on a song adapted from The Animals' *We Gotta Get Out Of This Place*. The verses revolved around a comparison of life on Signal Hill, where they were often cold, wet, under attack, and sometimes out of reach of the altitude-burdened helicopters, to their current lot at Fire Base Rubber, where, despite its own litany of drawbacks, a man could at least get medevacked for snake bite. Among the complaints both locations shared: neither had access to a whorehouse.

The festivities over, Contreras said to Jif, "The men are thrilled you're officially the BC, sir. I think they're taking it as a sign that there just might be some justice in this world after all."

"If they're looking for justice, Top, they'd better not get their expectations up too high. This is still the Army."

"I hear you, sir. And you know what they say about expectations, right? If you don't have any, you never get disappointed. But speaking of disappointments, does this mean Lieutenant Hammond is now the real XO?"

"Bloody right he is, Top. I mean, what's a guy got to do to get some recognition?"

"Do you really think he's ready, sir?"

"The Smoke does, Top…and so do I."

"Very well, sir. So be it." His words were delivered with a shrug that signaled reluctant acceptance.

Contreras brought up another personnel issue. "Now that we've got an actual BC and XO, that still leaves us short an assistant XO in FDC. Is Battalion gonna ship us some fresh butter bar for the role?"

Jif replied, "Negative. Rather than break in a rookie lieutenant in the middle of a combat operation, what I really want to do is promote Signorelli to spec-six and get another spec-four or spec-five computer with experience to work under him. I think the operation will run a lot smoother that way. He doesn't need the supervision of some greenhorn right now."

"You do realize that Battalion is going to have to sign off on his promotion, right, sir?"

"Do you really think they'll say no, Top?"

"Nah, you're right. I'll draw up the paperwork ASAP."

Jif replied, "Make it like bloody yesterday, okay?"

*****

The men of the firebase weren't the only ones who liked pumpkin pie. Rats were big fans, too. They seemed to come out of nowhere by the dozens, swarming over the pile of rinds and pulp outside the mess bunker that was the aftermath of all that baking.

Lieutenant Hammond, who grew up in suburbia and had never seen a rodent bigger than a squirrel until he got to Nam, couldn't believe how large these rats were. "They're the size of cats," he said. "I'll bet they weigh ten pounds apiece."

First Sergeant Contreras was already lambasting Panakis, the mess steward, for not burning the tasty garbage immediately. "Thanks a fucking lot, Nick," he said. "We're gonna have rats up our asses from now on. Like we don't have enough problems."

Hammond was still trying to grasp the rodent invasion. "I guess wherever there's trash, there'll be rats."

Contreras corrected him, saying, "The problem here is garbage, not trash, Lieutenant. Trash is non-edible refuse. Garbage is edible refuse. Wasn't that one of the first things you learned when pulling KP?"

"I guess I was lucky, Top, because I never pulled KP in ROTC. But how do we get rid of them?"

"We're never going to get rid of them now, Lieutenant. They've found our kitchen and they're here to stay."

"But we're in the middle of nowhere, Top. How do they get here?"

"There are all kinds of ways," Contreras replied. "A slew of them probably tagged along with the NVA and VC. Those people aren't real fastidious with their garbage. Or they came from base camp in our supply drops. You saw rats back at Camp Evans, didn't you?"

"Yeah, a few. But not like these. There's got to be something we can do, though."

"I'm fixing to do that something right now, Lieutenant. Mind you, it's not a permanent fix, just a culling of the herd." He pulled the pin on the white phosphorous grenade in his hand and lobbed it onto the pile of rat-infested garbage. Then he backed quickly away, pulling Hammond with him. In seconds, the heat and white smoke where they'd been standing were dangerously intense.

Watching the rats on the periphery of the blaze scurry away, the lieutenant asked, "What do we do with the ones that don't burn up?"

"Stab 'em, stomp 'em, or learn to live with 'em. If you feel one crawling on you while you're in the rack, don't antagonize it. It might not bite you then."

"Gee, Top, I don't know what's worse, the rats or the snakes."

"It's pretty much a toss-up, sir."

*****

The NVA sniper was hungry, restless, and aching. He'd spent the daylight hours of the last two days atop a ridge some seven hundred meters to the east of the American firebase, camouflaged high in the crook of a tree. His muscles were cramped from being wedged into the same uncomfortable position for hours on end, waiting for the shot that had yet to come.

It didn't help that the objective of his mission was based on faulty information. *My commander told me that place was an important base camp, with many high-ranking officers present. But that doesn't seem to be the case. I have yet to identify so much as a lieutenant or captain, let alone a colonel or general. To kill anyone of lesser rank would have no impact. I would give myself away for nothing.*

American patrols wander all around but have yet to see me. A few men seemed to be staring right at my nest but didn't recognize it for what it was. It's amazing they never heard my heart pounding.

I'm out of food. If I don't claim a worthwhile victim by sunset, I'll have to return to my regiment, where I will be severely punished for my failure. There's so little time left.

The boxy shape of a Chinook approaching Fire Base Condon gave the sniper one last infusion of hope. Dangling from the ship was a cargo bag that, no doubt, contained ammunition for the howitzers.

If I can cause that artillery ammunition to explode, the blast might devastate the base. But shooting the bag of ammo—while an easy target even when moving—might only get the job done if I used incendiary rounds.

And I have nothing but standard bullets.

But if I could make the helicopter crash, the result might be the same.

I should have tried this yesterday, when another helicopter brought artillery ammunition. I have a clear shot when they hover directly over the firebase, with my K44 stabilized against the tree. I don't have that advantage when the ships use the landing zone. I'd have to hand-hold the weapon while bracing myself to keep from falling. I'd probably miss.

But their cannon are hungry. They must be fed every day…

And that gives me another chance.

He waited until the Chinook settled into a hover, her cockpit facing him.

There are two pilots. Which do I shoot first?

I'll take the man in the left-hand seat. Surely he is the captain and not the co-pilot, so I'll cut off the head of the snake.

The rifle became an extension of himself. Pressing his eye to the telescopic sight, he breathed deeply, held that breath…

And squeezed the trigger with a gentle, practiced touch. The weapon's recoil struck his shoulder like a hammer's blow. The round's flight took just under a second.

Through the scope, he saw half the Chinook's windshield become a spiderweb of cracks around the imperceptible hole the bullet made. Instantly, the entire windshield turned opaque, as if a can of paint had been thrown against it.

A perfect headshot! Blood and brains everywhere!

The helicopter remained motionless, suspended in time and space, its sling load still dangling in the air. The sniper cycled the bolt for another shot. He didn't have to see the other pilot to know where he sat.

Chapter Seventeen

The NVA sniper had been wrong about who sat where in the cockpit of the Chinook. He thought his first shot had hit the aircraft commander—the captain, as he called him—in the left-hand seat. But the man sitting there was actually the co-pilot, now quite dead, with his brains splattered all over the cockpit. That hadn't brought the big helicopter down, though. Not yet.

The aircraft commander in the right seat, though stunned and barely able to see through the gore-splattered cockpit windows, was still in control of his ship. He had the presence of mind to punch off the sling load of ammunition in preparation for an escape maneuver. But then the second bullet pierced his windshield and shattered his right shoulder. His right hand now useless, he could no longer exert control forces on the cyclic stick, the one that pitched and rolled the helicopter. In excruciating pain, his efforts to control both sticks—the cyclic and collective—with his left hand alone were going terribly wrong.

The ship began a death dance, her nose pitching up and down in oscillations of increasing amplitude until a blade tip finally struck the ground. Shedding the forward rotor blades along with their pylon, the nose buried itself into the dirt just beyond the wire of Fire Base Rubber's eastern perimeter. The tail section, her rotors still intact and whirling, tried to overfly the grounded nose until the fuselage twisted and ripped apart at mid-cabin. The tail rotor's pylon buckled as if a giant, invisible hand had twisted it like a piece of taffy. Then it broke off and toppled onto the mangled fuselage, its three rotor blades flying off the hub as each tip hit the ground in rapid succession.

The sniper watched the devastation he'd caused. It wasn't what he hoped it would be. Despite destroying a helicopter, the firebase itself seemed unaffected. There had been no explosions, no spreading blaze.

I have failed, he told himself as he dropped from the tree, hastily gathered his gear, and fled west toward the Laotian border only a few kilometers away.

*****

Jif and Captain Wilton had been standing near the drop point at the center of the firebase, watching as Sergeant Pitrowski guided the hovering Chinook and her sling load into position. They saw the first bullet strike the windshield. There was no time to run for shelter as the cargo bag of ammunition came crashing to the ground from a height of thirty feet. The bag burst open on impact, sending its contents flying in all directions.

The wooden crates containing the rounds didn't bounce far, staying within a few feet of where they fell. Some of the crates broke open, revealing the olive drab projectiles they held.

Jif and Wilton had to dodge a hurtling powder canister but were untouched. Pitrowski, however, standing well in front of the wildly pitching ship that seemed headed straight for him, had visions of being crushed beneath her nose. He ran to the closest bunker—just yards away—and hurled himself in head first.

The chopper's crash evolved as a slow-motion calamity. The forward rotor blades had been flung away from the firebase. The aft blades were another story. Two of them came whizzing back into the perimeter like twenty-five-foot-long spears. One struck the sandbags of a gun parapet, breaking into several pieces while spewing fragments that mercifully cut no one.

The other blade flew straight toward the CP/FDC bunker. Spec-5 Signorelli had just stepped outside to see what all the commotion was, a move that placed him directly in the blade's path. But he was looking the wrong way and didn't see it coming. The only thing that saved him from being cut in half was the bruising tackle Jif delivered, sending them both sprawling as the blade passed over them by mere inches. It then bounced off the bunker and severed the thirty-foot aluminum masts of all four RC-292 antennas. When the dust settled, the blade had come to rest tangled in fallen guy ropes and coaxial cables. All the antenna heads were laying on the ground, rendering their receiver/transmitters useless.

As they picked themselves up off the ground, Jif told Signorelli, "Use one of the long-whip Prick Twenty-Fives and re-establish contact with Signal Hill immediately. Tell them we'll have something of a radio range problem until we get the two-niner-twos up and running again. They'll probably have to relay some fire missions for us until then."

As they looked at the tangled masts, Signorelli said, "I think we can splice two of these back together, LT. Done it before...just jam a strip of wood into the mast and then tape the shit out of it. But the other two...they're fucked."

"Maybe not," Jif replied as he eyed the sparse woods adjacent to the firebase. "Use the chainsaw, cut down a couple of those tall, scrawny trees to use as jury-rigged masts, strip them, and drag them over here. They won't be too heavy, and we've got plenty of wire to brace them up until we get replacement units. Get the commo guys to fix any coax cables or antenna heads that got broken. I want to be back to full capacity in no more than thirty minutes."

Signorelli looked skeptical as he said, "You don't ask for much, do you, LT? But we'll get it done, somehow."

Chief of Smoke McKay reported, "No damage or injuries at any section, sir. The battery landline network is intact, too."

"Outstanding, Smoke," Jif replied. "Be ready to loan Specialist Signorelli some manpower as needed to help fix those antennas and get us back on the air."

"Roger that, sir."

"And at first opportunity, get me a count on how much of that dropped ammo is useable."

"Will do, sir. But we can't use any of those fuzes, even if the boxes look okay. They've taken too much of a shock."

"Yeah, I know, Smoke."

First Sergeant Contreras was already rounding up the medics and a team of cannoneers to go to the wreck. Jif told Lieutenant Hammond, "I'll be going out to the chopper with the first sergeant. You stay and run the battery, like normal."

"That bird's blocking a lot of our direct fire sector to the east," the XO said. "We're going to have big problems if we get hit from that direction. How are we going to clear that mess out of the way?"

"Good question, Art. I'll let you know."

*****

Before following Contreras to the wreck, Jif checked in with Captain Wilton and 1SG Avery. The infantrymen were gearing up to deal with the sniper. "He can't be any farther than that ridge off to our east," Avery said. "We're about to hit it with mortars while a patrol heads out that way."

"Sounds like a plan," Jif replied. "I'll be out at the chopper, and I'm not taking an RTO with me. Anybody walking around with an antenna on his back is guaranteed to get special attention from our sniper. If you need me, use a runner."

"That shithook could start burning any second," Wilton said, "and when she does, all that fifty cal ammo on board will start cooking off. That's all we fucking need...those big-ass rounds whizzing all over the place."

"Don't sweat it," Jif replied. "As soon as we pull the crew out of there, those guns come next."

"Be fucking quick about it, Miles," the captain said.

*****

It took an ax to free the wounded aircraft commander from the crashed ship, cutting through mangled cockpit window frames and the collapsed instrument panel. One of the medics told Jif, "Between that shoulder wound and his leg crushed in all that twisted metal, he's lost a lot of blood, and he's in shock. He'll be as dead as his co-pilot if we don't medevac him real quick."

Contreras added, "I've already sent a man back to the CP to call for dustoff, sir. The crew chief and gunners are banged up, too. At least they're not bleeding badly. But that co-pilot…" He paused, trying to shake the horrific image from his head. But it wouldn't leave him.

"His fucking head's gone, sir," the first sergeant continued. "It's just gone. He's pinned in there, too. Nobody's worked up the balls to crawl in and cut him out yet."

The ground around the crash site had become soggy from leaked jet fuel wicking into the soil. Two men carrying a .50-caliber machine gun from the ship slipped and fell the moment they stepped from the wreckage, soaking their trousers.

"Those britches gotta come off ASAP," Contreras yelled to them. "That fuel's gonna start eating your skin." Then he told Jif, "I think some of the fuel may be running downslope, back toward the firebase. If this thing decides to burn…"

He didn't need to finish the sentence.

*****

The wounded men of the helicopter crew were carried to the firebase's LZ, arriving there just as the medevac ship touched down. Word of the sniper with a penchant for shooting pilots was all over the aviation frequencies. Not a moment was wasted loading the casualties on board, and the ship was airborne within seconds of its arrival. One of Jif's medics was still screaming instructions about when to loosen the Chinook pilot's leg tourniquet as the Huey lifted off. He had to leap from the skid to the ground to prevent his going on an involuntary ride.

The two first sergeants—Contreras and Avery—came to a mutual decision where to emplace the .50-caliber machine guns taken from the downed ship. Spread wide apart on the perimeter and mounted on stands fabricated from ammo crates and sandbags, they could provide interlocking fire along most of the eastern and southern quadrants. Avery was glad that Jif's men had not only taken all the ammo belts from the wreck but the tool kit for the guns, too. "We need that headspace gauge after the shock these babies took," he told Contreras. "All these ginormous rounds won't do us no good if they blow up in our faces. I'll have them both checked out in a couple minutes. What's the plan for getting rid of that wrecked bird out there? She sure is fucking up our field of fire in that direction."

"Lieutenant Miles is working that out with Brigade as we speak," Contreras replied. "It's going to take a while. Commo's slowed down because we've got to relay everything through Signal Hill. Once we get the two-niner-twos back up, we'll be back to normal."

Avery glanced across the firebase as men worked to repair and erect the antennas. "Looks like that won't be too much longer," he said. "Your boys seem to know the drill, Joe."

"Yeah…and we're still pulling out the dead co-pilot. That shouldn't be much longer, either."

*****

Despite their local problems, the war didn't pause for the men of Fire Base Rubber. They'd shot six fire missions for cav maneuver units to their south in the ninety minutes since the Chinook was brought down. They'd taken no incoming fire.

The patrol by one of Wilton's squads had reached the ridge but found no trace of the sniper, just some shattered trees and craters from the mortar barrage that preceded their arrival. When they called in that report, the captain replied, "Swing around to the south and keep looking."

"How far south, *Six*?"

"Go another klick...all the way down to the river."

"Roger that," the squad leader replied. Tossing the handset back to the RTO, he turned to his men and said, "Fuck that. We ain't getting any farther from home than we already are. War Crime Wilton can kiss my sweet ass." None of his men took issue with that sentiment.

Pilots were still leery about approaching the firebase, and the inconclusive reports on the sniper situation didn't inspire their confidence. The only helicopter that had come near since the medevac carried an aviation recovery team. The Huey didn't bother to land. It made just one quick pass over the wreck and declared the Chinook a total loss. "Nothing in that cockpit looks to be worth salvaging," the team leader radioed to Jif. "The engines and transmissions gotta be tore up bad, too." He had just one question: "Where are the fifty cals?"

"We've got them. Taking real good care of them, too."

"I'll make a note of that."

Then Jif asked, "So I reckon we have clearance to destroy her? She's kind of in our way."

The reply: "Affirmative. Knock yourself out. We're done here. Best of luck to y'all."

*****

First Sergeant Avery opened the discussion with, "So how are we gonna blow that bad girl away? Thermite's out of the question until after the next rain, whenever that's gonna be. With all that fuel soaked into the ground, we just might burn up our own damn asses if we go starting fires, am I right?"

Captain Wilton offered, "Let's hit her with a couple of LAW. That oughta blow her apart without setting the whole east side of the perimeter on fire."

Jif replied, "You sure you want to do that, sir? Aren't LAWs too valuable to your patrols to be wasting them shooting up a pile of junk? And there's no telling when we'll get resupplied, with the pilots all skittish like they are right now."

Avery said, "The lieutenant's got a point, sir. And while we're talking about wasting stuff, we don't want to use frags or forty-mike-mike grenades from the bloop guns, either. Too valuable to waste, and probably won't do shit to that carcass."

"Oh, yeah? Then maybe the lieutenant has a better idea?"

Jif replied, "How about this? Use your ninety-millimeter recoilless rifle section. They're not doing anything…except waiting for NVA tanks they probably can't stop, anyway. And those things aren't much good for patrolling. Their ammo's too big…you can't carry enough of it. At best, they'd be a two-shot weapon. LAWs are a lot lighter. A squad out in the bush can carry a bunch of them."

"The lieutenant's still got a point, sir," Avery added.

"You ever even seen a goddamn NVA tank, Miles?"

"I bloody well have, sir, last month back at Lang Vei, when we ambushed a column of them…with LAWs, I might add."

"Looks like we've got ourselves a regular freakin' war hero," Wilton said, trying to mock his way out of being upstaged. "Look…why the hell don't we all stop fiddle-fucking around here and just blow the thing with some C-4?"

Avery threw cold water on that suggestion. "I doubt we've got enough of the stuff on hand to do the job, sir, not after all we used to blow down trees and heat C rations. Better save what we got left for some threat that's a little more immediate, you know?"

Wilton threw up his hands and said, "All right…use the damn ricky-rifles. Those gunners need the practice, anyway."

Contreras chimed in with, "Just don't shoot one low and into the ground. We could still set the whole place on fire. If we just blow the tail section apart—all that junk that's sitting on top of the fuselage—that should do the job."

Twenty minutes later, it took the recoilless rifle section five shots to level the wreckage. Appraising their efforts, Jif said, "Close enough for government work, I reckon."

There was an unanticipated benefit to the demolition. As Contreras put it, "Look at all those hunks of scrap metal laying around. We can put them to good use in our position improvements. We'll have rain-proof metal roofs over every hole to pile sandbags on."

*****

At Lima 67, a CIA compound nestled on a Laotian mountaintop less than twenty kilometers from Fire Base Signal Hill, the contentious meeting came to an abrupt close. The Laotian colonel stormed from the hooch that was the site headquarters, sure he'd just been fed a packet of lies. But he couldn't disprove them.

Sylvie Bergerac, the site commander known to her people by the code name Françoise, was an operative well accomplished at snow-jobbing vain and foolish military officers, serving up fictions they took as gospel. She'd been doing it for over twenty years, first in the French Resistance against the Germans during WW2, then as an agent of the wartime OSS, and finally as a charter member of the CIA, where she'd been a clandestine operative on both sides of the Iron Curtain. Since France's Vietnam debacle in the early 1950s, she'd served multiple tours in Southeast Asia.

It was her people who'd called the "special" artillery mission fired by Signal Hill the night before. The team consisted of Hmong warriors and a CIA operator code-named Montana, who was ex-military and a trained artillery forward observer. As he decompressed post-mission after the long trek back through mountainous jungle, Montana was opening his third beer as he asked Sylvie, "How'd you bullshit ol' Vang this time, Frenchie?"

"Simple," she replied. "I fed him the company line that it was a strike by our Air America aircraft using secret infrared technology, specially adapted for night attacks."

"And he bought that load of crap?"

"Not at first. But after I promised a full technical overview by people far more knowledgeable than me at the coming conference in Vientiane, he withdrew the usual threat."

"You mean the one that says all CIA operators in Laos will be expelled if US ground troops, or their artillery fire, cross the border? How many times have we heard that one?"

"I've lost count," she replied. "One almost gets tired of watching them back down."

Montana laughed. "So they're going to keep playing both sides of the fence, hamstringing our grunts while letting the NVA stroll through their country at will. Just so the Agency helps them keep their two-bit prince on his throne. What a crock, eh?"

Sylvie replied, "Crockery is our business, Monty. I just served Vang a healthy portion of it with my talk of an airstrike, but who's to say it wasn't aerial bombs? Artillery shells are like hand grenades. They leave no fingerprints."

"Fingerprints or not, that NVA base camp is still blown to hell. That was a pretty sweet fire mission. Definitely worth the hump through the jungle. It ought to put a big roadblock in the Ho Chi Minh Trail for a while."

"There's a catch, though," she said. "I've gotten wind of a report claiming there was a friendly fire accident during our mission. A short round...several Americans were killed. That would be a crying shame."

Montana scowled as he said, "Don't tell me we're getting blamed for that."

"Of course not. Gunnery mistakes are not our problem. But it'll drive Washington crazy when it gets out that American servicemen died during an action contrary to the agreement with the Laotian government. Senators and congressmen will be screaming for heads to roll. You know how that works, don't you?"

"All too well, ma'am."

"Fortunately, we have General Jock Miles running interference for us at the State Department. He's quite adept at handling both American politicians and tin-pot warlords."

"Miles...that name sounds familiar," Montana said. "Wasn't he the guy you worked with in Saigon, right before Tet?"

"That's him. But you should also know the name from an encounter we had a few months back. Do you remember that young lieutenant one of our choppers pulled off the border with his team of Montagnards? They were dumped with us at Lima Fifty-Two. The lieutenant was General Miles' son. Talk about coincidences."

"Yeah, I remember him. The Australian kid, right? Didn't Colonel Vang almost catch us with him and the Yards, too, before we could fly them back to Nam?"

"Correct," Sylvie replied. "We scared off Vang's helicopter by pretending we were under attack. He fell for that ruse, too."

Then Montana said, "I think we can tell these clowns just about anything as long as we don't throw a monkey wrench into their opium trade."

"Ah, there it is," Sylvie replied. "We protect drug dealers to save the world from communism."

Chapter Eighteen

As the afternoon dragged on, Charlie Battery shot another half-dozen fire missions for maneuver units of the Cav that were pushing south down Route 548. They were closing in on the village of Kon Tom, which was just six kilometers short of the expected terminus of Operation Delaware, the destroyed airfield at A Sap. NVA resistance had been fierce, necessitating a great volume of artillery support. Jif added it all up: "We've fired over a hundred rounds already today. The choppers better hurry up with that ammo drop or another busy night could run us dry."

Just back from a briefing at Battalion, Captain Wilton added, "The NVA aren't giving up an inch of ground without a stiff fight. But once they break contact and withdraw, we're depending on you cannon-cockers to finish them off before they can beat feet to Laos. We can only chase them so far."

"That's why this firebase will continue to be a big target for the NVA in the coming days," Jif said. "We're the main source of fire support for this push. If we get knocked out of commission, this whole operation may go tits up. Good thing we're getting those quad-fifties tomorrow. That additional firepower should boost our defensive capabilities a whole lot. The terrain around here is perfect for them, too. It's mostly flat."

It was pushing sunset when the ammo resupply choppers finally arrived. Going over the delivery, Chief of Smoke McKay said, "This oughta last us a day or two,

LT. They even remembered to throw in extra fuzes to replace the ones that got dropped and ruined this morning. I'm still counting my lucky stars that only six of the rounds from that load aren't useable...too much damage to the rotating bands. Can't risk shooting one like that. It might not even come out of the tube."

Jif asked, "Did you ever have a round stuck like that, Smoke?"

"A few more than I care to remember, sir. Not so much on one-oh-fives, though. It's hard to screw up loading semi-fixed ammo. But it's still possible. Seen it happen."

"What's your opinion on the best way to get a stuck round out?"

"If it's traveled up the tube any distance at all, there's only one option—shoot it out. Take the gun to a safe place, point it downrange, put in a max charge, hook up a hundred-foot lanyard to the firing mechanism, and hope the tube doesn't blow apart when you pull it."

"Sounds pretty bleak, Smoke."

"Roger that, sir. It's bleak, all right. Like a whole lot of other things we have to do."

Jif smiled. He understood McKay wasn't just talking about gunnery.

*****

Nightfall brought no respite from the fire missions. Watching the target plots in FDC, Spec-5 Signorelli said, "*Vortex Two-Six* must have a bunch of NVA trapped between Kon Tom ville and the river. Some of these coordinates actually plot *in* the river. If those gooks get across, it's only about six klicks to

Laos." He asked Jif, "Do you think any cav units are going to get wet and chase them?"

"If I'm reading Captain Wilton correctly, they won't do that. And they definitely won't do it in the dark. Once *Vortex* loses contact, we'll be shifting to H&I fire, I reckon."

"You mean shooting blind, sir?"

"Yeah, that's right. But the brass prefer to think of it as an exercise with a high probability of success."

"I hope they're right, LT. Otherwise, it's just a fancy name for exterminating monkeys."

Jif's reckoning was correct. Within ten minutes, the fire mission shifted to unobserved H&I—harassment and interdiction fire—against preplanned coordinates, most of them along valleys that cut through jagged hills to the Laotian border. Growing weary from the day of non-stop activity, Signorelli told his section, "I'll bet we're going to be doing this all night. None of you guys really cared about sleeping much, did you?"

On one of the gun sections, a tired cannoneer complained, "Shooting like this all damn day and night…it's just like the factory assembly line I used to work on."

"Yeah," another gun-bunny replied, "but at that factory, nobody shot back at you."

*****

First Sergeants Avery and Contreras had pooled their expertise to establish four reference points in a roughly eight-hundred-meter radius around the firebase. These *Romeo* points—Alpha, Bravo, Charlie, and Delta—all on easily recognizable terrain features, served as surveyed locations; their coordinates had been determined by precise triangulation done with the battery's aiming circles. The security patrols sent out by Wilton's company used the Romeos as checkpoints for reporting their activity and suspected enemy positions. They also functioned as rally points should members of a patrol get separated. For the artillerymen, they were reference points of known direction and distance for battery defensive fires.

Just past 2300 hours, Charlie Battery was firing yet another H&I mission when an LP well outside the wire in the eastern sector reported over the landline, "We've got movement in the washboard, azimuth about zero-eight-zero degrees. Only saw silhouettes in the moonlight real quick, like dudes were running over the top and then dropping down into a dip or something. Do we have a patrol near there?"

Supposedly, Wilton's company did have a patrol in the area. Sergeant Eggers, the patrol leader, had called in a position report just five minutes before, saying he was at Romeo Alpha. That checkpoint was almost directly along the azimuth of the sighting the LP had just reported.

Thinking that the LP might've observed their own patrol, 1SG Avery radioed Eggers and asked him to confirm his position. The patrol leader's reply: "Like I just told you, Romeo Alpha, heading south toward Bravo."

"Copy that," Avery said. "Do you have line of sight with the base?"

There was hesitation before Eggers replied, "Affirmative."

"Then give me three red blinks on your flashlight."

Avery stepped outside the CP, watching and waiting. No flashes of red light could be seen from the direction of Romeo Alpha.

Back on the radio, the first sergeant said, "No joy. Repeat the flashes. Give me five this time, real slow."

There was still no light visible from the patrol. The LP was back on the landline, saying, "I've still got movement, definitely headed toward me and the firebase. Permission to come in?"

Avery asked the voice at the LP, "Any chance they might be friendlies?"

"They're moving pretty fast to be one of our patrols, Top." His voice took on heightened urgency as he added, "We need to come in."

"Can you tell how far out from the wire they are?"

"I'm guessing they're twice as far as I am, so let's say about five hundred meters. How about it, Top? It's getting too hairy out here."

"Okay, get your asses back inside the wire," Avery said.

Wilton's frustration was beginning to boil over. He asked, "What the hell's going on, Top?"

"Eggers is either lost or he's fucking the dog somewhere, sir. I don't think he's near Romeo Alpha, like he says. And if it ain't him the LP's caught wind of, we just might have gooks coming to visit."

Sergeant Eggers wasn't lost. He knew exactly where his patrol was, hunkered down just a hundred meters from the north side of the firebase, not far from where they'd walked out through the wire at the start of their patrol. Despite his orders, he never had any intention of patrolling between Romeo Alpha and Bravo, and the five men with him were just fine with that. His plan was to cool their heels a short distance from the perimeter, call in bogus position and activity reports, and saunter back inside the wire after two hours, when the allotted patrol time was up. He'd never flashed the red light. To do so would've revealed his deception. He didn't know that the LP had spotted another, unidentified group outside the wire; not a word about it had been broadcast over the radio yet.

Now Top's looking for me, Eggers told himself. *Better I say nothing and let this play out. Maybe I'll be able to get the whole thing chalked up to the fog of war once we come in. Who's to say I really wasn't where I said I was? Shit happens, right?*

Hell, I've heard stories that other guys blow these patrols off, too. It don't mean nothing.

But the fact that there was an unknown force approaching from the east definitely meant something to the firebase's command element. Jif told Hammond, "Have Guns One, Two, and Four prepare killer junior and beehive rounds, set to minimum range. Direction one-four-hundred mils. Do not—I repeat, do not—interrupt the H&I mission in progress to shoot defensive fires unless I tell you to do so. We may have friendlies in the zone. Nobody seems to know for sure right now."

Contreras said, "Good thing we flattened what was left of that Chinook. Looks like we could be firing killer junior right over what's left of her."

Avery shook his head. "You can't be firing nothing until we're sure who's coming. We ain't killing our own guys."

"I second that, Top," Jif replied.

Wilton snapped, "What are you two saying? That we're going to let the gooks stroll right in here and overrun us all because some patrol leader isn't sure where he is? I say fuck that and fuck Eggers. If he's in the way, that's tough shit."

Avery protested, "Begging your pardon, Captain, but we just don't know if those are gooks or friendlies coming in."

"We can fix that real quick," Wilton replied. He ordered his mortar section to fire illum rounds across the eastern sector.

But when Avery relayed to Eggers that an enemy unit might be in his vicinity—possibly between his patrol and the firebase—and they were about to be lit up, the patrol leader pushed his deceit to the next level, pleading, "Negative! No illum! You'll light my ass up, too."

No such thing would happen, though. Eggers and his men were hundreds of meters away.

Captain Wilton was unmoved. "Too fucking bad," he told Avery. "We'll take that risk. Are the men from the LP inside the wire yet?"

"Not sure, sir," the first sergeant replied.

"Son of a fucking bitch," Wilton roared. "Does anybody in this outfit know where the hell they are at the moment? By the way, where's our other patrol?"

"Denton's patrol ain't the issue, sir. They're on the other side of the firebase, near Romeo Charlie."

Wilton's skeptical reply: "Oh, yeah? Can I take that to the bank?"

A voice from the perimeter came over the landline, saying, "I've got the LP dudes with me, but there are people around that busted-up shithook. Who the hell are they? Our guys or gooks?"

"Engage them, First Sergeant," Wilton said.

A reluctant but dutiful Avery obeyed, relaying the captain's order to their men on the perimeter.

The battery had just fired another volley in the H&I mission. Contreras asked Jif, "Should we go to beehive now?" He had the flare gun in his hand already. A green star cluster from that gun would give the signal that beehive was to be fired.

"Not yet, Top," Jif replied. "We don't know what the bloody hell's going on here. Wait until the illum rounds pop and—"

Wilton interrupted, screeching, "Goddammit, Miles...what did I just say? Engage the fucking enemy. Give me beehive right fucking now."

"They might not be enemy, sir," Jif replied. "We've got to be bloody sure."

A second later, before any of the captain's infantrymen on the perimeter could start laying down defensive fire, an RPG was launched from the vicinity of the downed Chinook. It streaked over the CP to explode on the opposite side of the firebase near Gun Six. The only damage it caused was an aiming post that got knocked over.

From within the CP/FDC bunker, visibility outside was extremely limited. That was the price its occupants paid for the protection they enjoyed. Jif needed to get outside and see what was going on firsthand. He started for the entryway.

But Wilton stopped him, grabbing his arm and pulling him back while propelling himself toward the entrance. He snarled at Jif, saying, "I'm King Dick around here, Lieutenant. I'll decide what needs to be done."

The captain stepped from the bunker just as a second RPG hit it broadside. He became the first casualty of the night's attack. Jif pulled his unconscious, battered, and bleeding body back into the bunker.

The first flare from the mortars was drifting down, casting its brilliant light and dancing shadows across the terrain beyond the wire. "We've got illum, LT," Contreras said. "We've got to do something."

And it had to be done quickly, because friendlies don't fire RPGs into firebases. But Eggers' patrol might be in the beehive kill zone. Regardless of where they were, though, Wilton's orders in the last few moments had been based on shaky assumptions and hardcore fears, not facts. Jif didn't want his decision to be similarly uninformed.

If I'm going to use my howitzers in battery defense, I've got to decide right bloody now. I may have already taken too long.

Wilton's men still hadn't begun to fire. They could see nothing in the flare's light. They couldn't tell at what—or at who—they were supposed to be shooting.

Jif stepped outside the bunker, quickly circled to its west side—away from the incoming fire, hopefully—and scampered up the sandbags to a vantage point at the roof's edge. It was like sticking his head out of a fighting hole that was five feet above the ground.

The first thing he saw was the flash of yet another RPG being fired from the vicinity of the wrecked Chinook. The weapon malfunctioned, though, listlessly spitting the projectile and smoldering propellant just a few feet from the launch tube onto the fuel-soaked ground...

Which then erupted into a carpet of knee-high flames.

NVA soldiers, many of them on fire, sprang to their feet and started running toward the wire. Nobody could count exactly how many, but they seemed to number at least a platoon. A moment ago, lying prone and immobile beneath the flare's light, they'd been invisible. Now, they'd ignited their own funeral pyre.

Wilton's men on the perimeter finally had a visible enemy to engage. The volume of fire they inflicted on the attacking NVA was brutal. Only a few of the enemy got past the interlocking fire of the two .50-caliber machine guns. Those few were quickly cut down by M16s and M60s.

The crew of Gun One, closest to the attackers and the blaze, failed to fire their round in the latest H&I volley. Expecting the order any second to shoot beehive, half the crew had begun those preparations while the rest had become firefighters, racing to clear a firebreak with shovels and axes to prevent the spreading flames from endangering their pit.

Between the flare light and the fire, the situation became clear: the NVA's attack had literally gone up in smoke. At least twenty bodies lay scorched near the wreck; another dozen had been cut down trying to breach the wire.

Lieutenant Hammond jumped into the pit at Gun One, lending his help to the shorthanded gunners as they resumed their role in the H&I mission. SFC McKay marshaled additional men to expand the firebreak. Their efforts paid off; the flames got no closer than twenty feet to Gun One's parapet.

Convinced the situation was under control, Jif slid down from the roof and reentered the CP/FDC. He told Contreras, "We can stand down the beehive and killer junior, at least for now. That fire will burn itself out in a few minutes."

Signorelli said, "Battalion keeps shifting the H&I coordinates, LT. Have they actually got someone observing this stuff?"

"If they do, he's at a great distance," Jif replied. "More likely, they're just trying to hit points on a map."

"By the way, Signal Hill is shooting over our heads again," the FDC chief added. "They'd better not be dropping any short rounds tonight."

The cramped confines of the CP/FDC was a madhouse of raised voices, squawking radios, and two medics working resolutely to save Captain Wilton. "We called for the medevac," 1SG Avery told Jif. "We've got to get him to the LZ just as soon as the docs say he can be moved. He's bad, sir. Real bad."

"Yeah, I know, Top. Any idea where your lost patrol is now?"

"Nope. Ain't heard a word from them, but we're still trying. I hope to God we don't find their bodies out there mixed in with the dead gooks."

*****

At first, Sergeant Eggers thought the firebase was being overrun. But as the blaze around the downed Chinook burned out, the small arms fire dwindled, and the artillery battery continued to fire its H&I missions, he knew he was mistaken. It gave him an idea, though: *I can make it look like we helped beat the gooks. Just got to stay off the radio a little longer...and then stroll back into the firebase like we just saved the day.*

But a unit that had been in a fight wouldn't return to base with its ammunition load intact and its weapons unfired. He told his men, "We're going to mosey a couple hundred yards south, shoot off a mag or two each, and then work our way back to the firebase."

One of his men, a spec-4 named Switzer, asked, "Work our way back *how*? If we go south, we'll walk right over the ground where that fight was. There's bound to be some gooks still wandering around. Or maybe our own guys will think we're NVA trying to hit the base again."

"So we won't go too far south," Eggers replied. "Don't sweat it. When we get close, our radio will miraculously come back to life. We'll call in so they'll know it's us on our way back."

"Why don't we save all the bullshit and just call in now, Sarge? Shooting off our weapons out here will let the gooks know where we're at."

"Nah, we gotta make it sound like we helped out. Do as I say, Switzer...you might stay off my shit list that way."

"What are you gonna do to me, Sarge? Send me to the Nam?"

"Better cool your roll, dude. You might live longer. But in the meantime, I want you to walk point. Take us due south. Get moving."

The patrol *moseyed* for fifteen minutes, finally stopping on a shallow, treeless rise a few hundred meters west of the firebase. "This'll do," Eggers said. "They'll hear us real good back on Rubber. Point those weapons down into that depression and let 'er rip." As the firing began, he threw two frags into the darkness to heighten the aural illusion of a real fight.

They were done in seconds. Eggers told his point man, "All right, Switzer…take us home, azimuth two-six-zero."

"Are you gonna call in, Sarge?"

He never got to reply *Not yet*. The six-man patrol, silhouetted by moonlight in a neat line along the rise, was raked by AK-47 fire at close range.

Chapter Nineteen

Once the dustoff ship carrying the seriously wounded Captain Wilton was airborne, a medic asked 1SG Avery, "Are we sure there was no one else that needed medevac, Top? After that shitstorm, did we really luck out and only take one casualty?"

"For now, yeah, that's all we've got," Avery replied.

For now: nobody knew if Sergeant Eggers' patrol was among the charred bodies lying just beyond the eastside wire, or if they'd been involved in that brief and unexplained orgy of gunfire to the east, well beyond the perimeter. All they knew at the CP/FDC was the patrol was overdue and hadn't said a word over the radio since the last time Eggers insisted he was at Romeo Alpha. As Avery put it, "Ain't no point looking for them in the dark. Maybe we'll know something at daybreak."

That was still five hours away.

Battalion finally called a halt to Charlie Battery's H&I missions at 0230 hours. The night took on an uneasy stillness, occasionally punctuated by the distant booms of the 155-millimeter howitzers on Signal Hill echoing through the A Shau Valley. Jif told 1SG Contreras, "Let's put the men on fifty percent alert. Maybe they'll be able to get one sleep shift apiece by daybreak."

"Roger that, sir. We can hope, right?"

Since Captain Wilton had been wounded, 1SG Avery seemed to be in sole command of the infantry company. Jif knew there were at least two lieutenants from the company on the firebase, both of them platoon leaders. But neither had seemed to be much in command of anything. He asked Avery, "Who steps into Wilton's shoes, Top? Is your XO coming out to the field now?"

"Negative on that, sir. Lieutenant Prager's real short. His DEROS is in a week, so Captain Wilton let him skip out on this mission. I'm betting he's not even at Camp Evans anymore. Wouldn't be surprised if he was outprocessed and on his way to Da Nang or Tan Son Nhut by now to hop on the big bird back to The World. His replacement ain't been designated yet."

"But somebody's got to be next in line for command right now, Top."

Just then, an infantry second lieutenant entered the CP/FDC. He looked flustered, shuffling up to Avery as if some invisible hand was pushing him against his will.

"Speak of the devil," the first sergeant said. "Lieutenant Miles, I believe you've met Lieutenant Dowd? He was Second Platoon leader up until a little while ago. Now he's the new company commander."

"Yeah, we've met…briefly," Jif replied.

Then Dowd asked Avery, "Did you ask him yet?"

"No, sir, I figure that's your job." The first sergeant sounded like a teacher leading a befuddled pupil through an exercise.

Jif was growing amused with this charade. There was no doubt in his mind that Avery was the man running the company, and would be for a while. Dowd was nothing more than a temporary placeholder on the company manning chart.

"All right, if you say so, Top," Dowd said. Turning to Jif, he continued, "I think we should discontinue the security patrols for the night. Is that okay with you?"

"May I ask why?"

"It seems like it's getting a little dicey out there beyond the wire."

"It's been pretty dicey inside the wire, too," Jif replied. "How do you propose we make it less dicey without patrolling?"

Dowd didn't have an answer for that, but Avery did. "With the artillery quieting down for the night, sir, we can put our starlight scopes to use again. If we pool yours and ours, they can cover the whole perimeter."

"Sure," Jif said, "but I reckon you'll need to keep two patrols ready to go if the battery has to start shooting again and overloads the scopes. Can you do that?"

"Sure can," Avery replied. But then he looked at Dowd, asking, "If that's all right with you, Lieutenant?"

"Affirmative, Top. I'll get the men spooled up for that patrolling contingency right away."

"Excellent plan, sir," Avery called after Dowd as he headed for the exit. Once he was gone, the first sergeant shook his head and mumbled, "Yeah, you do that. Go spool them up, Howdy."

Jif asked, "Howdy? Is that his nickname?"

"Yes, sir. You ever see the TV show Howdy Doody?"

"Yeah, sure…like about ten years ago. My little sister watched it all the time when we were living in the States."

"Well, some of the men decided he looked like that peckerwood cowboy puppet, right down to the freckles and slicked-down red hair."

"I can see that," Jif said. "But I noticed you didn't call him *acting* company commander. How come?"

"Lieutenant, that acting title is nothing but an admin term. Out here, there ain't no *acting* anything. You're living the job, or you're dying in it. You should know that as well as anybody, am I right?"

"You've got a point, Top."

Within minutes, First Sergeants Avery and Contreras had worked out the details of the starlight scope surveillance and put the plan in motion. Satisfied that things were under control, Jif nestled into a corner of the CP, hoping to catch some sleep. But it proved elusive. Avery flopped down next to him only to find he couldn't sleep either. He felt sure the moment his eyes closed, Lieutenant Dowd would appear with some problem needing his attention. Abandoning any thought of sleep, he told Jif, "That sure was a tough break for Captain Wilton. Sure hope he makes it. They say he kinda regained consciousness when he was being put on the chopper, so that's something, right?"

"Maybe all that rotor noise woke him up, Top."

"Could be." Avery's tone became wistful as he added, "Did the captain ever tell you about his plan for the ovens?"

"What bloody ovens are we talking about?"

"The ones in the concentration camp, Lieutenant. He figures that him and his brethren will get to run them someday, once they take over completely. They've got one rule: if you don't have blond hair and blue eyes, you get thrown in the oven."

At first, Jif thought Avery might be pulling his leg. But he decided to play along.

"No, I never heard anything about that, Top. Isn't he from Georgia, though? Every other white person in those parts has blond hair and blue eyes. But the half that doesn't—is he planning to stuff them all in the oven?"

"No, there's an exception, Lieutenant. If he likes you, he'll let you operate the ovens. But the minute he don't like you no more…"

Avery made a sound like bacon sizzling in the pan.

Jif asked, "Did the captain like you, Top?"

His voice mimicking that of a Saigon hooker, the first sergeant replied, "He love me long time." Slipping back to his own sonorous tone, he added, "He better damn well have loved me. Picked him up off his lily-white ass more times than I can count."

"Copy that. But do you think he liked me?"

"You never did him no favors, Lieutenant. And with that dark hair and eyes, being smart as a whip with balls to match, plus talking funny and all, you didn't stand a chance. He hated you."

*****

Whatever little sleep Jif could find ended abruptly with the arrival of the first rocket. Feverish activity in the CP/FDC swirled around him as he staggered to his feet, trying to grasp what was happening. First Sergeant Contreras thrust a cup of coffee into his hands, saying, "Here, LT...you're going to need this. That incoming looks to be big caliber stuff, dammit. Maybe one-twenty-two millimeter. It's coming out of the south."

That first rocket had impacted well north of the firebase, near the intersection of Routes 548 and 547. Jif barely had time to take a few gulps of the coffee when the next one crashed down a few hundred meters to the west. The two explosions were nerve-shattering but harmless.

Spec-5 Signorelli was hunched over a firing chart, jarred from sleep and bleary-eyed just like his battery commander, trying to estimate the probable point of origin for the rockets. But it was a near-impossible task. "If they're one-twenty-twos, they've got a range of twenty klicks, right? That launcher could be up to ten klicks beyond the border in Laos. And if that's where the bastard is, we can't reach it, and we're not allowed to shoot there, anyway."

The stress of the attack knocked the last of the cobwebs from Jif's head. He realized Signorelli was right; there was nothing they could do to stop the incoming, just hope and pray that nothing impacted within the firebase.

A third rocket landed well to the south near the abandoned airfield. Contreras said, "Good thing those rockets are just area weapons. Their impacts have been scattered over a circle that's about a klick in diameter, so far." But knowing of their inherent inaccuracy didn't make him—or anyone else—feel any less threatened.

Then they heard sounds that allowed a trace of optimism: the muted thunder of big guns firing to their north, followed quickly by the faint whistle of rounds streaking high overhead, heading south.

"That's got to be Signal Hill shooting," Contreras said. "You don't suppose it's counter-battery fire on that rocket launcher, do you? Maybe somebody does know where the bastard is."

Signorelli was scanning the fire control frequencies, trying to eavesdrop on any fire mission that might be in progress. But he heard nothing except the occasional commo check, position report, and sitrep.

"This is just like the last time we heard the Hill shooting over our heads," the FDC chief said. "They must be on some super-secret freq again."

Over the next few minutes, two more volleys of friendly artillery arced through the sky above the firebase. Then it stopped.

The incoming rockets had stopped, too.

Contreras asked, "Anybody think that's a coincidence?"

No one could answer the question.

*****

At Lima Site 67, a CIA outpost across the Laotian border from the A Shau, Sylvie Bergerac—the station chief, code name Françoise—was monitoring the radio, too. She was providing a relay to Signal Hill for Montana—her unit's FO—and his team of four Hmong fighters as they once again sought out NVA and VC fleeing South Vietnam to sanctuary in Laos. Once the enemy was found, they'd attempt to bombard them with American artillery from across the border. The best hunting was at night, when the enemy tried to use the darkness to conceal their movements.

This night, however, the hunting was disappointing. The only potential target they'd discovered was an old truck with what appeared to be launch rails holding large-caliber rockets mounted on its bed. In the darkness, there was no telling if it was an NVA or VC vehicle. Trundling down a rough, narrow trail barely suitable for oxcarts, the truck made such slow progress that Montana and his team, concealed in the adjacent woods, could easily keep it in sight while following on foot.

Several times, the vehicle stopped and the five men on board dismounted to assess their location. They'd argue over a map for a few moments until one of them—the leader, apparently—ordered them all back onto the truck. Their slow journey down the trail would then continue.

I guess they're trying to find a specific firing point, Montana told himself. *For rocket artillery like that, they need to shoot from a location with established coordinates. Otherwise, they wouldn't come within a kilometer or two of their intended target, as inaccurate as those babies are. They're worse than those Honest Johns I used to work with in Germany back when I wore the Army green. The standard correction for those misguided missiles was "Drop a grid square."*

Since there doesn't seem to be anything else to shoot at tonight, I suppose that truck will do as a target. But they'll have to park that piece of shit somewhere before I can engage it. Don't want to be wasting rounds trying to nail a moving target. I'm having enough trouble as it is keeping track of my own coordinates in these hills, let alone that truck's. There's nothing but the moon and stars for landmarks out here, and I ain't no celestial navigator.

He called Sylvie on the radio, asking, "Is *Big Top* ready to play? We may have a bingo very shortly."

Big Top: the call sign for the CIA operators working with the 155-millimeter battery on Signal Hill.

She replied, "Affirmative. Standing by for tonight's game."

Just when Montana figured the truck was about to stop again, it sped up. The trail had apparently smoothed out, allowing for a faster ride. His team quickly outpaced, he told his Hmong warriors, "We'll try to keep following that vehicle. Maybe once they stop for good, we can catch up and call in the artillery."

Montana and his team abandoned the concealment of the woods to jog down the trail, hoping to move fast and close the gap. Fifteen minutes passed before they finally saw the blinking of flashlights a few hundred meters ahead. The truck had stopped; its crew was preparing to fire the rockets.

The Hmong seemed ready and eager to attack the rocket crew with only the weapons they carried, but Montana dissuaded them. His reasoning: *That would be suicide. My grease gun is only good for close-in fights, and my men's World War Two carbines would be badly outmatched by AK-Four-Sevens firing full auto. Besides, we're supposed to be a recon patrol, not an ambush team.*

But if we're going to bring hellfire down on that launcher, it's now or never.

He huddled beneath a poncho, trying to read his map by flashlight. *All I've got to do now is figure out exactly where the hell we are.*

It was a tough calculation. The trail's depiction on the map was only an approximation of its location, and he'd long since lost track of how far along it they'd traveled. He called in the target coordinates to Sylvie, hoping for all the world he wouldn't be bringing the rounds down on his own head. He told his men, "We'd best get down in the deepest ditch we can find."

The preparations at the truck were apparently complete. The crew had moved some distance to the side to avoid the backblast of a launch, dragging the cable for the trigger box with them. Within seconds, the first rocket was thrust into the night sky, the whooshing sound of its motor like water spraying from a high-pressure nozzle.

Montana expected a salvo of rockets to be launched in a matter of seconds. But there seemed to be a problem. After half a minute of tinkering with the trigger box, the second rocket was fired.

The problem with the launcher's firing system persisted. It took another minute of frantic activity to finally shoot the third rocket. In the brief flash of its motor's ignition, Montana thought he could see three more of the weapons on launch rails.

The first rounds from the American artillery at Signal Hill crashed down well to the west of both the launcher and Montana's team. The heavy thud of their impacts was heard but not seen. An adjustment of *right four hundred* was transmitted to Sylvie for relay.

While the crew continued to struggle with the launch controls, the second volley of American artillery came down, still unseen. But the roar of its explosions sounded so much closer this time. *I've got to bring it a little more to the right*, Montana decided.

The third volley of 155-millimeter rounds hit eighty seconds later. It fell closer still; the ground shook from its impact. But the explosions remained unseen.

The proximity of the artillery strikes threw the rocket crew into a panic. Convinced they were being zeroed in, they frantically returned the launcher to its traveling position, clambered on board, and drove away, backtracking in the direction from which they'd come. Montana and his men were still alongside the trail as the truck passed within thirty meters of them. The Hmong, swept up in the possibilities of the moment, began to riddle the cab as fast as their ancient, semi-automatic carbines could fire. The fusillade killed the driver, maybe others, and forced the vehicle to veer off the trail. Rolling into a gulley, it came to an inglorious halt on its side. As several survivors of the impromptu ambush stumbled from the wreck, they were dispatched at close range by Hmong rifle fire.

Montana called the artillery mission to a close. That done, he hurled two white phosphorous grenades onto the upended chassis and then led his team away from the expanding blaze with all the speed they could muster.

The titanic explosion of rocket propellant and warheads he'd expected took nearly two minutes to occur. By that time, they'd reached the back side of a hill and were safe from the blast.

At Lima Site 67, Sylvie relayed the termination of the fire mission to Signal Hill. It was only then that she decided to plot the coordinates of each volley on the map. To her horror, the second and third volley, with their huge shifts, had in all likelihood landed dangerously close to—or, perhaps, within—a Laotian hamlet. She only knew the hamlet existed because one of her operators had drawn it onto the map in the site's CP.

All these penciled-in changes are usually approximate, she told herself, *and Montana's map might not have been updated at all.*

Pardon me if I'm not optimistic. Violating Laotian territorial sovereignty to kill communists is one thing...

But killing Laotian civilians will be seen as something quite different.

This has fuckup written all over it.

*****

Fuckup: that was the same word that went through Montana's mind when his patrol stumbled upon the hamlet they'd just blown into oblivion. There was no doubt that this was where multiple 155-millimeter artillery shells had landed; the smoking craters formed a moonscape unmistakable even in the predawn darkness.

They found only dead people—twenty or so civilians; men, women, and children—among the shattered hooches. If anyone had survived the barrage, they'd already fled into the night. A few badly wounded animals wailed in pain; the Hmong put each one out of its misery.

Montana checked his map; the hamlet was indeed penciled in. But he recognized the reason for his error right away. The long trek through the mountainous forest in the dark had been more disorienting than he'd realized; *I was nearly a klick east of where I thought I was. And I didn't think I was anywhere near this damn ville.*

*****

Montana and his Hmong returned to Lima Site 67 just before 0800 hours. He didn't need to explain to Sylvie what had happened. She'd already figured it out.

He asked, "So, how do we cover our asses here?"

"We don't," she replied.

"Wait a damn minute. Are you saying you're not going to do the right thing and bullshit your way through this little mishap?"

"That's exactly right," Sylvie replied. "I'm going to report this to the ambassador and our country chief exactly as it happened. And then—"

Now irate, he interrupted, "In other words, Françoise, even after I did the mission and took out that launcher, you're hanging me out to dry."

"Nonsense," she replied. "Calm down. You didn't let me finish."

"All right...go ahead. Finish. I'm dying to hear this gem."

"Here's how it's going to work, Montana. We tell the story straight to our superiors, warts and all. Then *they* will concoct a cover-up...like they always do. You and I have nothing to worry about, since blaming us would still leave the Agency culpable. I wouldn't be surprised if by the time the dust settles on this incident, it'll be pinned on Pathet Lao guerrillas. The Laotian government will gladly accept that. It suits their agenda better than a CIA cock-up."

"But there hasn't been any Pathet Lao activity in this district the whole time we've been here. It's been all NVA and VC."

Sylvie replied, "Does that matter? They'll be writing fiction. Facts have little relevance. Now go get some sleep."

She took her own advice and retired to the privacy of her hooch. Even though it was the morning, she decided a beer would be more soothing than coffee. Settling onto her bunk with the cold brew, she thought, *There is nothing I hate more about this fucking business than collateral damage. I've seen too many of these tragedies over the years.*

She was surprised—and relieved—to find she could still cry.

Chapter Twenty

Lieutenant Dowd decided to personally lead the team that would search for Sergeant Eggers' lost patrol. After a brief moment of contemplation, 1SG Avery decided he wouldn't try to change his mind. As the team made their way outside the wire, Jif asked Avery, "Is that such a hot idea letting Dowd go out with them? That's really not his job, don't you think?"

The first sergeant replied, "What I think, sir, is that the young man needs the OJT. Nothing works better than learning by doing."

Jif still wasn't buying it. "And the sergeant whose leadership role is being stepped on? I would think he's pretty pissed that an officer is along for the ride."

"Sergeant Nye will get over it, sir," Avery replied. "Besides, who's going to teach a young lieutenant how to survive in combat better than a combat-experienced NCO? Nye is fully checked out on the process."

Despite his misgivings, Jif couldn't argue with that. He thought, *It kind of goes with what I've always been told: a green lieutenant may be technically in charge, but he's only in command when the NCO under him decides he's ready for it. But OJT in a combat situation is tricky. The men can easily get confused who they're supposed to listen to when the shit hits the fan.*

Lord knows I've had my share of NCO mentors. Without them, I probably would've been dead by now.

*****

The first thing Lieutenant Dowd had done to annoy Sergeant Nye was insist on using an entire squad to conduct the search. "We would've been much better off taking just a fire team, Lieutenant," Nye said as they paused once again for the straggling tail of the ten-man squad to catch up.

What the sergeant didn't add: *And we would've been better off even more if we hadn't taken you along, Howdy.*

The next cause of irritation: Dowd insisted the search begin at Romeo Alpha rather than the probable location of last night's mysterious firefight beyond the eastern perimeter. "That fight was a hell of a lot closer to Rubber than Romeo Alpha, Lieutenant. We may be doing a bunch of extra walking for nothing."

"Negative, Sergeant. We're going to do this search methodically, sticking as close to Eggers' suspected route as we can."

"We could be methodical as all hell in the other direction, too, LT."

Dowd pretended he didn't hear him. They were going to do it his way, and that was that.

It was nearly 0900 hours when they reached Romeo Alpha, which was deserted except for squadrons of ants and mosquitoes. Dowd was startled by a snake concealed on a low branch and reflexively blew it apart with a short burst from his M16. That prompted Nye to ask, "Did it bite you, sir? Don't look like it did."

After checking his person twice, the lieutenant replied, "No, I think I'm okay."

"Thank goodness for small favors, LT, because that little burst of yours just told the whole fucking world we're here. Next time you want to kill a snake, do it quietly, like with a knife. And if it's not bothering you, leave the fucking thing alone."

"But it was very close, Sergeant."

"Close only counts in horseshoes and hand grenades, sir. Now, since Eggers and his boys ain't here, how about we make a beeline for that firefight location? And maybe you should walk point. Show the men you've got a pair. I mean, what good is a leader who won't walk point every now and then?"

"But it's a leader's job to control his unit, Sergeant, and you can't do that effectively from the front."

"You can't effectively control a unit that doesn't think you have a hair on your ass, either, sir. Hypothetically speaking, of course."

Feeling the glare of ten pairs of eyes on him, the lieutenant succumbed to the pressure. He took up the point position and said, "All right, men, let's move out."

The squad hadn't traveled very far when Nye, who was two men behind Dowd, said, "Begging your pardon, LT, but we should be walking an azimuth of two-six-zero degrees. You're taking us too far south. We're gonna end up in Laos instead of back at the firebase."

While Nye was talking, the lieutenant, already sweating profusely, slathered his exposed skin with insect repellant for the fourth time since they'd set out on the patrol. When he was done, he took a big gulp of water, emptying one of his three canteens. Mother Nature was clearly getting the better of him.

Nye said, "With all due respect, sir, creature comforts got you by the ass. How do you expect to survive on a real patrol…one that goes out for a week or more?"

"It's just that everything seems so much worse today, Sergeant…the bugs, the heat…"

"It ain't nowhere near the hottest part of the day, Lieutenant. And as far as the insects go, well…better get used to them, because they ain't going away."

"But I can't keep the sweat out of my eyes," Dowd replied, "so I can't read the fucking compass right."

"That's why we drape a fucking towel around our neck, sir…to wipe off whatever needs drying." Turning to the next man in the column, he added, "Salcedo, you take point, amigo. The lieutenant's having a little episode here. Get going…we're already way behind schedule."

As the squad moved past them, Nye told Dowd, "Look, sir…the weather, the insects, they're all pains in the ass, for sure. But bad as they are, the fight ain't with them. It's with Luke the Gook and his AK. All the whining and crying about how hot you are, or how many leeches you picked off yourself, or how bad your jungle rot is don't mean shit when there's somebody trying to waste you. Do us all a favor and don't bitch like some fucking REMF whose beer at the club ain't cold enough or his Vietnamese maid didn't fold his laundry right. No offense or nothing, Lieutenant, but you won't last very long out here if you keep acting like this."

With PFC Salcedo leading the way, the patrol found Eggers and his men in a matter of minutes. The five bodies were sprawled in a line on low-lying ground between two shallow rises. They looked like victims of an execution.

But one of them—Spec-4 Switzer—was still alive. His leg was shattered and he'd lost a lot of blood, but he was conscious and able to speak. He told of playing dead as NVA soldiers scavenged the bodies, taking weapons, the radio, and any personal gear they could carry. After the enemy vanished into the night, he waited for minutes that seemed like an eternity before he felt safe to fashion a tourniquet with his belt. He'd thought about crawling back to the firebase—only four hundred meters away—but couldn't muster the strength. Calling out to the men on the perimeter wasn't a viable option, either. His voice was nothing but a hoarse whisper…and even at that, it might alert the NVA he was still alive.

"We've got to carry him to the firebase," Lieutenant Dowd said.

"No fucking way, sir," Nye replied, pausing his radio transmission for a moment. "I'm already bringing the dustoff to us. There's a clearing right over there she can land in."

The Huey arrived in five minutes, settling right on top of the yellow smoke grenade used to mark the emergency LZ. While they'd waited for the chopper, Switzer revealed what had happened to Eggers' patrol. His closing line: "The Sarge thought he was being real clever, trying to play games like that. He said everyone's been ducking out on these security patrols, but that's bullshit. I'm pretty sure he was the only son of a bitch doing it. He fucked us over big time. Fucked himself over, too."

After the medevac ship departed with Switzer and his dead squadmates on board, Nye said, "Well, Lieutenant, I guess we're done here. Do you want to lead us back?"

It wouldn't be much of a land navigation challenge; they could practically see the firebase in the distance. In a moment, they'd hear its roar, too, as the first fire mission of the new day commenced. But Dowd wasn't up to this most minor of challenges. He was still fighting back nausea from the encounter with Eggers' slaughtered patrol. He waved off Nye's suggestion to take point again.

*****

Back inside the wire at Fire Base Rubber, Lieutenant Dowd was still struggling to get his queasy stomach under control. At the CP/FDC, he fumbled his way through the debrief. At one point, he twisted Switzer's words about *everyone ducking out on these security patrols*, making it sound as if the dodge was endemic within the company. First Sergeant Avery promptly blew his cork. "Begging your pardon, Lieutenant," he roared, "but that's the biggest load of bullshit I've heard in a long, long time. You're putting a big black mark against every NCO in this company."

"Wait, Top...I didn't say *every* NCO is doing it."

"No, but you implied it, sir. Maybe you and Lieutenant Lawrence need to be going out on a few more patrols to see what's really going on."

Recoiling from the very thought, Dowd replied, "Oh, no, Top. We don't need to go that far."

"Damn straight we don't, Lieutenant. Let's not go making trouble where there ain't any. Whatever leadership problem we had just fixed itself. Sergeant Eggers saw to that himself, dammit. Now if you'll excuse me, sir..."

Avery turned away to join Contreras at a chart table. The two first sergeants were putting the finishing touches on how the firebase would employ the quad-50 machine gun truck. Word had already been received that it was on the road from the airfield at A Luoi and would be arriving shortly.

As operational planning and a fire mission's intense activity swirled around him, Dowd had no idea what to do with himself. He stood like an obstacle in the middle of the bunker, looking lost and understanding little, if anything, of what was going on. Taking pity on him, Jif said, "Why don't you come with me for a while? I'll check you out on perimeter defense."

"I should probably stay with the first sergeant, sir."

"You don't have to call me sir, Hank. We're both lieutenants, and there isn't any rank between the two grades. Come on...your first sergeant doesn't need you right now."

To himself, he added, *And probably won't in the foreseeable future.*

Outside the bunker, they met with Lieutenant Hammond, who kept one eye on the fire mission in progress while they talked. After filling Jif in on the battery's ammo status, the XO asked, "When is the mini-dozer supposed to show up?"

"Within the hour," Jif replied. "I told First Sergeant Contreras that its first order of business will be burying the barbequed NVA. Then it can dig the positions for the quad-fifty. Are you still okay with the mass grave site being just beyond the wrecked Chinook?"

"Yeah," Hammond replied. "Get those crispy critters as far away from us as we can. Did the first sergeants settle on how many positions they're going to make for the gun truck?"

"They sure did, and I've signed off on their plan. There'll be three...one south, one east-central, and one north by the LZ. We'll dig them in so they're kind of hull-down and then build up revetments so just the guns are sticking up."

Dowd asked, "Why three positions, Jif?" He sounded uncomfortable addressing a first lieutenant—and an actual commander—by his first name.

"So they can cover the entire perimeter without firing through howitzer positions, Hank. That would be a little nerve-rattling for my gunners. Have you ever heard a quad-fifty?"

Dowd shook his head.

"Let me tell you...it's a life-changing experience. The noise alone of four fifty-caliber machine guns will scare you half to death."

Jif had a question for Dowd. "Lieutenant Lawrence...is he still a platoon leader? Or is he now the acting XO?"

"He's still got First Platoon. It's the only one still led by an officer. The other three all have sergeants in charge."

"Nothing wrong with that," Jif said. "From what I've seen, it works pretty well most of the time."

"I'm not so sure," Dowd said. "Some of these sergeants, like Avery, like Nye...they don't hesitate to undercut me. They're downright rude most of the time. Maybe even insubordinate."

"I doubt that, Hank. Most NCOs worth their salt can tactfully chew an officer out without ever crossing the line to insubordination. Trust me on that one. You want my advice?"

"Sure. Why not?"

"You'd better listen to them," Jif continued. "They know what they're talking about. How long have you been in country, anyway?"

"Two months."

"And how long have you been outside of base camp?"

"Two weeks."

"So this is your first combat action," Jif said. "What about this guy Lawrence? How much time in country does he have?"

"About the same. I'm senior in grade to him by a couple of days."

Thank God that company has some good NCOs, Jif thought. *What's left of its officers are so green, they're fluorescent. Wilton was an asshole...but at least he'd been around the block a few times. And I kind of doubt they'll be getting any replacement officers with time under their belts until this operation is over.*

Probing cautiously, Dowd asked, "Hey, man...aren't you West Point?"

Jif tried but couldn't stifle his laugh. "Do I sound like I'm a ring-knocker? No, I'm ROTC...from Berkeley."

"BERKELEY? I thought nothing but hippies and leftist radicals went there. They had ROTC?" He pronounced it *rot-see*.

"You'd be surprised, Hank. It's true...a lot of the faculty and students are on the far left, and they make a lot of noise, but it's a very diverse environment. To be fair, though, the ROTC contingent is pretty small."

Dowd had another inquiry: "Is it true your father is a general?"

"A retired general, Hank, who's now an official at the State Department. By the way, he was a West Pointer."

"But don't you kind of become an automatic legacy if your dad went there?"

"Not exactly," Jif replied. "I had dual citizenship at the time—US and Australian—and I wasn't ready to renounce the Aussie side quite yet, so I wasn't eligible for a commission. Once it got to crunch time at Berkeley and I had to decide one way or the other, I went ahead and renounced. Pissed the hell out of my mother. But she got over it...sort of."

"So I guess you're going to be a lifer like your dad?"

"Not bloody likely, Hank."

"Ah, so you think the Army is all fucked up, too?"

"I didn't say that," Jif replied. "I do believe, though, that what it's being asked to do here is politically misguided. To the Vietnamese, our actions make us look like just another occupying imperial power who makes their lives miserable. So yeah, the Army's fucked up...but it's not FUBAR."

"FUBAR? What the hell does that mean?"

"Sorry," Jif replied. "It's a World War Two expression that my dad and his friends used all the time when I was just a kid. It was years before I realized it meant *fucked up beyond all recognition*."

Perhaps it was just his gastric distress lessening, but Dowd seemed confident to speak his mind now. He announced, "Well, I'm putting in my tour, then I'm getting the hell out of this nuthouse and going straight into law school. At the rate it's going, the Army will come crashing down of its own stupidity. And as far as I'm concerned, that's a good thing."

"No, Hank. We can't let that happen. The Army's too important…and very necessary in this world, I'm afraid."

"And you're going to be the one to save it, Jif?" He tried to make it sound like a lighthearted rib, but the snark was unmistakable. It made Jif bristle.

"I may be just a li'l ol' first lieutenant, Dowd, but I'm one who knows a bloody hell of a lot more about this Army and Vietnam than you do. I just hope you learn enough to survive your tour…and don't get any more of your men killed along the way."

"Hey, I'm not responsible for the patrol that got wasted."

"You're the company commander now, mate. You're responsible for everything that happens with your unit. Better start writing those condolence letters to your KIA's next of kin."

"I have to do that?"

"Damn right you do," Jif replied.

The air began to shudder with the sound of a Skycrane approaching the LZ, a minidozer slung beneath her. "She's clear to come on in out of the west," Hammond said, a phone to his ear.

Dowd asked, "We're going to keep that baby, right?"

"Get real, dude," Jif replied. "That dozer will be done with our little job in about two hours. Then that Crane will be back to take it someplace else."

The giant helicopter set the bulldozer down at the edge of the LZ and flew away. Right behind her was a Huey transporting the engineers who would crew the machine and their support equipment. The chopper was on the ground all of fifteen seconds.

The dozer was free of its slings and cranked up in just a few minutes. Under 1SG Contreras' guidance, it rumbled across the firebase to the site of the wrecked Chinook, where it was to dig the communal grave for the NVA dead. Jif recognized the driver right away: Sergeant Joseph Ka'anā'anā, aka Joey Aloha, from the engineer detachment on Signal Hill.

Contreras, standing on the deck behind the driver's seat, called out, "He followed me home, LT. Can I keep him?"

The machine came to a stop, allowing Jif to lean in and shake Aloha's hand. "Good to have you here, Sergeant," he said. "I'm a little surprised to see you, though. I figured you'd stay busy up on Signal Hill."

"Me and my boys haven't been up there in a couple days, sir. They shipped us down into the valley to work on the airstrip at A Luoi. Just as well…there's weird shit going on up there."

Jif asked, "What do you mean?"

"A bunch of civilians are walking around like they own the place. They gave us some horseshit story about being *government employees working with the Army*, but they gotta be CIA, right?"

"That would be my guess, Sergeant."

"The rumor is they're shooting fire missions into Laos, but nobody's talking about it."

"We've been thinking the same thing here," Jif said. "Those rounds going way over our heads have got to be coming down across the border."

"Hope they do some good, sir," Aloha said. "Let me get started on these holes you want dug. Won't take long." As he dropped the dozer into gear, he added, "It's good to be working with you guys again, LT."

*****

Interring the charred remains of the NVA attackers took all of twenty minutes. Joey Aloha then began carving out the first of three pits for the quad-50. Contreras told Jif, "Joey will give us a nice, shallow ramp into each pit so the deuce can get in and out easily. He's going to use the displaced dirt to put a three-sided berm around each one, too, so the truck will be protected right up to the bed. That'll stop us from having to fill a couple hundred sandbags."

"Outstanding, Top. Do you have the range cards for each pit done yet?"

"Just about, sir. We're putting the finishing touches on them right now."

"What about the no-fire areas? How'd they work out?"

"The only sectors we've got to be careful with are the northeast and southeast. To the southeast, rounds from the quad could easily hit friendlies. They're only about two klicks from here. Even bouncers could be dangerous to our guys down that way. And to the northeast, we've got that Yard village. Of course, we haven't had any enemy activity from that direction, not since the One-Oh-First cleared the gooks out. I'll make sure the quad crew safety-stakes the no-fire zones at each pit."

"Outstanding, Top. Make it happen."

"There's one more thing that's come up, sir," Contreras said with a hint of reluctance. "Avery wants to suspend night patrolling to the southeast. That includes Romeo Bravo."

"Negative, Top. *Negative*. The patrols will continue. LPs alone aren't going to be enough. That's where most of our troubles have come from. And you just told me the quad's field of fire is restricted there, so why do they want to ignore it?"

"After what happened last night, his boys are going to bitch up a storm about going out there after dark. They're calling it Ambush City."

"Come on, Top. Everybody knows what happened out there, and it was the squad leader's own bloody fault. Those patrols are still necessary. Last night's suspension was a one-off. We're going to keep running them."

"You want me to tell Avery, sir?"

"No. I'll do it myself."

Chapter Twenty-One

First Sergeant Avery took Jif's refusal of his request to suspend patrolling around Romeo Bravo stoically. His reply: "As you wish, sir."

"You're not fighting me very hard on this, Top," Jif said. "I was expecting some pushback. But you do see my point, don't you? It would be like leaving the door wide open for our Asian friends."

"Of course I see it, Lieutenant…and I'm not upset at all. I'm glad you made that decision."

The sly smile that followed those words proved the suspicion Jif was harboring. "All right, I bloody get it, First Sergeant. You want me to be the bad guy here and do your dirty work for you. When you give the order to go out and patrol in Ambush City and your men start bitching, you can blame the whole thing on me."

"That doesn't make me a bad person, sir, just a practical one. Whatever gets the job done, I always say."

"Speaking of getting the job done," Jif said, "can you guarantee that your men won't sandbag any future patrols around Romeo Bravo? It's not like it hasn't happened before."

"Now you're hurting my feelings, Lieutenant. I made sure that problem is never gonna happen again."

"You don't look hurt in the least, Top, but I believe it when you say the problem is fixed. I don't think either of us wants to deal with gooks in the wire again. The quad-fifty should be a big help on that score, but like the rest of us, its crew can't see in the dark. We still need early warning that an attack is coming. Only patrolling coupled with LPs can provide it."

"You're preaching to the choir, sir."

"Well, then...amen and hallelujah," Jif replied.

*****

The quad-50 deuce, the name *Hell To The Fourth Power* painted on its side, drove onto Fire Base Rubber just past 1200 hours. Its six-man crew was led by a staff sergeant named King. First Sergeant Contreras directed the vehicle to the east-central firing pit, the first one Joey Aloha and his dozer had dug.

As they drove, Contreras asked King, "How was the flight into A Luoi?"

"That Herc really bumped around coming over the mountains, Top. And the airfield's a real clusterfuck, being just opened up and all. They tried to snag us for base defense until some transportation officer finally looked at our orders. I'm glad to be away from that zoo."

They met Jif at the firing pit. Looking over the position, with its dirt berm that shielded the truck's chassis from the bed down, King was quite pleased. "Looks like you've got everything protected up to the gun mount and the cab, and they've got their own armor plate, anyway. We should be real happy here."

"Glad you like it, Sergeant," Jif said, "but don't get too bloody comfortable. There are two other positions just like it, and you'll be using all three."

King wasn't thrilled to hear it. "Why the hell is that, sir? You say your biggest threat vectors are from the south and east. We can cover that whole area from here without moving her an inch. And your antenna farm is behind us, so we won't shoot it down accidentally."

Jif replied, "It's for your own good, Sergeant. And ours, too. As they probably told you, we get hit a lot here…RPGs, mortars, big rockets…and we have to assume the gooks watch us during the day and know the layout of the place pretty well. With the dedicated threat your quad presents to them, the gooks are going to make it a target of the highest priority, so we don't want them to be certain where it is each night on the firebase. As soon as darkness falls, you'll reposition your vehicle to one of the other pits. If an attack comes that you can't fully counter from the pit you happen to be in, you'll move again."

"But what about your howitzers, Lieutenant? They're a threat to the gooks, too, with their beehive and shit. But you don't move them every night, do you?"

"Not that I wouldn't like to, Sergeant, but that's just not practical…or even possible. You, on the other hand, have a high degree of mobility on your side."

"That's a lot of potential driving around in the dark, all blacked out, while the shit's hitting the fan, Lieutenant. I'd hate to be running over any of your guys accidentally."

"I reckon my guys will be able to hear your deuce coming a mile away, Sergeant. Sure, we've all got artillery ears, but we're not bloody deaf."

"But what about accidentally ripping up the battery's telephone wiring?"

"Stick to the marked paths through the battery we made for you and you'll be fine. The wire's buried where it crosses them."

*****

Joey Aloha and his engineers were finished with their tasks at the firebase. He asked Jif and Contreras, "Are you sure there's nothing else we can do for you while we're here? The choppers coming to get us are held up for some bullshit reason. Their ETA's not for another hour."

"I can think of something," the first sergeant replied. "The ammo delivery choppers are inbound in a couple minutes. How about using the dozer to drag the pallets to each gun section? That way, the gun-bunnies can take what they need without having to hump it halfway across the firebase. It'll save us a bunch of time and effort."

"Be glad to, First Sergeant. I can hear those shithooks coming now."

"Sergeant McKay will tell you what goes where," Contreras said as he and Aloha left the CP/FDC.

At the situation map, Avery told Jif, "I've been looking at Brigade's latest movements to the south, sir. Once the lead battalion gets down near A Sap, your guns ain't gonna be no help to them. That's over twelve klicks from here...a little beyond your max range. Do you figure your battery's gonna be moving closer to them?"

"I don't reckon Divarty's decided who's going where yet, Top. And I've been hearing that no maneuver unit will reach A Sap for at least another week. Have you heard anything different?"

"Same-same, Lieutenant. But you know we never hear anything until the last minute, anyway. I don't believe we're at that minute yet."

Lieutenant Dowd, who'd been sitting in a corner working on some papers, asked Jif, "Do you have a minute to look at this?"

"Sure. What is it?"

Dowd motioned toward the entryway. "Maybe in private?"

He didn't realize how timely that request was. No sooner had he said it than a fire mission came down over the radio. The bunker started buzzing with FDC personnel shouting target information and firing data. The two lieutenants made their exit.

It wasn't any quieter outside, though. Supply helicopters fluttered overhead, queuing for the LZ. Trundling across the firebase, the quad-50 truck moved to another of its positions to set up azimuth markers and safety stakes. The bulldozer chugged by, dragging an ammo pallet. To cap it all off was the *POOM* of the base piece firing its first of several adjustment rounds.

But I reckon he doesn't want Avery in on this conversation for some reason, Jif thought, *so we'll have it out here.*

Dowd seemed surprised Jif was willing to help him while so much artillery business was going on. He asked, "Don't they need you?"

"No, Hank. The XO is in charge of the guns. With him and the chief of smoke watching over things, the firing battery takes care of itself. They don't need me at all."

"So what's the BC's job, then?"

"My job is to make sure they've got what's necessary to do theirs."

"You do mostly admin stuff, then?"

"Bingo. I'm their mother, father, lawyer, and priest all rolled into one. Plus, I have to make a command tactical decision every couple of minutes just to keep things interesting."

"Tactical...like the one to move the quad-fifty truck around?"

"Exactly," Jif replied. "And decisions like that will have to be made every couple of seconds when the outfit is moving to a new location. Fortunately, Charlie is an experienced battery that knows the drill, so tactical movements aren't too bad, just the usual chaos."

"Roger that. But getting back to admin tasks, I'm trying to draft a letter of condolence to the next of kin, and I'm kind of stuck. I've heard there's a recommended format for these things, but I've never seen it."

"Neither have I," Jif said, "but I'm told it's just more standard issue toilet paper. Let me have a look at what you've got so far."

He read it, poker-faced. When he was done, he said, "This needs a little work, Hank. In fact, it needs a lot of work."

"Okay, what do I need to change?"

"For starters, get rid of words like *hero* and *heroism*. They're never going to see their loved one alive again, and building him up like some Hollywood warrior is not comforting in the least. In fact, the next of kin would give anything for their son or husband *not* to have been a hero. Then he'd still be alive. Don't add to their grief, just try to share it with them. Leave the heroism bullshit to the guys who write the citations for medals."

As Dowd jotted down some notes, Jif added, "Something else to consider...there's a chance each next of kin will also receive a letter from their KIA, which he'd have written in advance and given to some other dude to mail if he bought the farm. It'll be a voice from the grave, probably full of how much he loved them, how much he missed home, how scared he was...things like that. Build on those sentiments and, like I said, share their grief honestly. Just try not to make it sound like bureaucratic boilerplate."

"Did you write an *if I die* letter, Jif?"

"Nope. My family already knows the score. How about you? Did you write one?"

Dowd hedged, but finally replied, "Thinking about it."

The fire mission was over in just a few minutes. Back inside the CP bunker, the men of the FDC section were taking a break, enjoying some fresh coffee one of the cooks had brought them.

Spec-5 Signorelli took advantage of the lull to ask Jif, "How long do you figure it'll be before we hear if Battalion's approved my promotion, LT?"

"I'm not sure, Frank. But the fact that they've waived the interview board is a real good sign. That should hurry things along."

"Why don't they promote you to captain while they're at it?"

"Not enough time in grade," Jif replied. "Got to have two years' service. I won't have that until April of Sixty-Nine...another eleven months."

"That sucks, LT. A guy doing the job should be wearing the rank. But I've got another question if you've got the time."

"Fire away, Frank."

"I heard a rumor you wanted to bring in someone from outside the battery for my old slot once I get promoted."

"That's not my preference, but we may have no choice in the matter once you move up a grade. The FDC computer is a spec-five slot. Neither of your two spec-fours are eligible for promotion yet. If there's a man already in grade in the personnel pipeline, he'll get the job."

"But the time in grade thing's not set in stone for enlisted men, LT. My guys could still be promoted into the job."

"I know that, Frank. But like I said, it may be out of our hands. For the sake of discussion, though, which of your spec-fours would you put up for promotion, knowing that the one you don't endorse will probably be pissed off for a long time?"

Signorelli started to disagree but changed his mind. "I hadn't looked at it like that," he said.

"Then let me put it this way. If it comes down to me to decide which of your guys to promote, I'm going to need your preference as to who it should be."

"Can I think about it, LT?"

"By all means, Frank."

Dowd had overheard the entire conversation. As Jif settled onto a stool with a cup of coffee, he asked him, "I guess that was an example of the admin a commander deals with on a regular basis?"

"Bloody right, Lieutenant."

"So what were you…his mother, father, lawyer, or priest?"

"None of the above. More of a Dutch uncle, I reckon."

*****

A Chinook occupied the LZ, offloading an assortment of supplies. Another orbited overhead, waiting its turn to land and unload. The CP staff found itself playing air traffic controller as yet another ship—a LOACH—demanded to land, as well.

"We told him to wait his damn turn," 1SG Avery said, "but he says he's landing one way or another."

Jif asked, "Is he having a mechanical? Or is there some big brass on board?"

"I asked both questions, sir, but he didn't give me any answers. Sounds pretty arrogant...a real hot stick. Or maybe he's just an asshole."

A further transmission denied landing rights on the firebase itself rather than the LZ. It went unheeded. The unwelcome LOACH set down right next to the CP/FDC bunker, blowing dust and debris in all directions. The chopper didn't shut down.

Jif and Avery ran out of the bunker to confront the flight crew. While another pilot remained in the right-hand seat, a major in flight suit, flying helmet, and reflective aviator sunglasses exited the left-hand seat and stormed toward them, bellowing, "WHO'S THE HONCHO OF THIS FUCKING CIRCUS?"

"I am, sir," Jif replied. "The name's Miles. Do you have a problem with your ship? Otherwise, you're really in the way."

The major recoiled in surprise when he heard the Aussie accent. "Yeah, I've got a problem, Lieutenant Wherever The Fuck You Come From. I'm the aviation company commander, First Brigade, and you've stolen two fifty-caliber machine guns from one of my aircraft."

The major hadn't bothered to introduce himself, but his name strip was plainly visible on the flight suit: Dempsey. The two machine guns in question had to be the ones from the crashed Chinook. They'd been deployed on the firebase perimeter ever since being salvaged from the wreck.

"I want those sons of bitches back right fucking now," Dempsey added.

"With all due respect, sir, you need to remove your aircraft from the firebase immediately. You're impeding our mission."

"It doesn't look like I'm impeding much of anything," the major said, his arm tracing a panoramic sweep of the idle gun sections. "Just give me my MGs and I'll be on my way, Miles…unless you're bucking to be brought up on charges for theft of government property."

Jif and Avery had to laugh. In their experience, they'd heard empty threats and they'd heard bullshit. Dempsey's pronouncement qualified as both.

Avery spoke up, saying, "Actually, Major, that Chinook of yours was declared a combat loss. That includes every damn piece of equipment on it, as you well know. You can't be court-martialed for stealing things that no longer exist."

"Look here, Sergeant—"

"That's *first sergeant*, sir."

"First, last, I don't give a flying fuck. I want those guns and I want them now. And I'll have both your insubordinate asses in—"

His words were interrupted by a horrific collage of sound, like the momentary snarl of a chainsaw followed by the squeals of damaged machinery. They were immediately pelted with droplets of blood and a pink substance they'd come to realize was brain tissue.

A soldier crossing the firebase had walked into the whirling tail rotor of the LOACH. His body was lying beneath the tail boom, the top of his head sheared off.

The damaged tail rotor, now dangerously out of balance, was shaking the whole helicopter. The pilot still on board promptly shut the shuddering ship down.

Dempsey, his mouth agape like a fish on the hook, was trembling as badly as his aircraft. But that didn't stop him from hurling invective in a terrified voice pitched well above normal. "Don't you train your troops how to behave around aircraft? The blame is on you people, not me."

Neither Jif, Avery, nor the others who'd streamed from the CP/FDC cared at the moment who'd be blamed. They all raced to the man lying below the tail boom, not wanting to believe he was dead but quickly resigning themselves to the obvious.

"He's one of mine," Avery said. "His name's Hurst." Since his helmet and dog tags were missing, the first sergeant had had to remove the dead man's belt and read the name stenciled on the inner side to make the identification. "Dammit...we drum into their heads how to walk around a Huey so they don't get nailed by the tail rotor, but the grunts are never told that a LOACH can bite them just the same. Must be because only officers ride around on LOACHes, right? Nobody else needs to know shit about the little fuckers."

They'd never know what possessed PFC Hurst to walk so close behind the tail boom. But in all likelihood, he'd never seen the tail rotor, which was nearly invisible when at normal operating speed. To further complicate things, when approaching the ship from the right side, a stabilizer fin partially obstructed half of the tail rotor's arc. The whirling blades were as unforgiving as a guillotine.

Fixing Dempsey in an angry gaze, Avery said, "This wouldn't have happened at all if this flying piece of crap wasn't sitting where it didn't belong. And it sure as hell didn't get here by itself."

Signorelli stuck his head from the bunker and shouted, "FDC dudes, get your asses back in here. We've got a fire mission coming in."

Jif asked, "What's the direction?"

"It ain't good, LT," the FDC chief replied. "Number Six could be shooting right through that fucking LOACH. Better check the boresight picture...see if it's got enough clearance."

Dempsey was still spewing denials. "You aren't going to pin this fuckup on me, I can promise you that." Then, talking to himself, he mumbled, "Fucking dumbass grunts don't even have the sense to look where they're walking."

Once the firing data was set on the guns, the battery fired, with the exception of Number Six, whose muzzle was pointed right at the LOACH. The section chief got down on his knees and looked up the still-unloaded tube through the open breech. He told the assistant gunner, "Bring her down, Jimmy, real slow."

The AG had barely cranked a quarter-turn on the handwheel when the chief said, "Stop. How many mils?"

"Thirty-three, Sarge."

Thirty-three mils: one and a half degrees until the top of the rotor head aligned with the tube at a distance of only fifteen meters. The section chief looked to the assembled brain trust of Jif, Contreras, and McKay. He didn't have to say a word; the expression on his face could only mean *What do we do now, boss?*

"No way that piece shoots, sir," McKay said.

Contreras chipped in, "I second that, Lieutenant."

Jif knew they were right. But they'd been down one tube the whole time they'd been at Rubber. That was enough of a compromise. Being down two could seriously weaken the battery's effectiveness.

"Number Six doesn't shoot," Jif announced. "Smoke, all other guns will double up their rounds." Instead of four rounds to a volley, there'd be eight, the last four impacting a few seconds behind the first.

"Copy that, sir," McKay replied.

Looking to Dempsey, Jif added, "Like I said before, Major, you're really in the way, and you're impeding our mission."

At that moment, the next volley roared from the other tubes like a bold-type exclamation point at the end of his sentence.

*****

A team of helicopter mechanics was dropped in by Huey an hour later. That same ship spirited a still-babbling Major Dempsey and his co-pilot away. In a cold but fitting rebuke, PFC Hurst's bagged body accompanied them on board. It took less than thirty minutes for the mechanics to rig the LOACH with lifting slings. An hour before sunset, a Chinook picked it up and flew away.

Chief of Smoke McKay asked, "You think that major's going to get his ass in a sling? I mean, his actions were flat out dangerous and contributed to a man's death. Could've been even worse. We could've had shrapnel from that tail rotor flying all over the place, hurting even more people."

"I doubt he'll get anything other than a verbal reprimand," Jif said. "The aviation boys will protect their own. They'll probably write the whole thing off as just another tragic aircraft accident for which the pilots weren't responsible."

"Yeah, but something else will come out of it, too, I'll bet," Avery added, "and it'll be aimed at us. I can smell it coming. Division will decide the blame falls on First Brigade's inadequate training of ground troops for helicopter operations, so we can expect to see mandatory instruction real soon on how to approach *all types* of aircraft, not just Hueys."

"I'll tell you one thing," Jif said. "They're getting those bloody fifty cals from that Chinook back over my dead body. Like Top Avery said, they don't even exist anymore."

*****

It was strangely quiet as the sun set. There hadn't been a fire mission for over an hour, and supply deliveries by helicopter were over for the day. Jif told Sergeant King, "You'll move your quad-fifty truck to the southern position in three-zero minutes."

"Copy that, sir." King had lost the combativeness he'd shown earlier. The handling of the LOACH incident had instilled in him a grudging respect for the leaders of the firebase. Put simply, *They know their shit...and they don't take any from higher-ups. I've got to respect that.*

Just after 2200 hours, a security patrol near Romeo Bravo came on the air to report, "We're watching *boo-coo* gooks out here...a company, maybe more, dancing in the moonlight. They're just south of Route Five-Four-Eight and following the road northwest." The coordinates he estimated for the enemy force put them squarely in the quad-50's no-fire zone.

Plotting the unfolding situation on the CP's map, Avery said, "If the gooks keep moving in the same direction, they'll be out of the red zone in a couple minutes and fair game for the quad. What do you want me to tell my patrol, Lieutenant? Keep tracking the gooks or get their asses clear?"

Dowd thought the first sergeant was addressing him. But he quickly realized he wasn't the lieutenant being asked.

Jif—the man the question was meant for—kept tapping a finger on the map at Romeo Bravo. Avery knew what that meant: *He's wondering if my guys are really there...or are they playing games again?*

"Tell them to keep tracking, Top, and get your mortars ready to shoot illum between Romeo Bravo and Romeo Charlie."

That wasn't what Avery wanted to hear. "Ain't that putting my men at risk, sir? They already did their recon job."

"They're not done with that job quite yet, Top."

Chapter Twenty-Two

Avery's prediction came true. Within minutes, the recon patrol reported that the enemy was now beyond the boundary of the no-fire zone and five hundred meters from the firebase's southern perimeter.

"They've stopped," the patrol leader, Sergeant Coleman, reported. "Can't read their minds, but it looks like they're forming up to make a move on the firebase."

Avery asked, "Can you tell if they're carrying any heavy weapons?"

"I can't see well enough for that. All I can make out is lots of little stick figures moving around...but they don't seem to be humping very much."

At the same time, the two LPs beyond the southern perimeter said there was no indication of enemy soldiers approaching. That could be significant; only riflemen, sappers, and light machine gunners could be stealthy in the bush. Heavy-weapons teams tended to sound like a herd of elephants. It was difficult to tread lightly when carrying great weight.

"I reckon the biggest things they've got are RPGs," Jif said, "so they're going to have to get closer before they try to launch them."

Avery asked, "Are my boys done *now*, Lieutenant?" It was not really a question but more a respectful insistence.

"Yeah," Jif replied. "Pull them back to Romeo Bravo. Pull the men on the southern LPs back inside the wire, too."

"How about we hold off on the illum rounds until we know all of them are clear?"

"Affirmative, Top," Jif replied.

First Sergeant Contreras added, "We've got killer juniors ready to load on Guns One, Four, and Six, set for minimum range. Beehive rounds are on standby, as well."

Sergeant Coleman's voice was back on the radio, sounding considerably less calm than it had just a few moments ago. "Things are getting a little fucked up here. I don't know if I'm clear of your fields of fire."

Avery replied, "Your escape azimuth is due east. Did you forget that already?"

"Negative, negative. I didn't forget…but I've lost orientation on the firebase. Can you help me out here?"

"Dammit," Jif said, "why do I suspect he was never at Romeo Bravo? The fact that the LPs can't hear a bloody thing doesn't add up. If those gooks are where the patrol says they are, at least one of the LPs should've heard something. Now Coleman's panicking because he has no bloody idea where he is. His patrol could be anywhere along a two-klick stretch of Five-Four-Eight. They could be walking *into* our field of fire now, not out of it."

"I hear you, Lieutenant," Avery said, "but let's help Coleman out before the gooks kill him…or we do. We can try to make sense of it later."

"Copy that, Top. I'm on your side here. Can anybody think of a good reason not to shoot him a star cluster so he can get oriented on the firebase again?"

Contreras replied, "Other than the fact that we might tip off the gooks we're on to them?"

"That might not be such a bad thing," Avery said. "They'll know they lost the element of surprise. Might make them a tad jumpy."

Lieutenant Dowd was already rummaging through the box of signal flares. He asked, "What color should I shoot?"

Jif held up his hand in a *wait* gesture, and then asked Contreras, "Are we still out of white clusters, Top?"

"Affirmative, sir. Resupply didn't show up yet."

"Then make it red," Jif told Dowd. Turning to Avery, he continued, "Top, tell Coleman the cluster is coming, and then assure the rest of the firebase that, at this particular moment, it doesn't mean there are gooks in the wire."

As those alerts went out, Dowd stepped outside the bunker, flare gun in hand.

"All clear, Lieutenant," Avery said. "Shoot that son of a bitch...then everybody better hold on to their asses. No telling how Luke the Gook's gonna react. Lord knows what direction he'll come from."

Dowd pointed the flare pistol straight up and pulled the trigger. But the star cluster that burst in the sky above the firebase wasn't red. It was green, the signal that beehive was about to be fired.

Cries of WHAT THE FUCK, OVER? rang from every radio, telephone, and mouth in the CP/FDC. But no one was more frightened by the signal than Sergeant Coleman, who shrieked into his handset, "YOU'RE NOT GONNA FIRE BEEHIVE AT US, ARE YOU?"

While Jif and Contreras calmed their battery personnel, some of whom were already ramming beehive rounds into the breech, Avery told Coleman,

"Negative, negative. We are not firing beehive. Hurry up and shoot your azimuth before the sumbitch dies out."

With unsteady hands, Coleman shot the azimuth to the star cluster. To his great relief and Avery's, too, he was safely in the quad-50's no-fire zone and in the vicinity of Romeo Bravo. Of course, there weren't any no-fire zones for beehive or killer junior, but Avery assured him those rounds weren't coming, either. At least not yet.

There was more good news: the LP teams were back inside the wire. "They must've set a new record for the hundred-meter dash," Avery mumbled.

After telling the quad-50 to engage, Jif was about to tear into Dowd for confusing the red and green star clusters, but he never got the chance. The ground beyond the southern perimeter was suddenly illuminated by a harsh white light...

And in that light was a startled assault line of NVA soldiers creeping toward the wire. They were still about a hundred meters out. Some of them had already gone to ground when the quad opened up, but it didn't save them. There was little in the way of cover or concealment in that area beyond the wire. The intense volume of .50-caliber bullets decimated the prone as well as the upright.

The source of the illumination—an NVA flare—hadn't gone very high in the air and was still burning when it returned to earth. The brilliant light at ground level caused each enemy soldier to cast a long shadow that seemed like an accusing finger pointing straight at him. The slaughter didn't stop; the large-caliber rounds chewed up flesh and dirt without mercy.

The attacking NVA managed to launch only one RPG. It impacted against the wall of Gun Three's sandbagged pit in the center of the firebase, wounding two cannoneers.

An NVA satchel charge was hurled into the wire. The man throwing it died in a hail of bullets before the charge even exploded. After it blew, the two sappers who tried to slip through the torn wire were riddled and became entangled corpses instead.

The engagement was over in twenty seconds.

Contreras asked, "What the fuck was that all about? Did the gooks actually light themselves up?"

"Must have," Avery replied. "We didn't fire that damn flare." Then he added, "Maybe they got a raw lieutenant who shoots the wrong shit, too."

There was no time to unravel the mysteries they'd just experienced. Another artillery fire mission request was spilling from the speakers, its target four kilometers to the southwest.

"Looks like it's going to be another night of assholes and elbows after all," Signorelli said as his FDC began the computations for the mission.

*****

The two wounded cannoneers didn't require medevac. They were patched up and returned to duty. That was fine with them, as they had no interest in a night ride on a helicopter with invisible walls of mountains all around. The doc's last words before cutting them loose: "Take two aspirin and call me in the morning, dudes."

Jif finally got the chance to give Dowd a righteous ass-chewing for his mistake, as would be standard military practice. But he let the opportunity pass; the green lieutenant was obviously mortified over the blunder. His only attempt at a defense: "Look, it was dark where we keep that box of flares, I knew we were in a hurry, and I really wanted to do something to help. I guess I couldn't read the markings on the canisters too well. Maybe all I saw was an *R* and an *E* and thought I had the right one."

"Yeah, but you had to walk through the rest of the bunker, which is lit up like Times Square on New Year's Eve, to get outside. You should've seen the problem then."

"I know. I really fucked up."

"That's true, Hank. You did. At least the whole bloody thing didn't go south...this time. But I hope you realize they're already calling you by a new nickname."

"Already? You mean they're not going to call me Howdy Doody anymore?"

"Nope. From now on, you're Captain Colorblind."

*****

After their debacle at the perimeter wire, the surviving NVA melted away into the night. Once at their rally point near the destroyed village of Ta Bat, a klick southwest of the firebase, the headcount revealed they'd lost over forty men, nearly half their original number.

One of the survivors was the company commander. Another was the platoon leader responsible for the colossal mistake. Like Dowd, he'd simply selected the wrong flare in the dark. It had been the first time he'd used this type of Chinese device and had trouble deciphering its markings while under pressure. To compound the mistake, he'd armed it incorrectly, so it didn't travel anywhere near its optimum height.

Unlike Dowd, however, he didn't get a sympathetic verbal reprimand or a chance to explain himself. The company commander said nothing, just drew his pistol and shot the platoon leader in the head.

*****

Lather, rinse, repeat.

That's what Jif mumbled to himself as he took his turn in the outdoor shower the next morning. That common expression found on shampoo bottles reminded him of the unrelenting routine of the past week: *fire missions all day and night; resupply choppers showing up several times a day; sleep in dribs and drabs. Tomorrow, do it all over again. Lather, rinse, repeat.*

The only thing missing was a repetition of the large-scale NVA attack of three nights ago. There hadn't been so much as a probe of the perimeter wire or incoming rounds of any sort since then, either. Even the day and night patrols outside the wire hadn't found any fresh evidence of enemy activity.

At least we got Joey Aloha and his bulldozer back for an hour yesterday to bury the remains of the gooks chewed up by the quad-fifty. Nobody was looking forward to digging a burial pit by hand, and Division put out the word to stop the burning of enemy bodies. Turns out we were offending the sensibilities of Catholic ARVN units, who don't believe in cremation. I don't see why they care...I don't think communist troopers go to church anymore, Catholic or otherwise. It seems the only things that don't offend the South Vietnamese these days is stuffing money in their pockets or dying for them.

Maybe those Christians need something to be angry about when they're not in a gang fight with the Buddhist ARVN battalions, and one outrage is as good as another. They certainly don't vent much of that anger on the enemy.

By 1000 hours, the first of the day's resupply choppers was dumping her sling load of ammo onto the firebase, late as usual. Then she drifted to the LZ to unload her internal cargo and six passengers, men of the battery returning from their twenty-four-hour leave at Camp Evans. They were in fine spirits. It was amazing what the meager comforts of base camp, even for one day, could do for a man's morale.

First Sergeant Contreras was the last man off the Chinook. He looked refreshed, like he'd just returned from R&R. Even his jungle boots were clean. Jif asked him, "What was the cargo...the perishables we should've gotten yesterday?"

"Some of it," Contreras replied. "Let's hope the stuff's still edible. You know the drill...the ammo gets priority. Everything else is backed up, waiting for a chopper to lift it."

"What else is new?" Jif replied. He was tired of the lagging supply train and the constant improvisations required to deal with it. *But at least we're still eating prepared meals fairly regularly, thanks to our ingenious mess steward*, he told himself. *I hear the maneuver units pushing south aren't that lucky. They're begging just to get C rations.*

"Any calamities while I was gone, LT?"

"Nope. Same-same, Top. It's almost like the NVA forgot we're here."

"The hot rumor floating around the REMFs at Evans is that the NVA have all gone over the border to Laos."

"Not bloody likely, Top. If that rumor's true, we're expending a shitload of ammunition shooting at nothing. I'm sure there are still plenty of bad guys in spitting distance of us."

"You know, sir, you really need to take a day off and ride the bird to Evans. Don't pass off your turn to somebody else like you did yesterday. By the way, the Divarty XO mentioned that some general wants to pin a Silver Star on you."

"I reckon he's going to have to come out here to do it, Top. I'd rather not go in. You know how it works…when the brass see an officer enjoying himself at base camp, they decide to volunteer him for some shit duty. In the boonies, you're out of sight, out of mind. Besides, I'm eating fairly regularly here, I get to shower every now and then, and you brought me clean clothes. Where are they, by the way? It's a shame I had to put these filthy rags back on this immaculately clean body."

"Pitrowski's got them. He's bringing them to the CP, along with a few duffels full of assorted goodies for the battery. I even got you some Hershey's with almonds."

"You're my bloody hero. Any word whether we're moving or not?"

"Nothing I could pick up on, sir. But I noticed that old sergeant major buddy of yours from MACV was there with a couple of colonels. Looks like they had the hatchets out. The division staff didn't seem terribly thrilled to have them around."

"Can't say I blame them, Top. Sergeant Major Moon is General Abrams' number one troubleshooter. He can smell a problem in an outfit quicker than a mouse can find cheese. And from what I can tell, the general takes his word as gospel. They've got that bond of trust that goes all the way back to World War Two."

"So you think there's trouble brewing at Division Headquarters?"

"Those teams from MACV don't stop by just to say hello, Top."

*****

As Jif surmised, the team from MACV wasn't interested in just saying hello. The progress—and hopefully, the final act—of Operation Delaware were the topics of discussion. Colonel O'Dell, the team leader, raised the high headquarters' major concerns in a meeting with 1st Cav's commander, Major General Alworth. "Although your forces occupy three-quarters of the targeted length of Route Five-Four-Eight, sir, the NVA is still able to challenge your movements, often in surprising force. The point of Delaware is to clear the enemy from the A Shau, cut if off as an avenue of infiltration, and allow its control to be passed to the ARVN. General Abrams feels certain that the continued persistence of the NVA indicates that they still have a base camp in the valley. The volume of their attacks would not be possible for units commuting to and from Laos. Your operation is halfway through its projected one-month timetable, and there is still no evidence that a base camp has been located, let alone destroyed."

Alworth was irritated by the suggestion of failure. He replied, "I discussed all of this with Eye Corps Command and General Abrams two days ago, Colonel. At that time, I stressed the two big difficulties I'm encountering. First, we lack all-weather, day and night operational capability for the airfield at A Luoi. Without the electronics to provide that capability, the limited sorties of fixed-wing cargo aircraft can barely fly in enough supplies to wrap up this operation. Second, my helicopter assets that distribute those supplies along the valley have been stretched to the breaking point. If I push them any harder, their attrition rate will skyrocket well above what it is already. Once that happens, my troops can't get the beans and bullets they need to keep fighting."

Sergeant Major Sean Moon, who rounded out the MACV team along with an aviator lieutenant colonel named Gradinsky, had to bite his tongue. What he wanted to say: *Your helicopter assets fell behind the eight ball from the get-go, when your logistics staff failed to catch an insufficient requisition of aviation fuel by Divarty. You've been playing catch-up ever since.*

But it wasn't his place to interject reality into the general's excuse-making and blame deflection. That job belonged to Colonel O'Dell, who replied, "The planned logistics for Delaware were not contingent on round-the-clock capability of the Air Force's transports, sir. The boys in blue made it quite clear back in the operation's planning phase that all-weather, day and night capability was not something they could create overnight. Now that they've begun flying into A Luoi, we've found even more operational issues than were originally envisioned, such as morning fog that persists well beyond the forecast and approach paths that have to be varied constantly due to artillery fire, friendly or otherwise. As a result, the operations you're requesting are neither safe nor feasible at this time…unless we're willing to decorate the mountains around the A Shau with a significant number of crashed cargo aircraft. MACV is certain the solution to your problem lies elsewhere." Turning to Sean Moon, he added, "The sergeant major should take it from here, sir."

Alworth seemed surprised—and miffed—that an NCO would have anything at all to say in this meeting. The general grumbled, "You have something to add, Moon?" He spoke the name dismissively, as if addressing a common private. Both colonels flinched when he did so.

Sergeant majors, the most senior of NCOs, were never addressed with anything other than their full rank, spoken with the utmost respect. But Sean shrugged off the insult. "Yes, sir," he replied. "Would I be right in assuming that it's more efficient to distribute supplies by truck from the airfield at A Luoi?"

Alworth rolled his eyes as if Sean's question was irrelevant. But he played along, replying, "You might be correct. Continue."

"In that case, General, it's possible to have your cake and eat it, too. Your problem is one of distribution capability, not the frequency of Air Force supply flights. The over-the-road distances involved here are not very great, no more than fifteen klicks in either direction from A Luoi. A small contingent of deuce and a halfs—say, twenty vehicles—with two shifts of drivers, about eighty men, could complete multiple runs day and night, in any weather, just like the Red Ball Express we used in Europe back in The Big One. We know you're now—"

Alworth interrupted, "This isn't Patton's march to the Rhine, Moon. Get with the program…it's an airmobile operation in mountainous jungle."

Colonel O'Dell provided the rebuttal. "It's an airmobile operation in danger of not achieving its objective, sir. Perhaps we should let the sergeant major finish what he was saying."

"If he must," the general replied.

Undaunted, Sean continued, "We know you're now putting emphasis on supplies and ammunition being flown into A Luoi on the fixed-wing aircraft, but maybe we should shift that emphasis to vehicles for just a day to create ground transportation capability. Once that capability is in place, fly in all the supplies and ammo you want between the morning fog burn-off and sundown. By the next morning, those supplies will all be distributed over the road, and the trucks will be ready for another day's operation. You won't have to wait on helicopters grounded by darkness, bad weather, or maintenance problems. Two deuces can carry as much as one Chinook, and unlike helicopters, they need little, if any, downtime for scheduled maintenance. You'll see a big increase in the delivered supply volume, guaranteed."

"But you're not taking into account the fuel I'll need for all those deuces," Alworth protested. "It's hard enough keeping my helicopters gassed up."

Sean replied, "The deuces run on diesel, General. Over distances as short as these, they'll go a couple days without gassing up, even with continuous use. One flight by a C-130 could bring in enough bladders of diesel fuel to keep those trucks running roughly four days. And if push comes to shove, they can run on aviation fuel or even gasoline. It just takes a simple adjustment any driver knows how to do."

Alworth turned angrily to Colonel O'Dell. "Does everyone at MACV endorse this pie-in-the-sky nonsense?"

"Affirmative, sir, but it's hardly pie in the sky. It's what we pay our logistics people the big bucks to figure out. And it has General Abrams' full support."

"Well, that's just fine and dandy, Colonel, but I think it stinks. Just one day's interruption in the flow of supplies will result in a lot of my boys suffering and dying for no goddamn reason. We feel sure the NVA base camp you're so worried about is in an area centered three klicks west of A Sap, and we're closing in on it steadily. But if I can't move and distribute an ever-increasing amount of supplies into the A Shau—even for a day—my operation comes to a grinding halt and my men are placed in extreme jeopardy. Once we lose momentum, who knows how long it'll take to get it back?"

"I think Colonel Gradinsky can fill in that gap for you, sir," O'Dell said. He passed the torch to his team's aviation expert, who continued, "Fourth Division will loan a company of Chinooks to temporarily augment your division's lift capability, sir. That will keep vital supplies moving into the A Shau until all the vehicles are delivered and the materiel flow by fixed-wing aircraft can resume. That should keep your logistics train moving without missing a beat."

"That's very generous of Fourth Division," the general said. "But only one deuce and a half can fit in a Herc at a time. Isn't that a colossal waste of transport capability?"

"Negative, sir," Gradinsky replied. "A deuce only fills a little more than half of the ship's cargo space. The rest can still be loaded with supplies. Nothing's wasted."

Alworth still wasn't on board. "And I suppose MACV is willing to take full responsibility when this genius plan of yours falls on its face? It depends entirely on complete cooperation from the Air Force and Fourth Division, and neither of those organizations dance to my drummer."

O'Dell replied, "But they dance to General Abrams' drummer, sir. Army, Air Force, Marines, Navy—we're all in this together. General Abe is seeing to that." He turned again to Sean, saying, "I believe you have something else to add, Sergeant Major?"

"Yes, sir. If you're going to be running convoys round the clock, they're going to need defensive firepower. Weather being what it is in the valley, we can't expect our helicopter gunships or the fighter-bombers of the US Air Force to always be there. Ordinarily, we'd detail armored forces to ride shotgun with the convoys, like we do along Route One on the coast. But getting tanks, Dusters, and their maintenance support into the A Shau is beyond our capabilities without a secure route for their ground transport. That route doesn't exist at the moment. But we can include quad-fifty gun trucks in the vehicle airlift. Four should do the trick. One's already been delivered to the valley."

"That's right, just one," the general said, "and it's protecting a crucial firebase."

Yeah, I know the place, Sean told himself. *The one Jif Miles commands. I was with him when he picked it out.*

"I'm sure we can see our way clear to give that firebase whatever substitute weaponry it needs to protect itself, sir," Sean continued, "but right now, we need that quad for something much more important. And according to your operational plans, that firebase—Condon—will become considerably less crucial in the coming days as you shift forces south toward A Sap."

"Tell that to the NVA, Sergeant Major."

"I think our adversaries are going to get the message loud and clear, sir," Sean replied.

Colonel O'Dell pushed to close the deal. "So it's agreed? We'll execute *Plan Road Ranger* in two days, commencing at oh-five-hundred hours of 7 May. Does that meet with your approval, General?"

Alworth gave no indication of agreement at first. Like any senior commander, he despised having the specifics of an operational plan dictated to him. Higher command was supposed to give him the objective of a mission and then butt out. It was then his job to formulate the detailed plan for that mission. And it was especially grating that these specifics were being delivered by a sergeant major, no matter how experienced and worldly-wise that senior NCO might be.

But Moon sits at the right hand of the MACV commander. Creighton Abrams himself might as well be across the table from me…and his word decides if I get that third star or not.

The general swallowed his pride—and his anger—and said, "Agreed."

*****

Sean stayed behind at Camp Evans while the two colonels jumped on the Huey back to MACV's forward HQ at Phu Bai. He sought out an old friend, a master sergeant and armorer with 1st Cav who owed him a long-standing favor. Together, they drafted equipment transfer paperwork and got an overworked and distracted captain in the division G4 shop to sign it without any questions. Per that paperwork, two .50-caliber machine guns, with tripods, were loaded into a jeep, which took Sean to the base camp's airstrip. Along the way, the jeep stopped at the Class VI warehouse, where eight cases of beer were sandwiched in with the machine guns. Collecting yet another favor from the aviation detachment commander, he commandeered a Huey to fly him to Fire Base Condon.

Chapter Twenty-Three

The voice on the field phone told Jif, "You might want to *dee-dee* up here to the LZ, Lieutenant. You've got a visitor."

Taking the suggestion to *hurry up* literally, Jif double-timed across the firebase to the idling Huey, assuming the arriving guest was his battalion commander or at least one of the colonel's staff officers. But from fifty meters away, he could make out the looming presence of Sean Moon, overseeing the unloading of the ship.

Eyeing the two .50-caliber machine guns, Jif said, "It's a little early for Christmas, isn't it, Sergeant Major? Something tells me this is one of those *I've got good news and bad news* scenarios."

"Can't fool you, can I, Lieutenant? Actually, it's not really bad news. You're gonna love it."

Sean explained the reason for his visit. Jif was less than thrilled. "So I'm losing the bloody gun truck in a couple of days?"

"But you're getting all-around fifty-cal coverage instead. The only thing better than that truck is the interlocking fire you're gonna get from four of these big bastards."

"Yeah, sure, Sergeant Major. But why do I feel I'm getting the shaft here, and all that beer is just the lubricant?"

"Hey, I had to call in a bunch of favors to get you this stuff. Don't look a gift horse in the mouth, Lieutenant."

"All right, I don't want to sound ungrateful. Thanks for looking out for us. But wait a minute…you said *four* fifty cals. You know that I already have two?"

"Yep."

"How in bloody hell does the whole world know what's going on at this firebase?"

"That little incident with the LOACH caused one hell of a ripple at MACV," Sean replied. "When one of our boys gets accidentally decapitated by one of our own machines, it's a big fucking deal. It's real hard to explain to the folks back home how something like that could happen. We know it was those fifty cals you salvaged that triggered the whole thing."

"I'm not in trouble for taking them, am I?"

"Fuck, no, Lieutenant. They were fair game. That pilot…what was his name? Dempster? Dumpster?"

"It's Dempsey, Sergeant Major."

"Well, Major Dempsey shouldn't have gotten his balls in an uproar over something like that. If he really wanted to make a federal case out of it, there were other ways, ones that didn't endanger your firebase. I saw the transcript from the initial inquest. Dempsey kept babbling about how much those fucking guns cost, like combat losses are coming out of his pocket. The colonel heading the panel shut him up by commenting that those guns were worth nothing compared to the value of a young man whose life was wasted due, in large part, to the major's recklessness. Your comments to the investigating officer kinda nailed the reckless part down tight. It didn't take long for the board to confirm he'd been refused permission to land on the firebase itself. That conversation was heard all the way to Signal Hill."

Surprised by all this, Jif asked, "So you're telling me the aviation community hasn't rallied to his support?"

"Not this time. He's gonna take it in the shorts, slowly but surely."

"Really? How?"

"In a month, he's gonna get passed over for promotion to light colonel for the second time. That'll be curtains for his career. In the meantime, he's been relieved of his command. He'll fly a desk at First Aviation Brigade until all the paperwork's done and he's forced out of the Army."

"Good riddance to him, I reckon," Jif said. Then he asked Sean, "Are you staying a while?"

"Yeah, I've got a little time." Pointing to the Huey, he added, "Let me cut this chopper loose. Get some dudes to hump this stuff and we'll set you up."

*****

First Sergeants Contreras and Avery needed no instruction on how to employ the four heavy machine guns in a 360-degree perimeter defensive scheme. The job was half complete before they'd even started; the two guns from the wrecked Chinook were already emplaced at the northeast and southeast corner. The two weapons Sean provided were being quickly dug in at the opposing corners.

"I'm gonna miss that gun truck, though," 1SG Avery said. "Just hearing those things shoot was like listening to victory. Still, unless we get hit from three sides at once, this setup will work just fine."

Contreras added, "Hell, if we did get hit from three sides at once, that quad truck would be shit out of luck, anyway."

Jif was coming around to the NCOs' collective wisdom. "We've still got more firepower than we're authorized," he admitted. "A lot more."

The only man not thrilled with the changes was SSG King, the gun truck section chief. "Me and my boys have had it pretty good here," he said. "Ain't looking forward to being ambush bait again."

"I wouldn't worry much if I were you, King," Sean said. "You're going to be the baddest son of a bitch on the roadway."

Jif was also warming to the concept of truck convoys augmenting the helicopter supply chain. "I see your point, Sergeant Major," he said. "Trucks don't get stopped cold by fog, rain, and darkness. How come Division didn't think of this before?"

"Don't be too hard on Division," Sean replied. "There wasn't a good way for the Cav to get the deuces here until the airfield at A Luoi opened up."

"But it's been opened for three days," Jif countered. "What took them so bloody long?"

"Let's just say that MACV had to prod them a little. Sometimes, you're so close to a problem you can't see the way around it. You get up a little higher, though, and the path becomes obvious."

"So it was MACV's idea," Jif said, "and I'll bet you had a lot to do with the plan. Can't say I'm surprised. Dad always said that when you need to get vehicles moving, you're the man."

Sean laughed. "Your dad was always a great judge of talent. But I'm not the only swinging dick who put this plan together. There are a whole bunch of whiz kids on General Abrams' staff. I've just been making things roll a hell of a lot longer than most, though, so I've seen about every mistake that can be made."

Contreras said, "Hey, the mess steward's giving me the high sign. Supper's ready. You going to be joining us, Sergeant Major?"

"Sure. What's on the menu, Top?"

"Chicken fricassee...sort of," the first sergeant replied.

"What do you mean, *sort of*?"

"It means we would've had fried chicken if we had any oil. But that's just one of the many items that haven't been delivered in the last few days. Maybe once we get your all-weather trucks bringing the goods, we can stop improvising with the menu."

"No maybes about it, First Sergeant," Sean replied. "I guaran-damn-tee it."

*****

Over supper, Jif asked Sean, "Is my battery moving or not?"

"Not real likely, Lieutenant. General Abrams is hot to keep this operation on schedule, which means it'll end in two weeks, give or take a day, because after, the rains start for real. Once that happens, it'll be tough going on the road, and the airfield at A Luoi will probably wash out, too. The runway's only packed dirt, for cryin' out loud. The big worry is that there's still an NVA base camp around here. Division thinks it's just west of A Sap, tucked into some valley that's a straight shot to Laos. Aerial recon hasn't been able to back that theory up. But here's a clue…every acoustic sensor in the area's gone dead. The odds of one dying without a little help from somebody is about one in five, and the odds of them all dying on their own is like zero."

"Most of our fire missions are in that direction," Jif said, "but A Sap itself is out of range. As First Brigade moves farther south, they're going to need at least one direct support battery moving with them."

"And I don't think that battery's gonna be yours, Lieutenant. You're taking care of business here damn well, so you own this place. It don't make much sense to pull you out just to plug in somebody else who'll have to start from scratch. I think we can expect one—or maybe two—of the batteries from up north to leapfrog you and emplace near A Sap."

"I don't reckon any of us will complain," Jif said, scanning the lieutenants and NCOs who were gathered around. Their assenting nods made it clear they liked that eventuality, too.

Sean added, "And you've done it all while short a howitzer. That's damn commendable."

"Speaking of the guns," Jif said to Chief of Smoke McKay, "some of them have to be wearing out. How close are they?"

"At the current rate, we're good for another couple of weeks. That should get us to the end of this operation, right?"

"That's the plan," Sean replied.

"Good," McKay said, "because if we're out here any longer than that, we'll be replacing tubes on site.

That'd be a lot easier to do in base camp than in the boonies."

"Actually," Sean added, "you guys just might have it knocked. Enemy activity against your perimeter has gone way down in the last few days, right?"

"That's true," Jif replied. "I reckon that's another reason we're losing the gun truck, right?"

"Again, I can't fool you, Lieutenant. But even though things have slowed down, don't you dare fall asleep out here. You might never wake up."

*****

Jif hadn't expected Sean to spend the night at the firebase. But the sergeant major explained, "Phu Bai knows where I am, and I'm not due back there until twelve hundred hours tomorrow. Even if the fog doesn't burn off until ten hundred hours, a chopper will still get me home before I turn into a pumpkin." They settled onto stools outside the CP/FDC, enjoying their coffee and the cool evening air. Only the faint, intermittent chatter of distant small arms fire disturbed the quiet.

"You know, my one-year anniversary on active duty is in two days," Jif said.

"Congratulations, Lieutenant," Sean replied. "I just chalked up my twenty-seventh year a few weeks back."

"Congratulations to you, too. Are you going for the full thirty?"

"Roger that. Once I hit twenty years, I said, *What the hell? Go for the full ticket*. My little brother's doing the same, too. He's a year behind me in time served."

"Your brother...the Air Force pilot?"

"That's him, Colonel Tommy Moon, F-105 jockey out of Thailand. His tour there is almost done, though. Same for his CIA spook wife. Her tour in Laos will be over soon, too."

"I remember Sylvie all too well," Jif said.

Agitated by that offhand comment, Sean said, "No, you don't, Lieutenant. You don't know her and you were never in Laos, understand? Please tell me you've been keeping all that shit under your hat."

"Of course I have. I know the bloody drill."

Sean relaxed and let out a sigh of relief. "That's good to hear, because information like that is dangerous. Those CIA operatives gotta fly under the radar. You're playing with people's lives if you blow their cover."

They fell quiet for a few moments. Then Sean asked, "So tell me, from your lofty perch of one year's service—and it's been one hell of a year, that's for damn sure—what do you think of the Army now?"

"Pretty much what I've always thought. It can be screwed up at times—like it is right now—but it's essential. There's no way around it. A strong, capable army is a necessity if you want to stay a superpower."

"Gee, you almost sound like a lifer. You're not planning on staying in after your two years are up, are you? Ain't your mother gonna kill you if you do that? Last I heard, she was still stirring the pacifist shit back in Washington."

"Probably not kill me…disown, maybe. But I'll tell you the truth, Sergeant Major…I really can't see very much beyond the end of this tour in Nam, and it's still got one hundred fifty-one days and a wake-up to go. But will I be staying in the Army? Let's just say I haven't ruled it out."

Sean was surprised to hear that but secretly delighted. Before he could say another word, Jif continued, "I had this moment of clarity when I was in Oz on R&R. I realized I belonged here in country. Up to that point, I'd looked at my tour as just doing a job for all it was worth. But belonging...that changes everything. I don't know how much I'll feel that I belong in the Army once I'm out of Nam, though. We'll find out, I reckon."

"Can't wait to hear that answer," Sean said.

*****

That night was as uneventful as the three that preceded it. Only two fire missions were shot during the early morning hours. One was an illumination mission that employed only a single howitzer. The other was an H&I utilizing the entire battery, the target being a trail junction they'd shot up several times before. But the sounds that floated on the night air left no doubt that the bulk of the action was well to the south, out of range for the guns of Fire Base Rubber.

On this night, as well, there wasn't even the hint of a probe at the perimeter.

Sean had racked out in 1SG Contreras' bunker but was wide awake at 0300 hours. He found Jif and several of the NCOs working in the CP/FDC. A discussion quickly ensued on the differences between Operation Pegasus—the relief of the Marines at Khe Sanh they'd been a part of last month—and the current operation, Delaware. Contreras asked Sean, "The rumor is that now we've taken it back, we're destroying the Khe Sanh Combat Base. Once that's done, that area is going to be abandoned completely. Can we take that to the bank?"

"You sure can, Top," Sean replied. "The place is strategically worthless. Always was. Westy could never see that, but General Abe can. The NVA didn't really want it, either. But as long as the Marines were sitting there as bait, they were hoping for another Dien Bien Phu."

"You mean we're not even going to go through the charade of turning it over to the ARVN?"

Sean replied, "Nope. Why bother? Like I said, it's strategically worthless."

Contreras continued, "Okay, but what about the A Shau, Sergeant Major? It's not worthless like Khe Sanh. Quite the opposite. Once we finish kicking ass here and get pulled out, are the ARVN coming in to take over?"

"That's the plan, Top."

"But will they actually be able to control the valley?"

"Of course not. They'll hang on for a while until the NVA builds up their strength again. Then the ARVN will get beat up bad and turn tail like they usually do."

Signorelli was overtired and irritable. When he heard what Sean said, he exploded, "Then why are we even fucking bothering with this place? We might as well save everyone the trouble and just hand this entire shitty valley back to the NVA right now."

His voice calm and steady, Sean replied, "You ain't the first genius to express that opinion, Specialist. But giving up ain't an option. We're gonna keep bothering because there's nothing else we can do. It's the cards we've been dealt. We win a few hands, then we pick up our chips and move to another table. Maybe one day, we'll get to stack the deck and clean house."

"So that's all this is? A fucking traveling card game?"

With one glance at the sergeant major, Signorelli immediately wished he'd kept his mouth shut. He braced himself, expecting the brutal tongue-lashing that was about to come his way. But Sean said nothing at first. He didn't need to; his towering, implacable presence could bend men to his will with nothing but steely-eyed silence. After a few fraught moments, though, he offered, "Lighten up, son. It's just a metaphor."

Nobody dared open his mouth until Jif said, "The moral of this story, men, is you should never play poker with anyone from MACV." Picking up the coffee pot from the makeshift stove, he added, "Anyone need a refill? It's still a long way to breakfast."

He was about to kid Sean about where he'd picked up the term metaphor, but decided against it. *I've never heard him use highbrow words like that*, he thought, *but this isn't the bloody time for ribbing. In fact, it'll probably never be the bloody time.*

*****

There was little fog that morning. Whatever had shrouded the valley burned off by 0830 hours. Sean's helicopter arrived to take him away just minutes later.

The last thing he said to Jif as he climbed on board: "That FDC chief of yours—the Italian kid—he knows his shit. I was watching him work. He's good people. A little mouthy, but still a keeper."

"Yeah, he's doing an excellent job. I'm promoting him."

"Outstanding," Sean replied. "Hey, if I run into your dad, you got any messages for him?"

"Yeah. Have him tell Washington to shit or get off the pot. Let us fight this thing to win or not fight at all."

Sean smiled, patted him on the shoulder, and said, "You'd be preaching to the choir, young man. He knows that story better than you and me put together." As he gave a thumbs up to the pilot, he added, "You watch your ass, Lieutenant Miles."

"You do the same, Sergeant Major. And thanks again for all that beer."

*****

The only excitement of the day came when a Chinook delivering a sling load of ammunition punched it off the hook while the cargo bag was still ten feet above the ground. The mistake infuriated SFC McKay, the signalman who'd not yet called for the release. The pilot not flying gave him a *sorry about that* gesture through the windshield, holding his hands up as if surrendering. McKay completed his *fly away* signal with a raised middle finger.

"We've got four boxes of HE busted open," Lieutenant Hammond told Jif. "Three out of eight canisters are damaged. Could be worse."

"Yeah, a lot worse," Jif replied.

Any hope for a fourth quiet night in a row evaporated just after 2200 hours. A patrol near Romeo Delta, the checkpoint west of the firebase, reported,

"You've got little people coming, about five hundred meters out, azimuth from you is about two-five-zero degrees. Doesn't sound like a lot of them, but I can't even see shadows. Not enough moon. They're making plenty of noise, jabbering like a bunch of girls. I'm going northeast pronto to get out of the way. I don't want to be catching any fifty cal tonight."

"Roger that," Avery replied. "Keep at least two hundred meters clear of the perimeter until you're level with the LZ. I'll alert the LP in that sector that you're coming."

He put the handset down and voiced his exasperation aloud to Jif: "Well, kiss my entire black ass. The gooks never showed any interest in hitting us from that direction before. What do you wanna do with the quad, Lieutenant?"

The quad-50 deuce had been sent to the eastern pit right after sundown. From there, its ability to counter a threat from anywhere in the western sector was practically nil. Guns 3, 6, and the CP/FDC bunker were blocking most of its field of fire.

"If we move the truck to the west side," Avery continued, "she's got no protection at all. There's no berm to hide it over there."

"Move her to the south pit," Jif said.

"You sure, sir? Gun Six is still gonna cut down her field of fire a whole bunch. We could shoot over the gun, I guess, but the crew will have to bail out. And once they do, we ain't got no beehive on that side of the perimeter."

As Jif mulled it over, Avery added, "Of course, putting the quad in the north pit's an even worse option.

Good chance they'll hit my patrol no matter how far out those guys stay."

"That's why we need the interlocking fifty cals to cover the west side," Jif said. "If your patrol keeps that two-hundred-meter interval, I reckon they'll be okay, even from beehive. Everybody agree?"

"I'm good with that," Avery replied.

"Me, too," Contreras added.

But Lieutenant Dowd asked, "What happens if you get a fire mission?"

"Same as always," Jif replied. "We shoot it with every gun not needed for perimeter defense. You've seen us do it before, haven't you?"

"I guess so. I've never seen how you control two missions at once, though."

"Watch and learn, Lieutenant," Jif said.

He was about to tell Contreras to get the gun truck moving to the south pit, but the first sergeant already had SSG King on the firebase landline. A few moments later, they heard the truck's diesel engine roar to life.

Dowd managed to ratchet up the tension in the bunker when he blurted, "I'll get the flares ready." As all eyes turned in horror to the signal flare box, he clarified his announcement with, "I mean illumination flares from the mortars, not the star clusters." After reading off the coordinates he intended to light up, he asked, "Do they sound about right?"

"Perfect, Lieutenant," Avery replied, "but do not—repeat, *do not*—hang those rounds yet. We've had enough accidental light around here to last a lifetime."

"Copy that, Top," Dowd replied. He realized the stigma of his last mistake would cling to him a long time.

*****

The waiting was the hardest part. It came to an end twenty minutes later when the LP beyond the southwest corner of the perimeter reported, "Gooks are two hundred meters out. We're coming in right fucking now. Don't shoot our asses."

Another anxious five minutes had ticked off when a trip flare in that same southwest corner went off, signaling that the intruders were at the outer ring of the wire. The quad-50, now at the southern pit, raked the southwest arc of the perimeter with a terrifying deluge of rounds. No one in the sector reported actually seeing any attackers.

Avery asked Jif, "Ready for the illum?"

"Affirmative, Top."

Within a minute, another trip flare was activated, this one in the center of the western sector. This time, the defenders in that sector actually saw a wave of figures trying to breach the wire, starkly backlit by the illumination flares from the mortars.

The gun truck couldn't repel this assault. Its field of fire was blocked by Gun 6.

So much for my brilliant placement of that vehicle, Jif told himself.

The defenders detonated several Claymore mines prematurely; the attackers were still beyond their kill zone. As one RPG and then another flew into the firebase, the men on the western perimeter responded with all the small arms at their disposal, augmented by the individual thunder of the .50-caliber machine guns at the northwest and southwest corners of the perimeter.

No American was sure if the attackers were shooting rifles or machine guns along with the RPGs. There was too much noise from their own weapons, and no muzzle flashes or green tracers were visible.

The action on the west side was over in less than two minutes. The echoes of the last stray shots died out quickly, like futile protests.

No longer did they need illum rounds to see; the fire raging at the mess bunker lit the entire firebase.

Chapter Twenty-Four

To Jif's relief, it wasn't the mess bunker itself on fire but the storage tent just next to it. The *Tent, GP Small* sat within a circular, chest-high wall of sandbags and was filled with canned goods, non-perishables, C rations, and kitchen equipment. Nothing inside should have burned with such ferocity after the RPG penetrated the canvas roof.

But 1SG Contreras figured out the cause of the intense blaze right away. "I'm going to wring Panakis' neck," he told Jif. "I told that damn fool to get those gas cans out of that tent. Now, everything in there's going to burn to the ground."

There'd been only one injury from what had seemed a two-pronged attack on the firebase. A KP was headed to the storage tent when the rocket hit. Though the sandbagged walls absorbed most of the fragments from the blast, one piece managed to hit him in the chest.

"The man wasn't wearing his flak jacket," Contreras said. "Wasn't wearing a helmet, either. Good thing he didn't get hit in the head."

Jif asked, "How bad is he, Top?"

"Concussed, a big hunk of skin is torn off his pecs, and it probably cracked his sternum. Doc says it could be a lot worse, but he's going to need medevac."

"Immediately?"

"Don't think so, sir. Let me get this mess sorted out, and I'll keep you posted."

First Sergeant Avery stuck his head out of the CP/FDC bunker and said, "You're gonna love this, LT. Over at the wire by Gun Six...we got ourselves some POWs."

While Avery went to work ensuring the perimeter was still intact, Jif hurried to Gun 6. He found several of his men working to free two NVA soldiers who were snared in the wire. The Americans had already taken the attackers' weapons. A sergeant told him, "They had satchel charges, too, sir. We tossed them away as far as we could...we were afraid they might've already been armed...but they never blew."

"Good move, anyway," Jif replied. "Do you remember where you threw them?"

"Yes, sir."

"When you're done with these clowns, blow those satchels up where they sit. I don't want anyone stumbling over them and getting hurt. Oh, and Sergeant..."

"Sir?"

"Tie the prisoners up, blindfold them, and bring them to the CP. Make bloody sure they don't accidentally get dead on the way."

"Yeah, sure, LT." Glancing toward the blaze, he asked, "How bad did the mess section get hit?"

"One wounded...and it looks like we'll be a little short on coffee, biscuits, and Cee's for a while." After he said it, he realized his assessment was probably overly optimistic.

*****

Jif beat the POWs back to the CP/FDC by a few minutes. He asked Contreras, "Does Avery think we're still secure all around, Top?"

"Affirmative, sir. Aside from those two caught in the wire, there's no sign of any other NVA. We'll have to wait until the sun comes up for a better picture."

"If we find anything at all, it'll probably just be blood trails and garbage they left behind," Jif replied.

The fire at the mess section was now nothing but ashes and embers. The first sergeant said, "Pretty much a total loss. We'll be okay for one more breakfast, but we don't have much to work with after that. No gasoline for the stoves, no food to cook. Not even Cee's. I'm putting together an emergency ration requisition."

Jif asked, "What did our mess sergeant have to say about the gas in the tent?"

"You mean our *mess private*, sir? He didn't say much, but he's well aware he crapped in my face. What do you think? Court-martial or Article Fifteen?"

"Any previous discipline in his *two-oh-one* file?"

"Negative, LT. He's been a pretty good troop, by the looks of it, even though I think he's here because some judge gave him the choice of jail or the Army back in Jersey. Since then, it seems like he's found a home here. And he is one hell of a cook."

"All right, then. Let's not crucify him for his first mistake. The stuff in that tent might've been shot to hell, anyway, even without the gasoline fire. I guess you've already chewed his ass?"

"Not as much as I plan to, sir."

"Well, finish it up, and then I'll write a letter of reprimand when I get a chance."

Contreras' reply: "As you wish, sir." But it couldn't have sounded less enthusiastic.

The radio burst into life: "*Backstop One-Eight-Zero,* this is *Banjo Two-Four*, fire mission, over."

"Here we go again," Signorelli said. "The war that never sleeps."

*****

No sooner had the POWs been brought to the CP than a medic rushed in, saying, "Change of plans, sir. The wounded guy—Staples—we've got to get him out of here. We think he's got a pierced lung. He's turning blue on us and coughing up blood."

"Can he be moved to the LZ?" Jif asked.

"I guess so."

"You guess? Or you know? Because I don't want to put a chopper into the middle of the firebase if I can help it. We've got missions to shoot, and she'll be in the way. We already learned that lesson the hard way."

"Understood, LT. Yeah, he can be moved."

Contreras added, "How about using the gun truck for an ambulance, sir? If we're bringing in a medevac with gooks on the perimeter, the LZ could be hot. The quad might be the ticket to cool things down. Moving it to the north side now kills two birds with one stone."

"Do it," Jif replied. He turned to Lieutenant Dowd and said, "I need you to get the medevac coming. Everybody else is a little busy right now."

Contreras asked, "What about the prisoners, sir?"

"They can wait. Brigade won't send anybody out for them tonight, anyway."

As he watched the chart operator plot the target coordinates, Signorelli said, "No surprise here...we'll be shooting southeast. The LZ is clear for a western approach." Dowd acknowledged with a nod and called for the dustoff.

Jif got his first good look at the POWs. The bound and blindfolded captives were squatting against the bunker wall, speaking to each other in tones that seemed tinged with terror.

"Stand them up," Jif told a trooper guarding them.

That's when he noticed something odd; the NVA soldiers were quite damp from the waist down.

Contreras noticed it, too. "LT, did these assholes piss themselves?"

"No. I reckon they might've come across the river not too long ago. Most of the gooks we've tangled with were either burned to a crisp or chewed up and soaked in blood. These are the first intact enemy we've seen, and they're wet from being in water. Something's strange here..."

The river in question was just over a klick to the southwest from Rubber. Called by several different names—some Laotian, some Vietnamese—it paralleled Route 548 from Ta Bat to A Sap. An American patrol had tried to ford it near the firebase but given up; the briskly flowing water came up to the chins of the tallest. It would be well over the heads of Vietnamese.

Intelligence estimates had always assumed that the NVA trying to hit the firebase had an assembly area on the near bank; no crossing of that unfordable river would then be necessary to stage their attacks.

And yet these gooks are only wet from the waist down.

What the fuck, over?

*****

PFC Staples, the cannoneer wounded while on KP, was on a dustoff chopper twenty minutes later. Once the Huey was gone, SSG King was told to bring the gun truck back to the south pit.

"Roger that," the sergeant replied. "I won't miss the nights on this firebase, that's for damn sure. You really keep a man busy."

"You know the drill, King," Contreras replied. "Keep the troops hopping and you keep them mad. That makes them fight better."

The battery averaged a fire mission an hour for the rest of the night. A search of the NVA prisoners for intel found only this revealing item among their effects: a sketch of the firebase wrapped in cellophane. It was quite accurate, right down to the three pits for the gun truck. The only things missing were the .50-caliber machine guns Sean Moon had supplied, emplaced yesterday at the northwest and southwest corners. Contreras asked Jif, "How much you want to bet those guns are on the next sketch the gooks draw?"

"Taking you up on that bet is a losing proposition, Top. But we might as well remove those blindfolds. They've already got the lay of the land."

One of the men guarding the prisoners said, "I'm pretty sure these gooks are trying to tell us they need to take a leak, LT. What should we do?"

Jif replied, "Take them to the latrine. I don't want them pissing themselves in here. It's pretty ripe as it is."

"Suppose they try to bolt? Can we shoot them?"

"Let's try to hold down on the gunfire inside the perimeter, okay? Leash them by their necks with rope. Leave their hands tied behind their backs."

"You mean I've got to hold their peckers for them when they pee, LT?"

His partner added, "And how're we gonna find their dicks, anyway? They're so fucking tiny."

"Just drop their drawers for them. The rest will take care of itself."

Contreras added, "It'll be part of the process, anyway. You're already going to swipe their belt buckles with those big red stars on them, right? I hear they're fetching a great price back at base camp."

*****

The sunrise revealed little evidence of an NVA attack in force. After a Huey arrived to take away the two POWs, the battalion S2—the intelligence officer, a captain—arrived in a LOACH. He told Jif, "Battalion's intrigued by what you reported, Miles, but everything points to nothing more than a probe at your position by a handful of sappers. I just took a look at the stretch of the river you suspect they crossed. I'm here to tell you that there's no evidence it's even possible. No bridge, no boats, no nothing in the area. Like all the other intel concludes, the gooks are coming from a base camp that's on the near side, probably south of here."

"How high up were you when you did the looking, sir?"

The question annoyed the S2. "If you're implying I gave the area a once over from five hundred feet up, you're full of shit, Miles. I've got tons of time as an AO. I know how to track troop movements."

The only thing full of shit was the captain. He'd actually done the recon from a thousand feet, a height from which trodden paths were rarely visible. What's more, his experience as an aerial observer amounted to a single familiarization flight at Fort Sill and two missions in country, where he adjusted rounds on registration points with no enemy in sight and no pressure.

"All right if I take a look for myself, sir?"

"If you've got your own chopper, knock yourself out, Miles. I'm taking mine and getting the hell out of here."

*****

It didn't take him long to find a helicopter. A Huey dropping off supplies at the LZ was piloted by a man Jif knew fairly well, a fellow first lieutenant named Gary Pitlock. They'd met during Pegasus and had shared more than a few beers after that operation at the Camp Evans O Club.

Standing on the skid-tip step of the idling chopper, Jif shouted at the pilot through the open cockpit window. "Can I borrow you and your ship for a few minutes, Gary?"

"Borrow? I don't like the sound of that, Jif."

After explaining what he had in mind, though, Pitlock lost all but a shade of his reluctance. He asked his crew if they had any problems taking Lieutenant Miles for a quick joyride. There were no objections.

"Sure, we'll help you out," the pilot said. Pointing to the man standing behind Jif with a radio on his back, he added, "Is he coming, too?"

"If that's okay?"

"Yeah, it's okay...but I've got radios on board, you know."

"I know, but I always like to have my own, too. You can never have enough commo."

"All right, welcome aboard," Pitlock said. "I'll give you ten minutes. Then I've got to split."

*****

Ninety seconds later, they were zipping along the river at an altitude of two hundred feet. Pitlock's voice was on the interphone, saying, "You do realize we can see Laos from up here, don't you? That means the triple-A gunners over there can see us, too."

"Sure, we can see it," Jif replied, "but the border's about eight klicks away, Gary. Don't sweat it."

"I'm not sweating it, my man, because we ain't gonna be here very long. Trust me on that."

Jif's RTO, Spec-4 Suggs, asked, "Is that really Laos over there, LT? It don't look a bit different from Nam."

"Yeah, tell me about it," Jif replied. "The mountains and jungle all look the bloody same."

But then Jif saw something that didn't look the same: stands of trees on either side of the river whose crowns seemed to have grown toward each other until they touched, forming a canopy over the flowing water.

"That's not natural," Jif said. "Gary, circle back. I need a better look at those trees."

"Why? Something wrong with them?"

"Bloody right there's something wrong with them. Do you remember the stories of the gooks hiding stretches of the Ho Chi Minh Trail from aerial observation by pulling treetops together over the roadway?"

"Yeah, sure. Everybody's heard about that."

As the chopper swung around, Jif added, "I think they've done the same thing over this river. I reckon there's some kind of crossing there…a bridge or something."

"And I reckon you've got a touch of jungle fever, dude. I don't see anything unusual about those trees."

"No, Gary, I'm telling you…it's unnatural for trees to grow like that. The ones on the east side…they're bending west, away from the strongest sunlight. That's just wrong. Even some of the fronds are facing the wrong way."

"Oh, excuse me, Jif. I didn't realize you were a forestry expert."

"Look, man…you remember where I spent half my childhood, don't you?"

"Yeah, Australia."

"Not just anyplace in Australia, but the Cape York Peninsula, a rain forest not unlike this place. Except, of course, there are mountains here."

Airborne, they couldn't see what was under the canopy of trees. Jif said, "Set me down in that clearing over there. I've got to have a look from ground level."

"Are you out of your fucking mind, Miles? Have you forgotten just where in the hell we are? This is Indian country, dude."

"Just set me down. I'll only take a minute."

Pitlock's frustrated sigh sounded more like a groan in the distortion of the Huey's interphone system. But he was already lining up to land in the clearing. "I'll give you a minute," he said, "but I'm not sitting there on the ground with my thumb up my ass. Call me when you're ready to be picked up."

Jif leaned into the cockpit and gave him a playful tap on the shoulder. "Now you understand why I never travel without my RTO."

"Yeah...and I understand how you set me up, pal. Let's pray this doesn't get us both fucked over."

The Huey touched down gently. Jif and Suggs had barely gotten beyond the rotor's arc when she popped into the air again to orbit nearby. Standing at the riverbank, they could plainly see the thick ropes pulling the tops of the trees together. More astounding was the change of the water's flow across a swath of the river; it degenerated from its smooth and unruffled appearance to a turbulent disruption for roughly six feet before resuming its tranquil procession downstream. The reason was obvious: a submerged bridge, built just beneath the surface, was upsetting the flow. Men on foot and vehicles could use it to cross the river's span with little difficulty.

"Call the chopper back," Jif told Suggs. "We're getting out of here."

A minute later, the Huey swept in. They were back on board before the skids ever touched the ground. "What'd you find?" Pitlock asked.

"Submerged bridge," Jif replied as he pointed to a rise a few hundred meters to the east. "Hold over there while I call in a fire mission. The ship will be out of the way, and I can adjust the rounds from the air."

Suggs was already calling the mission into Fire Base Rubber on his own radio.

Pitlock asked, "How long is this going to take, Jif?"

"Just a couple of minutes. You gave me ten. I've only taken five, so far."

"You owe me, man. Big time."

"Put it on my tab, Gary. You know I'm good for it."

Suggs held out the handset to Jif. "FDC needs to talk to you, LT."

It was Signorelli's voice in his ear. "Did we hear right? You requested *fuze delay* with fire for effect? The target's a bridge?"

"Affirmative, a submerged bridge. I need the rounds to blow up on the water and not in the trees."

Still sounding skeptical, Signorelli replied, "Ah…roger that. Hold one." In a matter of seconds, he added, "Shot, over."

Jif knew that Battalion FDC was monitoring the frequency. Brigade HQ was probably listening, too. It would be no secret what he was shooting at and where it was. They might even break into the conversation with their own questions…

But the rounds will already be in the air by the time that happens.

The adjustment round arrived seconds later. It was short but not by very much.

"Close enough for government work," Jif said. "Suggs, tell them add five-zero, fire for effect."

The time-delayed HE rounds ripped through the canopy of trees without exploding, penetrated the surface of the water, and detonated against the submerged bridge, just as Jif hoped they would. In a geyser of water, logs that had been part of the bridge's structure flew into the air, severing the ropes holding the trees together. Within seconds, the wreckage of the destroyed crossing site could be seen floating lazily downstream.

As Pitlock set the Huey down at the firebase's LZ a few minutes later, he told Jif, "You're a man of your word, pal. That little joyride took nine minutes and forty-two seconds. Eighteen seconds to spare. Let's hope you did some good."

*****

Within thirty minutes of his return to the firebase, two VIPs arrived, each in his own helicopter. One was Lieutenant Colonel Latimer, Jif's battalion commander. The other was Colonel Wilder, commanding 1st Brigade. Wilder stood petulantly, arms crossed, while Latimer did the questioning.

"Your little recon flight was an unauthorized use of an aircraft, Miles. What you found better be worth breaking Division SOP."

Ignoring the unexpected ingratitude, Jif began by explaining his theory: since the POWs captured at the firebase last night were living evidence that they'd walked across the river, there must've been some facility in place that enabled them to do it.

Latimer asked, "Don't you think it's possible your gooks just got wet sloshing through one of the several streams in this area?"

"Sir, a couple of those streams can be straddled, even by the Vietnamese. The rest aren't deep enough to get more than your feet wet. As I said before, the POWs were wet from the waist down."

"Maybe they just fell walking across a stream?"

"If that's the case, sir, they fell in an identical manner that left them both wet to exactly the same extent. That's not very likely. These guys were wading through waist-deep water shortly before hitting my firebase."

The two colonels exchanged hushed comments Jif could barely hear; the words *misappropriated* and *jeopardized an aircraft* were easy to understand, though. Then Colonel Wilder took over, asking, "So you found what you think was a submerged bridge?"

"I don't *think*, sir. I saw it with my own eyes and destroyed it."

"All right, I'll buy that. Did you draw any other conclusions from your escapade, Miles?"

"Sir, I wouldn't be surprised if there are more submerged bridges hidden along the river. Now that I know what I'm looking for, they shouldn't be too hard to spot. I'd be glad to make another recon flight that goes all the way down to A Sap. But there's just one problem. If I find a target beyond Kon Tom, none of our available artillery can reach it, not even the one-five-fives on Signal Hill. To knock them out, I'll need tac air with bombs, since I don't think our helicopter gunships can do the job. Rockets and machine guns won't cut it under water."

"I'll take you up on that offer, Miles," Colonel Wilder replied. "If it's okay with your boss here, I'd like you to take a ride on a FAC ship so you can show the Air Force what these targets look like. The zoomies will take care of the ones we can't hit with artillery."

LTC Latimer asked, "Can your battery spare you for an hour or two, Miles?"

"Yes, sir. I'm sure they can."

"Good. Say your goodbyes and come with me. We'll hook you up with a FAC at A Luoi."

Looking to Colonel Wilder, Jif asked a favor: "I take full responsibility for that unauthorized flight. I don't want Lieutenant Pitlock to get in any trouble. He was just helping me out."

The colonel smiled and said, "Don't worry, Miles. Neither you nor your pilot buddy are in trouble. Not anymore."

*****

The forward air control ship—a USAF O-2, distinctive with her two engines in tandem and twin tail booms—was waiting for Jif at the A Luoi airstrip. As he climbed into the right seat, the pilot, a captain named Bill Jones, told him, "Brief me once we're airborne. If we don't take off right now, we'll get stuck in the departure queue behind a bunch of Hercs. We'll be eating their dust for God knows how long." They were airborne two minutes later.

Jif asked, "Do you know where Fire Base Condon is, sir?"

"Yeah, it's penciled in on the chart," Jones replied, pointing to the folded map stowed on the glareshield. "You want to start there?"

"That's the plan," Jif replied.

Jones adjusted the ship's heading. "We'll be there in about two minutes, Miles. Where to from there?"

Jif told him they'd be following the river south to A Sap. He glanced at the airspeed indicator; they were going almost twice as fast as a recon helicopter's normal cruise. "At this speed, sir, we're going to have to fly a little higher than I thought to see what I'm looking for. How about eight hundred feet?"

"Sure, we can do that. You can call me Bill, by the way. You say your name's Jif?"

"Yep, that's it."

"How'd that happen?"

"Childhood nickname. It stuck."

"Whatever works. Nice to meet you, Jif. Now tell me what we're looking for."

He gave Jones the down and dirty on the submerged bridge and the unnatural tree cover that concealed it. After eight minutes of flying along the river, Jif spotted a similar oddity near Kon Tom. "Give me a right orbit," he said. "Let me check there are no friendlies in the area. If it's clear, my battery can take it out."

"This'll be fun," Jones said. "I've never called in artillery before, just jets and Skyraiders."

"Skyraiders...you mean *Spads*, right?"

"Oh, good. You know the lingo. You must've been around the block a few times."

"Yeah...rumor has it I've seen the elephant."

"I don't know what that means, Jif."

"I'll tell you later."

Within a minute, Brigade confirmed the target area was clear. Jif switched to Rubber's fire control frequency and called in the mission. After three adjustment rounds and one fire-for-effect volley, that submerged bridge became an assortment of trash floating downstream.

Nine minutes of flying later, they found two more likely targets near A Sap. Both were well out of range of the Cav's artillery. "Time to call in the zoomies," Jones said. "You taught me a new skill back there over Kon Tom, Jif—how to bracket a target. Now it's my turn to be teacher. You're going to learn how to mark a target for fast jets."

But school would have to be postponed. As they began a holding pattern to wait for the fighter-bombers, an arc of green tracers sketched their menacing line in the ship's path, daring her to cross it.

Chapter Twenty-Five

Captain Jones threw the agile O-2 into a violent right turn, but it only flung the ship deeper into what was now a web of tracers. The pilot's voice sounded surprisingly calm and focused as he told Jif, "Hold on, dude. This may get a little violent." Then, with a brisk, full-travel deflection of the control yoke, the aircraft suddenly stood on her left wingtip and reversed direction. Though harnessed to his seat, the forces of the maneuver slammed Jif's head against the side window. The impact left a smear of sweat and grime on the plexiglass. It knocked his headset off, too.

As he struggled to get the headset back over his ears, Jones shouted at him above the roaring engines, "Better hang on to something, dammit. I ain't shitting you, man."

Jif thought he saw stars, and for a moment, he probably did. But as his head cleared, he realized the brilliant lights he was seeing now were multiple streams of tracers enveloping the O-2. Some seemed only inches away.

They look the size of bloody basketballs when they're coming right at you.

She'd flown straight and level for only a split second before Jones reversed the ship's direction once again. It seemed a miracle that, so far, not one of the hundreds of large-caliber bullets in the air had hit the plane. Jif kept looking down through his side window, as if treetop height was where salvation might be. But the latticework of tracers beneath them dispelled that notion.

Jones seemed to be refuting Jif's fantasy of a plummeting escape to safety when he said, "There's an axiom among old fighter pilots…when you're in deep shit, don't dive, don't climb. Just turn."

No sooner had he said that, they were clear of the triple-A. Savoring the thrill of their getaway, the pilot added, "Those old fighter jockeys knew what they were talking about."

Jif asked, "So what do we do now? Do we go back and mark those sunken bridge sites?"

"Are you out of your fucking mind, Miles? Go back through all that shit again? No, thank you, Lieutenant. We're going to take a different approach."

"What would that be?"

"It's going to be up to your honchos to decide, Jif. I see you've got the coordinates for those bridges worked up already, but can you nail down the box where all that triple-A came from? I was a little busy flying to be doing any plotting."

Jif drew a goose egg on his map. As best as he could reconstruct the event, it encompassed the area where they'd nearly been shot down. He began to say, "Yeah, I reckon they're at—"

"Don't tell me, man," Jones interrupted. "Give those locations to your people at Brigade. Tell them we request Arc Light."

Arc Light: a bombing strike by a flight of B-52s; several hundred tons of concentrated high explosives that could cause massive devastation within a radius of half a kilometer.

*****

Twenty minutes later, Jones and Jif were back at A Luoi, explaining their request for the bombing strike. Colonel Wilder needed little convincing. "I agree with your contention, Captain," the brigade commander said. "There's an excellent chance you've located the NVA base camp that we've suspected all along is in that area. There's no other reason they would've thrown so much lead at you. They were trying to knock you down before you could report their position." He turned to Jif and asked, "Do you have anything to add, Miles?"

"Yes, sir. Are we still going after the bridges near A Sap?"

"Fuck the bridges, Lieutenant," the colonel replied. The possibility of wiping out the NVA's base camp was now the only thing on his mind.

Jones asked, "Should I get your air liaison to work up an Arc Light strike order, sir?"

"Negative. That decision will be made by Division HQ," Wilder replied.

"Time's of the essence, sir. If we file a preliminary order now, we should be able to get a strike tonight. If we wait too long, the NVA might be gone."

"Tell me something I don't know, Captain."

*****

The debrief of their recon flight completed, both aerial scouts were eager to be someplace other than A Luoi. Bill Jones needed to resume his FAC duties, but he had to wait while his O-2 was being refueled. Jif was looking for a ride back to Fire Base Rubber. A helicopter would be fastest; the flight would take just a few minutes. But there'd be no choppers going that way for a while, and lieutenants didn't rate personal air taxis. His other option was hitching a ride on a supply deuce; the next convoy was scheduled to depart in thirty minutes.

As he marked time in the operations shack, Jif put in a radio call to the firebase. His biggest concern: the status of their emergency ration request. Contreras confirmed it hadn't arrived, and he had no idea if and when it would. He concluded with, "The natives are getting restless. There's already been a fight over someone supposedly stealing food. I sorted it out, but there's more trouble to come, I'm sure."

Jif walked to the logistics section, where supplies were being staged for delivery to the field units via trucks and helicopters. The operation appeared to be total chaos, but he was able to figure out which trucks were going to Rubber. With a little more investigation, he could tell there were no rations among the cargo being loaded. In fact, the three deuces were being crammed full of building supplies: lumber, culvert half pipes, sandbags, and carpentry tools, all intended to be used for position improvements and hardening. A firebase didn't even need to order those items; they were automatically shipped whenever material was available.

An impatient voice called out, "Can I help you, Lieutenant?" The question wasn't meant to be taken as an offer of assistance; its subtext was more like, *Why the hell are you in my way?* The speaker, a staff sergeant, was the NCOIC of the convoy.

"I was wondering why there are no rations being loaded for Fire Base Condon," Jif said. "We placed an emergency requisition last night."

"And you are, sir?"

"I'm Miles, the battery commander of Condon. It's my men who got their food blown up in an NVA assault last night."

The irritated sergeant riffled through the papers on his clipboard. "Don't say nothing about that here, Lieutenant." He pointed to a large tent that was a beehive of admin activity. "Get with the major, sir. He's running this circus."

The major, a pompous REMF by the looks of him, was named Doggett. There was no doubt he considered Jif an irritating presence in his domain. Standing in starched utilities that looked like they'd just come from the laundry and boots marred by nothing more than a thin layer of dust, Doggett blustered, "What's your fucking problem, Lieutenant?"

Jif began to explain his need for the emergency ration requisition, but the major cut him off before he reached the second sentence. "What makes you think I've got the time to listen to everybody's piddling little troubles? Your bad planning does not constitute my emergency, Miles."

"Begging your pardon, sir, but we're not talking bad planning here. This is about replenishing combat losses. I didn't—"

Doggett interrupted him again, his voice raised as if he'd just been offended. "Listen to the balls on this kid! He's still talking! Let me tell you, Lieutenant, I ain't got time for any sad tales. Tell your story walking." He stormed off, leaving Jif standing alone.

At a nearby desk, an old chief warrant officer had overheard the encounter. He motioned for Jif to come over. The chief, a very senior CW4 named

Johnson, looked as if he'd been in the Army since WW2, or maybe even before. *Bloody hell, he looks older than Sergeant Major Moon*, Jif thought. *I'm kind of surprised to see a bloke like him out here in the boonies. Usually, warrant officers with that much time in service know how to wrangle jobs that never involve leaving base camp. Somebody very high up must've really sat on his head to get him out here, because I doubt Major Doggett had the juice to do it. Old chiefs screw assholes like him into the ground on a daily basis.*

Jif introduced himself and pleaded his case for the emergency ration shipment. As he spoke, Chief Johnson yawned, leaned back in his rickety folding chair, and rubbed his world-weary eyes. Without saying a word, he rummaged through the documents on his makeshift desk and came up with the requisition. It was in the bin marked *Priority Helicopter Lift*. "It's SOP to put loads declared urgent on the choppers, Lieutenant," Johnson explained.

"That's bloody great, Chief," Jif said, "but the next chopper lift to Condon won't be for hours. And if things go the way they've been going, it should probably contain nothing but ammo. No problem there...we certainly need the rounds. But my men need food right now, too. The truck will get it there faster."

He had no doubt he wasn't the first person to stand before this logistics wizard and spill a sob story. And he wasn't surprised when the wizard rolled his eyes.

But he was stunned when the chief said something other than *sorry about that*. Instead, Johnson offered a possible solution. A tenuous one, but still possible.

"Lieutenant, I feel for you," the chief said, "but I ain't got the people to be shuffling loads around once they're made up. But here's what you might do…you see that E-6 over there?" He was pointing to the staff sergeant Jif had first encountered. "His name's Blaine. He's running the convoy that's going south. If you can convince him to unload some of what they've already humped on board for Condon and put on your rations instead, that oughta solve your little problem. Then, I'll try to make sure that whatever gets taken off the trucks is airlifted down to you later today along with your ammo. Best I can do."

Jif had only one commodity to bargain with: beer. The eight cases Sean had provided were still unopened and stacked in the CP/FDC beneath the chart tables, where they were fairly safe from pilfering. The firebase command group—himself, Dowd, and the two first sergeants—hadn't yet arrived at a consensus on when to distribute it. Eight cases were just enough to allow one can per man.

Approaching SSG Blaine, Jif said, "I've got a proposition for you, Sergeant. Maybe we can do each other some good." He opened the negotiations at half a case to Blaine and his men. After a flurry of exorbitant counterbids, they shook hands on two cases. There was little grumbling as the convoy crew unloaded the building supplies on one of the deuces slated for Rubber and filled the truck bed with the emergency ration request.

Jones' aircraft was now fueled and ready for her next mission. As Jif gathered his personal gear for the truck ride back to the firebase, he asked the pilot, "Anything on Arc Light yet?"

"Nope. That's not the kind of stuff they broadcast, you know?"

"I know all too well, Bill. I nearly got nailed by one of those strikes a few months back. It was damn close...too damn close...and we had no idea it was coming when it did."

"And if this one comes, you won't know about it in advance, either, Jif."

As they prepared to part ways, Jones said, "You never did explain what *seeing the elephant* means."

"Well, in short, it means you've overcome a great obstacle but emerged the better for it."

"In that case, I guess I've seen the elephant myself a couple of times in this godforsaken place. You take care now...and just remember what my grandmother always told me."

"What's that?"

"She said, 'Son, don't fuck up.'"

*****

At Camp Evans, Major General Alworth, commander of 1st Cav, was salivating over the prospect of an Arc Light strike wiping out the suspected NVA base camp. His staff, however, was counseling caution. The G2—the intelligence officer, a lieutenant colonel—said, "The location is less than two klicks from the Laotian border, sir. It won't take much of an error by the Air Force to drop their eggs on the wrong side of the line. Then, there'll be hell to pay with Washington. We might never get another Arc Light mission within ten klicks of the border again."

The USAF liaison on Alworth's staff took umbrage at that suggestion. "Nobody complained when we were dropping our ordnance within a few hundred meters of the perimeter at Khe Sanh," the Air Force major said. "Not one American boy was ever endangered, and God only knows how many of their lives were saved by those *Buff* crewmen."

The G2 had another consideration. "There's also a complex of Montagnard villages a klick from the target area. Those people are our allies, General. There's no better way to turn them against us than kill a bunch of their people with friendly fire."

The G3—the division operations officer—scoffed at that assertion. "First off, Wally, those villes are on the other side of a mountain. They'll be shielded from the blast. And if they do get their brains rattled a little, who gives a shit? That should be the worst thing that happens to those savages in their sorry lives." Directing his attention to the general, he continued, "What worries me most, sir, is that we have no confirming intel on this base camp's location whatsoever. The fact that some observation plane got shot at by multiple weapons doesn't mean shit. I'd hate like hell to waste all that beautiful ordnance on bamboo trees and monkeys."

"But we can make logical assumptions," the G2 said. "The fact that our prime intelligence instruments—the acoustic sensors—have all gone inoperative is a very positive indicator that there are NVA massed in the suspect area. If there weren't, there wouldn't be enough manpower to find and neutralize all those devices. No doubt, we need to sweep that area clean, but I'm not sure Arc Light is the way to do it."

The general asked, "You're suggesting boots on the ground instead, Colonel?"

"Affirmative, sir."

The debate was interrupted by a host of urgent issues flaring throughout the division. Each one required immediate attention, diverting General Alworth and his staff for almost two hours. Although the division's Air Force liaison had filed a preliminary Arc Light strike order with his headquarters in Thailand, Alworth didn't activate that order until 1500 hours. The general had finally decided that the plusses of calling the strike far exceeded the minuses. The delay in making that decision, however, ensured the strike aircraft, flying from Guam, could not arrive over the target before 0400 hours of the following day.

*****

It was midafternoon when the supply convoy arrived at Fire Base Rubber. Nobody there had eaten much of anything since their meager breakfast, scraped together from what had survived last night's fire. If anything at all had been consumed afterward, it was little more than an item left over from a C ration meal, a snack brought back from a twenty-four-hour R&R at Camp Evans, or a gift of food that had arrived in a package from home. While no one was starving—not by a long shot—stomachs were grumbling all over the firebase. Not surprisingly, the infantrymen of the security company, who were often subjected to long patrols on a bare minimum of rations, took the lack of a midday meal—and the uncertainty of when they'd eat again—much better than the artillerymen. They might not hump the boonies like their infantry brothers, but the exhausting and monotonous exertions of the cannon-cockers were equivalent to humping freight on a loading dock twenty hours a day. Hungry, tired men got testy easily.

The news that Jif had given away two cases of beer in exchange for the timely delivery of fresh rations went over poorly with the men of the battery. "It's great that you brought in the food, sir," Contreras counseled, "but dammit, giving up a quarter of the beer supply to some convoy jockeys for just doing their jobs has the men more than a little riled."

Jif had no doubt his first sergeant was among the riled. Something else he was beginning not to doubt: *No good deed goes unpunished.*

Sergeant Pitrowski, one of the gun section chiefs, gave even more voice to the men's annoyance when he confronted his BC, saying, "With all due respect, Lieutenant, if you needed to cut a deal, you should've traded away something else."

Jif's exasperated reply: "Like what, Sergeant?"

"You know, LT…something…anything…but not that."

"Like maybe a future draft pick?"

"C'mon, LT, I'm being serious here."

"So am I, Sergeant. Since this isn't the NFL, and it's obvious we lack stuff to trade other than a windfall of beer, what was I supposed to do? Gamble that this firebase wouldn't eat for a day? Or maybe two days, if the weather socked in again, convoys got backed up, and choppers couldn't fly? Then I could listen to you complain about how I'm starving you. Sorry, but I like my way better."

"But it's *our* beer, LT."

"Correction, Sergeant. It's Uncle Sam's beer, and he's detailed me to dole it out as I see fit. And the stash isn't all gone, only a quarter of it. That means each man gets nine ounces instead of the entire twelve that's in a can. I'll give you a choice—I can pour those nine ounces into your canteen cup or a Dixie cup. And if it makes you feel better, you can sit an empty can in front of you while you drink it. You'll never feel the bloody three-ounce difference, and it'll taste just as good."

Pitrowski was beginning to wish he'd never opened his mouth.

Turning to the two first sergeants and Lieutenant Dowd, Jif asked, "Is today's supper a good time to consume our beer supply?"

"Sure," Contreras and Avery replied in unison with enthusiasm.

"And Panakis can pour out nine ounces per man on the serving line, right?"

"It won't be a problem, sir," Contreras affirmed.

"Bloody outstanding," Jif said. "Put it on the menu."

To himself, he added, *Get rid of that fucking beer before I hear any more candy-assed whining.*

*****

The day slipped into evening without the firebase receiving the promised helicopter delivery. Mechanical problems with the birds, and now darkness, forced the delivery of ammo and building supplies to be put off until tomorrow. If the battery had a night of constant firing, they'd be out of rounds to shoot by morning.

By 2000 hours, the supper of hamburgers and French fries was done, complete with its chaser of beer. A four-man detail was busy stomping flat the one hundred ninety-two empty beer cans and adding them to the firebase's burgeoning dump of non-flammable trash. As he watched them work, Lieutenant Hammond said, "I still can't believe how much garbage a firing battery generates. Between the wooden boxes, cardboard tubes, end caps, expended brass canisters, nose plugs, and fuze cans, every freakin' round we fire creates big loads of crap. If the Chinooks didn't haul away the stuff we can't burn every now and then, we'd be buried in our own junk by now."

Jif added, "Have you ever seen what the garbage pit at base camp looks like? How'd you like to be in charge of that place? There's a shit assignment for you...Division Refuse Officer."

But Hammond liked that idea. "How do I get that job? I think I'd love it. It wouldn't be so bad being a REMF, would it?"

"You've got to put in a lot more time in the boonies first, Arthur. Don't pack your bags quite yet." He added, "And yeah, being a REMF would be very bad...*Number Ten*, like the gooks say."

"Ten's my lucky number, Jif."

There hadn't been a fire mission since late afternoon. The gun crews looked relaxed, almost bored. Hammond said, "I guess the food and the beer helped mellow the boys out, eh?"

"I don't want to hear any more about that bloody beer, Art. I reckon they've been drinking plenty on their occasional overnights at Evans. I'm sure they're sneaking a few cans back, too, so I don't need to be playing barkeep out here. We've got enough to worry about."

"Speaking of worrying," Hammond said, "any update on when that Arc Light strike of yours is going to happen?"

"Arthur, it's not a question of when. I don't even know if it's going to happen."

"At least if it does come, it'll be pretty far away, right?"

"Yeah, let's hope," Jif replied.

*****

The battery fired one illumination mission around 0100. Then the night fell silent. The mostly cloudy sky was allowing little moonlight through, casting everything on and around the firebase in deep shades of charcoal gray.

It stayed that way until 0520, when the predawn darkness was obliterated by staccato flashes of brilliant light to the south, followed seconds later by an apocalyptic drumroll of explosions and unnerving tremors of the ground beneath their feet. The stupefying mayhem of the Arc Light strike lasted nearly twenty seconds. Then, after a few minutes of breathless silence, a steady rain began to fall, as if the earth had summoned the heavens to wash its wounds clean.

*****

At Lima Site 67 in Laos, across the border from A Sap, they felt the awesome power of the Arc Light strike, too. But Sylvie Bergerac—aka Françoise—and her five-man CIA team were too busy packing their gear and burning documents to dwell on it. Ever since yesterday evening, their Hmong scouts reported that NVA troops were crossing the border from South Vietnam in massive numbers. A scout team leader told her, "Several regiments, at least, if not an entire division, Madame Françoise. They are moving quickly and will swarm this mountain by late morning."

She didn't doubt he was right.

At first light, an Air America STOL aircraft would land on the site's postage-stamp runway and spirit the Americans to the US air base at Nakhon Phanom, Thailand. Their Hmong mercenaries had been paid; they'd scatter to mountain sanctuaries deeper into Laos when the plane departed. Once the ship was in range and calling for landing clearance, Sylvie's men would destroy the site's bulky radio equipment.

Right on schedule, the spindly Pilatus Porter aircraft lined up for landing, groping through the low clouds and early morning mist. The plane would barely come to a stop; she was back in the air with her passengers on board in less than a minute. Once airborne, the CIA operator code-named Montana asked, "How many NVA do you suppose that Arc Light strike took out, Frenchie?"

Sylvie thought of the vast numbers streaming over the border and replied, "How ever many, I doubt it was enough. It's never enough."

Chapter Twenty-Six

There'd be no post-strike bomb damage assessment that day. Weather conditions wouldn't permit it. Although the rain stopped by 1200 hours, low clouds and fog persisted, preventing reconnaissance by aircraft or ground troops inserted by helicopter.

Oddly enough, the resistance of the NVA in the A Shau seemed to increase. Charlie Battery received almost continuous fire mission requests in support of 1st Cav units attempting to advance on foot just south of Kon Tom, seven kilometers from the firebase. Watching the targets being plotted in FDC, Jif observed, "Two klicks more and they're out of range."

Chief of Smoke McKay brought even more sobering news: "At this rate, we'll be out of ammo in about four more missions."

"We're working on it, Smoke," Jif replied. But his repeated radio requests for the ammo resupply were getting the usual runaround: the choppers were down for weather; the trucks were all backed up as a result. A voice from A Luoi had reassured him with the same words several times: "You're priority one."

Bloody great, but I still don't have my ammo.

McKay said, "With all the gooks we're shooting at today, Lieutenant, it makes you wonder if that Arc Light strike of yours hit anything at all."

Of yours...if the strike had indeed been a worthless blunder, those words made it a personal one. The only reply Jif could manage: "There are no guarantees in life, Smoke." But that platitude did nothing to soothe the sting of failure implied in McKay's remark.

At 1345 hours, they heard the unexpected buzz of a LOACH groping its way toward the firebase, scud-running beneath the low cloud deck. The ship's call sign belonged to Colonel Wilder, 1st Brigade Commander. The pilot was requesting ground flares to mark the firebase's LZ.

Three minutes later, Jif was face to face with the colonel, who said, "I need a favor, Miles."

Colonels don't ask favors. He's going to order me to do something.

"Lieutenant, as soon as these clouds lift, I'm running an aerial recon of the Arc Light target area. The Air Force will eventually be doing their photo recon from high altitude, of course, but I want the down and dirty. It'll be a great help if the observer on board has already seen the terrain up close and personal. Can you think of anyone who might fit that bill?"

There were only two people who qualified: himself and Bill Jones. But the FAC pilot was, no doubt, unavailable, sitting on the ground somewhere with the rest of the Air Force, enjoying the foul weather.

"I reckon that'd be me, sir," Jif replied.

"Correct answer, Miles. I've already cleared it with your battalion commander. I'll keep you posted on when you'll be going."

"Just one thing, sir. My battery's almost out of HE, and we're still waiting on resupply. If we run dry, we'll be vulnerable as all hell. I can't leave them if that's the case."

"Don't worry," the colonel replied, "you'll get your ammo. My S4 is seeing to it."

An hour later, while a fire mission was in progress, three deuces drove up to the firebase. In charge of the convoy was SSG Blaine, the benefactor of yesterday's beer-for-food exchange. His trucks were loaded with the battery's needed ammo. It couldn't have come at a more opportune time, because the cannoneers were breaking open their last boxes of HE.

Blaine greeted Jif with, "Chief Johnson didn't forget about you, Lieutenant. He said he'd get you your ammo ASAP, and here it is."

"Actually, Sergeant, he said he'd get it to me yesterday."

"True, sir. Very true. But shit happens, you know? This is our first chance to get you the goods. Oh, and by the way, he thanks you for the beer."

"He thanks *me*? If anybody gave him beer, it was you."

"Gotta kick back a six-pack to the boss, sir. Otherwise, I could end up sucking hind tit."

Jif had to laugh. "That sounds more like how an organized crime setup works, Sergeant."

Blaine replied, "What do you think war is, sir? Sounds like the very definition of organized crime."

"And it sounds like you've been reading Smedley Butler, Sergeant."

"Affirmative, sir. He said *War is a racket*, and that general knew what he was talking about. We're all racketeers here."

*****

By evening, the clouds still hadn't lifted. Jif's aerial recon was postponed until tomorrow morning, weather permitting. But poor visibility didn't slow the pace of the fire missions Charlie Battery had to shoot.

It didn't slow the pace of enemy activity, either. When he heard the first NVA mortar round explode inside the perimeter, Jif's first thought was there'd been an ammo handling accident, with its inevitable catastrophic results. But when the second mortar round impacted a few moments later, there could only be one conclusion: *Incoming*.

The first round had landed between Guns 1 and 2. The second landed squarely in the unoccupied eastern pit once used by the quad-50 truck; that vehicle was now gone, assigned to convoy protection duty. Neither round had caused any damage or injuries, but if subsequent volleys were being adjusted onto choice targets by an observer, casualties were no longer a game of chance. Accurate fire would kill people.

First Sergeant Avery gave the LPs beyond the perimeter wire a warning over the landline: "If there's a gook FO out there, he could be anywhere around the perimeter. But odds are he's close to one of you."

That was quickly proven true. In hushed tones, an LP on the north side reported, "We've got somebody out in front of us, maybe fifty meters. You ain't gonna believe this, but he's standing at the intersection of Five-Four-Eight and Five-Four-Seven, right in the middle of the damn road, kinda walking around a little. If he stood still, we probably couldn't make him out."

Avery asked, "Any chance he's friendly, like he fell off a convoy?"

"No way, Top. No trucks have been by here since nightfall. He ain't no GI. Gotta be a gook...he looks like a little stick figure doing a jig. But I can't see no arms on the dude, like maybe he's using binoculars or something."

Avery asked, "Is he alone?"

"I can only see one, but I don't think he's humping a radio. If he's an FO, he must have an RTO somewhere nearby. Can I take this dude out? Or do you want the fifty cal to fuck him up?"

"You do it. One shot, one kill."

At the CP/FDC, they never heard the pop of an M16 from the north side. Maybe it was drowned out by the roar of howitzers, they thought...

Or maybe they never fired at all?

"Gimme a status," Avery asked the LP.

"Can't see him. Musta ducked down or...oh, shit! There he is!"

There was no trouble hearing the shots that time. In his excitement, the man on the phone had held the push-to-talk button down while his partner fired one three-round burst and then another in quick succession. The sound of the shots crackling from Avery's phone sounded like a series of mousetraps rapidly snapping closed.

When the rifle fell quiet, Avery demanded, "Status report."

"We're still here, Top. Don't know where the gook is."

A third mortar round fell into the firebase, landing in the trash pit. Again, there were no casualties, just waste material blown all over the place. The fourth arrived, too, landing on the LZ. It tore up a patch of dirt but nothing else.

"This son of a bitch's aim is all over the place," Contreras said to Avery. "If your LP guys didn't hit him, they must've shook him up real bad, at least."

"Gotta keep him shook up, then. Anybody got an idea where these mortars are? I wouldn't mind putting our own eighty-ones on them."

"Someone on Gun Two got a look at a crater," Jif replied. "He says the rounds are coming from somewhere out west, but no ballpark azimuth or range estimation."

The terrain to the west was a wooded washboard extending several kilometers from the firebase. A mortar section could easily conceal itself; nobody on Rubber would ever see the faint, momentary flash of a tube firing in the darkness. Shutting down the elusive FO seemed an easier proposition.

Contreras asked, "You want to pull a gun off the fire mission and spray some beehive at him, LT?"

"Spray it where, Top? No, I don't want to pull a gun off the mission. Not for just one or two gooks."

"But we can't let them keep shooting at us, LT," Contreras said. "Somebody's going to get hurt."

"No shit, Top," Jif replied, adding, "I'm taking a starlight scope and going over to Gun Six. Maybe I can spot that FO in between volleys."

Sounding doubtful, Contreras said, "Good luck with that, Lieutenant. You know how flaky those scopes can be when there's shooting going on, right?"

"I'm well aware, Top." To avoid the scope whiting out from muzzle flashes, he hoped that by being within earshot of a howitzer crew, the chatter between the assistant gunner and gunner as they confirmed their sighting adjustments would tell him when the battery was about to fire. That would give him an instant to cap the lens.

As he raced from the bunker, he thought, *If I mess up just once, though, this scope's out of action for a few minutes, at least.*

But I've got to try something.

Two mortar rounds crashed down almost simultaneously, one landing beyond the southern wire. The other fell very close to the CP/FDC bunker, toppling one of the four antenna masts. Jif yelled to the men inside, "One antenna's down, don't know which one. Keep the fire direction nets hot…swap the cables around if you need to. Don't try to put it back up until the incoming stops."

When he reached Gun 6, the crew was snatching nervous glances to the west as they prepared their howitzer for its next shot. The section chief explained, "The LP over that way says somebody's moseying south down the roadway. You think it's that gook, sir?"

"Nobody else would have the balls, Sergeant."

As he said that, new firing data came down to the gun. There'd be no time for a scan with the starlight scope until after this volley was shot. It took less than ten seconds for that to happen.

Before Jif even tried to use the scope, he made a startling discovery: *I can see the bastard moving without it! Wait…there's two of them, just strolling down the road!*

Then they stopped walking. By not moving, they became invisible.

"Give me the bloody phone," he told the gun chief. Once he had the handset, he asked the CP/FDC, "Are the men in the western LPs still down in their holes?" He didn't want to shoot one of his own accidentally.

The few seconds it took to get an answer seemed an eternity: "They're all down, looking out for the gooks."

All right, no friendlies in the way. I can't see the FO team anymore, so I reckon they're still standing there, probably calling in another adjustment. Am I really the only one who caught them?

Unslinging the M16 from his shoulder, Jif aimed into the void where he hoped they might still be and popped off three shots.

There was a shower of sparks downrange which quickly evolved into a ball of flames. Clearly visible in the light of the fire were two very small men, almost childlike in their slightness.

Definitely gooks.

One man ran, instantly vanishing into the darkness. The other stayed in place. He appeared to be consumed by the flames, gyrating wildly for a second or two until the ball of flames dropped to the ground in another explosion of sparks. Then he was gone, too, before Jif could get him in his sights.

The gun chief asked Jif, "What the fuck just happened, LT?"

"I shot a radio, I reckon."

"That's some fucking shooting, sir, considering we can't see shit."

"It's just luck, Sergeant. Just luck."

Charlie Battery was about to fire its next volley when Jif and every other man at Gun 6 sensed that barely perceptible millisecond of turbulence rippling the air around them; it signaled that in a moment too short to measure, the next mortar round would impact close by. They were already crouched down, seeking the shelter of the position's low parapet, an encircling wall of earth and sandbags two feet thick. It offered a fair degree of protection from anything except an explosive round dropped directly into the pit.

That exception nearly happened. The mortar shell struck the roof of the section's ammo hutch, a crude but sturdy structure of timbers supporting a sheet of aluminum from the crashed Chinook, covered high with sandbags. The ammo within the hutch was untouched, but the blast fractured the roof, which had absorbed the lion's share of its explosive force. The pit was showered with dirt from the bags but mercifully few shell fragments. All the men were dazed and some bled from the ears, but they were alive and composed enough to resume their duties in a matter of moments.

The only serious casualty was Jif's helmet. He couldn't find it until he shined his flashlight outside the parapet. It lay on the ground ten feet away, an arrowhead of shrapnel several inches long impaled in the front. Only then did he feel the trickle of blood running down his nose; the fragment had carved a shallow gouge in his scalp when the helmet was ripped from his head.

"You can get a Purple Heart for that, LT," the section chief said.

"I don't need another one, Sergeant. Too many of those and they send you home."

The sergeant looked at him like he was out of his mind. Or at least not thinking clearly. He asked, "You okay, LT?"

"Yeah, but I've had better days."

"Ain't we all," the sergeant replied.

Jif hadn't realized it, but another mortar round had struck the CP/FDC bunker. Just like at the ammo hutch at Gun 6, the roof withstood the blast, sacrificing sandbags to protect the men inside. It did punch a small hole through the aluminum base layer, allowing dirt from the ruptured bags to pour down into the bunker in a thin but steady stream. When Jif arrived, they were still sweeping it from the chart tables.

Choking dust from the breached roof hung in the air, coating everything and everyone inside. Signorelli watched as the cascade of dirt slowed to a trickle, mumbling, "Like sands through the hourglass…"

"I've heard that before," Jif said. "Who wrote that?"

"How the hell should I know, LT? It's just the intro from some soap opera my mother watches. She never misses her damn story. Even when I was home on leave, every afternoon I had to get lost when that show was on. Can you imagine that? Her son's going off to war on the other side of the world, but when it was TV time, he could go pound sand. She sure didn't mind pointing out that blue star flag in her front window to everybody and his brother, though. Pisses me off to be reminded of it."

Contreras asked, "You think you got that FO, sir? If anyone is marksman enough to nail him, it'd be you."

Jif replied, "I reckon I scared him off, that's all."

There'd be no more incoming mortar rounds that night. The battery's fire missions tapered off before ending completely around 2300 hours.

*****

At first light, they found the NVA FO's backpack radio laying on the side of the road. A bullet had pierced the battery, which had promptly ignited. The set was burned up almost completely. The only things recognizable were the antenna, a partially melted headset, and a data plate with Chinese characters.

The mist hugging the A Shau burned off by 0930 hours. Thirty minutes later, Jif was in a LOACH zooming low over the bombed-out zone. The chopper's pilot, a chief warrant 2 named Larry Ellerbee, didn't seem bothered by doing a recon of an area that might still be teeming with triple-A. Looking at the blast damage covering nearly a square kilometer, it was difficult to believe any living thing could've survived Arc Light.

Beneath the ship, there was nothing but scorched earth and shredded trees resembling toothpicks stuck in the ground. Little else was discernible from the fast-moving helicopter. They didn't expect to see corpses; men and animals caught in a blast like that would probably be vaporized.

"This is crazy," Jif said. "There's so much devastation, but NVA are still all over the A Shau. My firebase is as busy as ever, and we're still getting hit regularly."

"I wouldn't worry too much about it, Lieutenant," Ellerbee replied. "I'm thinking the NVA is like an old light bulb right about now…they get real bright just before they burn out. In a day or two, I'll bet we won't see a living, breathing gook in the A Shau."

Jif wished he could share that optimism.

More confident now that there'd be no triple-A, they quit the relative safety of their ground-hugging dash to climb higher, seeking a broader overview of the strike. With the suspected base camp nestled deep in a three-sided embrace of mountains, they needed altitude to do that. Passing over the fourth and final side of the enclave—open, flat terrain facing northeast toward Route 548—Jif thought, *That's right where we started to take fire in Bill Jones' O-2, as we began turning away from those mountains.*

As the LOACH rose past 2,000 feet, it was obvious the bombers had released their ordnance along a northwest-southeast track across the U-shaped enemy sanctuary. The long rectangular scar, slate gray in color, looked like a vast, shabby drop cloth laid over verdant terrain. "Those blue-suiters sure pasted the hell out of that base camp," Ellerbee said. "Just like they've been doing to North Vietnam."

But the bombers had blanketed more ground than perhaps they'd intended. The devastation they'd caused overlapped the peaks at the northern and southern ends of their run by hundreds of meters. On the overlapped peak to the south had been a cluster of Montagnard settlements, clearly marked on Jif's map.

Those villes weren't there anymore. They were now just smudges on that shabby drop cloth.

*****

They were back at A Luoi by 1100 hours, debriefing Colonel Wilder and his brigade staff. Jif's detailed report on what he'd seen could've gone on for half an hour. But once he stated there were no signs of life in the area and no triple-A, the colonel stopped him cold, turned to his staff, and said, "It's a go." From that point on, none of the senior officers in the HQ had any interest in what a mere lieutenant had to say.

I reckon we were just sacrificial lambs, Jif told himself. *They just wanted to see if we got shot up...or shot down. Now that we made it out alive, the whole world's going to be marching in there.*

He was exactly right. Within an hour, an infantry battalion made an airmobile insertion onto a hilltop that straddled a trail running from the base camp to the Laotian border, a distance of only two kilometers. "We're confident that's the route any surviving NVA are taking to withdraw from the battle area," Wilder explained to Jif, who had no doubt he was being patronized. "If there are any more of the bastards still around, we're going to cut off their escape and kill them."

"I understand, sir," Jif said, "but I need to point out something else."

"What's that, Miles?"

"The Montagnard villages to the south of the impact area...Arc Light destroyed them all." He made sure all the staff officers heard him, too.

Nobody gave a damn. Wilder and his entire staff seemed annoyed he'd brought it up. "Sorry about that, Lieutenant," the colonel said, not really sorry about anything. "But who gives a shit? The Yards in this province have been playing footsie with the commies, anyway, even while they pretend to be on our side. They're no fucking loss. Don't get bent out of shape over civilians, Miles. There haven't been any actual Vietnamese who weren't VC in the A Shau for a couple of years. And even if some happened to be there now, killing them wouldn't be any fucking loss, either."

Trying to keep his temper in check, Jif asked, "If that's the case, Colonel, who, exactly, are we fighting for?"

"We're fighting to keep all those sorry gook bastards from going communist, Lieutenant."

"Even if we kill them in the process, sir?"

"Damn right. You ever heard the expression *Better Dead than Red*?"

Of course he'd heard it. Stateside, it was a political dogma. Here in country, though, it had become an excuse for the incidental death of civilians.

"Yes, sir, I have," Jif replied.

"Do you believe it?"

"It's just another Cold War proverb, sir."

"Proverb, my ass. This is a hot war, young man, and I'm telling you one of its goddamn truths, which you'd better believe. You're dismissed."

*****

The battalion sent to block the NVA's escape found no enemy troops on that trail. Another battalion was then flown in to sweep the base camp. There was no point using the term *suspected* anymore, because by every indication, it was an actual base camp along the

NVA logistics pipeline from Laos into South Vietnam. Or at least it had been until a day or two ago. Thousands of meters square, it was now cratered and denuded like a moonscape. There was a motor pool containing dozens of burned-out trucks that blended into the charred ground on which they sat. Adjacent to it was a vehicle maintenance shop, its tooling scorched but unmistakable. The shop had probably been beneath a canvas roof that was incinerated in the bomb blasts.

A short distance from the shop was a severely burned-out area littered with the remains of blackened and fractured storage drums. It had been a petroleum and lubricants depot; the contents of the drums had either gone up in smoke or were coating the ground in a layer of oily soot.

One entire corner appeared to have been a bivouac area. While they found nothing in the way of soldiers' personal effects, the remnants of countless sleeping mats were scattered about. Numerous kitchen implements, all scorched by fire, indicated there had been a sizeable field mess. Further evidence was provided by numerous sacks of rice in disorderly mounds that were once neat stacks, some burned to a crisp; the others, too damp and moldy to burn with any ferocity, were merely seared.

The camp was ringed with defensive bunkers around its perimeter, each big enough for a machine gun team. None contained any weapons or ammo. In the center of the installation was a much larger storage bunker, dug deep into the ground. Mostly undamaged by the blasts, the Americans found within it nearly ten thousand rounds of Soviet and Chinese rifle and machine gun ammo, hundreds of Chinese hand grenades, and scores of rockets of various calibers up to 122 millimeters.

The only thing missing was people. There was no evidence a living soul had been in the camp when the bombs fell. Not even a belt buckle.

*****

That evening, as the reserve battalion of 1st Brigade geared up for its assault on A Sap the next morning, news of the *great victory*—the elimination of the NVA's base camp—was broadcast to all the units of 1st Cav. It was heralded as the climax of Operation Delaware. Missing from this announcement was the fact that the camp had been abandoned before the Arc Light strike.

The command group at Rubber knew the truth, however; the firebase had been close enough to the sweep operation to monitor its radio transmissions. Unit after unit had reported zero contact with the enemy, dead or alive. Nobody had expended so much as a round of ammunition.

To Jif, the Arc Light strike—and his involvement with it—still felt like a failure. He saw it this way:

Those bomber jockeys hit the target, all right. Too bad it wasn't there anymore.

Chapter Twenty-Seven

As he sat through yet another USAF briefing at Nakhon Phanom, Thailand, Major General (retired) Jock Miles found himself playing the naysayer once again. The unwieldy title he'd carried for the last few years—Chief of Staff to the Assistant Secretary of State for East Asian and Pacific Affairs—suggested someone who sat in a Washington office surrounded by stacks of official papers and constantly ringing telephones. But his role had become that of a traveling troubleshooter for the State Department, distilling the truth from the various inaccuracies the US military dispensed on a daily basis of their progress in Vietnam. It was time to challenge the willful deceits this Air Force briefer was dispensing about the brilliant successes of the Arc Light bombing campaign.

"Colonel, let me stop you here," General Miles told the briefer. "Even MACV doesn't buy your claims of how many NVA were killed as a result of your bombing. Case in point—you've claimed at least one thousand enemy KIA from a recent strike on a base camp near A Sap, not far from the border with Laos. First Cavalry Division, whose zone the strike was in, attempted to trumpet the same nonsense, but MACV rejected it outright. There was absolutely nothing in any of the after-action reports from troops on the ground to suggest so much as one enemy soldier being killed, let alone one thousand. There is no doubt there was a base camp there, but by all indications, it had been abandoned shortly before the strike. Once again, the NVA knew a strike was coming and evacuated the camp, with most, if not all, of its manpower going over the border. That exodus can be confirmed by our CIA chief in that area." He introduced Sylvie Bergerac—aka Françoise—who was seated next to him at the table.

"In fact," Jock continued, "the inflow of NVA troops was so great it was necessary to abandon the Lima site she commanded to prevent our people there from being sacrificed. The loss of this site will eliminate our ability to interdict enemy infiltration through the region for some time. In short, gentlemen, this looks like a losing proposition for our side. You did a great job destroying a finite amount of their equipment, but your effect on enemy manpower was nil, and it's cost us a vital observation and command post in Laos. Washington has already been notified of these amended findings."

Sure, they've been notified, he told himself, *as if that will change the minds of any of the chickenhawks roosting in the halls of government.*

The Air Force one-star chairing the briefing didn't bother hiding his annoyance. "I'll tell you what, sir," he said to Jock, "if you State Department types could wrangle permission for our B-52s to bomb over the border in Laos from ol' LBJ, we wouldn't be having this issue in the first place." Walking to the huge aerial photograph projected on the screen, an image showing nothing more than the hundreds of bomb craters meticulously blasted across the base camp area, he pounded his fist angrily against the wall while continuing, "We could turn the whole damn Ho Chi Minh Trail into the world's longest graveyard."

Jock replied, "General, you've already turned vast areas of North and South Vietnam into enormous graveyards, and it hasn't brought victory any closer. Just like in the past two wars, the enemy has proved incredibly resilient in the face of aerial bombing."

Then he stood and walked out of the briefing room, feeling so righteous that he didn't seem to need the support of his walking cane.

*****

Later, Jock and Sylvie relaxed over drinks at the base O Club. They hadn't seen each other in almost two months, since Jock had paid an official visit to her Lima site. But their working relationship had begun months earlier, shortly before Tet, when she was running a CIA honey trap in Saigon. It had ended with her being exposed as an agent and marked for death by the Viet Cong. Ever since, this highly experienced and multilingual operator had been managing Lima sites in Laos.

The delusional quality of the Air Force briefing had left the usual bad taste in their mouths, so they didn't want to talk shop. But she had to ask, "That friendly fire fiasco my team caused, dropping artillery on that village...I'm sure there have been repercussions. Nobody's said a word, though. I'm still waiting for the other shoe to drop."

"It won't be dropping," Jock reassured her. "The Laotians are giving it a pass, and so is Washington. You and your people are off the hook."

She took his terse explanation to mean, *You don't want to know what we had to do to smooth it over.* That was true; she didn't want to know the details. Whatever the solution was, however, she was sure it involved enhancing the drug-running revenues of some Laotian generals.

Eager to change the subject, she asked, "Have you seen your son?"

"About a month ago," Jock replied, "when he took his R&R in Australia. The whole family was there."

"It must've been wonderful for all of you to be together."

He smiled wistfully. "Actually, it got tenuous at times. Jif seemed to have been plucked from a world he wanted to be in and then dumped in a place he had little use for anymore."

"I know that feeling," she said. "I can sympathize with him." She half-expected that any second Jock would mention the fact that she and Jif had met during his son's brief but forbidden odyssey in Laos. Jock gave no clue he knew a thing about it, though.

I suspect young Jif Miles is a true soldier like his father and, from what I hear, his mother, too. He knows when to keep his mouth shut for the sake of the mission.

Then she asked, "Is my brother-in-law staying out of trouble?"

Jock laughed and replied, "Sergeant Major Moon is doing quite well at MACV. You've got to know he's in hog heaven being back with General Abrams again. And your husband? How's he doing?"

"Tommy's fine. I'll be visiting him in Korat the day after tomorrow. Miraculously, he's completed his hundredth mission in F-105s, so in a few weeks, he'll be going home for transition training to F-4s. My tour, well…it might not be over quite so quickly. I'm being ordered back to Saigon."

That news struck Jock like a punch. "What? There's a price on your head in that city. You can't go back!"

"Oh, I can, very easily. I've changed appearances before. Give me a few days, and you won't recognize me. Neither will the VC."

*****

It was a good thing that Operation Delaware had reached A Sap, its final objective, because the rainy season was hinting it would soon be returning in earnest. Constantly interrupted by brief but intense squalls, it had taken three days instead of one for helicopter airlifts to move 1st Brigade's entire reserve battalion into the area, along with two batteries of supporting artillery. Even the deuces had difficulties on the muddy roads, their progress sometimes blocked until engineers could breach the quagmires.

The brigade was being met with only dwindling resistance from the NVA. The communist forces took advantage of the Laotian border's close proximity to break contact rather than endure the all-weather menace of American artillery and fair-weather cremation from the napalm-dispensing Air Force. In a few days, the 1st Cav would withdraw to Camp Evans and turn the A Shau over to the ARVN for *safekeeping*. That was an unfortunate word to use, considering most American soldiers felt sure the valley would be safe only temporarily with the South Vietnamese on guard duty.

As expected, Jif's battery remained in place at Ta Bat. The bulk of combat action was now occurring well out of its range to the south. If there were NVA prowling their perimeter, the men of Fire Base Rubber were unaware. They spent the next few days firing H&I missions, unobserved bombardments of geographic coordinates on a predetermined schedule, the results of which were rarely known.

The prevailing attitude among Jif's men was the H&I missions were just busy work that wasted time and ammunition, performed to fill in the blanks on some MACV bean counter's status report. The more polite terms for those missions were *practice rounds* and *killing monkeys*. There were any number of profane expressions for them.

With marauding NVA ceasing to be the firebase's biggest problem, boredom had taken over its place at the head of the list. The disinterest it caused was leading to sloppiness; in the course of one afternoon, XO Hammond caught one gun cutting the wrong charge while another's elevation was set a hundred mils too low. Both errors would've resulted in short rounds if they'd been fired, creating danger for friendly units. "Good catches, Arthur," Jif told him. "You get extra points for those saves."

Contreras shared Jif's concern over the growing malaise infecting their men. "Everybody's got the attitude that we're as good as back at Camp Evans," the first sergeant said. "We've got to do something to snap them out of it, Lieutenant. Personally, I hate the chickenshit stuff a lot of commanders do when a unit gets slack…you know, *the beatings will continue until morale improves*…that kind of mentality. The Smoke has even found gun sections giving their tubes only a lick and a promise during maintenance. One of the gun chiefs had the balls to justify it by telling him, *Nothing cleans out a tube better than shooting a round down it.* There's a lot of truth to that, of course, but these weapons are worn out bad enough that we can't afford to be firing them dirty. If we keep doing it, pretty soon everything we shoot is going to go short, and that might get us killed if we have to defend this firebase one more time. You got any ideas how to fix this?"

"I might, Top," Jif replied. "If they're trying to short-change the howitzers on maintenance, I reckon they're not actually doing any maintenance on their M16s at all. By my count, I'm the only dude who's actually fired his lately. How about we turn that area where the Chinook went down into a rifle range?"

Contreras didn't look impressed. "You mean you want to have a marksmanship contest, sir?"

"No, Top. It'll be a serviceability contest. Let's see how many of those rifles function properly. If I'm right, they've been out there in dust and rain without much care at all. I'm betting a third of them will jam. Set it up, make it a surprise. It'll be a hell of a wake-up call when they realize their personal weapons don't work like they should."

Section by section, the men of Charlie Battery went to the makeshift rifle range to further shoot up the skeleton of the crashed Chinook. Jif's estimate wasn't far from wrong; of the seventy-two M16s, twenty-six of them jammed. Most malfunctioned after firing one shot. A few never fired at all.

"Break out the solvent and gun oil, Top," Jif said. "We're going to have ourselves a little cleaning party."

He'd expected some men to recite the mantra that the M16 was *a piece of shit, foisted on the American fighting man by the profit-hungry military-industrial complex*, and he wasn't disappointed. The loudest voice came from a gunner named McHugh, whose weapon had never even gotten off one shot; it had jammed trying to chamber a grimy bullet. Jif told him, "You're right, Specialist…the sixteen is far from perfect, but your weapon's a whole lot further from perfect. Let me see what that swab looks like after you've run it through."

After just one pass down the barrel, the white swab came out a crusty brown, not the oily light gray you'd expect from an unfired but well-maintained weapon.

"No weapon in any army's arsenal is going to work worth a damn if it's been neglected like that," Jif said. "It's a good thing you're finding it out now, McHugh, before your life depends on that rifle."

*****

It was still proving hard to motivate men who were convinced that the sudden decrease in enemy activity meant the fight was over. Even the infantrymen securing the perimeter were becoming lax. Lieutenant Dowd had shrugged off 1SG Avery's warning, saying, "I think you're overreacting, Top."

But the first sergeant knew better. "With all due respect, Lieutenant, maybe you oughta start walking the perimeter yourself sometime. Then you'll see how many of our troopers are dead asleep when they're supposed to be on watch. If you find less than five, the beer's on me. By the way, you do realize it only takes one sleeping man to get us all killed, don't you?"

"If the problem's that bad, Top, maybe we should be paying surprise visits to the men at the LPs, too."

"That would be great, Lieutenant, except there's a real good chance you'll get wasted doing it. That's Indian country out there, and if the gooks don't get you, some panicky dude in an LP hole probably will. We're better off just hounding the LPs on the landline every ten minutes. That'll keep them awake."

Late that night, one LP beyond the wire on the east side didn't respond when their phone was rung up. "We've got ourselves a worst-case scenario," Avery announced. "LP-Four's gone dead."

"Maybe their phone crapped out," Dowd offered, "or they deactivated the clacker."

"That's not our SOP, Lieutenant. You mute clackers, you don't deactivate them."

"Well, I guess somebody's got to go out there and check on them," Dowd said.

"That ain't SOP either, sir. We assume they've been neutralized. Otherwise, we could lose more people and still not know what the hell's going on. It's better you just go and tighten up the guys on the east wire."

Dowd did just that and found two men on the perimeter asleep in their holes. They were both black. After jarring the troopers awake, he announced his intention to court-martial them both. His threats were dramatically emphasized by the booms of howitzers firing yet another H&I mission.

Despite the unresponsive LP and the sleeping men on the perimeter, there seemed nothing out of order on the busy firebase…

Until Spec-4 McHugh, casually holding his now-functioning M16 by its handle, saw the darkened shapes of two men walking in front of him as he made his way to the latrine. He called out to them.

As they turned around, their faces were illuminated for just an instant by the muzzle flash of a howitzer. That instant was all it took to realize they weren't GIs.

McHugh didn't remember snapping his weapon to the firing position. He didn't remember shooting the long burst from it, either. It never crossed his mind that the weapon didn't jam.

He'd emptied the magazine on full auto. Six of the eighteen rounds killed the two NVA soldiers. The other twelve rounds embedded themselves in the sandbags covering the CP/FDC bunker. The dead NVA never got off a shot of their own.

It took a few minutes to sort out what had happened. Once Avery and Contreras felt sure that no more NVA were within the perimeter, Dowd insisted on leading a patrol to LP-4, despite it being against Avery's better judgment to do so. But at least the lieutenant had the good sense to follow the phone wire that ran to it. If he'd learned anything in his brief tenure, he knew he might never find the hole without the landline to guide him.

Both men at the LP were dead, their throats slashed.

"There's only one way this could've happened," the patrol's sergeant said. "They were asleep. The gooks crawled right up to the hole real quiet-like. Didn't make a sound killing them, either."

But Dowd was still unsure how NVA intruders had gotten onto the firebase. He asked, "How the hell did they get through the wire?"

"Carefully, Lieutenant," the sergeant replied. "Very carefully."

After bringing in the bodies of the two dead Americans and remanning the LP with frightened but wide-awake men, Dowd and the sergeant found where the perimeter wire had been breached. Just enough had been cut and bent away so the slender bodies of North Vietnamese soldiers could wiggle through. Noisemakers that hung in the wire had been cut free; a trip flare had been deactivated with a piece of wire slipped through the empty holes that once held its safety pin. Inside the barbed wire, two Claymore mines had been turned around so they faced a perimeter fighting hole, the same one where Dowd had been browbeating the two black troopers who'd been asleep.

The sergeant said, "The gooks crawled right past whoever was in this hole. It's a good thing they didn't hear the bastards coming, because if they'd blown those Claymores—"

He didn't get to finish the sentence. Dowd had thrown up on the sergeant's boots.

*****

Inside the CP/FDC, Avery and Dowd were nose to nose, exchanging angry words. The rift seemed deeper than the issue of the two dead men—dead *white* men—the medics had just bagged up in mattress covers.

The first sergeant said, "Can I assume you're gonna court-martial those two white boys posthumously,

Lieutenant? I mean, they were sleeping as well…just like those two black troopers you woke up." Avery usually came across like a force of nature, and nobody had ever seen him lose his cool. But he was getting close.

"That's apples and oranges, First Sergeant. Hypothetical nonsense."

"No, sir, when it comes right down to it, it's same-same. Sleeping on duty is sleeping on duty, regardless of color, right?"

Dowd had grown hot under the collar, too. He asked, "What do you want from those guys? They're KIA. How much more can we punish them?"

"I just want fair treatment for every last one of our men, sir," Avery replied. "You're saying that in your eyes, it's only a crime for black troopers to be asleep at the wheel."

"Negative, Top. Negative. I didn't say that. You're just protecting them because they're—"

Avery wasn't going to rise to that bait. He'd cut the lieutenant off, saying, "With all due respect, sir, you're being harder on those men because of their color."

"So let me get this straight," Dowd replied. "You're telling me it's okay for men to sleep when they're on perimeter duty?"

Again, the first sergeant wouldn't be suckered into fallacious arguments. Instead, he replied, "Maybe I made a bad assumption before, Lieutenant, but I'll give you a chance to set me straight. Not counting tonight, how many nights have you actually walked the perimeter?"

Dowd hesitated, not wanting to answer. If he'd performed that task in darkness, the number of times would be quite low, if there was a number at all.

"I'm guessing the answer is pretty close to zero," Avery said. "Am I right?"

"I don't know…maybe. But what does that have to do with anything, First Sergeant?"

"It has every damn thing in the world to do with it, Lieutenant. If you did it enough, you'd know that there are *always* gonna be men asleep when they shouldn't be. Black, white, blue, purple, it don't matter. It goes with the territory. That's why the Lord made NCOs and officers…to kick their asses awake. If you catch a man sleeping out here, justice is a swift boot in the ass, not threatening him with some bullshit court-martial." He was going to say *some racist court-martial*, but stopped himself. It wasn't necessary; it was implicit in his tone of voice.

Clearly cowed, the green lieutenant retreated, saying, "We'll see about this, First Sergeant." Then he left the bunker…

And walked right into Jif.

Dowd asked, "Did you hear the shit Avery's trying to pull on me?"

"Like what, Hank?" Jif was playing dumb. He'd overheard the whole discussion.

"Those jigaboos, man…always angling for special treatment they're not entitled to. But when you call them on it, they accuse you of being racist."

"Not entitled to what, Hank?"

Dowd began to rehash the whole story, but Jif stopped him after a few sentences, saying, "Look, man, I'm not getting in the middle of your company's business. But I will say this…if you're going to start court-martialing men for sleeping on the perimeter, you'd better set aside a big block of time, because just about every swinging dick in Uncle Sam's Army is guilty of it at one time or another. I'm talking officers and NCOs, as well."

"So you think I'm being racist, too? I can't be…I'm not even from the South."

Jif, like Avery, wouldn't play the fallacy game. "It doesn't matter what I think, Hank," he replied. "And it doesn't matter where you're from, either. But do you really think you're ready to claim the crown?"

"The crown? What the hell are you talking about now, Jif?"

"I don't know what they told you back in training, but here's the deal…the top kick runs an outfit until he decides the rookie officer technically in command is ready. You've got a very strong first sergeant…and dude, I hate to be the Dutch uncle here, but he doesn't think you're ready to take command yet. Neither do I. You need a lot more seasoning before Avery hands over the reins. By the way, you've still got some puke on your britches."

"But he doesn't want to enforce discipline against the soul brothers…*his* soul brothers. He's undermining my authority."

Jif tried not to laugh. "What authority, Hank? The company is dancing to his tune, not yours. He cracks the whip when—and only when—it's necessary. Pay attention to him, because you need to learn that skill, and he's one hell of a teacher."

It was like talking to the wall. Dowd said, "I can't let the inmates run the asylum, Jif. Especially not the black ones."

"Then you'd better let Avery handle them until you can do it without causing a riot...or a fragging."

As Dowd fumed like a spoiled teenager, Jif added, "Maybe you ought to consider this, Hank. A wise commander once said that when he looked at his troops, the only color he saw was green."

He paused before saying, "And you've probably noticed everybody's blood is the same color, too, right?"

Chapter Twenty-Eight

Holding the message that had just come over the command net, 1SG Contreras made a tongue-in-cheek announcement: "Ladies and gentlemen, we have our marching orders. Charlie Battery will stand down at 0700 hours tomorrow, 17 May 68. The evacuation of the firebase will commence at 0930 hours, when the first of ten Chinooks will arrive in sequence to airlift the battery to Camp Evans. All battery equipment and personnel are to be removed from the firebase by 1200 hours, when airlifts to evacuate the security company will begin."

"Sounds like a pretty ambitious schedule," Jif said. "Are they guaranteeing the weather will cooperate?"

Contreras made a theatrical show of flipping the message form over and then upside down while pretending to read it. "Negatory, sir. No contingency plans listed. I guess we'll be playing this one by ear, as always."

Jif asked, "Any special instructions about turning over the place to the ARVN?"

"Not really, sir. Just a line instructing us to leave all fortifications in place for immediate use by allied forces."

Contreras read a little further and added, "And you'll love this, LT…it says ARVN forces are already in the area, patrolling the major arteries."

"Major arteries? That's a hell of a way to describe the one dirt road that runs through this valley. Has anybody actually seen an ARVN?"

Every man in the CP/FDC shook his head.

"Sounds like we're off to a magnificent start," Jif said, "as usual."

*****

There would be no evacuation choppers at 0930 hours the next morning. Fog and rain would persist until at least noon, with visibility at Fire Base Rubber down to practically nothing. Jif read the latest message from Divarty, announcing that Charlie Battery's stand-down time had been rescinded, its rescheduling subject to improvements in the weather.

"I hope they give us at least a thirty-minute warning before the first *shithook* shows up," SFC McKay, the chief of smoke, said to Jif. "I hate closing up shop in a rush. You always lose something when you're short on time."

"I hear you, Smoke, so let's do this…pack up and sling Guns Two and Six at 1000 hours. That'll leave us three guns as a safety cushion until official stand-down, and we'll be ready for the first two lifts on a moment's notice. It's a gamble, but I think we can pull it off without getting our tits caught in the wringer."

"Outstanding, LT," McKay replied. "I'll get the XO up to speed on the plan. He's catching his forty winks right now."

*****

Something did arrive at 0930 hours, however: a lone deuce pulled out of the mist and onto the firebase. The gate guards, assuming it was a standard delivery, waved it through without noticing the two men in the cab were Vietnamese. But when a man in the back of the truck peeked out from the canvas cover, it was obvious he wasn't American. For all the guards knew, the truck could be full of VC or NVA. One of them began screaming, "GOOKS IN THE DEUCE." Then, too uncertain to start shooting, he hurled a red smoke grenade that was supposed to land in front of the slow-moving vehicle. Instead, his frantic throw went through the open rear curtain and onto the bed.

The truck rolled another fifty feet before it was forced to a halt. There were at least six Americans with weapons at the ready blocking its path, two of them with M60s. Three soldiers in ARVN fatigues bailed out the back, choking on the red smoke. The two in the cab exited, as well; the M16s they held by the handles posed no immediate threat. They were both wearing ARVN uniforms, too, and one was a lieutenant. He was furious, yelling in passable English a demand to see whoever was in charge.

As one of the GIs went to get Lieutenant Miles, the ARVN officer directed the three who'd jumped from the bed to climb back in, reclaim their rifles, kick the smoke grenade out, and report back to him. They did as they were told, but reluctantly.

The ARVN lieutenant then pointed to the .50-caliber machine gun pit nearby and instructed his men in Vietnamese to take the weapon and put it on the truck.

The two GIs manning the fifty cal were Jif's men. When two of the ARVN tried to lift the heavy weapon, they were quickly overpowered, stripped of their rifles, and thrown out of the pit. A third ARVN leveled his M16 nervously at the Americans, looking for all the world like he intended to fire it.

But he was standing too close. One of the GIs—a muscular twenty-year-old buck sergeant who bragged of being a state wrestling champion in high school—ripped the rifle from the ARVN's hands and contorted the much smaller man into a half-nelson. The move dislocated the man's shoulder, and he began to wail in pain. The ARVN lieutenant was foolish enough to suddenly point his weapon at the Americans but was met with at least a dozen muzzles in his face. As the rifle was taken from him, he shrieked, "YOU ALL GO TO JAIL."

When Jif passed through the cloud of red smoke that had blocked his view of the altercation, he wasn't sure what to make of the standoff. But his uncertainty cleared up quickly when the ARVN officer turned to him and asked, "Are you in charge of these criminals? They assault me and my men, steal our weapons. They go to jail."

"First things first, mate," Jif replied. "How about you tell me what the fuck you're doing on my firebase?"

"Not your firebase! Now belongs to Republic of Vietnam." Still trying to process Jif's accent, he added, "You are not even American!"

"The hell I'm not," Jif replied. "Answer my question, dipshit."

The wrestler spoke up. "They were trying to steal the fifty cal, LT."

"NOT STEAL! NOT STEAL! It is ours now. All machine guns are ours."

"Bloody hell they are," Jif replied. "You just want to take stuff you can sell to the Victor Charlies. Actually, you might be Victor Charlie yourself. I'm going to tell you just one more time, wanker…get the fuck off my firebase before I kick your ass all the way back to Saigon."

"NOT VC, NOT VC," the ARVN lieutenant implored as he pulled some paperwork from his pocket. "It says here…*all fortifications are to be left in place*."

"A fifty cal's not a fortification," Jif replied. "It's a weapon. You see that hole with the sandbags all around it? *That's* a bloody fortification, and you're welcome to it once we leave. But not the gun that's in the hole, though. That's mine, Marvin."

"My name is not Marvin. It is Thong."

Jif found that funny. "Isn't that bloody perfect? Marvin the ARVN is named Lieutenant Thong. I'll bet your men call you *Flip-Flop*." The Americans burst out laughing, but the joke was lost on the Vietnamese.

Then Jif asked, "By the way, where'd you steal the truck from? It's got US Army markings all over it."

"Not stolen. *Given* to us by your division."

That almost made sense. There was no practical way to transport the deuces out of the A Shau at the moment; the deteriorating weather was severely limiting the C-130 flights in and out of A Luoi. To drive them back east to an American base camp involved a long, hazardous trip along Route 547, where the road was probably washed out in numerous places and the threat of ambush was great. Rather than just abandon the vehicles, turning them over in an orderly manner to the

ARVN, who might actually get some good use out of them, wasn't such a bad idea...

Provided, of course, that they don't sell them to the Victor Charlies.

Then Thong insisted, "You will give me machine guns now."

When Jif refused, Thong added, "You are under arrest for stealing from Republic of—"

He didn't get to finish the sentence. Jif hit him with a right cross squarely to the jaw, toppling the diminutive officer.

"Wow! Killer punch, LT," the wrestler said. "I think you broke his fucking face. How about we just shoot 'em all and be done with it?"

"Nah, don't waste the bullets," Jif replied. "And the last thing we need right now is CID up our asses over murder charges." Pointing to the wailing man with the arm clutched to his chest, he asked, "What's his problem?"

"I think I popped his shoulder, LT. Didn't mean to. I was just—"

"Forget it, Sergeant. Just get the medic to fix him up, then load them all on that deuce and send them back where they came from."

"We're not going to give them back their sixteens, are we, sir?"

"Sure we are. We're not thieves like them. But break them down first and remove the bolts."

"So we keep the bolts, right?"

"Negative," Jif replied, "give them back, too. But separately."

The wrestler seemed confused for a moment, but then his face lit up with recognition. "Oh, I get it,

LT…they won't know which bolt came from which rifle. Match them up wrong and the things might blow up in their faces. They'll need an armorer to put them back together."

"You've got it, Sergeant," Jif said.

Lieutenant Thong had recovered from his post-coldcock daze. He realized the possible hazards of mismatched rifle parts, too. "This is not allowed," he said, his aching jaw making the words difficult. "You cannot disarm us in the face of the enemy."

"I wouldn't worry too much about the enemy, pal," Jif replied. "The only reason you're here is because we kicked them all out. Try not to fuck that up too quickly, okay?"

A few minutes later, he told the men in the CP/FDC what had transpired, capping the story with, "I'm growing more confident by the day that we're fighting the wrong gooks."

*****

The sun was finally beginning to burn through the haze. At 1030 hours, the radio crackled with the order for Charlie Battery to stand down. Once decoded, the message advised *first wave choppers ETA 1100 hours*. It seemed like a taunt, betting they wouldn't be ready for the lift.

SFC McKay raised his hands over his head, rejoicing like he'd just scored a touchdown. Then he said, "What did I tell you? I figured the bastards wouldn't give us more than thirty minutes' warning, and that's all we got." Then he told Jif, "By the way, LT, that was a great call to stand down two guns at ten hundred. Not like they were doing anything, anyway. Getting real quiet around here."

"It was a gamble, Smoke," Jif replied, "but we lucked out and won. Now, let's get out of this bloody place."

*****

By 1400 hours, the entire battery was back at Camp Evans, as was most of 1st Cav. For the first time in three weeks, all of Jif's men would be showered and in clean utilities at the same time. "Enjoy it while you can, men," 1SG Contreras told the troopers, "because I've got a hunch we aren't going to be hanging out here very long."

A runner told Jif, "Meeting for all commanders at 1800 hours, Lieutenant, at Battalion CP. The old man says you'd better have supper first, because it's going to be a long one."

Lieutenant Hammond asked Jif, "You think we're going out again right away?"

"Depends on how you define *right away*, Art. We're not exactly ready for another operation...and we won't be until we get ourselves some new tubes."

The first two hours of the meeting were a detailed description of how two of the battalion's three firing batteries would be deployed to LZs within a ten-kilometer radius of Evans. From those LZs, they'd be providing fire support to maneuver battalions engaged in sweeping enemy forces from the coastal flats to the east and the heavily wooded foothills to the west. One battery—at the moment, Jif's outfit—would remain at Evans to provide the base camp with defensive support.

The assignment had an inherent convenience: with Charlie at Evans, the logistics of replacing its worn-out tubes was a much easier undertaking.

Battalion had a plan to make it even easier. Lieutenant Colonel Latimer, the battalion commander, told Jif, "Since you're already short after the flyboys were nice enough to dump one of your guns into the A Shau, we need to bring you back to full strength. But there's a bit of a problem with that. We can't scrape up another M102 for a few weeks, and since the howitzers you do have are at serviceability limits, rather than swap those tubes out, we're converting your Charlie Battery back to M101s. That will save a ton of time and effort. Any problem with that?"

Actually, Jif was delighted in concept with the exchange. But he knew the older model howitzers wouldn't be brand new, so he didn't want to seem too enthused until he had their whole story. He asked, "What's the tube life on the one-oh-ones I'll be getting, sir?"

Latimer deferred that question to his S4, who explained that all six guns had seventy-five to eighty percent of their tube life remaining.

"All right, when can I have them?"

"You'll receive all six weapons over the course of the next four days, Lieutenant. Three of them have to be driven up from Nha Trang. The rest are at Da Nang, a little closer."

"Sounds like a plan, sir."

The meeting moved on to personnel matters. The colonel told his officers, "We're getting a number of replacements in the coming days. Fortunately, Divarty's combat losses from Operation Delaware were fairly low, but fifteen percent of our manpower have a DEROS within two weeks. Be advised…we can expect the motivation levels of the new arrivals to be somewhat lower than we're used to. This batch of snuffies is mostly draftees, gentlemen, the largest influx we've seen since being in country. Some of them may well be from the pool known as McNamara's Misfits, the result of a harebrained scheme from our recently departed Secretary of Defense. They're real bottom-of-the-barrel types in terms of intelligence and physical conditioning. Make sure you get them with the program from the get-go, because they'll need a lot of guidance if they're going to keep themselves and others from getting killed outright. The S1 will break down the numbers for you."

The last item on the administrative agenda: "There will be a Divarty awards ceremony tomorrow at 1300 hours. VIPs will be present. The following people from this battalion are to be decorated…"

There were three names on the list. The last name read off was *Miles, John F., First Lieutenant*.

It was just after 2100 hours when the meeting finally wrapped up. LTC Latimer asked Jif to stay behind. "A couple of items, Miles," he said. "First off, congratulations on the Silver Star. I'm sorry it was so long in coming."

He really does seem sorry, Jif thought, *but I reckon the colonel didn't have anything to do with the political bullshit that held up that medal.*

"Thank you, sir."

"Young as you are, that's a lot of fruit salad to hang on your chest. But you've certainly earned it all. I'm proud to have you in my battalion."

"I'm proud to be here, sir...but there's something I've got to confess. I'm afraid you might not be so proud after you hear it."

"Oh? What'd you do?"

"I wanted you to hear this from me, sir, so you don't get blindsided...I punched out an ARVN lieutenant this morning at Fire Base Condon. Just one punch, actually, but it was a good one. In all honesty, I'd say he had it coming. He was trying to appropriate our *Ma Deuces*."

Latimer smiled. "Really? You smacked him one good?"

"Yes, sir."

"Well, I'm glad to hear it. In fact, join the club. Yours wasn't the only outfit those crooks—excuse me, our steadfast allies—tried to rip off. The ARVN battalion commander filed a complaint with Brigade over his men being assaulted by various units, but he was told to get stuffed. Politely, of course. Then, the whole thing was written off as a misunderstanding of the transition orders. But that was just a face-saving gesture for the gooks. The ARVN battalion commander was advised, however, that if there were any more reports of pilfering, he'd be held personally accountable."

"So I'm not in any hot water, sir?"

"Absolutely not, Miles. Don't lose any sleep over it. You did good."

Then, with a wink, he added, "But don't ever fucking do it again. There...you've been reprimanded."

*****

Jif found it bizarre to be playing toy soldier on a makeshift parade ground when, just yesterday, he was still in the bush, being a soldier for real. He'd heard that the commanding general wanted an awards ceremony with the full division in attendance—over eighteen thousand men—but practical considerations prevented it. First off, the only place to have a formation that big would've been on the airstrip's runway, which couldn't be closed down—even for an hour—without further disrupting the flow of air traffic already ravaged by weather. Secondly, the Cav hadn't scraped up enough suitably clean utilities yet to fully outfit every battalion, two of whom had just flown in this morning after serving as rear guard in the A Shau. The final reason: several hundred of the troopers were needed to pull security duty at Evans around the clock. As a result, the brigades would be holding their own ceremonies when convenient.

As scheduled, Division Artillery assembled on the open field behind its HQ at 1300 hours. When the command came for *persons to be decorated, front and center*, Jif joined eleven other awardees to stand before Major General Alworth, the 1st Cav commander, and an assortment of field grade officers. Seeing the others who'd be getting medals, he thought, *A little heavy on the officers, aren't we? There are only two enlisted men to be decorated. That seems way out of balance...unless we've started giving out medals to officers for standing around with hands on hips, trying to look tough.*

A short distance behind the general was a small crowd of VIPs invited to witness the awards ceremony.

It took Jif a few moments to realize that his father and SGM Sean Moon were among that group. Completely surprised by their presence, he couldn't help but smile. Seeing them meant more to him at the moment than the medal about to be pinned to his chest.

The ceremony was quick. After a rendition of *The Field Artillery March* by the division's band, a John Phillips Sousa tune Jif had only heard once before during a ceremony at Fort Sill, the medals were handed out. Then the formation was dismissed. Jif made a beeline to his father and Sean Moon.

But he couldn't get close; every high-ranking officer in attendance wanted a few words with the man from the State Department. Sean eased Jif away, saying, "This could take a while. Retired generals get a lot of attention, especially one who's a big wheel from DC and knows things the resident brass would just love to hear about. Besides, if you went rushing right in there, his guards might have to shoot you. You know that those snake-eaters shoot first and don't bother asking questions later, right?"

Jif had to laugh. He hadn't noticed the two Special Forces NCOs keeping close watch over his father until that moment. He asked Sean, "How'd you guys get here, anyway?"

"That C-7 that landed about thirty minutes ago brought us up from Saigon. General Abe gave me the sweet duty of being your dad's escort again. He heard the Cav was in from the A Shau and wanted a debrief...and to pay you a quick visit, of course. Hey...what's this I hear about you punching out some ARVN officer?"

"Bloody hell...do they know about that at MACV, too?"

"Nah, I heard about it right here, just a little while ago. You're all the buzz up at Divarty HQ. But it's a good thing the dude you decked was of equal rank. That makes it a lot simpler if somebody wants to make a stink. It's just simple assault, not like striking a superior or a subordinate. I hear it was just one killer punch, too."

"Oh, for cryin' out loud. Can't anybody keep a secret around here?"

"You're in the Army, sir. The only guys allowed to have secrets wear stars on their collar."

The seas had finally parted around his father. Jock's first words: "Congratulations on the medal, son. I promise not to tell your mother what you did to earn it."

That startled Jif. "You know what I got it for?"

"Sergeant Major Moon filled me in. You really like to push the envelope, don't you?"

"It didn't seem like a big deal at the time, Dad. Still doesn't."

Jock just smiled. That's what brave men—or men who didn't realize they were doing something extraordinary—always said.

Jif noticed his father's new walking cane, which featured a military unit crest on its handle. He recognized it as the one from the regimental combat team Jock had commanded during the Korean War. A larger version of it hung in a place of honor in each of his childhood homes, whether in the States or Australia.

"Nice cane, Dad. Very distinctive."

"Your mother had it made up for me. It was a nice surprise. She sends her love, of course, and really appreciates your letters. We've got a few hours before we fly back. Can you join us for a drink at the NCO club? You know how the sergeant major refuses to set foot in an officers club."

"Yeah, I know he does. And sure, I can join you, Dad. The NCO club suits me just fine. It's more fun there, anyway. Give me a second to tell my XO where I'll be."

*****

Their money was no good at the NCO club. In tribute to Jif's Silver Star, their drinks were on the house. Sean asked, "You realize what an honor that is, don't you, Lieutenant?"

"I bloody well do, Sergeant Major."

Sean raised his glass in a toast. "To Lieutenant Jif Miles, another bright star in the galaxy of his brilliant family."

After they drank on that, Jock said, "I'm impressed, Sergeant Major. That didn't even come out of the book of standard Army toasts. You thought that one up all by yourself?"

"What can I say, sir? When you hang out in the exalted atmosphere of MACV, even an old Brooklyn thug like me can pick up some verbal skills."

Jock added, "Be careful, though, or you might find yourself in line for Sergeant Major of the Army."

"Big fucking deal, sir. There's no jump in pay grade. It's still just another E-9 slot. Besides, I don't feel like rubbing elbows with the Joint Chiefs on a regular basis...or ol' LBJ, either."

"President Johnson will be gone by January," Jock said. "Now that he's taken himself out of the game, you'd be rubbing elbows with Bobby Kennedy, I imagine."

"You're probably right, sir. I guess LBJ's just another casualty of this war, right?"

When Sean excused himself to use the latrine, Jock asked, "Well, son, do you still think you belong here in this man's Army?"

"I do. One way or another, I've been in the Army my whole life. There's no denying that it's pretty screwed up right now, but it's too important an institution to watch it go down the tubes like this. However Nam finally ends, some of us will have to put the pieces back together."

"Do you think that *some of us* might include you?"

"It could be, Dad."

Jock raised his glass. "I'll drink to that, son."

Chapter Twenty-Nine

While Jif was saying goodbye to his father and Sergeant Major Moon, Lieutenant Hammond emplaced the battery in its defensive role at Camp Evans, still with the same five, nearly worn-out M102 howitzers they'd brought in from the A Shau. As replacement M101s arrived over the next few days, the one-oh-deuces would be carted off to the maintenance depot at Da Nang.

An unforeseen benefit of the weapons swap: the vast majority of the gun-bunnies were thrilled to be getting the older weapons back. The ability to work standing up rather than hunched over or on their knees outweighed the occasional backbreaking work of trail shifting when large changes in azimuth of fire were necessary.

On Jif's return to the battery, Hammond asked him, "Why do we have to build parapets around the guns, BC? We're in the middle of a damn base camp, for cryin' out loud."

Jif knew that his XO was only repeating the bitching he'd been getting all day from the battery's enlisted men, who, after the never-ending exertions of creating a fortress at Fire Base Rubber, didn't see the need to do it all over again in the middle of Camp Evans. He told Hammond, "Two reasons, Arthur. First off, base camps can be overrun, too, or at least infiltrated. And if either of those things happen, you'll wish you had parapets and fighting holes protecting you. Second, you're doing it because I said so. But let me ask you something…why the hell do you have the men humping all those sandbags?"

The XO seemed confused by the question. Hesitantly, he answered with another one: "How else are we supposed to build parapets?"

Jif shook his head sadly as he patted Hammond on the shoulder. "Arthur, Arthur, Arthur, as you've already mentioned, we're on a damn base camp, right?"

The tentative reply: "Yeah?" Hammond knew it was a loaded question, but one to which he didn't know the answer.

"So if this is a base camp, the whole bloody division is within spitting distance," Jif continued. "Have our engineers bring a bulldozer and a backhoe over here to build earthen berms. It won't take them long, and the men wouldn't need to be humping all those extra sandbags."

"But the first sergeant already asked the engineers. They said they'd put us on the list. Last I checked, that list was like a week long already."

"So what do they want? Beer, ice cream, or pizza?"

"What are you talking about, Jif?"

"Lesson one, Art…at our humble level, the Army is a transactional organization. If you want your transaction to occur in a reasonable time frame, you've got to grease the skids."

"You mean bribe them?"

"Call it whatever you like," Jif replied. "Come with me to the CP for a minute. You're about to sign for a fistful of MPCs from the unit fund. Find out what the engineer crew wants and go buy it at the PX, the O Club, or the Class Six store. Unless, of course, you'd rather the men devolve into an Army work party. You know what that is, right?"

"Yeah, it's when the troops get so uncooperative that you can't possibly give enough commands to get even the simplest job done. But wouldn't every other unit on this base be trying to bribe the engineers, too?"

"Then outbid them, Arthur. It's only Uncle Sam's money. You don't want your men to think you're screwing them because you're a cheapskate, do you?"

"But what if the engineers want women instead?"

"Then you'll have to talk with the ARVN. They do the pimping around here."

"What about the donut dollies? Are they available?"

"Put that thought right out of your head, Lieutenant. Those good ladies are off limits. Do not mess with them, period."

"So they're just here to fuel our wet dreams?"

"You say that like it's a bad thing, Arthur. Better than reading a bloody spank book, isn't it? Be thankful the Red Cross sends them…and they're innocent enough to come."

*****

The next night, just after 2230 hours, the first rocket crashed down onto Camp Evans. Landing uncomfortably close to the camp's vast ammo storage depot, it did no damage other than taxing everyone's nerves. The second rocket struck just seconds later, again coming down harmlessly but on the opposite side of the depot, bracketing it. Jif had been studying maps of the area in the battery CP when 1SG Contreras raced in, still half-dressed, fumbling to pull on a flak jacket. He was told, "Wake up the sleep shift, Top. Put everyone on full alert. I'm going up to Battalion...see if I can get a handle on what the bloody hell's going on."

The first sergeant asked, "Any idea what direction the stuff's coming from? We could start spinning the guns if we knew."

"Not a clue, Top."

Grabbing his helmet and rifle, Jif plunged into the street that ran between the hooches. Another rocket impacted, this time squarely in the ammo dump. He'd only run three steps when a secondary explosion from that direct hit knocked him off his feet, the shock wave like a whack from an invisible club. Jif staggered to his feet and kept moving toward Battalion, wishing he were wearing a flak jacket like his first sergeant.

I'm not even sure where the bloody thing is at the moment. I hardly ever wear it.

It wasn't bravado that made him shuck the cumbersome armored vest; it was purely a case of creature comfort, nurtured by the time he'd spent in the bush as an FO. Out there, they were just another source of sweaty, exhausting misery...

And they don't actually stop bullets, anyway.

At Battalion CP, no one knew where the rockets were coming from, either. One thing was clear, though; these were well-targeted missiles of large caliber, probably 122 millimeter. That first direct hit had started a conflagration in the ammo dump the Americans were powerless to extinguish. If the fire took hold fully, several million pounds of ammunition would cook off in a fireworks display like no other.

The only chance to control the devastation was to stop the incoming with counter-battery artillery fire before the enemy could do more damage. But none of the post's several watchtowers could catch sight of the telltale flash of a rocket's launch.

And then, that sole possibility of limiting the carnage evaporated. Two more rockets dropped into the ammo dump, at least one of them scoring another direct hit inside a storage revetment. The flames now turned night into day, blinding the observers to any distant flashes.

A request for a Spooky gunship with its own flare-dropping capability was rejected outright by the Air Force. Without a precise target location, the AC-47 wouldn't be committed to the fight.

More secondary explosions rocked the camp, shooting flaming debris in all directions and forcing the observers in the towers to flee the rickety structures for their lives.

A conference call between all major units based at Evans quickly deteriorated into an exercise in helpless frustration. As irritated voices spilled from the squawk box, Colonel Latimer told his assembled staff, "Cutting to the chase, gentlemen, the general wants scout choppers in the air immediately, if not sooner, to find that launch site so we can blow it up with counter-battery fire. But there's a bit of a problem...it seems that at least half our choppers are already destroyed or damaged where they sit on the ramp. And the blaze is spreading to engulf even more of them. We have a full-fledged debacle on our hands. The Cav is being crippled before our eyes."

The battalion XO spoke up. "Hold on, sir…your personal LOACH is sitting right out back of this hooch. Nothing's stopping her from flying."

"Great," Latimer replied, "but where's the pilot?"

A sleepy voice floated from the back of the room. "I'm right here, sir."

"Is that you, Mister Ellerbee?"

"Yes, sir."

It was the same CW2 Larry Ellerbee who'd flown the Arc Light bomb damage assessment with Jif a few days ago. Seated on the wooden floor, his back against the wall, he'd been catching a nap. As far as he was concerned, he was a taxi driver, not a decision-maker.

"Pardon me for asking, Chief," the colonel asked, "but how the hell can you sleep through this bombardment?"

"I guess I'm just blessed that way, sir. What do you need me to do?"

"I need you to fly Captain Hutchins wherever he needs to go to find that launch site."

Captain Hutchins, the battalion S3-Air, had been trying to hide in a corner, hoping no one knew or cared he was there. But it was a fool's dream. Colonel Latimer was telling him, "Step over to the map, Captain. We need to go over the target acquisition plan you're about to execute."

Hutchins rose from the field box he was sitting on and began to shuffle unsteadily toward the chart table. His words slurred and inappropriately flippant, he called out, "What is it you want to show me, boss?"

When the captain reached the table, the first thing Latimer noticed were his eyes. In the harsh, bare-bulb lighting, they looked glassy and red. The colonel asked, "Are you drunk, Hutchins?"

He didn't reply but seemed amused, as if enjoying a private joke.

The battalion XO took one look at the captain and told Latimer, "He's not drunk, Colonel. He's stoned."

"Stoned? Like on drugs?"

"Affirmative, sir. Marijuana. Pot. Grass. Weed."

The battalion commander overcame his initial shock quickly. His voice brimming with disgust, he told the battalion sergeant major, "Confine Captain Hutchins to his quarters immediately. I'll deal with him later. Get him out of my sight."

That didn't solve the problem of who'd be the aerial observer conducting the search for the launch site. Normally, it was the S3-Air's role to locate enemy positions from the air. It was, by most accounts, the least desirable job on the staff, as the scout helicopters were frequently shot up and sometimes shot down. The job tended to be filled by a captain or lieutenant nobody wanted. That's how Hutchins had gotten the job; he was rated too below par as a manager of people to be given a battery, and his administrative skills were considered too weak to hold a primary staff position. His future as an Army officer was, to say the least, already tenuous even before showing up high on marijuana.

The job of S3-Air, risky in the best of times, was thought to be suicidal now. When Latimer took a quick glance around the room, there was only one man who seemed even remotely interested in the mission; he'd actually made eye contact with the colonel. The fact that he was experienced at aerial observation, as well, seemed a gift.

"Are you raising your hand, Miles?"

Jif replied, "If Chief Ellerbee's going to fly it, I'll take the observer's seat."

The collective air of relief—a *better him than me* state of mind—was palpable in the CP. The other officers graciously cleared a path for Jif and Ellerbee to join the colonel at the map.

From the outset, Jif thought the colonel's plan was an exercise in frustration and futility. Five concentric rings, centered on Camp Evans, had been drawn at two-thousand-meter intervals, encompassing an area of over three hundred square kilometers. Colonel Latimer said, "I want you to fly each ring in succession, starting with the closest one. Between the fire raging on this post and the lights of all the villes along Route One, you should have no trouble staying oriented over the ground. We'll give you illum rounds and WP as necessary to provide landmarks in the dark."

Ellerbee was shaking his head. "With all due respect, sir, no illum, please. It'll light up the chopper too well. I plan to stay as invisible as possible. High as we'll have to fly, the flares would make us an easy target." The chief might've been considered a young, fearless daredevil, but he wasn't crazy.

Jif added, "Besides, our best chance of finding the site is to see flashes from the rocket launches. The less ambient light, the better they'll show up."

The operations officer/S3—the stoned Captain Hutchins' boss—didn't appreciate mere lieutenants and warrant officers contradicting his plans, even if they were hastily drawn. But as he began to object, the colonel cut him off, saying, "It'll be their call, Major. We'll just have to be ready when they change their minds."

The S3 wasn't happy. He backed off with, "As you wish, sir."

"Another thing, sir," Ellerbee said, "I don't have a full tank, and with all the shit burning on the airstrip, I don't know if and when I'll be able to refuel." Doing some quick figuring on his clipboard, he added, "If we have to travel the circumferences of all those circles, that adds up to almost two hundred klicks of flying. That'll take much more gas than I have on board."

Jif did some figuring of his own. "It would take about an hour and a half to fly it, right? The gooks would need a shitload of rockets on hand to be firing that long. They could run out and we might never get a chance to spot a launch."

"I've got a feeling those launch sites probably aren't as far away as you think, Miles," Latimer said. "Still, the only way to do this is methodically. Stick with the program, gentlemen."

As they ran to the LOACH, two more rockets crashed down into the ammo dump, which was now totally ablaze. As a new wave of flying debris forced them to briefly take cover in the nearest ditch, Jif told Ellerbee, "We're not going to do that bullshit search pattern by the numbers. These rockets are too bloody accurate. They've got to be coming from proper launchers mounted on vehicles, not some bamboo contraptions the gooks cobbled together in the jungle. Those trucks aren't going to be in swamps or on sandy dunes, so that rules out half the colonel's search area right off the bat. I reckon they'll be near roads that branch off Route One, so that'll narrow our search down to the southeast and northwest. Are you okay with that, Chief?"

"Yeah, I'm good...but you might as well start calling me Larry."

"Sure, but only if you call me Jif."

"I can do that, no sweat."

After a quick preflight inspection to ensure the ongoing bombardment had caused no damage to the LOACH, the little ship was cranked up. In another minute, they were airborne. Ellerbee asked, "You want eight hundred feet?"

"Yeah. Let's see how that works. If it's no good, we'll go higher. We're invisible, right?"

"Let's hope so, Jif."

They flew south at first to get away from the impact zone Camp Evans had become. The carnage looked even worse from the air. Flames were shooting hundreds of feet into the sky and growing higher. "Son of a bitch...it looks like the whole flight line got torched," Ellerbee said.

"No shit," Jif replied. "And look...the POL dump across the road is starting to light off, too. The Cav is in a world of hurt, man. All it took was a handful of rockets, and the whole bloody division is combat ineffective. Who had the bright idea to put an airfield, an ammo dump, and all that fuel and oil right next to each other? I'm betting the G4's going to be looking for a new job by morning."

"Maybe the division commander, too," the pilot added. "Okay, I think we're clear enough. Which way you want to go, Jif?"

"Let's try southeast first," Jif replied, "heading one-three-zero toward Ap Long Khe."

"How the hell do you know which of those clusters of lights is Ap Long Khe, man?"

"It's the only one that's not smack on the river. It's set back about half a klick."

The river in question, the *Song Bo*, looked like a shimmering snake in the moonlight once they got high enough to see it. The twinkling lights of villages lining its banks reflected off the water's surface, enhancing the serpentine illusion.

Ellerbee said, "Oh, yeah…I see what you mean. How far past Ap Long Khe can we go and still be in the colonel's goose egg?"

"About two klicks. We can use where the river bends back to the east as a signpost."

They kept waiting for green tracers to arc through the sky, searching blindly for the buzz saw sound of the LOACH's high-speed rotor. But those rounds never materialized.

With the ship settled into the desired altitude and heading, Ellerbee said, "That captain with the weed…talk about bad timing. This was the wrong night to get high, dude."

The offhandedness of the comment stunned Jif. "You make it sound like pot use is commonplace among officers. That's not what I've seen."

"Then you haven't spent much time in base camp, Jif. Tons of people are getting stoned, even your captains and majors."

That stunned Jif even more. He asked, "Do you smoke grass, Larry?"

"Not really. I'm more into booze. We warrant officer pilots are mainly juicers."

"What about the commissioned officer pilots?"

"Most of them are college boys, so they're potheads. You're a college boy, too, right? You know the score, don't you?"

"Yes and yes," Jif replied, "but it's different in the boonies. We don't have much problem with drugs out there because it's easy to cut it off at the source. I reckon base camp is becoming a very different scene, though."

"You'd better believe it, Jif. The ARVNs are all over the place, and they're the biggest pushers on the planet. Pot, hash, heroin, pills...you name it."

They scoured the area around Ap Long Khe for nearly fifteen minutes but found nothing. There hadn't been any impacts on Camp Evans since they'd lifted off. "We may be spinning our wheels, man," Ellerbee said. "How much you want to bet the gooks ran out of rockets?"

"Could be, Larry. How we doing on fuel?"

"Another thirty minutes before I get brown drawers. You ready to look someplace else?"

"Roger that. Turn to heading three-zero-zero. Minimum altitude en route is five hundred feet, so we're still golden."

"Copy. How far do you want to go this time?"

"Once we cross that third river, that'll be about it. That launch site has to be somewhere in that box...if they haven't done a runner by now, that is."

As they flew over invisible scrub hills midway to that next objective, Ellerbee asked, "You don't think those launchers could be right around here, do you?"

"Nope. There's no good way to drive in or out. My money's on the area near the third river, around Doc Dau. Tactically, it's a logical spot…sparsely populated, easily accessible on roads that are rarely patrolled, gentle hills, with good tree cover. Actually, I think I screwed up…we should've gone there first."

"Don't be too hard on yourself, man. This is needle in a haystack stuff."

"It sure is…but you know what's really pissing me off? The NVA couldn't beat us in the A Shau, so they waited until we were all sitting around back at Evans with our thumbs up our bums. Then, in the blink of an eye, they destroy our ammo, our choppers, and our fuel. It happens over and over again…we win a fight, kick the gooks out, but then it all turns full bloody circle when they come back and tear us a new one. We end up right back where we started."

"Don't give them too much credit, Jif. North Vietnam's getting the shit bombed out of it every damn day. I give them six more months. Then the fat lady's going to sing."

"You mean like *it ain't over until the fat lady sings*?"

"Yep."

"Ever the optimist, eh, Larry? The trouble is, I haven't seen any fat ladies in this whole bloody country."

"Then maybe we'd better ship Kate Smith over here, because—"

He stopped talking when Jif lurched forward in his seat, straining against the shoulder straps for a better view of something far beyond their plexiglass bubble. Then Ellerbee saw it, too, the vivid flash like distant lightning, and then the glowing, pencil-thin streak of rocket exhaust crossing far ahead of the ship's nose.

Jif was already calling in the fire mission to the 155-millimeter battery at Evans: "*Mallet Eight-Zero*, this is *White Star One Seven...*"

The transmission complete, he told the pilot, "Give us a tight orbit left. I need to lock onto that spot so I can adjust fire."

He could hear the smirk in Ellerbee's voice as the pilot asked, "So you want to fly a full circle...or should I say a full *bloody* circle? Okay, we can play that game."

Those words triggered a bittersweet memory: a song he'd loved when, fresh from Berkeley, he'd begun his active duty. It was called *The Circle Game*, a Joni Mitchell composition sung by Buffy Sainte-Marie. Vulnerable in this floating plastic bubble, shielded only by darkness, the lyrics might have seemed uncomfortably close to home...

Especially the parts about a frightened child beholding a sky roiled by thunder, knowing the sadness of a falling star, and the sobering realization that growing older and wiser offered no escape from the inevitable circle of life and death.

But as the first round of the fire mission impacted very near its target, a quiet confidence settled in, telling him that he hadn't been a frightened child for some time, he'd grown used to the thunder, and the odds of his star falling tonight were probably not that great. The apprehensions of a warrior would never fully go away...

But facing up to them comes with the "older and wiser" part, I reckon.

After calling in the required adjustment, he told Ellerbee, "Yeah, give me another full bloody circle. But this one, at least, is going to be a victory lap."

* * * * *

* * * * *

Upcoming Releases

Don't miss Book #5 in the
Miles to Vietnam
series

Available November 2023

Sign up to be added to the Mailing List for New Release Announcements at williampgrasso@gmail.com, with Mailing List as the subject

About the Author

A lifelong student of history, William Peter Grasso served in the US Army and is retired after a career in the aircraft maintenance industry. His devotion to all things historical, military, and aviation remains unabated and continues to inspire his fiction.

Visit the Author's Webpage at:
https://williampetergrasso.com

Connect with the Author on Facebook:
https://www.facebook.com/AuthorWilliamPeterGrasso

Follow the Author on Amazon:
https://amazon.com/author/williampetergrasso

More Novels by William Peter Grasso

Miles to Vietnam

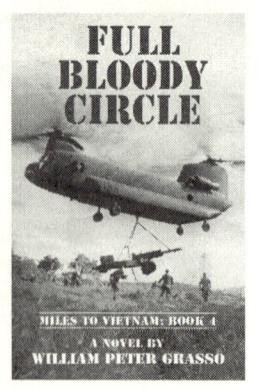

Jock Miles-Moon Brothers Korean War Story
4-Book Series

Moon Brothers WWII Adventure Series
4-Book Series

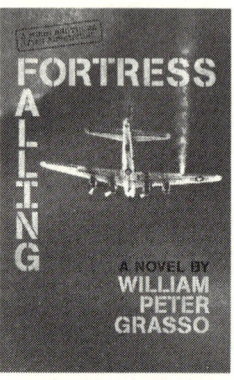

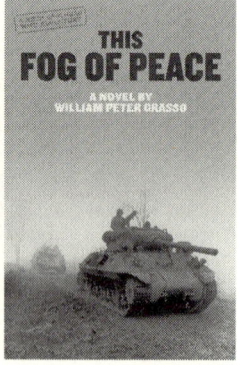

Jock Miles WW2 Adventure Series
5-Book Series

WW2 Standalone Novels

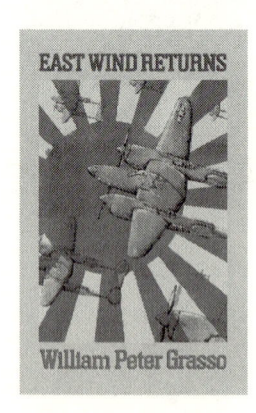

Made in United States
Troutdale, OR
02/29/2024

18079955R00268